LARGE
PRINT
EDITION

RANDOM
HOUSE

Also available in Random House Large Print
RISING SUN

DISCLOSURE

DISCLOSURE

A NOVEL BY
MICHAEL CRICHTON

Published by Random House Large Print
in association with Alfred A. Knopf, Inc.
New York 1994

Copyright © 1993 by Michael Crichton

Library of Congress Cataloging-in-Publication Data
Crichton, Michael, [date]
Disclosure : a novel / by Michael Crichton.—1st large print ed.
p. cm.
Simultaneously published with: New York : Knopf, 1994
ISBN 0-679-75143-2
1. Sexual harassment—United States—Fiction.
2. Computer industry—United States—Fiction. 3. Large type books.
I. Title.
[PS3553.R48D57 1994b]
813'.54—dc20 93-33218 CIP

Manufactured in the United States of America
FIRST LARGE PRINT EDITION

This Large Print Book carries the
Seal of Approval of N.A.V.H.

For Douglas Crichton

It shall be an unlawful employment practice for an employer: (1) to fail or refuse to hire or to discharge any individual, or otherwise to discriminate against any individual with respect to his compensation, terms, conditions or privileges of employment because of such individual's race, color, religion, sex, or national origin or (2) to limit, segregate, or classify his employees or applicants for employment in any way which would deprive or tend to deprive any individual of employment opportunities or otherwise adversely affect his status as an employee, because of such individual's race, color, religion, sex, or national origin.

Title VII, Civil Rights Act of 1964

Power is neither male nor female.

Katharine Graham

DISCLOSURE

MONDAY

From: DC/M
ARTHUR KAHN
TWINKLE/KUALA LUMPUR/MALAYSIA

To: DC/S
TOM SANDERS
SEATTLE (AT HOME)

TOM:

CONSIDERING THE MERGER, I THOUGHT YOU SHOULD GET THIS AT HOME AND NOT THE OFFICE:

TWINKLE PRODUCTION LINES RUNNING AT 29% CAPACITY DESPITE ALL EFFORTS TO INCREASE. SPOT CHECKS ON DRIVES SHOW AVG SEEK TIMES IN 120–140 MILLISECOND RANGE WITH NO CLEAR INDICATION WHY WE ARE NOT STABLE AT SPECS. ALSO, WE STILL HAVE POWER FLICKER IN SCREENS WHICH APPEARS TO COME FROM HINGE DESIGN DESPITE IMPLEMENTATION OF DC/S FIX LAST WEEK. I DON'T THINK IT'S SOLVED YET.

HOW'S THE MERGER COMING? ARE WE GOING TO BE RICH AND FAMOUS?

CONGRATULATIONS IN ADVANCE ON YOUR PROMOTION.

ARTHUR

Tom Sanders never intended to be late for work on Monday, June 15. At 7:30 in the morning, he stepped into the shower at his home on Bainbridge Island. He knew he had to shave, dress, and leave the house in ten minutes if he was to make the 7:50 ferry and arrive at work by 8:30, in time to go over the remaining points with Stephanie Kaplan before they went into the meeting with the lawyers from Conley-White. He already had a full day at work, and the fax he had just received from Malaysia made it worse.

Sanders was a division manager at Digital Communications Technology in Seattle. Events at work had been hectic for a week, because DigiCom was being acquired by Conley-White, a publishing conglomerate in New York. The merger would allow Conley to acquire technology important to publishing in the next century.

But this latest news from Malaysia was not good, and Arthur had been right to send it to him at home. He was going to have a problem explaining it to the Conley-White people because they just didn't—

"Tom? Where are you? Tom?"

His wife, Susan, was calling from the bedroom. He ducked his head out of the spray.

"I'm in the shower!"

She said something in reply, but he didn't hear it. He stepped out, reaching for a towel. "What?"

"I said, Can you feed the kids?"

His wife was an attorney who worked four days a week at a downtown firm. She took Mondays off, to spend more time with the kids, but she was not good at managing the routine at home. As a result, there was often a crisis on Monday mornings.

"Tom? Can you feed them for me?"

"I can't, Sue," he called to her. The clock on the sink said 7:34. "I'm already late." He ran water in the basin to shave, and lathered his face. He was a handsome man, with the easy manner of an athlete. He touched the dark bruise on his side from the company touch football game on Saturday. Mark Lewyn had taken him down; Lewyn was fast but clumsy. And Sanders was getting too old for touch football. He was still in good shape—still within five pounds of his varsity weight—but as he ran his hand through his wet hair, he saw streaks of gray. It was time to admit his age, he thought, and switch to tennis.

Susan came into the room, still in her bathrobe. His wife always looked beautiful in the morning, right out of bed. She had the kind of fresh beauty that required no makeup. "Are you sure you can't feed them?" she said. "Oh, nice bruise. Very butch." She kissed him lightly, and pushed a fresh mug of coffee onto the counter for him. "I've got to get Matthew to the pediatrician by eight-fifteen, and neither one of them has eaten a thing, and I'm not dressed. Can't you please feed them? Pretty please?" Teasing, she ruffled his hair, and her bathrobe fell open. She left it open and smiled. "I'll owe you one . . ."

"Sue, I can't." He kissed her forehead distractedly. "I've got a meeting, I can't be late."

She sighed. "Oh, all right." Pouting, she left.

Sanders began shaving.

A moment later he heard his wife say, "Okay, kids, let's go! Eliza, put your shoes on." This was followed by whining from Eliza, who was four, and didn't like to wear shoes. Sanders had almost finished shaving when he heard, "Eliza, you put on those shoes and take your brother downstairs right now!" Eliza's reply was indistinct, and then Susan said, "Eliza Ann, I'm talking to you!" Then Susan began slamming drawers in the hall linen closet. Both kids started to cry.

Eliza, who was upset by any display of tension, came into the bathroom, her face scrunched up, tears in her eyes. "Daddy . . . ," she sobbed. He put his hand down to hug her, still shaving with his other hand.

"She's old enough to help out," Susan called, from the hallway.

"Mommy," she wailed, clutching Sanders's leg.

"Eliza, will you *cut it out.*"

At this, Eliza cried more loudly. Susan stamped her foot in the hallway. Sanders hated to see his daughter cry. "Okay, Sue, I'll feed them." He turned off the water in the sink and scooped up his daughter. "Come on, Lize," he said, wiping away her tears. "Let's get you some breakfast."

He went out into the hallway. Susan looked relieved. "I just need ten minutes, that's all," she said. "Consuela is late again. I don't know what's the matter with her."

Sanders didn't answer her. His son, Matt, who was nine months old, sat in the middle of the hallway banging his rattle and crying. Sanders scooped him up in his other arm.

"Come on, kids," he said. "Let's go eat."

When he picked up Matt, his towel slipped off, and he clutched at it. Eliza giggled. "I see your penis, Dad." She swung her foot, kicking it.

"We don't kick Daddy there," Sanders said. Awkwardly, he wrapped the towel around himself again, and headed downstairs.

Susan called after him: "Don't forget Matt needs vitamins in his cereal. One dropperful. And don't give him any more of the rice cereal, he spits it out. He likes wheat now." She went into the bathroom, slamming the door behind her.

His daughter looked at him with serious eyes. "Is this going to be one of those days, Daddy?"

"Yeah, it looks like it." He walked down the stairs, thinking he would miss the ferry and that he would be late for the first meeting of the day. Not very late, just a few minutes, but it meant he wouldn't be able to go over things with Stephanie before they started, but perhaps he could call her from the ferry, and then—

"Do I have a penis, Dad?"

"No, Lize."

"Why, Dad?"

"That's just the way it is, honey."

"Boys have penises, and girls have vaginas," she said solemnly.

"That's right."

"Why, Dad?"

"Because." He dropped his daughter on a chair at the kitchen table, dragged the high chair from the corner, and placed Matt in it. "What do you want for breakfast, Lize? Rice Krispies or Chex?"

"Chex."

Matt began to bang on his high chair with his spoon. Sanders got the Chex and a bowl out of the cupboard, then the box of wheat cereal and a smaller bowl for Matt. Eliza watched him as he opened the refrigerator to get the milk.

"Dad?"

"What."

"I want Mommy to be happy."

"Me too, honey."

He mixed the wheat cereal for Matt, and put it in front of his son. Then he set Eliza's bowl on the table, poured in the Chex, glanced at her. "Enough?"

"Yes."

He poured the milk for her.

"No, Dad!" his daughter howled, bursting into tears. "*I* wanted to pour the milk!"

"Sorry, Lize—"

"Take it out—take the milk out—" She was shrieking, completely hysterical.

"I'm sorry, Lize, but this is—"

"I wanted to pour the milk!" She slid off her seat to the ground, where she lay kicking her heels on the floor. "Take it out, take the milk out!"

His daughter did this kind of thing several times a day. It was, he was assured, just a phase. Parents were advised to treat it with firmness.

"I'm sorry," Sanders said. "You'll just have to eat it, Lize." He sat down at the table beside Matt to feed him. Matt stuck his hand in his cereal and smeared it across his eyes. He, too, began to cry.

Sanders got a dish towel to wipe Matt's face. He noticed that the kitchen clock now said five to eight. He thought that he'd better call the office, to warn them he would be late. But he'd have to quiet Eliza first: she was still on the floor, kicking and screaming about the milk. "All right, Eliza, take it easy. Take it easy." He got a fresh bowl, poured more cereal, and gave her the carton of milk to pour herself. "Here."

She crossed her arms and pouted. "I don't want it."

"Eliza, you pour that milk *this minute*."

His daughter scrambled up to her chair. "Okay, Dad."

Sanders sat down, wiped Matt's face, and began to feed his son. The boy immediately stopped crying, and swallowed the cereal in big gulps. The poor kid was hungry. Eliza stood on her chair, lifted the milk carton, and splashed it all over the table. "Uh-oh."

"Never mind." With one hand, he wiped the table with the dish towel, while with the other he continued to feed Matt.

Eliza pulled the cereal box right up to her bowl, stared fixedly at the picture of Goofy on the back, and began to eat. Alongside her, Matt ate steadily. For a moment, it was calm in the kitchen.

Sanders glanced over his shoulder: almost eight o'clock. He should call the office.

Susan came in, wearing jeans and a beige sweater. Her face was relaxed. "I'm sorry I lost it," she said. "Thanks for taking over." She kissed him on the cheek.

"Are you happy, Mom?" Eliza said.

"Yes, sweetie." Susan smiled at her daughter,

and turned back to Tom. "I'll take over now. You don't want to be late. Isn't today the big day? When they announce your promotion?"

"I hope so."

"Call me as soon as you hear."

"I will." Sanders got up, cinched the towel around his waist, and headed upstairs to get dressed. There was always traffic in town before the 8:20 ferry. He would have to hurry to make it.

He parked in his spot behind Ricky's Shell station, and strode quickly down the covered walkway to the ferry. He stepped aboard moments before they pulled up the ramp. Feeling the throb of the engines beneath his feet, he went through the doors onto the main deck.

"Hey, Tom."

He looked over his shoulder. Dave Benedict was coming up behind him. Benedict was a lawyer with a firm that handled a lot of high-tech companies. "Missed the seven-fifty, too, huh?" Benedict said.

"Yeah. Crazy morning."

"Tell me. I wanted to be in the office an hour ago. But now that school's out, Jenny doesn't know what to do with the kids until camp starts."

"Uh-huh."

"Madness at my house," Benedict said, shaking his head.

There was a pause. Sanders sensed that he and Benedict had had a similar morning. But the two men did not discuss it further. Sanders often wondered why it was that women discussed the most intimate details of their marriages with their friends, while men maintained a discreet silence with one another.

"Anyway," Benedict said. "How's Susan?"

"She's fine. She's great."

Benedict grinned. "So why are you limping?"

"Company touch football game on Saturday. Got a little out of hand."

"That's what you get for playing with children," Benedict said. DigiCom was famous for its young employees.

"Hey," Sanders said. "I scored."

"Is that right?"

"Damn right. Winning touchdown. Crossed the end zone in glory. And then I got creamed."

At the main-deck cafeteria, they stood in line for coffee. "Actually, I would've thought you'd be in bright and early today," Benedict said. "Isn't this the big day at DigiCom?"

Sanders got his coffee, and stirred in sweetener. "How's that?"

"Isn't the merger being announced today?"

"What merger?" Sanders said blandly. The merger was secret; only a handful of DigiCom executives knew anything about it. He gave Benedict a blank stare.

"Come on," Benedict said. "I heard it was pretty much wrapped up. And that Bob Garvin was announcing the restructuring today, including a bunch of new promotions." Benedict sipped his coffee. "Garvin is stepping down, isn't he?"

Sanders shrugged. "We'll see." Of course Benedict was imposing on him, but Susan did a lot of work with attorneys in Benedict's firm; Sanders couldn't afford to be rude. It was one of the new complexities of business relations at a time when everybody had a working spouse.

The two men went out on the deck and stood by the port rail, watching the houses of Bainbridge Island slip away. Sanders nodded toward the house on Wing Point, which for years had been Warren Magnuson's summer house when he was senator.

"I hear it just sold again," Sanders said.

"Oh yes? Who bought it?"

"Some California asshole."

Bainbridge slid to the stern. They looked out at the gray water of the Sound. The coffee steamed in the morning sunlight. "So," Benedict said. "You think maybe Garvin won't step down?"

"Nobody knows," Sanders said. "Bob built the company from nothing, fifteen years ago. When he started, he was selling knockoff modems from Korea. Back when nobody knew what a modem was. Now the company's got three buildings downtown, and big facilities in California, Texas, Ireland, and Malaysia. He builds fax modems the size of a dime, he markets fax and e-mail software, he's gone into CD-ROMs, and he's developed proprietary algorithms that should make him a leading provider in education markets for the next century. Bob's come a long way from some guy hustling three hundred baud modems. I don't know if he can give it up."

"Don't the terms of the merger require it?"

Sanders smiled. "If you know about a merger, Dave, you should tell me," he said. "Because I haven't heard anything." The truth was that Sanders didn't really know the terms of the impending merger. His work involved the development of CD-ROMs and electronic databases. Although these were areas vital to the future of the company—they were the main reason Conley-White was acquiring DigiCom—they were essentially technical areas. And Sanders was essentially a technical manager. He was not informed about decisions at the highest levels.

For Sanders, there was some irony in this. In earlier years, when he was based in California, he had been closely involved in management decisions. But since coming to Seattle eight years ago, he had been more removed from the centers of power.

Benedict sipped his coffee. "Well, I hear Bob's definitely stepping down, and he's going to promote a woman as chairman."

Sanders said, "Who told you that?"

"He's already got a woman as CFO, doesn't he?"

"Yes, sure. For a long time, now." Stephanie Kaplan was DigiCom's chief financial officer. But it seemed unlikely she would ever run the company. Silent and intense, Kaplan was competent, but disliked by many in the company. Garvin wasn't especially fond of her.

"Well," Benedict said, "the rumor I've heard is he's going to name a woman to take over within five years."

"Does the rumor mention a name?"

Benedict shook his head. "I thought you'd know. I mean, it's your company."

On the deck in the sunshine, he took out his cellular phone and called in. His assistant, Cindy Wolfe, answered. "Mr. Sanders's office."

"Hi. It's me."

"Hi, Tom. You on the ferry?"

"Yes. I'll be in a little before nine."

"Okay, I'll tell them." She paused, and he had the sense that she was choosing her words carefully. "It's pretty busy this morning. Mr. Garvin was just here, looking for you."

Sanders frowned. "Looking for me?"

"Yes." Another pause. "Uh, he seemed kind of surprised that you weren't in."

"Did he say what he wanted?"

"No, but he's going into a lot of offices on the floor, one after another, talking to people. Something's up, Tom."

"What?"

"Nobody's telling me anything," she said.

"What about Stephanie?"

"Stephanie called, and I told her you weren't in yet."

"Anything else?"

"Arthur Kahn called from KL to ask if you got his fax."

"I did. I'll call him. Anything else?"

"No, that's about it, Tom."

"Thanks, Cindy." He pushed the END button to terminate the call.

Standing beside him, Benedict pointed to Sanders's phone. "Those things are amazing. They just get smaller and smaller, don't they? You guys make that one?"

Sanders nodded. "I'd be lost without it. Especially these days. Who can remember all the numbers? This is more than a telephone: it's my telephone book. See, look." He began to demonstrate the features for Benedict. "It's got a memory for two hundred numbers. You store them by the first three letters of the name." Sanders punched in K-A-H to bring up the international number for Arthur Kahn in Malaysia. He pushed SEND, and heard a long string of electronic beeps. With the country code and area code, it was thirteen beeps.

"Jesus," Benedict said. "Where are you calling, Mars?"

"Just about. Malaysia. We've got a factory there."

DigiCom's Malaysia operation was only a year old, and it was manufacturing the company's new CD-ROM players—units rather like an audio CD player, but intended for computers. It was widely agreed in the business that all information was soon going to be digital, and much of it was going to be stored on these compact disks. Computer programs, databases, even books and magazines—everything was going to be on disk.

The reason it hadn't already happened was that CD-ROMs were notoriously slow. Users were obliged to wait in front of blank screens while the drives whirred and clicked—and computer users didn't like waiting. In an industry where speeds reliably doubled every eighteen months, CD-ROMs had improved much less in the last five years. DigiCom's SpeedStar technology addressed that problem, with a new generation of drives code-named Twinkle (for "Twinkle, twinkle, little SpeedStar"). Twinkle drives were twice as fast as any in the world. Twinkle was packaged as a small, stand-alone multimedia player with its own screen. You could carry it in your hand, and use it on a bus or a train. It was going to be revolutionary. But now the Malaysia plant was having trouble manufacturing the new fast drives.

Benedict sipped his coffee. "Is it true you're the only division manager who isn't an engineer?"

Sanders smiled. "That's right. I'm originally from marketing."

"Isn't that pretty unusual?" Benedict said.

"Not really. In marketing, we used to spend a lot of time figuring out what the features of the new products were, and most of us couldn't talk to the engineers. I could. I don't know why. I don't have a technical background, but I could talk to the guys. I knew just enough so they couldn't bullshit me. So pretty soon, I was the one who talked to the engineers. Then eight years ago, Garvin asked me if I'd run a division for him. And here I am."

The call rang through. Sanders glanced at his watch. It was almost midnight in Kuala Lumpur. He hoped Arthur Kahn would still be awake. A moment later there was a click, and a groggy voice said, "Uh. Hello."

"Arthur, it's Tom."

Arthur Kahn gave a gravelly cough. "Oh, Tom. Good." Another cough. "You got my fax?"

"Yes, I got it."

"Then you know. I don't understand what's going on," Kahn said. "And I spent all day on the line. I had to, with Jafar gone."

Mohammed Jafar was the line foreman of the Malaysia plant, a very capable young man. "Jafar is gone? Why?"

There was a crackle of static. "He was cursed."

"I didn't get that."

"Jafar was cursed by his cousin, so he left."

"What?"

"Yeah, if you can believe that. He says his cousin's sister in Johore hired a sorcerer to cast a spell on him, and he ran off to the Orang Asli witch doctors for a counter-spell. The aborigines run a hospital at Kuala Tingit, in the jungle about three hours outside of KL. It's very famous. A lot of politicians go out there when they get sick. Jafar went out there for a cure."

"How long will that take?"

"Beats me. The other workers tell me it'll probably be a week."

"And what's wrong with the line, Arthur?"

"I don't know," Kahn said. "I'm not sure anything's wrong with the line. But the units coming off are very slow. When we pull units for IP checks, we consistently get seek times above the hundred-millisecond specs. We don't know why they're slow, and we don't know why there's a variation. But the engineers here are guessing that there's a compatibility problem with the controller chip that positions the split optics, and the CD-driver software."

"You think the controller chips are bad?" The controller chips were made in Singapore and trucked across the border to the factory in Malaysia.

"Don't know. Either they're bad, or there's a bug in the driver code."

"What about the screen flicker?"

Kahn coughed. "I think it's a design problem, Tom. We just can't build it. The hinge connectors that carry current to the screen are mounted inside the plastic housing. They're supposed to maintain electrical contact no matter how you move the screen. But the current cuts in and out. You move the hinge, and the screen flashes on and off."

Sanders frowned as he listened. "This is a pretty standard design, Arthur. Every damn laptop in the world has the same hinge design. It's been that way for the last ten years."

"I know it," Kahn said. "But ours isn't working. It's making me crazy."

"You better send me some units."

"I already have, DHL. You'll get them late today, tomorrow at the latest."

"Okay," Sanders said. He paused. "What's your best guess, Arthur?"

"About the run? Well, at the moment we can't make our production quotas, and we're turning out a product thirty to fifty percent slower than specs. Not good news. This isn't a hot CD player, Tom. It's only incrementally better than what Toshiba and Sony already have on the market. They're making theirs a lot cheaper. So we have major problems."

"We talking a week, a month, what?"

"A month, if it's not a redesign. If it's a redesign, say four months. If it's a chip, it could be a year."

Sanders sighed. "Great."

"That's the situation. It isn't working, and we don't know why."

Sanders said, "Who else have you told?"

"Nobody. This one's all yours, my friend."

"Thanks a lot."

Kahn coughed. "You going to bury this until after the merger, or what?"

"I don't know. I'm not sure I can."

"Well, I'll be quiet at this end. I can tell you that. Anybody asks me, I don't have a clue. Because I don't."

"Okay. Thanks, Arthur. I'll talk to you later."

Sanders hung up. Twinkle definitely presented a political problem for the impending merger with Conley-White. Sanders wasn't sure how to handle it. But he would have to deal with it soon enough; the ferry whistle blew, and up ahead, he saw the black pilings of Colman Dock and the skyscrapers of downtown Seattle.

Digicom was located in three different buildings around historic Pioneer Square, in downtown Seattle. Pioneer Square was actually shaped like a triangle, and had at its center a small park, dominated by a wrought-iron pergola, with antique clocks mounted above. Around Pioneer Square were low-rise red-brick buildings built in the early years of the century, with sculpted façades and chiseled dates; these buildings now housed trendy architects, graphic design firms, and a cluster of high-tech companies that included Aldus, Advance HoloGraphics, and DigiCom. Originally, DigiCom had occupied the Hazzard Building, on the south side of the square. As the company grew, it expanded into three floors of the adjacent Western Building, and later, to the Gorham Tower on James Street. But the executive offices were still on the top three floors of the Hazzard Building, overlooking the square. Sanders's office was on the fourth floor, though he expected later in the week to move up to the fifth.

He got to the fourth floor at nine in the morning, and immediately sensed that something was wrong. There was a buzz in the hallways, an electric tension in the air. Staff people clustered at the laser printers and whispered at the coffee machines; they turned away or stopped talking when he walked by.

He thought, Uh-oh.

But as a division head, he could hardly stop to ask an assistant what was happening. Sanders walked on, swearing under his breath, angry with himself that he had arrived late on this important day.

Through the glass walls of the fourth-floor conference room, he saw Mark Lewyn, the thirty-three-year-old head of Product Design, briefing some of the Conley-White people. It made a striking scene: Lewyn, young, handsome, and imperious, wearing black jeans and a black Armani T-shirt, pacing back and forth and talking animatedly to the blue-suited Conley-White staffers, who sat rigidly before the product mock-ups on the table, and took notes.

When Lewyn saw Sanders he waved, and came over to the door of the conference room and stuck his head out.

"Hey, guy," Lewyn said.

"Hi, Mark. Listen—"

"I have just one thing to say to you," Lewyn said, interrupting. "Fuck 'em. Fuck Garvin. Fuck Phil. Fuck the merger. Fuck 'em all. This reorg sucks. I'm with you on this one, guy."

"Listen, Mark, can you—"

"I'm in the middle of something here." Lewyn

jerked his head toward the Conley people in the room. "But I wanted you to know how I feel. It's not right, what they're doing. We'll talk later, okay? Chin up, guy," Lewyn said. "Keep your powder dry." And he went back into the conference room.

The Conley-White people were all staring at Sanders through the glass. He turned away and walked quickly toward his office, with a sense of deepening unease. Lewyn was notorious for his tendency to exaggerate, but even so, the—

It's not right, what they're doing.

There didn't seem to be much doubt what that meant. Sanders wasn't going to get a promotion. He broke into a light sweat and felt suddenly dizzy as he walked along the corridor. He leaned against the wall for a moment. He wiped his forehead with his hand and blinked his eyes rapidly. He took a deep breath and shook his head to clear it.

No promotion. Christ. He took another deep breath, and walked on.

Instead of the promotion he expected, there was apparently going to be some kind of reorganization. And apparently it was related to the merger.

The technical divisions had just gone through a major reorganization nine months earlier, which had revised all the lines of authority, upsetting the hell out of everybody in Seattle. Staff people didn't know who to requisition for laser-printer paper, or to degauss a monitor. There had been months of uproar; only in the last few weeks had the tech groups settled down into some semblance of good working routines. Now . . . to reorganize again? It didn't make any sense at all.

Yet it was last year's reorganization that placed Sanders in line to assume leadership of the tech divisions now. That reorganization had structured the Advanced Products Group into four subdivisions—Product Design, Programming, Data Telecommunications, and Manufacturing—all under the direction of a division general manager, not yet appointed. In recent months, Tom Sanders had informally taken over as DGM, largely because as head of manufacturing, he was the person most concerned with coordinating the work of all the other divisions.

But now, with still another reorganization . . . who knew what might happen? Sanders might be broken back to simply managing DigiCom's production lines around the world. Or worse—for weeks, there had been persistent rumors that company headquarters in Cupertino was going to take back all control of manufacturing from Seattle, turning it over to the individual product managers in California. Sanders hadn't paid any attention to those rumors, because they didn't make a lot of sense; the product managers had enough to do just pushing the products, without also worrying about their manufacture.

But now he was obliged to consider the possibility that the rumors were true. Because if they were true, Sanders might be facing more than a demotion. He might be out of a job.

Christ: out of a job?

He found himself thinking of some of the things Dave Benedict had said to him on the ferry earlier that morning. Benedict chased rumors, and he had seemed to know a lot. Maybe even more than he had been saying.

Is it true you're the only division manager who isn't an engineer?

And then, pointedly:

Isn't that pretty unusual?

Christ, he thought. He began to sweat again. He forced himself to take another deep breath. He reached the end of the fourth-floor corridor and came to his office, expecting to find Stephanie Kaplan, the CFO, waiting there for him. Kaplan could tell him what was going on. But his office was empty. He turned to his assistant, Cindy Wolfe, who was busy at the filing cabinets. "Where's Stephanie?"

"She's not coming."

"Why not?"

"They canceled your nine-thirty meeting because of all the personnel changes," Cindy said.

"What changes?" Sanders said. "What's going on?"

"There's been some kind of reorganization," Cindy said. She avoided meeting his eyes, and looked down at the call book on her desk. "They just scheduled a private lunch with all the division heads in the main conference room for twelve-thirty today, and Phil Blackburn is on his way down to talk to you. He should be here any minute. Let's see, what else? DHL is delivering drives from Kuala Lumpur this afternoon. Gary Bosak wants to meet with you at ten-thirty." She ran her finger down the call book. "Don Cherry called twice about the Corridor, and you just got a rush call from Eddie in Austin."

"Call him back." Eddie Larson was the production supervisor in the Austin plant, which made cellular telephones. Cindy placed the call; a moment later he heard the familiar voice with the Texas twang.

"Hey there, Tommy boy."

"Hi, Eddie. What's up?"

"Little problem on the line. You got a minute?"

"Yes, sure."

"Are congratulations on a new job in order?"

"I haven't heard anything yet," Sanders said.

"Uh-huh. But it's going to happen?"

"I haven't heard anything, Eddie."

"Is it true they're going to shut down the Austin plant?"

Sanders was so startled, he burst out laughing. *"What?"*

"Hey, that's what they're saying down here, Tommy boy. Conley-White is going to buy the company and then shut us down."

"Hell," Sanders said. "Nobody's buying anything, and nobody's selling anything, Eddie. The Austin line is an industry standard. And it's very profitable."

He paused. "You'd tell me if you knew, wouldn't you, Tommy boy?"

"Yes, I would," Sanders said. "But it's just a rumor, Eddie. So forget it. Now, what's the line problem?"

"Diddly stuff. The women on the production line are demanding that we clean out the pinups in the men's locker room. They say it's offensive to them. You ask me, I think it's bull," Larson said. "Because women never go into the men's locker room."

"Then how do they know about the pinups?"

"The night cleanup crews have women on 'em. So now the women working the line want the pinups removed."

Sanders sighed. "We don't need any complaints about being unresponsive on sex issues. Get the pinups out."

"Even if the women have pinups in *their* locker room?"

"Just do it, Eddie."

"You ask me, it's caving in to a lot of feminist bullshit."

There was a knock on the door. Sanders looked up and saw Phil Blackburn, the company lawyer, standing there.

"Eddie, I have to go."

"Okay," Eddie said, "but I'm telling you—"

"Eddie, I'm sorry. I have to go. Call me if anything changes."

Sanders hung up the phone, and Blackburn came into the room. Sanders's first impression was that the lawyer was smiling too broadly, behaving too cheerfully.

It was a bad sign.

Philip Blackburn, the chief legal counsel for DigiCom, was a slender man of forty-six wearing a dark green Hugo Boss suit. Like Sanders, Blackburn had been with DigiCom for over a decade, which meant that he was one of the "old guys," one of those who had "gotten in at the beginning." When Sanders first met him, Blackburn was a brash, bearded young civil rights lawyer from Berkeley. But Blackburn had long since abandoned protest for profits, which he pursued with singleminded intensity—while carefully emphasizing the new corporate issues of diversity and equal opportunity. Blackburn's embrace of the latest fashions in clothing and correctness made "PC Phil" a figure of fun in some quarters of the company. As one executive put it, "Phil's finger is chapped from wetting it and holding it to the wind." He was the first with Birkenstocks, the first with bell-bottoms, the first with sideburns off, and the first with diversity.

Many of the jokes focused on his mannerisms. Fussy, preoccupied with appearances, Blackburn was always running his hands over himself, touching his hair, his face, his suit, seeming to caress himself, to smooth out the wrinkles in his suit.

This, combined with his unfortunate tendency to rub, touch, and pick his nose, was the source of much humor. But it was humor with an edge: Blackburn was mistrusted as a moralistic hatchet man.

Blackburn could be charismatic in his speeches, and in private could convey a convincing impression of intellectual honesty for short periods. But within the company he was seen for what he was: a gun for hire, a man with no convictions of his own, and hence the perfect person to be Garvin's executioner.

In earlier years, Sanders and Blackburn had been close friends; not only had they grown up with the company, but their lives were intertwined personally as well: when Blackburn went through his bitter divorce in 1982, he lived for a while in Sanders's bachelor apartment in Sunnyvale. A few years later, Blackburn had been best man at Sanders's own wedding to a young Seattle attorney, Susan Handler.

But when Blackburn remarried in 1989, Sanders was not invited to the wedding, for by then, their relationship had become strained. Some in the company saw it as inevitable: Blackburn was a part of the inner power circle in Cupertino, to which Sanders, based in Seattle, no longer belonged. In addition, the two men had had sharp disputes about setting up the production lines in Ireland and Malaysia. Sanders felt that Blackburn ignored the inevitable realities of production in foreign countries.

Typical was Blackburn's demand that half the workers on the new line in Kuala Lumpur should be women, and that they should be intermingled with the men; the Malay managers wanted the women segregated, allowed to work only on certain parts of the line, away from the men. Phil strenuously objected. Sanders kept telling him, "It's a Muslim country, Phil."

"I don't give a damn," Phil said. "DigiCom stands for equality."

"Phil, it's their country. They're Muslim."

"So what? It's our factory."

Their disagreements went on and on. The Malaysian government didn't want local Chinese hired as supervisors, although they were the best-qualified; it was the policy of the Malaysian government to train Malays for supervisory jobs. Sanders disagreed with this blatantly discriminatory policy, because he wanted the best supervisors he could get for the plant. But Phil, an outspoken opponent of discrimination in America, immediately acquiesced to the Malay government's discriminatory policy, saying that DigiCom should embrace a true multicultural perspective. At the last minute, Sanders had had to fly to Kuala Lumpur and meet with the Sultans of Selangor and Pahang, to agree to their demands. Phil then announced that Sanders had "toadied up to the extremists."

It was just one of the many controversies that surrounded Sanders's handling of the new Malaysia factory.

Now, Sanders and Blackburn greeted each other with the wariness of former friends who had long since ceased to be anything but superficially cordial. Sanders shook Blackburn's hand as the company lawyer stepped into the office. "What's going on, Phil?"

"Big day," Blackburn said, slipping into the chair facing Sanders's desk. "Lot of surprises. I don't know what you've heard."

"I've heard Garvin has made a decision about the restructuring."

"Yes, he has. Several decisions."

There was a pause. Blackburn shifted in his chair and looked at his hands. "I know that Bob wanted to fill you in himself about all this. He came by earlier this morning to talk to everyone in the division."

"I wasn't here."

"Uh-huh. We were all kind of surprised that you were late today."

Sanders let that pass without comment. He stared at Blackburn, waiting.

"Anyway, Tom," Blackburn said, "the bottom line is this. As part of the overall merger, Bob has decided to go outside the Advanced Products Group for leadership of the division."

So there it was. Finally, out in the open. Sanders took a deep breath, felt the bands of tightness in his chest. His whole body was tense. But he tried not to show it.

"I know this is something of a shock," Blackburn said.

"Well," Sanders shrugged. "I've heard rumors." Even as he spoke, his mind was racing ahead. It was clear now that there would not be a promotion, there would not be a raise, he would not have a new opportunity to—

"Yes. Well," Blackburn said, clearing his throat. "Bob has decided that Meredith Johnson is going to head up the division."

Sanders frowned. "Meredith *Johnson*?"

"Right. She's in the Cupertino office. I think you know her."

"Yes, I do, but . . ." Sanders shook his head. It didn't make any sense. "Meredith's from sales. Her background is in sales."

"Originally, yes. But as you know, Meredith's been in Operations the last couple of years."

"Even so, Phil. The APG is a technical division."

"You're not technical. You've done just fine."

"But I've been involved in this for years, when I was in Marketing. Look, the APG is basically programming teams and hardware fabrication lines. How can she run it?"

"Bob doesn't expect her to run it directly. She'll oversee the APG division managers, who will report to her. Meredith's official title will be Vice President for Advanced Operations and Planning. Under the new structure, that will include the entire APG Division, the Marketing Division, and the TelCom Division."

"Jesus," Sanders said, sitting back in his chair. "That's pretty much everything."

Blackburn nodded slowly.

Sanders paused, thinking it over. "It sounds," he said finally, "like Meredith Johnson's going to be running this company."

"I wouldn't go *that* far," Blackburn said. "She won't have direct control over sales or finance or distribution in this new scheme. But I think there is no question Bob has placed her in direct line for succession, when he steps down as CEO sometime in the next two years." Blackburn shifted in his chair. "But that's the future. For the present—"

"Just a minute. She'll have four APG division managers reporting to her?" Sanders said.

"Yes."

"And who are those managers going to be? Has that been decided?"

"Well." Phil coughed. He ran his hands over his chest, and plucked at the handkerchief in his breast pocket. "Of course, the actual decision to name the division managers will be Meredith's."

"Meaning I might not have a job."

"Oh hell, Tom," Blackburn said. "Nothing of the sort. Bob wants everyone in the divisions to stay. Including you. He'd hate very much to lose you."

"But it's Meredith Johnson's decision whether I keep my job."

"Technically," Blackburn said, spreading his hands, "it has to be. But I think it's pretty much pro forma."

Sanders did not see it that way at all. Garvin could easily have named all the division managers at the same time he named Meredith Johnson to run the APG. If Garvin decided to turn the company over to some woman from Sales, that was certainly his choice. But Garvin could still make sure he kept his division heads in place—the heads who had served him and the company so well.

"Jesus," Sanders said. "I've been with this company twelve years."

"And I expect you will be with us many more," Blackburn said smoothly. "Look: it's in everybody's interest to keep the teams in place. Because as I said, she can't run them directly."

"Uh-huh."

Blackburn shot his cuffs and ran his hand through his hair. "Listen, Tom. I know you're disappointed that this appointment didn't come to you. But let's not make too much of Meredith appointing the division heads. Realistically speaking, she isn't going to make any changes. Your situation is secure." He paused. "You know the way Meredith is, Tom."

"I used to," Sanders said, nodding. "Hell, I lived with her for a while. But I haven't seen her in years."

Blackburn looked surprised. "You two haven't kept contact?"

"Not really, no. By the time Meredith joined the company, I was up here in Seattle, and she was based in Cupertino. I ran into her once, on a trip down there. Said hello. That's about it."

"Then you only know her from the old days," Blackburn said, as if it all suddenly made sense. "From six or seven years ago."

"It's longer than that," Sanders said. "I've been in Seattle eight years. So it must be . . ." Sanders thought back. "When I was going out with her, she worked for Novell in Mountain View. Selling Ethernet cards to small businesses for local area networks. When was that?" Although he remembered the relationship with Meredith Johnson vividly, Sanders was hazy about exactly when it had occurred. He tried to recall some memorable event—a birthday, a promotion, an apartment move—that would mark the date. Finally he remembered watching election returns with her on television: balloons rising up toward the ceiling, people cheering. She was drinking beer. That had been early in their relationship. "Jesus, Phil. It must be almost ten years ago."

"That long," Blackburn said.

When Sanders first met Meredith Johnson, she was one of the thousands of pretty saleswomen working in San Jose—young women in their twenties, not long out of college, who started out doing the product demos on the computer while a senior man stood beside her and did all the talking to the customer. Eventually, a lot of those women learned enough to do the selling themselves. At the time Sanders first knew Meredith, she had acquired enough jargon to rattle on about token rings and 10BaseT hubs. She didn't really have any deep knowledge, but she didn't need to. She was good-looking, sexy, and smart, and she had a kind of uncanny self-possession that carried her through awkward moments. Sanders had admired her, back in those days. But he never imagined that she had the ability to hold a major corporate position.

Blackburn shrugged. "A lot's happened in ten years, Tom," he said. "Meredith isn't just a sales exec. She went back to school, got an MBA. She worked at Symantec, then Conrad, and then she came to work with us. The last couple of years, she's been working very closely with Garvin. Sort of his protégé. He's been pleased with her work on a number of assignments."

Sanders shook his head. "And now she's my boss . . ."

"Is that a problem for you?"

"No. It just seems funny. An old girlfriend as my boss."

"The worm turns," Blackburn said. He was smiling, but Sanders sensed he was watching him closely. "You seem a little uneasy about this, Tom."

"It takes some getting used to."

"Is there a problem? Reporting to a woman?"

"Not at all. I worked for Eileen when she was head of HRI, and we got along great. It's not that. It's just funny to think of Meredith Johnson as my boss."

"She's an impressive and accomplished manager," Phil said. He stood up, smoothed his tie. "I think when you've had an opportunity to become reacquainted, you'll be very impressed. Give her a chance, Tom."

"Of course," Sanders said.

"I'm sure everything will work out. And keep your eye on the future. After all, you should be rich in a year or so."

"Does that mean we're still spinning off the APG Division?"

"Oh yes. Absolutely."

It was a much-discussed part of the merger plan that after Conley-White bought DigiCom, it would spin off the Advanced Products Division and take it public, as a separate company. That would mean enormous profits for everyone in the division. Because everyone would have the chance to buy cheap options before the stock was publicly sold.

"We're working out the final details now," Blackburn said. "But I expect that division managers like yourself will start with twenty thousand shares vested, and an initial option of fifty thousand shares at twenty-five cents a share, with the right to purchase another fifty thousand shares each year for the next five years."

"And the spin-off will go forward, even with Meredith running the divisions?"

"Trust me. The spin-off will happen within eighteen months. It's a formal part of the merger plan."

"There's no chance that she may decide to change her mind?"

"None at all, Tom." Blackburn smiled. "I'll tell you a little secret. Originally, this spin-off was Meredith's idea."

Blackburn left Sanders's office and went down the hall to an empty office and called Garvin. He heard the familiar sharp bark: "Garvin here."

"I talked to Tom Sanders."

"And?"

"I'd say he took it well. He was disappointed, of course. I think he'd already heard a rumor. But he took it well."

Garvin said, "And the new structure? How did he respond?"

"He's concerned," Blackburn said. "He expressed reservations."

"Why?"

"He doesn't feel she has the technical expertise to run the division."

Garvin snorted, "Technical expertise? That's the last goddamn thing I care about. Technical expertise is not an issue here."

"Of course not. But I think there was some uneasiness on the personal level. You know, they once had a relationship."

"Yes," Garvin said. "I know that. Have they talked?"

"He says, not for several years."

"Bad blood?"

"There didn't seem to be."

"Then what's he concerned about?"

"I think he's just getting used to the idea."

"He'll come around."

"I think so."

"Tell me if you hear otherwise," Garvin said, and hung up.

Alone in the office, Blackburn frowned. The conversation with Sanders left him vaguely uneasy. It had seemed to go well enough, and yet . . . Sanders, he felt sure, was not going to take this reorganization lying down. Sanders was popular in the Seattle division, and he could easily cause trouble. Sanders was too independent, he was not a team player, and the company needed team players now. The more Blackburn thought about it, the more certain he was that Sanders was going to be a problem.

Tom Sanders sat at his desk, staring forward, lost in thought. He was trying to put together his memory of a pretty young saleswoman in Silicon Valley with this new image of a corporate officer running company divisions, executing the complex groundwork required to take a division public. But his thoughts kept being interrupted by random images from the past: Meredith smiling, wearing one of his shirts, naked beneath it. An opened suitcase on the bed. White stockings and white garter belt. A bowl of popcorn on the blue couch in the living room. The television with the sound turned off.

And for some reason, the image of a flower, a purple iris, in stained glass. It was one of those hackneyed Northern California hippie images. Sanders knew where it came from: it was on the glass of the front door to the apartment where he had lived, back in Sunnyvale. Back in the days when he had known Meredith. He wasn't sure why he should keep thinking of it now, and he—

"Tom?"

He glanced up. Cindy was standing in the doorway, looking concerned.

"Tom, do you want coffee?"

"No, thanks."

"Don Cherry called again while you were with Phil. He wants you to come and look at the Corridor."

"They having problems?"

"I don't know. He sounded excited. You want to call him back?"

"Not right now. I'll go down and see him in a minute."

She lingered at the door. "You want a bagel? Have you had breakfast?"

"I'm fine."

"Sure?"

"I'm fine, Cindy. Really."

She went away. He turned to look at his monitor, and saw that the icon for his e-mail was blinking. But he was thinking again about Meredith Johnson.

Sanders had more or less lived with her for about six months. It had been quite an intense relationship for a while. And yet, although he kept having isolated, vivid images, he realized that in general his memories from that time were surprisingly vague. Had he really lived with Meredith for six months? When exactly had they first met, and when had they broken up? Sanders was surprised at how difficult it was for him to fix the chronology in his mind. Hoping for clarity, he considered other aspects of his life: what had been his position at DigiCom in those days? Was he still working in Marketing, or had he already moved to the technical divisions? He wasn't sure, now. He would have to look it up in the files.

He thought about Blackburn. Blackburn had left his wife and moved in with Sanders around the time Sanders was involved with Meredith. Or was it afterward, when things had gone bad? Maybe Phil had moved into his apartment around the time he was breaking up with Meredith. Sanders wasn't sure. As he considered it, he realized he wasn't sure about anything from that time. These events had all happened a decade ago, in another city, at another period in his life, and his memories were in disarray. Again, he was surprised at how confused he was.

He pushed the intercom. "Cindy? I've got a question for you."

"Sure, Tom."

"This is the third week of June. What were you doing the third week of June, ten years ago?"

She didn't even hesitate. "That's easy: graduating from college."

Of course that would be true. "Okay," he said. "Then how about June, nine years ago."

"Nine years ago?" Her voice sounded suddenly cautious, less certain. "Gee . . . Let's see, June . . . Nine years ago? . . . June . . . Uh . . . I think I was with my boyfriend in Europe."

"Not your present boyfriend?"

"No . . . This guy was a real jerk."

Sanders said, "How long did that last?"

"We were there for a month."

"I mean the relationship."

"With him? Oh, let's see, we broke up . . . oh, it must have been . . . uh, December . . . I think it was December, or maybe January, after the holidays . . . Why?"

"Just trying to figure something out," Sanders said. Already he was relieved to hear the uncertain tone of her voice, as she tried to piece together the past. "By the way, how far back do we have office records? Correspondence, and call books?"

"I'd have to check. I know I have about three years."

"And what about earlier?"

"Earlier? How much earlier?"

"Ten years ago," he said.

"Gee, that'd be when you were in Cupertino. Do they have that stuff in storage down there? Did they put it on fiche, or was it just thrown out?"

"I don't know."

"You want me to check?"

"Not now," he said, and clicked off. He didn't want her making any inquiries in Cupertino now. Not right now.

Sanders rubbed his eyes with his fingertips. His thoughts drifting back over time. Again, he saw the stained-glass flower. It was oversize, bright, banal. Sanders had always been embarrassed by the banality of it. In those days, he had lived in one of the apartment complexes on Merano Drive. Twenty units clustered around a chilly little swimming pool. Everybody in the building worked for a high-tech company. Nobody ever went in the pool. And Sanders wasn't around much. Those were the days when he flew with Garvin to Korea twice a month. The days when they all flew coach. They couldn't even afford business class.

And he remembered how he would come home, exhausted from the long flight, and the first thing he would see when he got to his apartment was that damned stained-glass flower on the door.

And Meredith, in those days, was partial to white stockings, a white garter belt, little white flowers on the snaps with—

"Tom?" He looked up. Cindy was at the doorway. She said, "If you want to see Don Cherry, you'd better go now because you have a ten-thirty with Gary Bosak."

He felt as if she was treating him like an invalid. "Cindy, I'm fine."

"I know. Just a reminder."

"Okay, I'll go now."

As he hurried down the stairs to the third floor, he felt relieved at the distraction. Cindy was right to get him out of the office. And he was curious to see what Cherry's team had done with the Corridor.

The Corridor was what everyone at DigiCom called VIE: the Virtual Information Environment. VIE was the companion piece to Twinkle, the second major element in the emerging future of digital information as envisioned by DigiCom. In the future, information was going to be stored on disks, or made available in large databases that users would dial into over telephone lines. At the moment, users saw information displayed on flat screens—either televisions or computer screens. That had been the traditional way of handling information for the last thirty years. But soon, there would be new ways to present information. The most radical, and the most exciting, was virtual environments. Users wore special glasses to see computer-generated, three-dimensional environments which allowed them to feel as though they were literally moving through another world. Dozens of high-tech companies were racing to develop virtual environments. It was exciting, but very difficult, technology. At DigiCom, VIE was one of Garvin's pet projects; he had thrown a lot of money at it; he had had Don Cherry's programmers working on it around the clock for two years.

And so far, it had been nothing but trouble.

The sign on the door said "VIE" and underneath, "When Reality Is Not Enough." Sanders inserted his card in the slot, and the door clicked open. He passed through an anteroom, hearing a half-dozen voices shouting from the main equipment room beyond. Even in the anteroom, he noticed a distinctly nauseating odor in the air.

Entering the main room, he came upon a scene of utter chaos. The windows were thrown wide; there was the astringent smell of cleaning fluid. Most of the programmers were on the floor, working with disassembled equipment. The VIE units lay scattered in pieces, amid a tangle of multicolored cables. Even the black circular walker pads had been taken apart, the rubber bearings being cleaned one by one. Still more wires descended from the ceiling to the laser scanners which were broken open, their circuit boards exposed. Everyone seemed to be talking at once. And in the center of the room, looking like a teenage Buddha in an electric blue T-shirt that said "Reality Sucks," was Don Cherry, the head of Programming. Cherry was twenty-two years old, widely acknowledged to be indispensable, and famous for his impertinence.

When he saw Sanders he shouted: "Out! Out! Damned management! Out!"

"Why?" Sanders said. "I thought you wanted to see me."

"Too late! You had your chance!" Cherry said. "Now it's over!"

For a moment, Sanders thought Cherry was referring to the promotion he hadn't gotten. But Cherry was the most apolitical of the DigiCom division heads, and he was grinning cheerfully as he walked toward Sanders, stepping over his prostrate programmers. "Sorry, Tom. You're too late. We're fine-tuning now."

"Fine-tuning? It looks like ground zero here. And what's that terrible smell?"

"I know." Cherry threw up his hands. "I ask the boys to wash every day, but what can I say. They're programmers. No better than dogs."

"Cindy said you called me several times."

"I did," Cherry said. "We had the Corridor up and running, and I wanted you to see it. But maybe it's just as well you didn't."

Sanders looked at the complex equipment scattered all around him. "You had it *up*?"

"That was then. This is now. Now, we're fine-tuning." Cherry nodded to the programmers on the floor, working on the walker pads. "We finally got the bug out of the main loop, last night at midnight. The refresh rate doubled. The system really rips now. So we have to adjust the walkers and the servos to update responsiveness. It's a *mechanical* problem," he said disdainfully. "But we'll take care of it anyway."

The programmers were always annoyed when they had to deal with mechanical problems. Living almost entirely in an abstract world of computer code, they felt that physical machinery was beneath them.

Sanders said, "What is the problem, exactly?"

"Well, look," Cherry said. "Here's our latest implementation. The user wears this headset," he said, pointing to what looked like thick silver sunglasses. "And he gets on the walker pad, here."

The walker pad was one of Cherry's innovations. The size of a small round trampoline, its surface was composed of tightly packed rubber balls. It functioned like a multidirectional treadmill; walking on the balls, users could move in any direction. "Once he's on the walker," Cherry said, "the user dials into a database. Then the computer, over there—" Cherry pointed to a stack of boxes in the corner, "takes the information coming from the database and constructs a virtual environment which is projected inside the headset. When the user walks on the pad, the projection changes, so you feel like you're walking down a corridor lined with drawers of data on all sides. The user can stop anywhere, open any file drawer with his hand, and thumb through data. Completely realistic simulation."

"How many users?"

"At the moment, the system can handle five at one time."

"And the Corridor looks like what?" Sanders said. "Wire-frame?" In the earlier versions, the Corridor was outlined in skeletal black-and-white outlines. Fewer lines made it faster for the computer to draw.

"Wire-frame?" Cherry sniffed. "*Please*. We dumped that two weeks ago. Now we are talking 3-D surfaces fully modeled in 24-bit color, with anti-alias texture maps. We're rendering true curved surfaces—no polygons. Looks completely real."

"And what're the laser scanners for? I thought you did position by infrared." The headsets had infrared sensors mounted above them, so that the system could detect where the user was looking and adjust the projected image inside the headset to match the direction of looking.

"We still do," Cherry said. "The scanners are for body representation."

"Body representation?"

"Yeah. Now, if you're walking down the Corridor with somebody else, you can turn and look at them and you'll see them. Because the scanners are capturing a three-dimensional texture map in real time: they read body and expression, and draw the virtual face of the virtual person standing beside you in the virtual room. You can't see the person's eyes, of course, because they're hidden by the headset they're wearing. But the system generates a face from the stored texture map. Pretty slick, huh?"

"You mean you can see other users?"

"That's right. See their faces, see their expressions. And that's not all. If other users in the system aren't wearing a headset, you can still see them, too. The program identifies other users, pulls their photo out of the personnel file, and pastes it onto a virtual body image. A little kludgey, but not bad." Cherry waved his hand in the air. "And that's not all. We've also built in virtual help."

"Virtual help?"

"Sure, users always need online help. So we've made an angel to help you. Floats alongside you, answers your questions." Cherry was grinning. "We thought of making it a blue fairy, but we didn't want to offend anybody."

Sanders stared thoughtfully at the room. Cherry was telling him about his successes. But something else was happening here: it was impossible to miss the tension, the frantic energy of the people as they worked.

"Hey, Don," one of the programmers shouted. "What's the Z-count supposed to be?"

"Over five," Cherry said.

"I got it to four-three."

"Four-three sucks. Get it above five, or you're

fired." He turned to Sanders. "You've got to encourage the troops."

Sanders looked at Cherry. "All right," he said finally. "Now what's the *real* problem?"

Cherry shrugged. "Nothing. I told you: finetuning."

"Don."

Cherry sighed. "Well, when we jumped the refresh rate, we trashed the builder module. You see, the room is being built in real time by the box. With a faster refresh off the sensors, we have to build objects much faster. Otherwise the room seems to lag behind you. You feel like you're drunk. You move your head, and the room swooshes behind you, catching up."

"And?"

"And, it makes the users throw up."

Sanders sighed. "Great."

"We had to take the walker pads apart because Teddy barfed all over everything."

"Great, Don."

"What's the matter? It's no big deal. It cleans up." He shook his head. "Although I do wish Teddy hadn't eaten huevos rancheros for breakfast. That was unfortunate. Little bits of tortilla everywhere in the bearings."

"You know we have a demo tomorrow for the C-W people."

"No problem. We'll be ready."

"Don, I can't have their top executives throwing up."

"Trust me," Cherry said. "We'll be ready. They're going to love it. Whatever problems this company has, the Corridor is not one of them."

"That's a promise?"

"That," Cherry said, "is a guarantee."

Sanders was back in his office by ten-twenty, and was seated at his desk when Gary Bosak came in. Bosak was a tall man in his twenties, wearing jeans, running shoes, and a Terminator T-shirt. He carried a large fold-over leather briefcase, the kind that trial attorneys used.

"You look pale," Bosak said. "But everybody in the building is pale today. It's tense as hell around here, you know that?"

"I've noticed."

"Yeah, I bet. Okay to start?"

"Sure."

"Cindy? Mr. Sanders is going to be unavailable for a few minutes."

Bosak closed the office door and locked it. Whistling cheerfully, he unplugged Sanders's desk phone, and the phone beside the couch in the corner. From there, he went to the window and closed the blinds. There was a small television in the corner; he turned it on. He snapped the latches on his briefcase, took out a small plastic box, and flipped the switch on the side. The box began to blink, and emitted a low white noise hiss. Bosak set it in the middle of Sanders's desk. Bosak never gave information until the white noise scrambler was in place, since most of what he had to say implied illegal behavior.

"I have good news for you," Bosak said. "Your boy is clean." He pulled out a manila file, opened it up, and started handing over pages. "Peter John Nealy, twenty-three, DigiCom employee for sixteen months. Now working as a programmer in APG. Okay, here we go. His high school and college transcripts . . . Employment file from Data General, his last employer. All in order. Now, the recent stuff . . . Credit rating from TRW . . . Phone bills from his apartment . . . Phone bills for his cellular line . . . Bank statement . . . Savings account . . . Last two 1040s . . . Twelve months of credit card charges, VISA and Master . . . Travel records . . . E-mail messages inside the company, and off the Internet . . . Parking tickets . . . And this is the clincher . . . Ramada Inn in Sunnyvale, last three visits, his phone charges there, the numbers he called . . . Last three car rentals with mileage . . . Rental car cellular phone, the numbers called . . . That's everything."

"And?"

"I ran down the numbers he called. Here's the breakdown. A lot of calls to Seattle Silicon, but Nealy's seeing a girl there. She's a secretary, works in sales, no conflict. He also calls his brother, a programmer at Boeing, does parallel processing stuff for wing design, no conflict. His other calls are to suppliers and code vendors, and they're all appropriate. No calls after hours. No calls to pay phones. No overseas calls. No suspicious pattern in the calls. No unexplained bank transfers, no sudden new purchases. No reason to think he's looking for a move. I'd say he's not talking to anybody you care about."

"Good," Sanders said. He glanced down at the sheets of paper, and paused. "Gary . . . Some of this stuff is from our company. Some of these reports."

"Yeah. So?"

"How'd you get them?"

Bosak grinned. "Hey. You don't ask and I don't tell you."

"How'd you get the Data General file?"

Bosak shook his head. "Isn't this why you pay me?"

"Yes it is, but—"

"Hey. You wanted a check on an employee, you got it. Your kid's clean. He's working only for you. Anything else you want to know about him?"

"No." Sanders shook his head.

"Great. I got to get some sleep." Bosak collected all the files and placed them back in his folder. "By the way, you're going to get a call from my parole officer."

"Uh-huh."

"Can I count on you?"

"Sure, Gary."

"I told him I was doing consulting for you. On telecommunications security."

"And so you are."

Bosak switched off the blinking box, put it in his briefcase, and reconnected the telephones. "Always a pleasure. Do I leave the bill with you, or Cindy?"

"I'll take it. See you, Gary."

"Hey. Anytime. You need more, you know where I am."

Sanders glanced at the bill, from NE Professional Services, Inc., of Bellevue, Washington. The name was Bosak's private joke: the letters NE stood for "Necessary Evil." Ordinarily, high-tech companies employed retired police officers and private investigators to do background checks, but occasionally they used hackers like Gary Bosak, who could gain access to electronic data banks, to get information on suspect employees. The advantage of using Bosak was that he could work quickly, often making a report in a matter of hours, or overnight. Bosak's methods were of course illegal; simply by hiring him, Sanders himself had broken a half-dozen laws. But background checks on employees were accepted as standard practice in high-tech firms, where a single document or product development plan might be worth hundreds of thousands of dollars to competitors.

And in the case of Pete Nealy, a check was

particularly crucial. Nealy was developing hot new compression algorithms to pack and unpack video images onto CD-ROM laser disks. His work was vital to the new Twinkle technology. High-speed digital images coming off the disk were going to transform a sluggish technology and produce a revolution in education. But if Twinkle's algorithms became available to a competitor, then DigiCom's advantage would be greatly reduced, and that meant—

The intercom buzzed. "Tom," Cindy said. "It's eleven o'clock. Time for the APG meeting. You want the agenda on your way down?"

"Not today," he said. "I think I know what we'll be talking about."

In the third-floor conference room, the Advanced Products Group was already meeting. This was a weekly meeting in which the division heads discussed problems and brought everyone up to date. It was a meeting that Sanders ordinarily led. Around the table were Don Cherry, the chief of Programming; Mark Lewyn, the temperamental head of Product Design, all in black Armani; and Mary Anne Hunter, the head of Data Telecommunications. Petite and intense, Hunter was dressed in a sweatshirt, shorts, and Nike running tights; she never ate lunch, but ordinarily went on a five-mile run after each meeting.

Lewyn was in the middle of one of his storming rages: "It's insulting to everybody in the division. I have no idea why she got this position. I don't know what her qualifications could be for a job like this, and—"

Lewyn broke off as Sanders came into the room. There was an awkward moment. Everyone was silent, glancing at him, then looking away.

"I had a feeling," Sanders said, smiling, "you'd be talking about this."

The room remained silent. "Come on," he said, as he slipped into a chair. "It's not a funeral."

Mark Lewyn cleared his throat. "I'm sorry, Tom. I think it's an outrage."

Mary Anne Hunter said, "Everybody knows it should have been you."

Lewyn said, "It's a shock to all of us, Tom."

"Yeah," Cherry said, grinning. "We've been trying like hell to get you sacked, but we never really thought it would work."

"I appreciate all this," Sanders said, "but it's Garvin's company, and he can do what he wants with it. He's been right more often than not. And I'm a big boy. Nobody ever promised me anything."

Lewyn said, "You're really okay with this?"

"Believe me. I'm fine."

"You talked with Garvin?"

"I talked with Phil."

Lewyn shook his head. "That sanctimonious asshole."

"Listen," Cherry said, "did Phil say anything about the spin-off?"

"Yes," Sanders said. "The spin-off is still happening. Eighteen months after the merger, they'll structure the IPO, and take the division public."

There were little shrugs around the table. Sanders could see they were relieved. Going public meant a lot of money to all the people sitting in the room.

"And what did Phil say about Ms. Johnson?"

"Not much. Just that she's Garvin's choice to head up the technical side."

At that moment Stephanie Kaplan, DigiCom's Chief Financial Officer, came into the room. A tall woman with prematurely gray hair and a notably silent manner, she was known as Stephanie Stealth, or the Stealth Bomber—the latter a reference to her habit of quietly killing projects she did not consider profitable enough. Kaplan was based in Cupertino, but she generally sat in once a month on the Seattle division meetings. Lately, she had been up more often.

Lewyn said, "We're trying to cheer up Tom, Stephanie."

Kaplan took a seat, and gave Sanders a sympathetic smile. She didn't speak.

Lewyn said, "Did *you* know this Meredith Johnson appointment was coming?"

"No," Kaplan said. "It was a surprise to everybody. And not everybody's happy about it." Then, as if she had said too much, she opened her briefcase, and busied herself with her notes. As usual, she slid into the background; the others quickly ignored her.

"Well," Cherry said, "I hear Garvin's got a real thing for her. Johnson's only been with the company four years, and she hasn't been especially outstanding. But Garvin took her under his wing. Two years ago, he began moving her up, fast. For some reason, he just thinks Meredith Johnson is *great*."

Lewyn said, "Is Garvin fucking her?"

"No, he just likes her."

"She must be fucking somebody."

"Wait a minute," Mary Anne Hunter said, sitting up. "What's this? If Garvin brought in some guy from Microsoft to run this division, nobody'd say he must be fucking somebody."

Cherry laughed. "It'd depend on who he was."

"I'm serious. Why is it when a woman gets a promotion, she must be fucking somebody?"

Lewyn said, "Look: if they brought in Ellen Howard from Microsoft, we wouldn't be having this conversation because we all know Ellen's very competent. We wouldn't like it, but we'd accept it. But nobody even *knows* Meredith Johnson. I mean, does anybody here know her?"

"Actually," Sanders said, "I know her."

There was silence.

"I used to go out with her."

Cherry laughed. "So *you're* the one she's fucking."

Sanders shook his head. "It was years ago."

Hunter said, "What's she like?"

"Yeah," Cherry said, grinning lasciviously. "What's she like?"

"Shut up, Don."

"Lighten up, Mary Anne."

"She worked for Novell when I knew her,"

Sanders said. "She was about twenty-five. Smart and ambitious."

"Smart and ambitious," Lewyn said. "That's fine. The world's full of smart and ambitious. The question is, can she run a technical division? Or have we got another Screamer Freeling on our hands?"

Two years earlier, Garvin had put a sales manager named Howard Freeling in charge of the division. The idea was to bring product development in contact with customers at an earlier point, to develop new products more in line with the emerging market. Freeling instituted focus groups, and they all spent a lot of time watching potential customers play with new products behind one-way glass.

But Freeling was completely unfamiliar with technical issues. So when confronted with a problem, he screamed. He was like a tourist in a foreign country who didn't speak the language and thought he could make the locals understand by shouting at them. Freeling's tenure at APG was a disaster. The programmers loathed him; the designers rebelled at his idea for neon-colored product boxes; the manufacturing glitches at factories in Ireland and Texas didn't get solved. Finally, when the production line in Cork went down for eleven days, Freeling flew over and screamed. The Irish managers all quit, and Garvin fired him.

"So: is that what we have? Another Screamer?"

Stephanie Kaplan cleared her throat. "I think Garvin learned his lesson. He wouldn't make the same mistake twice."

"So you think Meredith Johnson is up to the job?"

"I couldn't say," Kaplan replied, speaking very deliberately.

"Not much of an endorsement," Lewyn said.

"But I think she'll be better than Freeling," Kaplan said.

Lewyn snorted. "This is the Taller Than Mickey Rooney Award. You can still be very short and win."

"No," Kaplan said, "I think she'll be better."

Cherry said, "Better-looking, at least, from what I hear."

"Sexist," Mary Anne Hunter said.

"What: I can't say she's good-looking?"

"We're talking about her competence, not her appearance."

"Wait a minute," Cherry said. "Coming over here to this meeting, I pass the women at the espresso bar, and what are they talking about? Whether Richard Gere has better buns than Mel Gibson. They're talking about the crack in the ass, lift and separate, all that stuff. I don't see why they can talk about—"

"We're drifting afield," Sanders said.

"It doesn't matter what you guys say," Hunter said, "the fact is, this company is dominated by males; there are almost no women except Stephanie in high executive positions. I think it's great that Bob has appointed a woman to run this division, and I for one think we should support her." She looked at Sanders. "We all love you, Tom, but you know what I mean."

"Yeah, we all love you," Cherry said. "At least, we did until we got our cute new boss."

Lewyn said, "I'll support Johnson—if she's any good."

"No you won't," Hunter said. "You'll sabotage her. You'll find a reason to get rid of her."

"Wait a minute—"

"No. What is this conversation *really* about? It's about the fact that you're all pissed off because now you have to report to a woman."

"Mary Anne . . ."

"I mean it."

Lewyn said, "I think Tom's pissed off because he didn't get the job."

"I'm not pissed off," Sanders said.

"Well, I'm pissed off," Cherry said, "because Meredith used to be Tom's girlfriend, so now he has a special in with the new boss."

"Maybe." Sanders frowned.

Lewyn said, "On the other hand, maybe she hates you. All my old girlfriends hate me."

"With good reason, I hear," Cherry said, laughing.

Sanders said, "Let's get back to the agenda, shall we?"

"What agenda?"

"Twinkle."

There were groans around the table. "Not again."

"Goddamn Twinkle."

"How bad is it?" Cherry said.

"They still can't get the seek times down, and they can't solve the hinge problems. The line's running at twenty-nine percent."

Lewyn said, "They better send us some units."

"We should have them today."

"Okay. Table it till then?"

"It's okay with me." Sanders looked around the table. "Anybody else have a problem? Mary Anne?"

"No, we're fine. We still expect prototype card-phones off our test line within two months."

The new generation of cellular telephones were not much larger than a credit card. They folded open for use. "How's the weight?"

"The weight's now four ounces, which is not great, but okay. The problem is power. The batteries only run 180 minutes in talk mode. And the keypad sticks when you dial. But that's Mark's headache. We're on schedule with the line."

"Good." He turned to Don Cherry. "And how's the Corridor?"

Cherry sat back in his chair, beaming. He

crossed his hands over his belly. "I am pleased to report," he said, "that as of half an hour ago, the Corridor is fan-fucking-*tastic*."

"Really?"

"That's great news."

"Nobody's throwing up?"

"*Please*. Ancient history."

Mark Lewyn said, "Wait a minute. Somebody threw up?"

"A vile rumor. That was then. This is now. We got the last delay bug out half an hour ago, and all functions are now fully implemented. We can take any database and convert it into a 3-D 24-bit color environment that you can navigate in real time. You can walk through any database in the world."

"And it's stable?"

"It's a rock."

"You've tried it with naïve users?"

"Bulletproof."

"So you're ready to demo for Conley?"

"We'll blow 'em away," Cherry said. "They won't fucking believe their eyes."

Coming out of the conference room, Sanders ran into a group of Conley-White executives being taken on a tour by Bob Garvin.

Robert T. Garvin looked the way every CEO wanted to look in the pages of *Fortune* magazine. He was fifty-nine years old and handsome, with a craggy face and salt-and-pepper hair that always looked windblown, as if he'd just come in from a fly-fishing trip in Montana, or a weekend sailing in the San Juans. In the old days, like everyone else, he had worn jeans and denim work shirts in the office. But in recent years, he favored dark blue Caraceni suits. It was one of the many changes that people in the company had noticed since the death of his daughter, three years before.

Brusque and profane in private, Garvin was all charm in public. Leading the Conley-White executives, he said, "Here on the third floor, you have our tech divisions and advanced product laboratories. Oh, Tom. Good." He threw his arm around Sanders. "Meet Tom Sanders, our division manager for advanced products. One of the brilliant young men who's made our company what it is. Tom, say hello to Ed Nichols, the CFO for Conley-White . . ."

A thin, hawk-faced man in his late fifties, Nichols carried his head tilted back, so that he seemed to be pulling away from everything, as if there were a bad smell. He looked down his nose through half-frame glasses at Sanders, regarding him with a vaguely disapproving air, and shook hands formally.

"Mr. Sanders. How do you do."

"Mr. Nichols."

". . . and John Conley, nephew of the founder, and vice president of the firm . . ."

Sanders turned to a stocky, athletic man in his late twenties. Wire-frame spectacles. Armani suit. Firm handshake. Serious expression. Sanders had the impression of a wealthy and very determined man.

"Hi there, Tom."

"Hi, John."

". . . and Jim Daly, from Goldman, Sachs . . ."

A balding, thin, storklike man in a pinstripe suit. Daly seemed distracted, befuddled, and shook hands with a brief nod.

". . . and of course, Meredith Johnson, from Cupertino."

She was more beautiful than he had remembered. And different in some subtle way. Older, of course, crow's-feet at the corners of her eyes, and faint creases in her forehead. But she stood straighter now, and she had a vibrancy, a confidence, that he associated with power. Dark blue suit, blond hair, large eyes. Those incredibly long eyelashes. He had forgotten.

"Hello, Tom, nice to see you again." A warm smile. Her perfume.

"Meredith, nice to see you."

She released his hand, and the group swept on, as Garvin led them down the hall. "Now, just ahead is the VIE Unit. You'll be seeing that work tomorrow."

Mark Lewyn came out of the conference room and said, "You met the rogues' gallery?"

"I guess so."

Lewyn watched them go. "Hard to believe those guys are going to be running this company," he said. "I did a briefing this morning, and let me tell you, they don't know *anything*. It's scary."

As the group reached the end of the hallway, Meredith Johnson looked back over her shoulder at Sanders. She mouthed, "I'll call you." And she smiled radiantly. Then she was gone.

Lewyn sighed. "I'd say," he said, "that you have an in with top management there, Tom."

"Maybe so."

"I just wish I knew why Garvin thinks she's so great."

Sanders said, "Well, she certainly looks great."

Lewyn turned away. "We'll see," he said. "We'll see."

At twenty past twelve, Sanders left his office on the fourth floor and headed toward the stairs to go down to the main conference room for lunch. He passed a nurse in a starched white uniform. She was looking in one office after another. "Where is he? He was just here a minute ago." She shook her head.

"Who?" Sanders said.

"The professor," she replied, blowing a strand of hair out of her eyes. "I can't leave him alone for a minute."

"What professor?" Sanders said. But by then he heard the female giggles coming from a room farther down the hall, and he already knew the answer. "Professor Dorfman?"

"Yes. Professor Dorfman," the nurse said, nodding grimly, and she headed toward the source of the giggles.

Sanders trailed after her. Max Dorfman was a German management consultant, now very elderly. At one time or another, he had been a visiting professor at every major business school in America, and he had gained a particular reputation as a guru to high-tech companies. During most of the 1980s, he had served on the board of directors of DigiCom, lending prestige to Garvin's upstart company. And during that time, he had been a mentor to Sanders. In fact, it was Dorfman who had convinced Sanders to leave Cupertino eight years earlier and take the job in Seattle.

Sanders said, "I didn't know he was still alive."

"Very much so," the nurse said.

"He must be ninety."

"Well, he doesn't act a day over eighty-five."

As they approached the room, he saw Mary Anne Hunter coming out. She had changed into a skirt and blouse, and she was smiling broadly, as if she had just left her lover. "Tom, you'll never guess who's here."

"Max," he said.

"That's right. Oh, Tom, you should see him: he's exactly the same."

"I'll bet he is," Sanders said. Even from outside the room, he could smell the cigarette smoke.

The nurse said, "Now, Professor," in a severe tone, and strode into the room. Sanders looked in; it was one of the employee lounges. Max Dorfman's wheelchair was pulled up to the table in the center of the room. He was surrounded by pretty assistants. The women were making a fuss over him, and in their midst Dorfman, with his shock of white hair, was grinning happily, smoking a cigarette in a long holder.

"What's he doing here?" Sanders said.

"Garvin brought him in, to consult on the merger. Aren't you going to say hello?" Hunter said.

"Oh, Christ," Sanders said. "You know Max. He can drive you crazy." Dorfman liked to challenge conventional wisdom, but his method was indirect. He had an ironic way of speaking that was provocative and mocking at the same moment. He was fond of contradictions, and he did not hesitate to lie. If you caught him in a lie, he would immediately say, "Yes, that's true. I don't know what I was thinking of," and then resume talking in the same maddening, elliptical way. He never really said what he meant; he left it for you to put it together. His rambling sessions left executives confused and exhausted.

"But you were such friends," Hunter said, looking at him. "I'm sure he'd like you to say hello."

"He's busy now. Maybe later." Sanders looked at his watch. "Anyway, we're going to be late for lunch."

He started back down the hallway. Hunter fell into step with him, frowning. "He always got under your skin, didn't he?"

"He got under everybody's skin. It was what he did best."

She looked at him in a puzzled way, and seemed about to say more, then shrugged. "It's okay with me."

"I'm just not in the mood for one of those conversations," Sanders said. "Maybe later. But not right now." They headed down the stairs to the ground floor.

In keeping with the stripped-down functionality of modern high-tech firms, DigiCom maintained no corporate dining room. Instead, lunches and dinners were held at local restaurants, most often at the nearby Il Terrazzo. But the need for secrecy about the merger obliged DigiCom to cater a lunch in the large, wood-paneled conference room on the ground floor. At twelve-thirty, with the principal managers of the DigiCom technical divisions, the Conley-White executives, and the Goldman, Sachs bankers all present, the room was crowded. The egalitarian ethos of the company meant that there was no assigned seating, but the principal C-W executives ended up at one side of the table near the front of the room, clustered around Garvin. The power end of the table.

Sanders took a seat farther down on the opposite side, and was surprised when Stephanie Kaplan slid into the chair to his right. Kaplan usually sat much closer to Garvin; Sanders was distinctly further down the pecking order. To Sanders's left was Bill Everts, the head of Human Resources—a nice, slightly dull guy. As white-coated waiters served the meal, Sanders talked about fishing on Orcas Island, which was Everts's passion. As usual, Kaplan was quiet during most of the lunch, seeming to withdraw into herself.

Sanders began to feel he was neglecting her. Toward the end of the meal, he turned to her and said, "I notice you've been up here in Seattle more often the last few months, Stephanie. Is that because of the merger?"

"No." She smiled. "My son's a freshman at the university, so I like to come up because I get to see him."

"What's he studying?"

"Chemistry. He wants to go into materials chemistry. Apparently it's going to be a big field."

"I've heard that."

"Half the time I don't know what he's talking about. It's funny, when your child knows more than you do."

He nodded, trying to think of something else to ask her. It wasn't easy: although he had sat in meetings with Kaplan for years, he knew little about her personally. She was married to a professor at San Jose State, a jovial chubby man with a mustache, who taught economics. When they were together, he did all the talking while Stephanie stood silently by. She was a tall, bony, awkward woman who seemed resigned to her lack of social graces. She was said to be a very good golfer—at least, good enough that Garvin wouldn't play her anymore. No one who knew her was surprised that she had made the error of beating Garvin too often; wags said that she wasn't enough of a loser to be promoted.

Garvin didn't really like her, but he would never think of letting her go. Colorless, humorless, and tireless, her dedication to the company was legendary; she worked late every night and came in most weekends. When she had had a bout of cancer a few years back, she refused to take even a single day off. Apparently she was cured of the cancer; at least, Sanders hadn't heard anything more about it. But the episode seemed to have increased Kaplan's relentless focus on her impersonal domain, figures and spreadsheets, and heightened her natural inclination to work behind the scenes. More than one manager had come to work in the morning, only to find a pet project killed by the Stealth Bomber, with no lingering trace of how or why it had happened. Thus her tendency to remain aloof in social situations was more than a reflection of her own discomfort; it was also a reminder of the power she wielded within the company, and how she wielded it. In her own way, she was mysterious—and potentially dangerous.

While he was trying to think of something to say, Kaplan leaned toward him confidentially and lowered her voice, "In the meeting this morning, Tom, I didn't really feel I could say anything. But I hope you're okay. About this new reorganization."

Sanders concealed his surprise. In twelve years, Kaplan had never said anything so directly personal to him. He wondered why she would do so now. He was instantly wary, unsure of how to respond.

"Well, it was a shock," he said.

She looked at him with a steady gaze. "It was a shock to many of us," she said quietly. "There was an uproar in Cupertino. A lot of people questioned Garvin's judgment."

Sanders frowned. Kaplan never said anything even obliquely critical of Garvin. Never. But now this. Was she testing him? He said nothing, and poked at his food.

"I can imagine you're uneasy about the new appointment."

"Only because it was so unexpected. It seemed to come out of the blue."

Kaplan looked at him oddly for a moment, as if he had disappointed her. Then she nodded. "It's always that way with mergers," she said. Her tone was more open, less confidential. "I was at CompuSoft when it merged with Symantec, and it was exactly the same: last-minute announcements, switches in the organization charts. Jobs promised, jobs lost. Everybody up in the air for weeks. It's not easy to bring two organizations together—especially these two. There are big differences in corporate cultures. Garvin has to make them comfortable." She gestured toward the end of the table where Garvin was sitting. "Just look at them," she said. "All the Conley people are wearing suits. Nobody in our company wears suits, except lawyers."

"They're East Coast," Sanders said.

"But it goes deeper than that. Conley-White likes to present itself as a diversified communications company, but it's really not so grand. Its primary business is textbooks. That's a lucrative business, but you're selling to school boards in Texas and Ohio and Tennessee. Many of them are deeply conservative. So Conley's conservative, by instinct and experience. They want this merger because they need to acquire a high-tech capacity going into the next century. But they can't get used to the idea of a very young company, where the employees work in T-shirts and jeans, and everybody goes by first names. They're in shock. Besides," Kaplan added, lowering her voice again, "there are internal divisions within Conley-White. Garvin has to deal with that, too."

"What internal divisions?"

She nodded toward the head of the table. "You may have noticed that their CEO isn't here. The big man hasn't honored us with his presence. He won't show up until the end of the week. For now, he's only sent his minions. Their highest-ranking officer is Ed Nichols, the CFO."

Sanders glanced over at the suspicious, sharp-faced man he had met earlier. Kaplan said, "Nichols doesn't want to buy this company. He thinks we're overpriced and underpowered. Last year, he tried to form a strategic alliance with Microsoft, but Gates blew him off. Then Nichols tried to buy InterDisk, but that fell through: too many problems, and InterDisk had that bad publicity about the fired employee. So they ended up with us. But Ed isn't happy about where he landed."

"He certainly doesn't look happy," Sanders said.

"The main reason is he hates the Conley kid."

Seated beside Nichols was John Conley, the bespectacled young lawyer in his twenties. Distinctly younger than anyone around him, Conley was speaking energetically, jabbing his fork in the air as he made a point to Nichols.

"Ed Nichols thinks Conley's an asshole."

"But Conley's only a vice president," Sanders said. "He can't have that much power."

Kaplan shook her head. "He's the heir, remember?"

"So? What does that mean? His grandfather's picture is on some boardroom wall?"

"Conley owns four percent of C-W stock, and controls another twenty-six percent still held by the family or vested in trusts controlled by the family. John Conley has the largest voting block of Conley-White stock."

"And John Conley wants the deal?"

"Yes." Kaplan nodded. "Conley handpicked our company to acquire. And he's going forward fast, with the help of his friends like Jim Daly at Goldman, Sachs. Daly's very smart, but investment bankers always have big fees riding on a merger. They'll do their due diligence, I'm not saying they won't. But it'd take a lot to get them to back out of the deal now."

"Uh-huh."

"So Nichols feels he's lost control of the acquisition, and he's being rushed into a deal that's a lot richer than it should be. Nichols doesn't see why C-W should make us all wealthy. He'd pull out of this deal if he could—if only to screw Conley."

"But Conley's driving this deal."

"Yes. And Conley's abrasive. He likes to make little speeches about youth versus age, the coming digital era, a young vision for the future. It enrages Nichols. Ed Nichols feels he's doubled the net worth of the company in a decade, and now this little twerp is giving him lectures."

"And how does Meredith fit in?"

Kaplan hesitated. "Meredith is suitable."

"Meaning what?"

"She's Eastern. She grew up in Connecticut and went to Vassar. The Conley people like that. They're comfortable with that."

"That's all? She has the right accent?"

"You didn't hear it from me," Kaplan said.

"But I think they also see her as weak. They think they can control her once the merger is completed."

"And Garvin's going along with that?"

Kaplan shrugged. "Bob's a realist," she said. "He needs capitalization. He's built his company skillfully, but we're going to require massive infusions of cash for the next phase, when we go head-to-head with Sony and Philips in product development. Conley-White's textbook operation is a cash cow. Bob looks at them and sees green—and he's inclined to do what they want, to get their money."

"And of course, Bob likes Meredith."

"Yes. That's true. Bob likes her."

Sanders waited while she poked at her food for a while. "And you, Stephanie? What do you think?"

Kaplan shrugged. "She's able."

"Able but weak?"

"No." Kaplan shook her head. "Meredith has ability. That's not in question. But I'm concerned about her experience. She's not as seasoned as she might be. She's being put in charge of four major technical units that are expected to grow rapidly. I just hope she's up to it."

There was the clink of a spoon on a glass, and Garvin stepped to the front of the room. "Even though you're still eating dessert, let's get started, so we can finish by two o'clock," he said. "Let me remind you of the new timetable. Assuming everything continues as planned, we expect to make the formal announcement of the acquisition at a press conference here on Friday noon. And now, let me introduce our new associates from Conley-White . . ."

As Garvin named the C-W people, and they stood up around the table, Kaplan leaned over and whispered to Tom, "This is all fluff and feathers. The real reason for this lunch is you-know-who."

". . . and finally," Garvin said, "let me introduce someone that many of you know, but some of you do not, the new Vice President for Advanced Operations and Planning, Meredith Johnson."

There was scattered, brief applause as Johnson got up from her seat and walked to a podium at the front of the room. In her dark blue suit, she looked the model of corporate correctness, but she was strikingly beautiful. At the podium, she put on horn-rimmed glasses and lowered the conference room lights.

"Bob has asked me to review the way the new structure will work," she said, "and to say something about what we see happening in the coming months." She bent over the podium, where a computer was set up for presentations. "Now, if I can just work this thing . . . let me see . . ."

In the darkened room, Don Cherry caught Sanders's eye and shook his head slowly.

"Ah, okay, here we are," Johnson said, at the podium. The screen behind her came to life. Animated images generated by the computer were projected onto the screen. The first image showed a red heart, which broke into four pieces. "The heart of DigiCom has always been its Advanced Products Group, which consists of four separate divisions as you see here. But as all information throughout the world becomes digital, these divisions will inevitably merge." On the screen, the pieces of the heart slid back together, and the heart transformed itself into a spinning globe. It began to throw off products. "For the customer in the near future, armed with cellular phone, built-in fax modem, and hand-held computer or PDA, it will be increasingly irrelevant where in the world he or she is and where the information is coming from. We are talking about the true globalization of information, and this implies an array of new products for our major markets in business and education." The globe expanded and dissolved, became classrooms on all continents, students at desks. "In particular, education will be a growing focus of this company as technology moves from print to digital displays to virtual environments. Now, let's review exactly what this means, and where I see it taking us."

And she proceeded to do it all—hypermedia, embedded video, authoring systems, work-group structures, academic sourcing, customer acceptance. She moved on to the cost structures—projected research outlays and revenues, five-year goals, offshore variables. Then to major product challenges—quality control, user feedback, shorter development cycles.

Meredith Johnson's presentation was flawless, the images blending and flowing across the screen, her voice confident, no hesitation, no pauses. As she continued, the room became quiet, the atmosphere distinctly respectful.

"Although this is not the time to go into technical matters," she said, "I want to mention that new CD-drive seek times under a hundred milliseconds, combined with new compression algorithms, should shift the industry standard for CD to full-res digitized video at sixty fields per second. And we are talking about platform-independent RISC processors supported by 32-bit color active-matrix displays and portable hard copy at 1200 DPI and wireless networking in both LAN and WAN configurations. Combine that with an autonomously generated virtual database—especially when ROM-based software agents for object definition and classification are in place—and I think we can agree we are looking at prospects for a very exciting future."

Sanders saw that Don Cherry's mouth was hanging open. Sanders leaned over to Kaplan. "Sounds like she knows her stuff."

"Yes," Kaplan said, nodding. "The demo

queen. She started out doing demos. Appearance has always been her strongest point." Sanders glanced at Kaplan; she looked away.

But then the speech ended. There was applause as the lights came up, and Johnson went back to her seat. The room broke up, people heading back to work. Johnson left Garvin, and went directly to Don Cherry, said a few words to him. Cherry smiled: the charmed geek. Then Meredith went across the room to Mary Anne, spoke briefly to her, and then to Mark Lewyn.

"She's smart," Kaplan said, watching her, "touching base with all the division heads—especially since she didn't name them in her speech."

Sanders frowned. "You think that's significant?"

"Only if she's planning to make changes."

"Phil said she wasn't going to."

"But you never know, do you?" Kaplan said, standing up, dropping her napkin on the table. "I've got to go—and it looks like you're next on her list."

Kaplan moved discreetly away as Meredith came up to Sanders. She was smiling. "I wanted to apologize, Tom," Meredith said, "for not mentioning your name and the names of the other division heads in my presentation. I don't want anybody to get the wrong idea. It's just that Bob asked me to keep it short."

"Well," Sanders said, "it looks like you won

everybody over. The reaction was very favorable."

"I hope so. Listen," she said, putting her hand on his arm, "we've got a slew of due diligence sessions tomorrow. I've been asking all the heads to meet with me today, if they can. I wonder if you're free to come to my office at the end of the day for a drink. We can go over things, and maybe catch up on old times, too."

"Sure," he said. He felt the warmth of her hand on his arm. She didn't take it away.

"They've given me an office on the fifth floor, and with any luck there should be furniture in by later today. Six o'clock work for you?"

"Fine," he said.

She smiled. "You still partial to dry chardonnay?"

Despite himself, he was flattered that she remembered. He smiled, "Yes, I still am."

"I'll see if I can get one. And we'll go over some of the immediate problems, like that hundred-millisecond drive."

"Okay, fine. About that drive—"

"I know," she said, her voice lower. "We'll deal with it." Behind her, the Conley-White executives were coming up. "Let's talk tonight."

"Good."

"See you then, Tom."

"See you then."

As the meeting broke up, Mark Lewyn drifted over to him. "So, let's hear it: what'd she say to you?"

"Meredith?"

"No, the Stealthy One. Kaplan was bending your ear all during lunch. What's up?"

Sanders shrugged. "Oh, you know. Just small talk."

"Come on. Stephanie doesn't do small talk. She doesn't know how. And Stephanie talked more to you than I've seen her talk in years."

Sanders was surprised to see how anxious Lewyn was. "Actually," he said, "we talked mostly about her son. He's a freshman at the university."

But Lewyn wasn't buying it. He frowned and said, "She's up to something, isn't she. She never talks without a reason. Is it about me? I know she's critical of the design team. She thinks we're wasteful. I've told her many times that it's not true—"

"Mark," Sanders said. "Your name didn't even come up. Honest."

To change the subject, Sanders asked, "What'd

you think of Johnson? Pretty strong presentation, I thought."

"Yes. She's impressive. There was only one thing that bothered me," Lewyn said. He was still frowning, still uneasy. "Isn't she supposed to be a late-breaking curve, forced on us by management at Conley?"

"That's what I heard. Why?"

"Her presentation. To put together a graphic presentation like that takes two weeks, at a minimum," Lewyn said. "In my design group, I get the designers on it a month in advance, then we run it through for timing, then say a week for revisions and re-do's, then another week while they transfer to a drive. And that's my own in-house group, working fast. For an executive, it'd take longer. They pawn it off on some assistant, who tries to make it for them. Then the executive looks at it, wants it all done over again. And it takes more time. So if this was her presentation, I'd say she's known about her new job for a while. Months."

Sanders frowned.

"As usual," Lewyn said, "the poor bastards in the trenches are the last to know. I just wonder what *else* we don't know."

Sanders was back at his office by 2:15. He called his wife to tell her he would be home late, that he had a meeting at six.

"What's happening over there?" Susan said. "I got a call from Adele Lewyn. She says Garvin's screwing everybody, and they're changing the organization around."

"I don't know yet," he said cautiously. Cindy had just walked in the room.

"Are you still getting a promotion?"

"Basically," he said, "the answer is no."

"I can't believe it," Susan said. "Tom, I'm sorry. Are you okay? Are you upset?"

"I would say so, yes."

"Can't talk?"

"That's right."

"Okay. I'll leave soup on. I'll see you when you get here."

Cindy placed a stack of files on his desk. When Sanders hung up, she said, "She already knew?"

"She suspected."

Cindy nodded. "She called at lunchtime," she said. "I had the sense. The spouses are talking, I imagine."

"I'm sure everybody's talking."

Cindy went to the door, then paused. Cautiously, she said, "And how was the lunch meeting?"

"Meredith was introduced as the new head of all the tech divisions. She gave a presentation. She says she's going to keep all the division heads in place, all reporting to her."

"Then there's no change for us? Just another layer on top?"

"So far. That's what they're telling me. Why? What do you hear?"

"I hear the same."

He smiled. "Then it must be true."

"Should I go ahead and buy the condo?" She had been planning this for some time, a condo in Queen Anne's Hill for herself and her young daughter.

Sanders said, "When do you have to decide?"

"I have another fifteen days. End of the month."

"Then wait. You know, just to be safe."

She nodded, and went out. A moment later, she came back. "I almost forgot. Mark Lewyn's office just called. The Twinkle drives have arrived from KL. His designers are looking at them now. Do you want to see them?"

"I'm on my way."

The Design Group occupied the entire second floor of the Western Building. As always, the atmosphere there was chaotic; all the phones were ringing, but there was no receptionist in the little waiting area by the elevators, which was decorated with faded, taped-up posters for a 1929 Bauhaus Exhibition in Berlin and an old science-fiction movie called *The Forbin Project*. Two Japanese visitors sat at a corner table, speaking rapidly, beside the battered Coke machine and the junk food dispenser. Sanders nodded to them, used his card to open the locked door, and went inside.

The floor was a large open space, partitioned at unexpected angles by slanted walls painted to look like pastel-veined stone. Uncomfortable-looking wire chairs and tables were scattered in odd places. Rock-and-roll music blared. Everybody was casually dressed; most of the designers wore shorts and T-shirts. It was clearly A Creative Area.

Sanders went through to Foamland, the little display of the latest product designs the group had made. There were models of tiny CD-ROM drives and miniature cellular phones. Lewyn's teams were charged with creating product designs for the future, and many of these seemed absurdly small: a cellular phone no larger than a pencil, and another that looked like a postmodern version of Dick Tracy's wrist radio, in pale green and gray; a pager the size of a cigarette lighter; and a micro-CD player with a flip-up screen that could fit easily in the palm of the hand.

Although these devices looked outrageously tiny, Sanders had long since become accustomed to the idea that the designs were at most two years in the future. The hardware was shrinking fast; it was difficult for Sanders to remember that when he began working at DigiCom, a "portable" computer was a thirty-pound box the size of a carry-on suitcase—and cellular telephones didn't exist at all. The first cellular phones that DigiCom manufactured were fifteen-pound wonders that you lugged around on a shoulder strap. At the time, people thought they were a miracle. Now, customers complained if their phones weighed more than a few ounces.

Sanders walked past the big foam-cutting machine, all twisted tubes and knives behind Plexiglas shields, and found Mark Lewyn and his team bent over three dark blue CD-ROM players from Malaysia. One of the players already lay in pieces on the table; under bright halogen lights, the team was poking at its innards with tiny screwdrivers, glancing up from time to time to the scope screens.

"What've you found?" Sanders said.

"Ah, hell," Lewyn said, throwing up his hands in artistic exasperation. "Not good, Tom. Not good."

"Talk to me."

Lewyn pointed to the table. "There's a metal rod inside the hinge. These clips maintain contact with the rod as the case is opened; that's how you maintain power to the screen."

"Yes . . ."

"But power is intermittent. It looks like the rods are too small. They're supposed to be fifty-four millimeters. These seem to be fifty-two, fifty-three millimeters."

Lewyn was grim, his entire manner suggesting unspeakable consequences. The bars were a millimeter off, and the world was coming to an end. Sanders understood that he would have to calm Lewyn down. He'd done it many times before.

He said, "We can fix that, Mark. It'll mean opening all the cases and replacing the bars, but we can do that."

"Oh sure," Lewyn said. "But that still leaves the clips. Our specs call for 16/10 stainless, which has requisite tension to keep the clips springy and maintain contact with the bar. These clips seem to be something else, maybe 16/4. They're too stiff.

So when you open the cases the clips bend, but they don't spring back."

"So we have to replace the clips, too. We can do that when we switch the bars."

"Unfortunately, it's not that easy. The clips are heat-pressed into the cases."

"Ah, hell."

"Right. They are integral to the case unit."

"You're telling me we have to build new housings just because we have bad clips?"

"Exactly."

Sanders shook his head. "We've run off thousands so far. Something like four thousand."

"Well, we've got to do 'em again."

"And what about the drive itself?"

"It's slow," Lewyn said. "No doubt about it. But I'm not sure why. It might be power problems. Or it might be the controller chip."

"If it's the controller chip . . ."

"We're in deep shit. If it's a primary design problem, we have to go back to the drawing board. If it's only a fabrication problem, we have to change the production lines, maybe remake the stencils. But it's months, either way."

"When will we know?"

"I've sent a drive and power supply to the Diagnostics guys," Lewyn said. "They should have a report by five. I'll get it to you. Does Meredith know about this yet?"

"I'm briefing her at six."

"Okay. Call me after you talk to her?"

"Sure."

"In a way, this is good," Lewyn said.

"How do you mean?"

"We're throwing her a big problem right away," Lewyn said. "We'll see how she handles it."

Sanders turned to go. Lewyn followed him out. "By the way," Lewyn said. "*Are* you pissed off that you didn't get the job?"

"Disappointed," Sanders said. "Not pissed. There's no point being pissed."

"Because if you ask me, Garvin screwed you. You put in the time, you've demonstrated you can run the division, and he put in someone else instead."

Sanders shrugged. "It's his company."

Lewyn threw his arm over Sanders's shoulder, and gave him a rough hug. "You know, Tom, sometimes you're too reasonable for your own good."

"I didn't know being reasonable was a defect," Sanders said.

"Being *too* reasonable is a defect," Lewyn said. "You end up getting pushed around."

"I'm just trying to get along," Sanders said. "I want to be here when the division goes public."

"Yeah, true. You got to stay." They came to the elevator. Lewyn said, "You think she got it because she's a woman?"

Sanders shook his head. "Who knows."

"Pale males eat it again. I tell you. Sometimes I get so sick of the constant pressure to appoint women," Lewyn said. "I mean, look at this design group. We've got forty percent women here, better than any other division, but they always say, why don't you have more. More women, more—"

"Mark," he said, interrupting. "It's a different world now."

"And not a better one," Lewyn said. "It's hurting everybody. Look: when I started in DigiCom, there was only one question. Are you good? If you were good, you got hired. If you could cut it, you stayed. No more. Now, ability is only one of the priorities. There's also the question of whether you're the right sex and skin color to fill out the company's HR profiles. And if you turn out to be incompetent, we can't fire you. Pretty soon, we start to get junk like this Twinkle drive. Because no one's accountable anymore. No one is responsible. You can't build products on a *theory*. Because the product you're making is real. And if it stinks, it stinks. And no one will buy it."

Coming back to his office, Sanders used his electronic passcard to open the door to the fourth floor. Then he slipped the card in his trouser pocket, and headed down the hallway. He was moving quickly, thinking about the meeting with Lewyn. He was especially bothered by one thing that Lewyn had said: that he was allowing himself to be pushed around by Garvin—that he was being too passive, too understanding.

But Sanders didn't see it that way. When Sanders had said it was Garvin's company, he meant it. Bob was the boss, and Bob could do what he wanted. Sanders was disappointed not to get the job, but no one had promised it to him. Ever. He and others in the Seattle divisions had come, over a period of weeks, to assume that Sanders would get the job. But Garvin had never mentioned it. Nor had Phil Blackburn.

As a result, Sanders felt he had no reason to gripe. If he was disappointed, it was only because he had done it to himself. It was classic: counting your chickens before they hatched.

And as for being too passive—what did Lewyn expect him to do? Make a fuss? Yell and scream? That wouldn't do any good. Because clearly

Meredith Johnson had this job, whether Sanders liked it or not. Resign? That *really* wouldn't do any good. Because if he quit, he would lose the profits pending when the company went public. That would be a real disaster.

So on reflection, all he could do was accept Meredith Johnson in the new job, and get on with it. And he suspected that if the situation were reversed, Lewyn, for all his bluster, would do exactly the same thing: grin and bear it.

But the bigger problem, as he thought it over, was the Twinkle drive. Lewyn's team had torn up three drives that afternoon, and they still didn't have any idea why they were malfunctioning. They had found some non-spec components in the hinge, which Sanders could track down. He'd find out soon enough why they were getting non-spec materials. But the real problem—the slowness of the drives—remained a mystery to which they had no clue, and that meant that he was going to—

"Tom? You dropped your card."

"What?" He looked up absently. An area assistant was frowning, pointing back down the hall.

"You dropped your card."

"Oh." He saw the passcard lying there, white against the gray carpet. "Thanks."

He went back to retrieve it. Obviously, he must be more upset than he realized. You couldn't get anywhere in the DigiCom buildings without a passcard. Sanders bent over, picked it up, and slipped it in his pocket.

Then he felt the second card, already there. Frowning, he took both cards out and looked at them.

The card on the floor wasn't his card, it was someone else's. He paused for a moment, trying to decide which was his. By design, the passcards were featureless: just the blue DigiCom logo, a stamped serial number, and a magstripe on the back.

He ought to be able to remember his card number, but he couldn't. He hurried back to his office, to look it up on his computer. He glanced at his watch. It was four o'clock, two hours before his meeting with Meredith Johnson. He still had a lot to do to prepare for that meeting. He frowned as he walked along, staring at the carpet. He would have to get the production reports, and perhaps also the design detail specs. He wasn't sure she would understand them, but he should be prepared with them, anyway. And what else? He did not want to go into this first meeting having forgotten something.

Once again, his thoughts were disrupted by images from his past. An opened suitcase. The bowl of popcorn. The stained-glass window.

"So?" said a familiar voice. "You don't say hello to your old friends anymore?"

Sanders looked up. He was outside the glass-walled conference room. Inside the room, he saw a solitary figure hunched over in a wheelchair, staring at the Seattle skyline, his back to Sanders.

"Hello, Max," Sanders said.

Max Dorfman continued to stare out the window. "Hello, Thomas."

"How did you know it was me?"

Dorfman snorted. "It must be magic. What do you think? Magic?" His voice was sarcastic. "Thomas: I can *see* you."

"How? You have eyes in the back of your head?"

"No, Thomas. I have a reflection in *front* of my head. I see you in the glass, of course. Walking with your head down, like a defeated *putz*." Dorfman snorted again, and then wheeled his chair around. His eyes were bright, intense, mocking. "You were such a promising man. And now you are hanging your head?"

Sanders wasn't in the mood. "Let's just say this hasn't been one of my better days, Max."

"And you want everybody to know about it? You want sympathy?"

"No, Max." He remembered how Dorfman had ridiculed the idea of sympathy. Dorfman used to say that an executive who wanted sympathy was not an executive. He was a sponge, soaking up something useless.

Sanders said, "No, Max. I was thinking."

"Ah. *Thinking*. Oh, I like thinking. Thinking is good. And what were you thinking about, Thomas: the stained glass in your apartment?"

Despite himself, Sanders was startled: "How did you know that?"

"Maybe it's magic," Dorfman said, with a rasping laugh. "Or perhaps I can read minds. You think I can read minds, Thomas? Are you stupid enough to believe that?"

"Max, I'm not in the mood."

"Oh well, then I must stop. If you're not in the mood, I must stop. We must at all costs preserve your mood." He slapped the arm of his wheelchair irritably. "*You told me, Thomas*. That's how I knew what you were thinking."

"I told you? When?"

"Nine or ten years ago, it must have been."

"What did I tell you?"

"Oh, you don't remember? No wonder you have problems. Better stare at the floor some more. It may do you good. Yes. I think so. Keep staring at the floor, Thomas."

"Max, for Christ's sake."

Dorfman grinned at him. "Do I irritate you?"

"You always irritate me."

"Ah. Well. Then perhaps there is hope. Not for you, of course—for me. I am old, Thomas. Hope has a different meaning, at my age. You wouldn't understand. These days, I cannot even get around by myself. I must have someone *push* me. Preferably a pretty woman, but as a rule they do not like to do such things. So here I am, with no pretty woman to push me. *Unlike you.*"

Sanders sighed. "Max, do you suppose we can just have an ordinary conversation?"

"What a good idea," Dorfman said. "I would like that very much. What is an ordinary conversation?"

"I mean, can we just talk like normal people?"

"If it will not bore you, Thomas, yes. But I am worried. You know how old people are worried about being boring."

"Max. What did you mean about the stained glass?"

He shrugged. "I meant Meredith, of course. What else?"

"What about Meredith?"

"How am I to know?" Dorfman said irritably. "All I know of this is what you told me. And all you told me is that you used to take trips, to Korea or Japan, and when you came back, Meredith would—"

"Tom, I'm sorry to interrupt," Cindy said, leaning in the door to the conference room.

"Oh, don't be sorry," Max said. "Who is this beautiful creature, Thomas?"

"I'm Cindy Wolfe, Professor Dorfman," she said. "I work for Tom."

"Oh, what a lucky man he is!"

Cindy turned to Sanders. "I'm really sorry,

Tom, but one of the executives from Conley-White is in your office, and I thought you would want to—"

"Yes, yes," Dorfman said immediately. "He must go. Conley-White, it sounds *very* important."

"In a minute," Sanders said. He turned to Cindy. "Max and I were in the middle of something."

"No, no, Thomas," Dorfman said. "We were just talking about old times. You better go."

"Max—"

"You want to talk more, you think it's important, you come visit me. I am at the Four Seasons. You know that hotel. It has a *wonderful* lobby, such high ceilings. Very grand, especially for an old man. So, you go right along, Thomas." His eyes narrowed. "And leave the beautiful Cindy with me."

Sanders hesitated. "Watch out for him," he said. "He's a dirty old man."

"As dirty as possible," Dorfman cackled.

Sanders headed down the hallway to his office. As he left, he heard Dorfman say, "Now beautiful Cindy, please take me to the lobby where I have a car waiting. And on the way, if you don't mind indulging an old man, I have a few little questions. So many *interesting* things are happening in this company. And the secretaries always know everything, don't they?"

Mr. Sanders." Jim Daly stood quickly, as Sanders came into the room. "I'm glad they found you."

They shook hands. Sanders gestured for Daly to sit down, and slid behind his own desk. Sanders was not surprised; he had been expecting a visit from Daly or one of the other investment bankers for several days. Members of the Goldman, Sachs team had been speaking individually with people in various departments, going over aspects of the merger. Most of the time they wanted background information; although high technology was central to the acquisition, none of the bankers understood it very well. Sanders expected Daly to ask about progress on the Twinkle drive, and perhaps the Corridor.

"I appreciate your taking the time," Daly said, rubbing his bald head. He was a very tall, thin man, and he seemed even taller sitting down, all knees and elbows. "I wanted to ask you some things, ah, off the record."

"Sure," Sanders said.

"It's to do with Meredith Johnson," Daly said, in an apologetic voice. "If you, ah, don't mind, I'd prefer we just keep this conversation between us."

"All right," Sanders said.

"I understand that you have been closely involved with setting up the plants in Ireland and Malaysia. And that there has been a little controversy inside the company about how that was carried out."

"Well." Sanders shrugged. "Phil Blackburn and I haven't always seen eye to eye."

"Showing your good sense, in my view," Daly said dryly. "But I gather that in these disputes you represent technical expertise, and others in the company represent, ah, various other concerns. Would that be fair?"

"Yes, I'd say so." What was he getting at?

"Well, it's along those lines that I'd like to hear your thoughts. Bob Garvin has just appointed Ms. Johnson to a position of considerable authority, a step which many in Conley-White applaud. And certainly it would be unfair to prejudge how she will carry out her new duties within the company. But by the same token, it would be derelict of me not to inquire about her past duties. Do you get my drift?"

"Not exactly," Sanders said.

"I'm wondering," Daly said, "what you feel about Ms. Johnson's past performance with regard to the technical operations of the company. Specifically, her involvement in the foreign operations of DigiCom."

Sanders frowned, thinking back. "I'm not

aware that she's had much involvement," he said. "We had a labor dispute two years ago in Cork. She was part of the team that went over to negotiate a settlement. She lobbied in Washington about flat-panel display tariffs. And I know she headed the Ops Review Team in Cupertino, which approved the plans for the new plant at Kuala Lumpur."

"Yes, exactly."

"But I don't know that her involvement goes beyond that."

"Ah. Well. Perhaps I was given wrong information," Daly said, shifting in his chair.

"What did you hear?"

"Without going into specifics, let me say a question of judgment was raised."

"I see," Sanders said. Who would have said anything to Daly about Meredith? Certainly not Garvin or Blackburn. Kaplan? It was impossible to know for sure. But Daly would be talking only to highly placed officers.

"I was wondering," Daly said, "if you had any thoughts on her technical judgment. Speaking privately, of course."

At that moment, Sanders's computer screen beeped three times. A message flashed:

ONE MINUTE TO DIRECT VIDEO LINKUP: DC / M-DC / S
SEN: A. KAHN
REC: T. SANDERS

Daly said, "Is something wrong?"

"No," Sanders said. "It looks like I have a video feed coming in from Malaysia."

"Then I'll be brief and leave you to it," Daly said. "Let me put it to you directly. Within your division, is there any concern whether Meredith Johnson is qualified for this post?"

Sanders shrugged. "She's the new boss. You know how organizations are. There's always concern with a new boss."

"You're very diplomatic. I mean to say, is there concern about her expertise? She's relatively young, after all. Geographic move, uprooting. New faces, new staffing, new problems. And up here, she won't be so directly under Bob Garvin's, ah, wing."

"I don't know what to say," Sanders said. "We'll all have to wait and see."

"And I gather that there was trouble in the past when a non-technical person headed the division . . . a man named, ah, Screamer Freeling?"

"Yes. He didn't work out."

"And there are similar concerns about Johnson?"

Sanders said, "I've heard them expressed."

"And her fiscal measures? These cost-containment plans of hers? That's the crux, isn't it?"

Sanders thought: what cost-containment plans? The screen beeped again.

30 SECONDS TO DIRECT VIDEO LINKUP: DC/M-DC/S

"There goes your machine again," Daly said, unfolding himself from the chair. "I'll let you go. Thank you for your time, Mr. Sanders."

"Not at all."

They shook hands. Daly turned and walked out of the room. Sanders's computer beeped three times in rapid succession:

15 SECONDS TO DIRECT VIDEO LINKUP: DC/M-DC/S

He sat down in front of the monitor and twisted his desk lamp so that the light shone on his face. The numbers on the computer were counting backward. Sanders looked at his watch. It was five o'clock—eight o'clock in Malaysia. Arthur would probably be calling from the plant.

A small rectangle appeared in the center of the screen and grew outward in progressive jumps. He saw Arthur's face, and behind him, the brightly lit assembly line. Brand-new, it was the epitome of modern manufacturing: clean and quiet, the workers in street clothes, arranged on both sides of the green conveyor belt. At each workstation there was a bank of fluorescent lights, which flared a little in the camera.

Kahn coughed and rubbed his chin. "Hello, Tom. How are you?" When he spoke, his image blurred slightly. And his voice was out of sync, since the bounce to the satellite caused a slight delay in the video, but the voice was transmitted immediately. This unsynchronized quality was very distracting for the first few seconds; it gave the linkup a dreamy quality. It was a little like talking to someone under water. Then you got used to it.

"I'm fine, Arthur," he said.

"Well, good. I'm sorry about the new organization. You know how I feel personally."

"Thank you, Arthur." He wondered vaguely how Kahn in Malaysia would have heard already. But in any company, gossip traveled fast.

"Yeah. Well. Anyway, Tom, I'm standing here on the floor," Kahn said, gesturing behind him. "And as you can see, we're still running very slow. And the spot checks are unimproved. What do the designers say? Have they gotten the units yet?"

"They came today. I don't have any news yet. They're still working on it."

"Uh-huh. Okay. And have the units gone to Diagnostics?" Kahn asked.

"I think so. Just went."

"Yeah. Okay. Because we got a request from Diagnostics for ten more drive units to be sent in heat-sealed plastic bags. And they specified that they wanted them sealed inside the factory. Right as they came off the line. You know anything about that?"

"No, this is the first I heard of it. Let me find out, and I'll get back to you."

"Okay, because I have to tell you, it seemed strange to me. I mean, ten units is a lot. Customs is going to query it if we send them all together. And I don't know what this sealing is about. We send them wrapped in plastic anyway. But not sealed. Why do they want them sealed, Tom?" Kahn sounded worried.

"I don't know," Sanders said. "I'll get into it. All I can think is that it's a full-court press around here. People really want to know why the hell those drives don't work."

"Hey, us too," Kahn said. "Believe me. It's making us crazy."

"When will you send the drives?"

"Well, I've got to get a heat-sealer first. I hope I can ship Wednesday, you can have them Thursday."

"Not good enough," Sanders said. "You should ship today, or tomorrow at the latest. You want me to run down a sealer for you? I can probably get one from Apple." Apple had a factory in Kuala Lumpur.

"No. That's a good idea. I'll call over there and see if Ron can loan me one."

"Fine. Now what about Jafar?"

"Hell of a thing," Kahn said. "I just talked to the hospital, and apparently he's got cramps and vomiting. Won't eat anything. The abo doctors say they can't figure out anything except, you know, a spell."

"They believe in spells?"

"Damn right," Kahn said. "They've got laws against sorcery here. You can take people to court."

"So you don't know when he'll be back?"

"Nobody's saying. Apparently he's really sick."

"Okay, Arthur. Anything else?"

"No. I'll get the sealer. And let me know what you find out."

"I will," Sanders said, and the transmission ended. Kahn gave a final wave, and the screen went blank.

SAVE THIS TRANSMISSION TO DISK OR DAT?

He clicked DAT, and it was saved to digital tape. He got up from the desk. Whatever all this was about, he'd better be informed before he had his meeting with Johnson at six. He went to the outer area, to Cindy's desk.

Cindy was turned away, laughing on the phone. She looked back and saw Sanders, and stopped laughing. "Listen, I got to go."

Sanders said, "Would you mind pulling the

production reports on Twinkle for the last two months? Better yet, just pull everything since they opened the line."

"Sure."

"And call Don Cherry for me. I need to know what his Diagnostics group is doing with the drives."

He went back into his office. He noticed his e-mail cursor was blinking, and pushed the key to read them. While he waited, he looked at the three faxes on his desk. Two were from Ireland, routine weekly production reports. The third was a requisition for a roof repair at the Austin plant; it had been held up in Operations in Cupertino, and Eddie had forwarded it to Sanders to try and get action.

The screen blinked. He looked up at the first of his e-mail messages.

OUT OF NOWHERE WE GOT A BEAN COUNTER FROM OPERATIONS DOWN HERE IN AUSTIN. HE'S GOING OVER ALL THE BOOKS, DRIVING PEOPLE MAD. AND THE WORD IS WE GOT MORE COMING DOWN TOMOR- ROW. WHAT GIVES? THE RUMORS ARE FLYING, AND SLOWING HELL OUT OF THE LINE. TELL ME WHAT TO SAY. IS THIS COMPANY FOR SALE OR NOT?

EDDIE

Sanders did not hesitate. He couldn't tell Eddie what was going on. Quickly, he typed his reply:

THE BEAN COUNTERS WERE IN IRELAND LAST
WEEK, TOO. GARVIN'S ORDERED A COMPANY-WIDE
REVIEW, AND THEY'RE LOOKING AT EVERYTHING.
TELL EVERYBODY DOWN THERE TO FORGET IT AND
GO BACK TO WORK.

TOM

He pushed the SEND button. The message disappeared.

"You called?" Don Cherry walked into the room without knocking, and dropped into the chair. He put his hands behind his head. "Jesus, what a day. I've been putting out fires all afternoon."

"Tell me."

"I got some dweebs from Conley down there, asking my guys what the difference is between RAM and ROM. Like they have time for this. Pretty soon, one of the dweebs hears 'flash memory' and he goes, 'How often does it flash?' Like it was a flashlight or something. And my guys have to put up with this. I mean, this is high-priced talent. They shouldn't be doing remedial classes for lawyers. Can't you stop it?"

"Nobody can stop it," Sanders said.

"Maybe Meredith can stop it," Cherry said, grinning.

Sanders shrugged. "She's the boss."

"Yeah. So—what's on your mind?"

"Your Diagnostics group is working on the Twinkle drives."

"True. That is, we're working on the bits and pieces that're left after Lewyn's nimble-fingered *artistes* tore the hell out of them. Why did they go to design first? Never, *ever*, let a designer near an actual piece of electronic equipment, Tom. Designers should only be allowed to draw pictures on pieces of paper. And only give them one piece of paper at a time."

"What have you found?" Sanders said. "About the drives."

"Nothing yet," Cherry said. "But we got a few ideas we're kicking around."

"Is that why you asked Arthur Kahn to send you ten drives, heat-sealed from the factory?"

"You bet your ass."

"Kahn was wondering about that."

"So?" Cherry said. "Let him wonder. It'll do him good. Keep him from playing with himself."

"I'd like to know, too."

"Well look," Cherry said. "Maybe our ideas won't amount to anything. At the moment, all we have is one suspicious chip. That's all Lewyn's clowns left us. It's not very much to go on."

"The chip is bad?"

"No, the chip is fine."

"What's suspicious about it?"

"Look," Cherry said. "We've got enough rumors flying around as it is. I can report that we're working on it, and we don't know yet. That's all. We'll get the sealed drives tomorrow or Wednesday, and we should know within an hour. Okay?"

"You thinking big problem, or little problem? I've got to know," Sanders said. "It's going to come up in the meetings tomorrow."

"Well, at the moment, the answer is we don't know. It could be anything. We're working on it."

"Arthur thinks it might be serious."

"Arthur might be right. But we'll solve it. That's all I can tell you."

"Don . . ."

"I understand you want an answer," Cherry said. "Do you understand that I don't have one?"

Sanders stared at him. "You could have called. Why'd you come up in person?"

"Since you asked," Cherry said, "I've got a small problem. It's delicate. Sexual harassment thing."

"*Another* one? It seems like that's all we have around here."

"Us and everybody else," Cherry said. "I hear UniCom's got fourteen suits going right now. Digital Graphics has even more. And MicroSym, look out. They're all pigs over there, anyway. But I'd like your read on this."

Sanders sighed. "Okay."

"In one of my programming groups, the remote DB access group. The group's all pretty old: twenty-five to twenty-nine years old. The supervisor for the fax modem team, a woman, has been asking one of the guys out. She thinks he's cute. He keeps turning her down. Today she asks him again in the parking lot at lunch; he says no. She gets in her car, rams his car, drives off. Nobody hurt, and he doesn't want to make a complaint. But he's worried, thinks it's a little out of hand. Comes to me for advice. What should I do?"

Sanders frowned. "You think that's the whole story? She's just mad at him because he turned her down? Or did he do something to provoke this?"

"He says no. He's a pretty straight guy. A little geeky, not real sophisticated."

"And the woman?"

"She's got a temper, no question. She blows at the team sometimes. I've had to talk to her about that."

"What does she say about the incident in the parking lot?"

"Don't know. The guy's asked me not to talk to her. Says he's embarrassed and doesn't want to make it worse."

Sanders shrugged. "What can you do? People are upset but nobody will talk . . . I don't know, Don. If a woman rammed his car, I'd guess he must have done something. Chances are he slept with her once, and won't see her again, and now she's pissed. That's my guess."

"That would be my guess, too," Cherry said, "but of course, maybe not."

"Damage to the car?"

"Nothing serious. Broken taillight. He just doesn't want it to get any worse. So, do I drop it?"

"If he won't file charges, I'd drop it."

"Do I speak to her informally?"

"I wouldn't. You go accusing her of impropriety—even informally—and you're asking for trouble. Nobody's going to support you. Because the chances are, your guy *did* do something to provoke her."

"Even though he says he didn't."

Sanders sighed. "Listen, Don, they always say they didn't. I never heard of one who said, 'You know, I deserve this.' Never happens."

"So, drop it?"

"Put a note in the file that he told you the story, be sure you characterize the story as alleged, and forget it."

Cherry nodded, turned to leave. At the door, he stopped and looked back. "So tell me this. How come we're both so convinced this guy must have done something?"

"Just playing the odds," Sanders said. "Now fix that damned drive for me."

At six o'clock, he said good night to Cindy and took the Twinkle files up to Meredith's office on the fifth floor. The sun was still high in the sky, streaming through the windows. It seemed like late afternoon, not the end of the day.

Meredith had been given the big corner office, where Ron Goldman used to be. Meredith had a new assistant, too, a woman. Sanders guessed she had followed her boss up from Cupertino.

"I'm Tom Sanders," he said. "I have an appointment with Ms. Johnson."

"Betsy Ross, from Cupertino, Mr. Sanders," she said. She looked at him. "Don't say anything."

"Okay."

"Everybody says something. Something about the flag. I get really sick of it."

"Okay."

"My whole life."

"Okay. Fine."

"I'll tell Miss Johnson you're here."

Tom." Meredith Johnson waved from behind her desk, her other hand holding the phone. "Come in, sit down."

Her office had a view north toward downtown Seattle: the Space Needle, the Arly towers, the SODO building. The city looked glorious in the afternoon sun.

"I'll just finish this up." She turned back to the phone. "Yes, Ed, I'm with Tom now, we'll go over all of that. Yes. He's brought the documentation with him."

Sanders held up the manila folder containing the drive data. She pointed to her briefcase, which was lying open on the corner of the desk, and gestured for him to put it inside.

She turned back to the phone. "Yes, Ed, I think the due diligence will go smoothly, and there certainly isn't any impulse to hold anything back . . . No, no . . . Well, we can do it first thing in the morning if you like."

Sanders put the folder in her briefcase.

Meredith was saying, "Right, Ed, right. Absolutely." She came toward Tom and sat with one hip on the edge of the desk, her navy blue skirt riding up her thigh. She wasn't wearing stockings.

"Everybody agrees that this is important, Ed. Yes." She swung her foot, the high heel dangling from her toe. She smiled at Sanders. He felt uncomfortable, and moved back a little. "I promise you, Ed. Yes. Absolutely."

Meredith hung up the phone on the cradle behind her, leaning back across the desk, twisting her body, revealing her breasts beneath the silk blouse. "Well, that's done." She sat forward again, and sighed. "The Conley people heard there's trouble with Twinkle. That was Ed Nichols, flipping out. Actually, it's the third call I've had about Twinkle this afternoon. You'd think that was all there was to this company. How do you like the office?"

"Pretty good," he said. "Great view."

"Yes, the city's beautiful." She leaned on one arm and crossed her legs. She saw that he noticed, and said, "In the summer, I'd rather not wear stockings. I like the bare feeling. So much cooler on a hot day."

Sanders said, "From now to the end of summer, it will be pretty much this way."

"I have to tell you, I dread the weather," she said. "I mean, after California . . ." She uncrossed her legs again, and smiled. "But you like it here, don't you? You seem happy here."

"Yes." He shrugged. "You get used to rain." He pointed to her briefcase. "Do you want to go over the Twinkle stuff?"

"Absolutely," she said, sliding off the desk, coming close to him. She looked him directly in the eyes. "But I hope you don't mind if I impose on you first. Just a little?"

"Sure."

She stepped aside. "Pour the wine for us."

"Okay."

"See if it's chilled long enough." He went over to the bottle on the side table. "I remember you always liked it cold."

"That's true," he said, spinning the bottle in the ice. He didn't like it so cold anymore, but he did in those days.

"We had a lot of fun back then," she said.

"Yes," he said. "We did."

"I swear," she said. "Sometimes I think that back when we were both young and trying to make it, I think that was the best it ever was."

He hesitated, not sure how to answer her, what tone to take. He poured the wine.

"Yes," she said. "We had a good time. I think about it often."

Sanders thought: I never do.

She said, "What about you, Tom? Do you think about it?"

"Of course." He crossed the room carrying the glasses of wine to her, gave her one, clinked them. "Sure I do. All us married guys think of the old days. You know I'm married now."

"Yes," she said, nodding. "Very married, I hear. With how many kids? Three?"

"No, just two." He smiled. "Sometimes it seems like three."

"And your wife is an attorney?"

"Yes." He felt safer now. The talk of his wife and children made him feel safer somehow.

"I don't know how somebody can be married," Meredith said. "I tried it." She held up her hand. "Four more alimony payments to the son of a bitch and I'm free."

"Who did you marry?"

"Some account executive at CoStar. He was cute. Amusing. But it turned out he was a typical gold digger. I've been paying him off for three years. *And* he was a lousy lay." She waved her hand, dismissing the subject. She looked at her watch. "Now come and sit down, and tell me how bad it is with the Twinkle drive."

"You want the file? I put it in your briefcase."

"No." She patted the couch beside her. "You just tell me yourself."

He sat down beside her.

"You look good, Tom." She leaned back and kicked off her heels, wiggled her bare toes. "God, what a day."

"Lot of pressure?"

She sipped her wine and blew a strand of hair from her face. "A lot to keep track of. I'm glad we're working together, Tom. I feel as though you're the one friend I can count on in all this."

"Thanks. I'll try."

"So: how bad is it?"

"Well. It's hard to say."

"Just tell me."

He felt he had no choice but to lay it all out for her. "We've built very successful prototypes, but the drives coming off the line in KL are running nowhere near a hundred milliseconds."

Meredith sighed, and shook her head. "Do we know why?"

"Not yet. We're working on some ideas."

"That line's a start-up, isn't it?"

"Two months ago."

She shrugged. "Then we have problems on a new line. That's not so bad."

"But the thing is," he said, "Conley-White is buying this company for our technology, and especially for the CD-ROM drive. As of today, we may not be able to deliver as promised."

"You want to tell them *that*?"

"I'm concerned they'll pick it up in due diligence."

"Maybe, maybe not." She leaned back in the couch. "We have to remember what we're really looking at. Tom, we've all seen production problems loom large, only to vanish overnight. This may be one of those situations. We're shaking out the Twinkle line. We've identified some early problems. No big deal."

"Maybe. But we don't know that. In reality, there may be a problem with controller chips, which means changing our supplier in Singapore. Or there may be a more fundamental problem. A design problem, originating here."

"Perhaps," Meredith said, "but as you say, we don't know that. And I don't see any reason for us to speculate. At this critical time."

"But to be honest—"

"It's not a matter of honesty," she said. "It's a matter of the underlying reality. Let's go over it, point by point. We've told them we have a Twinkle drive."

"Yes."

"We've built a prototype and tested the hell out of it."

"Yes."

"And the prototype works like gangbusters. It's twice as fast as the most advanced drives coming out of Japan."

"Yes."

"We've told them we're in production on the drive."

"Yes."

"Well, then," Meredith said, "we've told them all that anybody knows for sure, at this point. I'd say we are acting in good faith."

"Well, maybe, but I don't know if we can—"

"Tom." Meredith placed her hand on his arm. "I always liked your directness. I want you to know how much I appreciate your expertise and your frank approach to problems. All the more reason why I'm sure the Twinkle drive will get ironed out. We know that fundamentally it's a good product that performs as we say it does. Personally, I have complete confidence in it, and in your ability to make it work as planned. And I have no problem saying that at the meeting tomorrow." She paused, and looked intently at him. "Do you?"

Her face was very close to him, her lips half-parted. "Do I what?"

"Have a problem saying that at the meeting?"

Her eyes were light blue, almost gray. He had forgotten that, as he had forgotten how long her lashes were. Her hair fell softly around her face. Her lips were full. She had a dreamy look in her eyes. "No," he said. "I don't have a problem."

"Good. Then at least *that's* settled." She smiled and held out her glass. "Do the honors again?"

"Sure."

He got up from the couch and went over to the wine. She watched him.

"I'm glad you haven't let yourself go, Tom. You work out?"

"Twice a week. How about you?"

"You always had a nice tush. Nice hard tush."

He turned. "Meredith . . ."

She giggled. "I'm sorry. I can't help it. We're old friends." She looked concerned. "I didn't offend you, did I?"

"No."

"I can't imagine you ever getting prudish, Tom."

"No, no."

"Not you." She laughed. "Remember the night we broke the bed?"

He poured the wine. "We didn't exactly break it."

"Sure we did. You had me bent over the bottom of the footboard and—"

"I remember—"

"And first we broke the footboard, and then the bottom of the bed crashed down—but you didn't want to stop so we moved up and then when I was grabbing the headboard it all came—"

"I remember," he said, wanting to interrupt her, to stop this. "Those days were great. Listen, Meredith—"

"And then the woman from downstairs called up? Remember her? The old Lithuanian lady? She vanted ta know if somebody had died or vhat?"

"Yeah. Listen. Going back to the drive . . ."

She took the wineglass. "I *am* making you uncomfortable. What—did you think I was coming on to you?"

"No, no. Nothing like that."

"Good, because I really wasn't. I promise." She gave him an amused glance, then tilted her head back, exposing her long neck, and sipped the wine. "In fact, I—ah! Ah!" She winced suddenly.

"What is it?" he said, leaning forward, concerned.

"My neck, it goes into spasm, it's right there . . ." With her eyes still squeezed shut in pain, she pointed to her shoulder, near the neck.

"What should I—"

"Just rub it, squeeze—there—"

He put down his wineglass and rubbed her shoulder. "There?"

"Yes, ah, harder—squeeze—"

He felt the muscles of her shoulder relax, and she sighed. Meredith turned her head back and forth slowly, then opened her eyes. "Oh . . . Much better . . . Don't stop rubbing."

He continued rubbing.

"Oh, thanks. That feels good. I get this nerve thing. Pinched something, but when it hits, it's really . . ." She turned her head back and forth. Testing. "You did that very well. But you were always good with your hands, Tom."

He kept rubbing. He wanted to stop. He felt everything was wrong, that he was sitting too close, that he didn't want to be touching her. But it also felt good to touch her. He was curious about it.

"Good hands," she said. "God, when I was married, I thought about you all the time."

"You did?"

"Sure," she said. "I told you, he was terrible in bed. I hate a man who doesn't know what he's doing." She closed her eyes. "That was never your problem, was it."

She sighed, relaxing more, and then she seemed to lean into him, melting toward his body, toward his hands. It was an unmistakable sensation. Immediately, he gave her shoulder a final friendly squeeze, and took his hands away.

She opened her eyes. She smiled knowingly. "Listen," she said, "don't worry."

He turned and sipped his wine. "I'm not worried."

"I mean, about the drive. If it turns out we really have problems and need agreement from higher management, we'll get it. But let's not jump the gun now."

"Okay, fine. I think that makes sense." He felt secretly relieved to be talking once again about the drive. Back on safe ground. "Who would you take it to? Directly to Garvin?"

"I think so. I prefer to deal informally." She looked at him. "You've changed, haven't you."

"No . . . I'm still the same."

"I think you've changed." She smiled. "You never would have stopped rubbing me before."

"Meredith," he said, "it's different. You run the division now. I work for you."

"Oh, don't be silly."

"It's true."

"We're colleagues." She pouted. "Nobody around here really believes I'm superior to you. They just gave me the administrative work, that's all. We're colleagues, Tom. And I just want us to have an open, friendly relationship."

"So do I."

"Good. I'm glad we agree on that." Quickly, she leaned forward and kissed him lightly on the lips. "There. Was that so terrible?"

"It wasn't terrible at all."

"Who knows? Maybe we'll have to go to Malaysia together, to check on the assembly lines. They have very nice beaches in Malaysia. You ever been to Kuantan?"

"No."

"You'd love it."

"I'm sure."

"I'll show it to you. We could take an extra day or two. Stop over. Get some sun."

"Meredith—"

"Nobody needs to know, Tom."

"I'm married."

"You're also a man."

"What does that mean?"

"Oh Tom," she said, with mock severity,

"don't ask me to believe you never have a little adventure on the side. I *know* you, remember?"

"You knew me a long time ago, Meredith."

"People don't change. Not *that* way."

"Well, I think they do."

"Oh, come on. We're going to be working together, we might as well enjoy ourselves."

He didn't like the way any of this was going. He felt pushed into an awkward position. He felt stuffy and puritanical when he said: "I'm married now."

"Oh, I don't care about your personal life," she said lightly. "I'm only responsible for your on-the-job performance. All work and no play, Tom. It can be bad for you. Got to stay playful." She leaned forward. "Come on. Just one little kiss . . ."

The intercom buzzed. "Meredith," the assistant's voice said.

She looked up in annoyance. "I told you, no calls."

"I'm sorry. It's Mr. Garvin, Meredith."

"All right." She got off the couch and walked across the room to her desk, saying loudly, "But after this, Betsy, no more calls."

"All right, Meredith. I wanted to ask you, is it okay if I leave in about ten minutes? I have to see the landlord about my new apartment."

"Yes. Did you get me that package?"

"I have it right here."

"Bring it in, and then you can leave."

"Thank you, Meredith. Mr. Garvin is on two."

Meredith picked up the phone and poured more wine. "Bob," she said. "Hi. What's up?" It was impossible to miss the easy familiarity in her voice.

She spoke to Garvin, her back turned to Sanders. He sat on the couch, feeling stranded, foolishly passive and idle. The assistant entered the room carrying a small package in a brown paper bag. She gave the package to Meredith.

"Of course, Bob," Meredith was saying. "I couldn't agree more. We'll certainly deal with that."

The assistant, waiting for Meredith to dismiss her, smiled at Sanders. He felt uncomfortable just sitting there on the couch, so he got up, walked to the window, pulled his cellular phone out of his pocket, and dialed Mark Lewyn's number. He had promised to call Lewyn anyway.

Meredith was saying, "That's a very good thought, Bob. I think we should act on it."

Sanders heard his call dial, and then an answering machine picked up. A male voice said, "Leave your message at the beep." Then an electronic tone.

"Mark," he said, "it's Tom Sanders. I've talked about Twinkle with Meredith. Her view is that we're in early production and we are shaking out the lines. She takes the position that we can't say for sure that there are any significant problems to be flagged, and that we should treat the situation as standard procedure for the bankers and C-W people tomorrow . . ."

The assistant walked out of the room, smiling at Sanders as she passed him.

". . . and that if we have problems with the drive later on that we have to get management involved with, we'll face that later. I've given her your thoughts, and she's talking to Bob now, so presumably we'll go into the meeting tomorrow taking that position . . ."

The assistant came to the door to the office. She paused briefly to twist the lock in the doorknob, then left, closing the door behind her.

Sanders frowned. *She had locked the door on her way out.* It wasn't so much the fact that she had done it, but the fact that he seemed to be in the middle of an arrangement, a planned event in which everyone else understood what was going on and he did not.

". . . Well, anyway, Mark, if there is a significant change in all this, I'll contact you before the meeting tomorrow, and—"

"Forget that phone," Meredith said coming up suddenly, very close to him, pushing his hand down, and pressing her body against his. Her lips mashed against his mouth. He was vaguely aware of dropping the phone on the windowsill as they kissed and she twisted, turning away, and they tumbled over onto the couch.

"Meredith, wait—"

"Oh God, I've wanted you all day," she said intensely. She kissed him again, rolling on top of him, lifting one leg to hold him down. His position was awkward but he felt himself responding to her. His immediate thought was that someone might come in. He had a vision of himself, lying on his back on the couch with his boss half-straddling him in her businesslike navy suit, and he was anxious about what the person seeing them would think, and then he was truly responding.

She felt it too, and it aroused her more. She pulled back for a breath. "Oh God, you feel so *good*, I can't stand the bastard touching me. Those stupid glasses. Oh! I'm so *hot*, I haven't had a decent fuck—" and then she threw herself back on him, kissing him again, her mouth mashed on him. Her tongue was in his mouth and he thought, *Jesus, she's pushing it.* He smelled her perfume, and it immediately brought back memories.

She shifted her body so she could reach down and touch him, and she moaned when she felt him through his trousers. She fumbled at the zipper. He had suddenly conflicting images, his desire for her, his wife and his kids, memories of the past, of being with her in the apartment in Sunnyvale, of breaking the bed. Images of his wife.

"Meredith—"

"*Oooh.* Don't talk. No! No . . ." She was gasping in little breaths, her mouth puckering rhythmically like a goldfish. He remembered that she got that way. He had forgotten until now. He felt her hot panting breath on his face, saw her flushed cheeks. She got his trousers open. Her hot hand on him.

"Oh, Jesus," she said, squeezing him, and she slid down his body, running her hands over his shirt.

"Listen, Meredith."

"Just let me," she said hoarsely. "Just for a minute." And then her mouth was on him. She was always good at this. Images flooding back to him. The way she liked to do it in dangerous places. While he was driving on the freeway. In the men's room at a sales conference. On the beach at Napili at night. The secret impulsive nature, the secret heat. When he was first introduced to her, the exec at ConTech had said, *She's one of the great cocksuckers.*

Feeling her mouth on him, feeling his back arch as the tension ran through his body, he had the uneasy sense of pleasure and danger at once. So much had happened during the day, so many changes, everything was so sudden. He felt dominated, controlled, and at risk. He had the feeling as he lay on his back that he was somehow agreeing to a situation that he did not understand fully, that was not fully recognized. There would be trouble later. He did not want to go to Malaysia with her. He did not want an affair with his boss. He did not even want a one-night stand. Because what always happened was that people found out, gossip at the water cooler, meaningful looks in the hallway. And sooner or later the spouses found out. It always happened. Slammed doors, divorce lawyers, child custody.

And he didn't want any of that. His life was arranged now, he had things in place. He had commitments. This woman from his past understood none of that. She was free. He was not. He shifted his body.

"Meredith—"

"God, you taste good."

"Meredith—"

She reached up, and pressed her fingers over his lips. "Ssshhh. I know you like it."

"I do like it," he said, "but I—"

"Then let me."

As she sucked him, she was unbuttoning his shirt, pinching his nipples. He looked down and saw her straddling his legs, her head bent over him. Her blouse was open. Her breasts swung free. She reached up, took his hands, and pulled them down, placing them on her breasts.

She still had perfect breasts, the nipples hard under his touch. She moaned. Her body squirming as she straddled him. He felt her warmth. He began to hear a buzzing in his ears, a suffusing intoxicated flush in his face as sounds went dull, the room seemed distant, and there was nothing but this woman and her body and his desire for her.

In that moment he felt a burst of anger, a kind of male fury that he was pinned down, that she was dominating him, and he wanted to be in control, to take her. He sat up and grabbed her hair roughly, lifting her head and twisting his body. She looked in his eyes and saw instantly.

"Yes!" she said, and she moved sideways, so he could sit up beside her. He slipped his hand between her legs. He felt warmth, and lacy underpants. He tugged at them. She wriggled, helping him, and he slid them down to her knees; then she kicked them away. Her hands were caressing his hair, her lips at his ear. "Yes," she whispered fiercely. "Yes!"

Her blue skirt was bunched up around her waist. He kissed her hard, pulling her blouse wide, pressing her breasts to his bare chest. He felt her heat all along his body. He moved his fingers, probing between her lips. She gasped as they kissed, nodding her head *yes*. Then his fingers were in her.

For a moment he was startled: she was not very wet, and then he remembered that, too. The way she would start, her words and body immediately passionate, but this central part of her slower to respond, taking her eventual arousal from his.

She was always turned on most by his desire for her, and always came after he did—sometimes within a few seconds, but sometimes he struggled to stay hard while she rocked against him, pushing to her own completion, lost in her own private world while he was fading. He always felt alone, always felt as if she were using him. Those memories gave him pause, and she sensed his hesitation and grabbed him fiercely, fumbling at his belt, moaning, sticking her hot tongue in his ear.

But reluctance was seeping back into him now, his angry heat was fading, and unbidden the thought flashed through his mind: *It's not worth it.*

All his feelings shifted again, and now he had a familiar sensation. Going back to see an old lover, being attracted over dinner, then getting involved again, feeling desire and, suddenly, in the heat of the moment, in the press of flesh, being reminded of all the things that had been wrong with the relationship, feeling old conflicts and angers and irritations rise up again, and wishing that he had never started. Suddenly thinking of how to get out of it, how to stop what was started. But usually there was no way to get out of it.

Still his fingers were inside her, and she was moving her body against his hand, shifting to be sure he would touch the right place. She was wetter, her lips were swelling. She opened her legs wider for him. She was breathing very hard, stroking him with her fingers. "Oh God, I love the way you feel," she said.

Usually there was no way to get out of it.

His body was tense and ready. Her hard nipples brushed against his chest. Her fingers caressed him. She licked the bottom of his earlobe with a quick dart of her tongue and instantly there was nothing but his desire, hot and angry, more intense for the fact that he didn't really want to be there, that he felt she had manipulated him to this place. Now he would fuck her. He wanted to fuck her. Hard.

She sensed his change and moaned, no longer kissing him, leaning back on the couch, waiting. She watched him through half-closed eyes, nodding her head. His fingers still touched her, rapidly, repeatedly, making her gasp, and he turned, pushed her down on her back on the couch. She hiked up her skirt and spread her legs for him. He crouched over her and she smiled at him, a knowing, victorious smile. It made him furious to see this sense that she had somehow won, this watchful detachment, and he wanted to catch her, to make her feel as out of control as he felt, to make her part of this, to wipe that smug detachment from her face. He spread her lips but did not enter her, he held back, his fingers moving, teasing her.

She arched her back, waiting for him. "No, no . . . please . . ."

Still he waited, looking at her. His anger was

fading as quickly as it had come, his mind drifting away, the old reservations returning. In an instant of harsh clarity, he saw himself in the room, a panting middle-aged, married man with his trousers down around his knees, bent over a woman on an office couch that was too small. What the hell was he doing?

He looked at her face, saw the way the makeup cracked at the corners of her eyes. Around her mouth.

She had her hands on his shoulders, tugging him toward her. "Oh please . . . No . . . No . . ." And then she turned her head aside and coughed.

Something snapped in him. He sat back coldly. "You're right." He got off the couch, and pulled up his trousers. "We shouldn't do this."

She sat up. "What are you doing?" She seemed puzzled. "You want this as much as I do. You know you do."

"No," he said. "We shouldn't do this, Meredith." He was buckling his belt. Stepping back.

She stared at him in dazed disbelief, like someone awakened from sleep. "You're not serious . . ."

"This isn't a good idea. I don't feel good about it."

And then her eyes were suddenly furious. "You fucking *son of a bitch.*"

She got off the couch fast, rushing at him, hitting him hard with bunched fists. "You bastard!

You prick! You fucking bastard!" He was trying to button his shirt, turning away from her blows. "You shit! You bastard!"

She moved around him as he turned away, grabbing his hands, tearing at his shirt to keep him from buttoning it.

"You can't! You can't do this to me!"

Buttons popped. She scratched him, long red welts running down his chest. He turned again, avoiding her, wanting only to get out of there. To get dressed and get out of there. She pounded his back.

"You fucker, you can't leave me like this!"

"Cut it out, Meredith," he said. "It's over."

"*Fuck* you!" She grabbed a handful of his hair, pulling him down with surprising strength, and she bit his ear hard. He felt an intense shooting pain and he pushed her away roughly. She toppled backward, off balance, crashing against the glass coffee table, sprawling on the ground.

She sat there, panting. "You fucking son of a bitch."

"Meredith, just leave me alone." He was buttoning his shirt again. All he could think was: *Get out of here*. Get your stuff and get out of here. He reached for his jacket, then saw his cellular phone on the windowsill.

He moved around the couch and picked up the phone. The wineglass crashed against the window near his head. He looked over and saw her standing in the middle of the room, reaching for something else to throw.

"I'll kill you!" she said. "I'll fucking kill you."

"That's enough, Meredith," he said.

"The hell." She threw a small paper bag at him. It thunked against the glass and dropped to the floor. A box of condoms fell out.

"I'm going home." He moved toward the door.

"That's right," she said. "You go home to your wife and your little fucking family."

Alarms went off in his head. He hesitated for a moment.

"Oh yes," she said, seeing him pause. "I know *all* about you, you asshole. Your wife isn't fucking you, so you come in here and lead me on, you set me up and then you walk out on me, you hostile violent fucking asshole. You think you can treat women this way? You asshole."

He reached for the doorknob.

"You walk out on me, you're dead!"

He looked back and saw her leaning unsteadily on the desk, and he thought, *She's drunk.*

"Good night, Meredith," he said. He twisted the knob, then remembered that the door had been locked. He unlocked the door and walked out, without looking back.

In the outer room, a cleaning woman was emptying trash baskets from the assistants' desks.

"I'll fucking kill you for this!" Meredith called after him.

The cleaning woman heard it, and stared at Sanders. He looked away from her, and walked straight to the elevator. He pushed the button. A moment later, he decided to take the stairs.

Sanders stared at the setting sun from the deck of the ferry going back to Winslow. The evening was calm, with almost no breeze; the surface of the water was dark and still. He looked back at the lights of the city and tried to assess what had happened.

From the ferry, he could see the upper floors of the DigiCom buildings, rising behind the horizontal gray concrete of the viaduct that ran along the water's edge. He tried to pick out Meredith's office window, but he was already too far away.

Out here on the water, heading home to his family, slipping back into his familiar daily routine, the events of the previous hour had already begun to take on an unreal quality. He found it hard to believe that it had happened. He reviewed the events in his mind, trying to see just where he had gone wrong. He felt certain that it was all his fault, that he had misled Meredith in some important way. Otherwise, she would never have come on to him. The whole episode was an embarrassment for him, and probably for her, too. He felt guilty and miserable—and deeply uneasy about the future. What would happen now? What would she do?

He couldn't even guess. He realized then that he didn't really know her at all. They had once been lovers, but that was a long time ago. Now she was a new person, with new responsibilities. She was a stranger to him.

Although the evening was mild, he felt chilled. He went back inside the ferry. He sat in a booth and took out his phone to call Susan. He pushed the buttons, but the light didn't come on. The battery was dead. For a moment he was confused; the battery should last all day. But it was dead.

The perfect end to his day.

Feeling the throb of the ferry engines, he stood in the bathroom and stared at himself in the mirror. His hair was messed; there was a faint smear of lipstick on his lips, and another on his neck; two buttons of his shirt were missing, and his clothes were rumpled. He looked as if he had just gotten laid. He turned his head to see his ear. A tiny bruise marked where she had bitten him. He unbuttoned the shirt and looked at the deep red scratches running in parallel rows down his chest.

Christ.

How was he going to keep Susan from seeing this?

He dampened paper towels and scrubbed away the lipstick. He patted down his hair, and buttoned his sport coat, hiding most of his shirt.

Then he went back outside, sat down at a booth by the window, and stared into space.

"Hey, Tom."

He looked up and saw John Perry, his neighbor on Bainbridge. Perry was a lawyer with Marlin, Howard, one of the oldest firms in Seattle. He was one of those irrepressibly enthusiastic people, and Sanders didn't much feel like talking to him. But Perry slipped into the seat opposite him.

"How's it going?" Perry asked cheerfully.

"Pretty good," Sanders said.

"I had a *great* day."

"Glad to hear it."

"Just *great*," Perry said. "We tried a case, and I tell you, we kicked ass."

"Great," Sanders said. He stared fixedly out the window, hoping Perry would take the hint and go away.

Perry didn't. "Yeah, and it was a damned tough case, too. Uphill all the way for us," he said. "Title VII, Federal Court. Client's a woman who worked at MicroTech, claimed she wasn't promoted because she was a female. Not a very strong case, to tell the truth. Because she drank, and so on. There were problems. But we have a gal in our firm, Louise Fernandez, a Hispanic gal, and she is just *lethal* on these discrimination cases. Lethal. Got the jury to award our client nearly half a million. That Fernandez can work the case law like nothing you've ever seen. She's won fourteen of her last sixteen cases. She acts so sweet and demure, and inside, she's just *ice*. I tell you, sometimes women scare the hell out of me."

Sanders said nothing.

He came home to a silent house, the kids already asleep. Susan always put the kids to bed early. He went upstairs. His wife was sitting up in bed, reading, with legal files and papers scattered across the bedcovers. When she saw him, she got out of bed and came over to hug him. Involuntarily, his body tensed.

"I'm really sorry, Tom," she said. "I'm sorry about this morning. And I'm sorry about what happened at work." She turned her face up and kissed him lightly on the lips. Awkwardly, he turned away. He was afraid she would smell Meredith's perfume, or—

"You mad about this morning?" she asked.

"No," he said. "Really, I'm not. It was just a long day."

"Lot of meetings on the merger?"

"Yes," he said. "And more tomorrow. It's pretty crazy."

Susan nodded. "It must be. You just got a call from the office. From a Meredith Johnson."

He tried to keep his voice casual. "Oh yes?"

"Uh-huh. About ten minutes ago." She got back in bed. "Who is she, anyway?" Susan was always suspicious when women from the office called.

Sanders said, "She's the new veep. They just brought her up from Cupertino."

"I wondered . . . She acted like she knew me."

"I don't think you've ever met." He waited, hoping he wouldn't have to say more.

"Well," she said, "she sounded very friendly. She said to tell you everything is fine for the due diligence meeting tomorrow morning at eight-thirty, and she'll see you then."

"Okay. Fine."

He kicked off his shoes, and started to unbutton his shirt, then stopped. He bent over and picked his shoes up.

"How old is she?" Susan asked.

"Meredith? I don't know. Thirty-five, something like that. Why?"

"Just wondered."

"I'm going to take a shower," he said.

"Okay." She picked up her legal briefs, and settled back in bed, adjusting the reading light.

He started to leave.

"Do you know her?" Susan asked.

"I've met her before. In Cupertino."

"What's she doing up here?"

"She's my new boss."

"*She's* the one."

"Yeah," he said. "She's the one."

"She's the woman that's close to Garvin?"

"Yeah. Who told you? Adele?" Adele Lewyn, Mark's wife, was one of Susan's best friends.

She nodded. "Mary Anne called, too. The phone never stopped ringing."

"I'll bet."

"So is Garvin fucking her or what?"

"Nobody knows," he said. "The general belief is that he's not."

"Why'd he bring her in, instead of giving the job to you?"

"I don't know, Sue."

"You didn't talk to Garvin?"

"He came around to see me in the morning, but I wasn't there."

She nodded. "You must be pissed. Or are you being your usual understanding self?"

"Well." He shrugged. "What can I do?"

"You can quit," she said.

"Not a chance."

"They passed over you. Don't you *have* to quit?"

"This isn't the best economy to find another job. And I'm forty-one. I don't feel like starting over. Besides, Phil insists they're going to spin off the technical division and take it public in a year. Even if I'm not running it, I'd still be a principal in that new company."

"And did he have details?"

He nodded. "They'll vest us each twenty thousand shares, and options for fifty thousand more. Then options for another fifty thousand shares each additional year."

"At?"

"Usually it's twenty-five cents a share."

"And the stock will be offered at what? Five dollars?"

"At least. The IPO market is getting stronger. Then, say it goes to ten. Maybe twenty, if we're hot."

There was a brief silence. He knew she was good with figures. "No," she said finally. "You can't possibly quit."

He had done the calculations many times. At a minimum, Sanders would realize enough on his stock options to pay off his mortgage in a single payment. But if the stock went through the roof, it could be truly fantastic—somewhere between five and fourteen million dollars. That was why going public was the dream of anyone who worked in a technical company.

He said, "As far as I'm concerned, they can bring in Godzilla to manage that division, and I'll still stay at least two more years."

"And is that what they've done? Brought in Godzilla?"

He shrugged. "I don't know."

"Do you get along with her?"

He hesitated. "I'm not sure. I'm going to take a shower."

"Okay," she said. He glanced back at her: she was reading her notes again.

Afrer his shower, he plugged his phone into the charger unit on the sink, and put on a T-shirt and boxer shorts. He looked at himself in the mirror; the shirt covered his scratches. But he was still worried about the smell of Meredith's perfume. He splashed after-shave on his cheeks.

Then he went into his son's room to check on him. Matthew was snoring loudly, his thumb in his mouth. He had kicked down the covers. Sanders pulled them back up gently and kissed his forehead.

Then he went into Eliza's room. At first he could not see her; his daughter had lately taken to burrowing under a barricade of covers and pillows when she slept. He tiptoed in, and saw a small hand reach up, and wave to him. He came forward.

"Why aren't you asleep, Lize?" he whispered.

"I was having a dream," she said. But she didn't seem frightened.

He sat on the edge of the bed, and stroked her hair. "What kind of a dream?"

"About the beast."

"Uh-huh . . ."

"The beast was really a prince, but he was placed under a powerful spell by a 'chantress."

"That's right . . ." He stroked her hair.

"Who turned him into a hideous beast."

She was quoting the movie almost verbatim.

"That's right," he said.

"Why?"

"I don't know, Lize. That's the story."

"Because he didn't give her shelter from the bitter cold?" She was quoting again. "Why didn't he, Dad?"

"I don't know," he said.

"Because he had no love in his heart," she said.

"Lize, it's time for sleep."

"Give me a dream first, Dad."

"Okay. There's a beautiful silver cloud hanging over your bed, and—"

"That dream's no good, Dad." She was frowning at him.

"Okay. What kind of dream do you want?"

"With Kermit."

"Okay. Kermit is sitting right here by your head, and he is going to watch over you all night."

"And you, too."

"Yes. And me, too." He kissed her forehead, and she rolled away to face the wall. As he left the room he could hear her sucking her thumb loudly.

He went back to the bedroom and pushed aside his wife's legal briefs to get into bed.

"Was she still awake?" Susan asked.

"I think she'll go to sleep. She wanted a dream. About Kermit."

His wife nodded. "Kermit is a very big deal now."

She didn't comment on his T-shirt. He slipped under the covers and felt suddenly exhausted. He lay back against the pillow and closed his eyes. He felt Susan picking up the briefs on the bed, and a moment later she turned off the light.

"Mmm," she said. "You smell good."

She snuggled up against him, pressing her face against his neck, and threw her leg over his side. This was her invariable overture, and it always annoyed him. He felt pinned down by her heavy leg.

She stroked his cheek. "Is that after-shave for me?"

"Oh, Susan . . ." He sighed, exaggerating his fatigue.

"Because it works," she said, giggling. Beneath the covers, she put her hand on his chest. He felt it slide down, and slip under the T-shirt.

He had a burst of sudden anger. What was the matter with her? She never had any sense about these things. She was always coming on to him at inappropriate times and places. He reached down and grabbed her hand.

"Something wrong?"

"I'm really tired, Sue."

She stopped. "Bad day, huh?" she said sympathetically.

"Yeah. Pretty bad."

She got up on one elbow, and leaned over him. She stroked his lower lip with one finger. "You don't want me to cheer you up?"

"I really don't."

"Not even a little?"

He sighed again.

"You sure?" she asked, teasingly. "Really, *really* sure?" And then she started to slide beneath the covers.

He reached down and held her head with both hands. "Susan. Please. Come on."

She giggled. "It's only eight-thirty. You can't be *that* tired."

"I am."

"I bet you're not."

"Susan, damn it. I'm not in the mood."

"Okay, okay." She pulled away from him. "But I don't know why you put on the after-shave, if you're not interested."

"For Christ's sake."

"We hardly ever have sex anymore, as it is."

"That's because you're always traveling." It just slipped out.

"I'm not 'always traveling.' "

"You're gone a couple of nights a week."

"That's not 'always traveling.' And besides, it's

my job. I thought you were going to be more supportive of my job."

"I am supportive."

"Complaining is not supportive."

"Look, for Christ's sake," he said, "I come home early whenever you're out of town, I feed the kids, I take care of things so you don't have to worry—"

"*Sometimes*," she said. "And sometimes you stay late at the office, and the kids are with Consuela until all hours—"

"Well, I have a job, too—"

"So don't give me this 'take care of things' crap," she said. "You're not home anywhere near as much as I am, I'm the one who has two jobs, and mostly you do exactly what you want, just like every other fucking man in the world."

"Susan . . ."

"Jesus, you come home early once in a while, and you act like a fucking martyr." She sat up, and turned on her bedside light. "Every woman I know works harder than any man."

"Susan, I don't want to fight."

"Sure, make it *my* fault. I'm the one with the problem. Fucking *men*."

He was tired, but he felt suddenly energized by anger. He felt suddenly strong, and got out of bed and started pacing. "What does being a man have to do with it? Am I going to hear how oppressed you are again now?"

"Listen," she said, sitting straighter. "Women are oppressed. It's a fact."

"Is it? How are you oppressed? You never wash a load of clothes. You never cook a meal. You never sweep a floor. Somebody does all that for you. You have somebody to do everything for you. You have somebody to take the kids to school and somebody to pick them up. You're a partner in a law firm, for Christ's sake. You're about as oppressed as Leona Helmsley."

She was staring at him in astonishment. He knew why: Susan had made her oppression speech many times before, and he had never contradicted her. Over time, with repetition it had become an accepted idea in their marriage. Now he was disagreeing. He was changing the rules.

"I can't believe you. I thought you were different." She squinted at him, her judicious look. "This is because a woman got your job, isn't it."

"What're we going to now, the fragile male ego?"

"It's true, isn't it? You're threatened."

"No it's not. It's crap. Who's got the fragile ego around here? Your ego's so fucking fragile, you can't even take a rejection in bed without picking a fight."

That stopped her. He saw it instantly: she had no comeback. She sat there frowning at him, her face tight.

"Jesus," he said, and turned to leave the room.

"You picked this fight," she said.

He turned back. "I did not."

"Yes, you did. You were the one who started in with the traveling."

"No. You were complaining about no sex."

"I was *commenting*."

"Christ. Never marry a lawyer."

"And your ego *is* fragile."

"Susan, you want to talk fragile? I mean, you're so fucking self-involved that you had a shitfit this morning because you wanted to look pretty for the *pediatrician*."

"Oh, there it is. Finally. You *are* still mad because I made you late. What is it? You think you didn't get the job because you were late?"

"No," he said, "I didn't—"

"You didn't get the job," she said, "because Garvin didn't give it to you. You didn't play the game well enough, and somebody else played it better. That's why. A woman played it better."

Furious, shaking, unable to speak, he turned on his heel and left the room.

"That's right, leave," she said. "Walk away. That's what you always do. Walk away. Don't stand up for yourself. You don't want to hear it, Tom. But it's the truth. If you didn't get the job, you have nobody to blame but yourself."

He slammed the door.

He sat in the kitchen in darkness. It was quiet all around him, except for the hum of the refrigerator. Through the kitchen window, he could see the moonlight on the bay, through the stand of fir trees.

He wondered if Susan would come down, but she didn't. He got up and walked around, pacing. After a while, it occurred to him that he hadn't eaten. He opened the refrigerator door, squinting in the light. It was stacked with baby food, juice containers, baby vitamins, bottles of formula. He poked among the stuff, looking for some cheese, or maybe a beer. He couldn't find anything except a can of Susan's Diet Coke.

Christ, he thought, not like the old days. When his refrigerator was full of frozen food and chips and salsa and lots of beer. His bachelor days.

He took out the Diet Coke. Now Eliza was starting to drink it, too. He'd told Susan a dozen times he didn't want the kids to get diet drinks. They ought to be getting healthy food. Real food. But Susan was busy, and Consuela indifferent. The kids ate all kinds of crap. It wasn't right. It wasn't the way he had been brought up.

Nothing to eat. Nothing in his own damned

refrigerator. Hopeful, he lifted the lid of a Tupperware container and found a partially eaten peanut butter and jelly sandwich, with Eliza's small toothmarks in one side. He picked the sandwich up and turned it over, wondering how old it was. He didn't see any mold.

What the hell, he thought, and he ate the rest of Eliza's sandwich, standing there in his T-shirt, in the light of the refrigerator door. He was startled by his own reflection in the glass of the oven. "Another privileged member of the patriarchy, lording it over the manor."

Christ, he thought, where did women come up with this crap?

He finished the sandwich and rubbed the crumbs off his hands. The wall clock said 9:15. Susan went to sleep early. Apparently she wasn't coming down to make up. She usually didn't. It was his job to make up. He was the peacemaker. He opened a carton of milk and drank from it, then put it back on the wire shelf. He closed the door. Darkness again.

He walked over to the sink, washed his hands, and dried them on a dish towel. Having eaten a little, he wasn't so angry anymore. Fatigue crept over him. He looked out the window and through the trees and saw the lights of a ferry, heading west toward Bremerton. One of the things he liked about this house was that it was relatively isolated. It had some land around it. It was good for the kids. Kids should grow up with a place to run and play.

He yawned. She definitely wasn't coming down. It'd have to wait until morning. He knew how it would go: he'd get up first, fix her a cup of coffee, and take it to her in bed. Then he'd say he was sorry, and she would reply that she was sorry, too. They'd hug, and he would go get dressed for work. And that would be it.

He went back up the dark stairs to the second floor, and opened the door to the bedroom. He could hear the quiet rhythms of Susan's breathing.

He slipped into bed, and rolled over on his side. And then he went to sleep.

TUESDAY

It rained in the morning, hard sheets of drumming downpour that slashed across the windows of the ferry. Sanders stood in line to get his coffee, thinking about the day to come. Out of the corner of his eye, he saw Dave Benedict coming toward him, and quickly turned away, but it was too late. Benedict waved, "Hey, guy." Sanders didn't want to talk about DigiCom this morning.

At the last moment, he was saved by a call: the phone in his pocket went off. He turned away to answer it.

"Fucking A, Tommy boy." It was Eddie Larson in Austin.

"What is it, Eddie?"

"You know that bean counter Cupertino sent down? Well, get this: there's *eight* of 'em here now. Independent accounting firm of Jenkins, McKay, out of Dallas. They're going over all the books, like a swarm of roaches. And I mean everything: receivables, payables, A and L's, year to date, *everything*. And now they're going back through every year to 'eighty-nine."

"Yeah? Disrupting everything?"

"Better believe it. The gals don't even have a place to sit down and answer the phone. Plus, everything from 'ninety-one back is in storage, downtown. We've got it on fiche here, but they say they want original documents. They want the damned paper. And they get all squinty and paranoid when they order us around. Treating us like we're thieves or something trying to pull a fast one. It's insulting."

"Well," Sanders said, "hang in there. You've got to do what they ask."

"The only thing that really bothers me," Eddie said, "is they got another seven more coming in this afternoon. Because they're also doing a complete inventory of the plant. Everything from the furniture in the offices to the air handlers and the heat stampers out on the line. We got a guy there now, making his way down the line, stopping at each work station. Says, 'What's this thing called? How do you spell it? Who makes it? What's the model number? How old is it? Where's the serial number?' You ask me, we might as well shut the line down for the rest of the day."

Sanders frowned. "They're doing an *inventory*?"

"Well, that's what they call it. But it's beyond any damn inventory I ever heard of. These guys have worked over at Texas Instruments or someplace, and I'll give 'em one thing: they know what they're talking about. This morning, one of the Jenkins guys came up and asked me what kind of glass we got in the ceiling skylights. I said, 'What kind of glass?' I thought he was shitting me. He says, 'Yeah, is it Corning two-forty-seven, or two-forty-seven slash nine.' Or some damned thing like that. They're different kinds of UV glass, because UV can affect chips on the production line. I never even heard that UV can affect chips. 'Oh yeah,' this guy says. 'Real problem if your ASDs get over two-twenty.' That's annual sunny days. Have you heard of that?"

Sanders wasn't really listening. He was thinking about what it meant that somebody—either Garvin, or the Conley-White people—would ask for an inventory of the plant. Ordinarily, you called for an inventory only if you were planning to sell a facility. Then you had to do it, to figure your writedowns at the time of transfer of assets, and—

"Tom, you there?"

"I'm here."

"So I say to this guy, I never heard that. About the UV and the chips. And we been putting chips in the phones for years, never any trouble. And then the guy says, 'Oh, not for installing chips. UV affects it if you're *manufacturing* chips.' And I say, we don't do that here. And he says, 'I know.' So, I'm wondering: what the hell does he care what kind of glass we have? Tommy boy? You with me? What's the story?" Larson said. "We're going to have fifteen guys crawling all over us by the end of the day. Now don't tell me this is *routine.*"

"It doesn't sound like it's routine, no."

"It sounds like they're going to sell the plant to somebody who makes chips, is what it sounds like. And that ain't us."

"I agree. That's what it sounds like."

"Fucking A," Eddie said. "I thought you told me this wasn't going to happen. Tom: people here are getting upset. And I'm one of 'em."

"I understand."

"I mean, I got people asking me. They just bought a house, their wife's pregnant, they got a baby coming, and they want to know. What do I tell 'em?"

"Eddie, I don't have any information."

"Jesus, Tom, you're the division head."

"I know. Let me check with Cork, see what the accountants did there. They were out there last week."

"I already talked to Colin an hour ago. Operations sent two people out there. For one day. Very polite. Not like this at all."

"No inventory?"

"No inventory."

"Okay," Sanders said. He sighed. "Let me get into it."

"Tommy boy," Eddie said. "I got to tell you right out. I'm concerned you don't already know."

"Me, too," Sanders said. "Me, too."

He hung up the phone. Sanders pushed K-A-P

for Stephanie Kaplan. She would know what was going on in Austin, and he thought she would tell him. But her assistant said Kaplan was out of the office for the rest of the morning. He called Mary Anne, but she was gone, too. Then he dialed the Four Seasons Hotel, and asked for Max Dorfman. The operator said Mr. Dorfman's lines were busy. He made a mental note to see Max later in the day. Because if Eddie was right, then Sanders was out of the loop. And that wasn't good.

In the meantime, he could bring up the plant closing with Meredith at the conclusion of the morning meeting with Conley-White. That was the best he could do, for the moment. The prospect of talking to her made him uneasy. But he'd get through it somehow. He didn't really have a choice.

When he got to the fourth-floor conference room, nobody was there. At the far end, a wall board showed a cutaway of the Twinkle drive and a schematic for the Malaysia assembly line. There were notes scribbled on some of the pads, open briefcases beside some of the chairs.

The meeting was already under way.

Sanders had a sense of panic. He started to sweat.

At the far end of the room, an assistant came in, and began moving around the table, setting out glasses and water.

"Where is everybody?" he asked.

"Oh, they left about fifteen minutes ago," she said.

"Fifteen minutes ago? When did they start?"

"The meeting started at eight."

"Eight?" Sanders said. "I thought it was supposed to be eight-thirty."

"No, the meeting started at eight."

Damn.

"Where are they now?"

"Meredith took everybody down to VIE, to demo the Corridor."

Entering VIE, the first thing Sanders heard was laughter. When he walked into the equipment room, he saw that Don Cherry's team had two of the Conley-White executives up on the system. John Conley, the young lawyer, and Jim Daly, the investment banker, were both wearing headsets while they walked on the rolling walker pads. The two men were grinning wildly. Everyone else in the room was laughing too, including the normally sour-faced CFO of Conley-White, Ed Nichols, who was standing beside a monitor which showed an image of the virtual corridor that the users were seeing. Nichols had red marks on his forehead from wearing the headset.

Nichols looked over as Sanders came up. "This is *fantastic*."

Sanders said, "Yes, it's pretty spectacular."

"Simply fantastic. It's going to wipe out all the criticism in New York, once they see this. We've been asking Don if he can run this on our own corporate database."

"No problem," Cherry said. "Just get us the programming hooks for your DB, and we'll plug you right in. Take us about an hour."

Nichols pointed to the headset. "And we can get one of these contraptions in New York?"

"Easy," Cherry said. "We can ship it out later today. It'll be there Thursday. I'll send one of our people to set it up for you."

"This is going to be a *great* selling point," Nichols said. "Just great." He took out his half-frame glasses. They were a complicated kind of glasses that folded up very small. Nichols unfolded them carefully and put them on his nose.

On the walker pad, John Conley was laughing. "Angel," he said. "How do I open this drawer?" Then he cocked his head, listening.

"He's talking to the help angel," Cherry said. "He hears the angel through his earphones."

"What's the angel telling him?" Nichols said.

"That's between him and his angel," Cherry laughed.

On the walker pad, Conley nodded as he listened, then reached forward into the air with his hand. He closed his fingers, as if gripping something, and pulled back, pantomiming someone opening a file drawer.

On the monitor, Sanders saw a virtual file drawer slide out from the wall of the corridor. Inside the drawer he saw neatly arranged files.

"Wow," Conley said. "This is amazing. Angel: can I see a file? . . . Oh. Okay."

Conley reached out and touched one of the file labels with his fingertip. Immediately the file popped out of the drawer and opened up, apparently hanging in midair.

"We have to break the physical metaphor sometimes," Cherry said. "Because users have only one hand. And you can't open a regular file with one hand."

Standing on the black walker pad, Conley moved his hand through the air in short arcs, mimicking someone turning pages with his hand. On the monitor, Sanders saw Conley was actually looking at a series of spreadsheets. "Hey," Conley said, "you people ought to be more careful. I have all your financial records here."

"Let me see that," Daly said, turning around on the walker pad to look.

"You guys look all you want," Cherry laughed. "Enjoy it while you can. In the final system, we'll have safeguards built in to control access. But for now, we bypass the entire system. Do you notice that some of the numbers are red? That means they have more detail stored away. Touch one."

Conley touched a red number. The number zoomed out, creating a new plane of information that hung in the air above the previous spreadsheet.

"Wow!"

"Kind of a hypertext thing," Cherry said, with a shrug. "Sort of neat, if I say so myself."

Conley and Daly were giggling, poking rapidly at numbers on the spreadsheet, zooming out dozens of detail sheets that now hung in the air all around them. "Hey, how do you get rid of all this stuff?"

"Can you find the original spreadsheet?"

"It's hidden behind all this other stuff."

"Bend over, and look. See if you can get it."

Conley bent at the waist, and appeared to look under something. He reached out and pinched air. "I got it."

"Okay, now you see a green arrow in the right corner. Touch it."

Conley touched it. All the papers zoomed back into the original spreadsheet.

"Fabulous!"

"I want to do it," Daly said.

"No, you can't. I'm going to do it."

"No, me!"

"Me!"

They were laughing like delighted kids.

Blackburn came up. "I know this is enjoyable for everyone," he said to Nichols, "but we're falling behind our schedule and perhaps we ought to go back to the conference room."

"All right," Nichols said, with obvious reluctance. He turned to Cherry. "You sure you can get us one of these things?"

"Count on it," Cherry said. "Count on it."

Walking back to the conference room, the Conley-White executives were in a giddy mood; they talked rapidly, laughing about the experience. The DigiCom people walked quietly beside them, not wanting to disrupt the good mood. It was at that point that Mark Lewyn fell into step alongside Sanders and whispered, "Hey, why didn't you call me last night?"

"I did," Sanders said.

Lewyn shook his head. "There wasn't any message when I got home," he said.

"I talked to your answering machine, about six-fifteen."

"I never got a message," Lewyn said. "And then when I came in this morning, you weren't here." He lowered his voice. "Christ. What a mess. I had to go into the meeting on Twinkle with no idea what the approach was going to be."

"I'm sorry," Sanders said. "I don't know what happened."

"Fortunately, Meredith took over the discussion," Lewyn said. "Otherwise I would have been in deepest shit. In fact, I— We'll do this later," he said, seeing Johnson drop back to talk to Sanders. Lewyn stepped away.

"Where the hell were you?" Johnson said.

"I thought the meeting was for eight-thirty."

"I called your house last night, specifically because it was changed to eight. They're trying to catch a plane to Austin for the afternoon. So we moved everything up."

"I didn't get that message."

"I talked to your wife. Didn't she tell you?"

"I thought it was eight-thirty."

Johnson shook her head, as if dismissing the whole thing. "Anyway," she said, "in the eight o'clock session, I had to take another approach to Twinkle, and it's very important that we have some coordination in the light of—"

"Meredith?" Up at the front of the group, Garvin was looking back at her. "Meredith, John has a question for you."

"Be right there," she said. With a final angry frown at Sanders, she hurried up to the head of the group.

Back in the conference room, the mood was light. They were all still joking as they took their seats. Ed Nichols began the meeting by turning to Sanders. "Meredith's been bringing us up to date on the Twinkle drive. Now that you're here, we'd like your assessment as well."

I had to take another approach to Twinkle, Meredith had said. Sanders hesitated. "My assessment?"

"Yes," Nichols said. "You're in charge of Twinkle, aren't you?"

Sanders looked at the faces around the table, turned expectantly toward him. He glanced at Johnson, but she had opened her briefcase and was rummaging through her papers, taking out several bulging manila envelopes.

"Well," Sanders said. "We built several prototypes and tested them thoroughly. There's no doubt that the prototypes performed flawlessly. They're the best drives in the world."

"I understand that," Nichols said. "But now you are in production, isn't that right?"

"That's right."

"I think we're more interested in your assessment of the production."

Sanders hesitated. What had she told them? At the other end of the room, Meredith Johnson closed her briefcase, folded her hands under her chin, and stared steadily at him. He could not read her expression.

What had she told them?

"Mr. Sanders?"

"Well," Sanders began, "we've been shaking out the lines, dealing with the problems as they arise. It's a pretty standard start-up experience for us. We're still in the early stages."

"I'm sorry," Nichols said. "I thought you've been in production for two months."

"Yes, that's true."

"Two months doesn't sound like 'the early stages' to me."

"Well—"

"Some of your product cycles are as short as nine months, isn't that right?"

"Nine to eighteen months, yes."

"Then after two months, you must be in full production. How do you assess that, as the principal person in charge?"

"Well, I'd say the problems are of the order of magnitude we generally experience at this point."

"I'm interested to hear that," Nichols said, "because earlier today, Meredith indicated to us that the problems were actually quite serious. She said you might even have to go back to the drawing board."

Shit.

How should he play it now? He'd already said that the problems were not so bad. He couldn't back down. Sanders took a breath and said, "I hope I haven't conveyed the wrong impression to Meredith. Because I have full confidence in our ability to manufacture the Twinkle drive."

"I'm sure you do," Nichols said. "But we're looking down the barrel at competition from Sony and Philips, and I'm not sure that a simple expression of your confidence is adequate. How many of the drives coming off the line meet specifications?"

"I don't have that information."

"Just approximately."

"I wouldn't want to say, without precise figures."

"Are precise figures available?"

"Yes. I just don't have them at hand."

Nichols frowned. His expression said: why don't you have them when you knew this is what the meeting was about?

Conley cleared his throat. "Meredith indicated that the line is running at twenty-nine percent capacity, and that only five percent of the drives meet specifications. Is that your understanding?"

"That's more or less how it has been. Yes."

There was a brief silence around the table. Abruptly, Nichols sat forward. "I'm afraid I need some help here," he said. "With figures like that, on what do you base your confidence in the Twinkle drive?"

"The reason is that we've seen all this before," Sanders replied. "We've seen production problems that look insurmountable but then get resolved quickly."

"I see. So you think your past experience will hold true here."

"Yes, I do."

Nichols sat back in his seat and crossed his arms over his chest. He looked extremely dissatisfied.

Jim Daly, the thin investment banker, sat forward and said, "Please don't misunderstand, Tom. We're not trying to put you on the spot," he said. "We have long ago identified several reasons for acquisition of this company, irrespective of any specific problem with Twinkle. So I don't think Twinkle is a critical issue today. We just want to know where we stand on it. And we'd like you to be as frank as possible."

"Well, there *are* problems," Sanders said. "We're in the midst of assessing them now. We have some ideas. But some of the problems may go back to design."

Daly said, "Give us worst case."

"Worst case? We pull the line, rework the housings and perhaps the controller chips, and then go back on."

"Causing a delay of?"

Nine to twelve months. "Up to six months," Sanders said.

"Jesus," somebody whispered.

Daly said, "Johnson suggested that the maximum delay would be six *weeks.*"

"I hope that's right. But you asked for worst case."

"Do you really think it will take six months?"

"You asked for worst case. I think it's unlikely."

"But possible?"

"Yes, possible."

Nichols sat forward again and gave a big sigh. "Let me see if I understand this right. If there *are* design problems with the drive, they occurred under your stewardship, is that correct?"

"Yes, it is."

Nichols shook his head. "Well. Having gotten us into this mess, do you really think you're the person to clean it up?"

Sanders suppressed a surge of anger. "Yes I do," he said. "In fact, I think I'm the best possible person to do it. As I said, we've seen this kind of situation before. And we've handled it before. I'm close to all the people involved. And I am sure we can resolve it." He wondered how he could explain to these people in suits the reality of how products were made. "When you're working the cycles," he said, "it's sometimes not so serious to go back to the boards. Nobody likes to do it, but it may have advantages. In the old days, we made a complete generation of new products every year or so. Now, more and more, we also make incremental changes within generations. If we have to redo the chips, we may be able to code in the video compression algorithms, which weren't available when we started. That will enhance the end-user perception of speed by more than the simple drive specs. We won't go back to build a hundred-millisecond drive. We'll go back to build an eighty-millisecond drive."

"But," Nichols said, "in the meantime, you won't have entered the market."

"No, that's true."

"You won't have established your brand name, or established market share for your product stream. You won't have your dealerships, or your OEMs, or your ad campaign, because you won't have a product line to support it. You may have a better drive, but it'll be an unknown drive. You'll be starting from scratch."

"All true. But the market responds fast."

"And so does the competition. Where will Sony be by the time you get to market? Will they be at eighty milliseconds, too?"

"I don't know," Sanders said.

Nichols sighed. "I wish I had more confidence about where we are on this thing. To say nothing of whether we're properly staffed to fix it."

Meredith spoke for the first time. "I may be a

little bit at fault here," she said. "When you and I spoke about Twinkle, Tom, I understood you to say that the problems were quite serious."

"They are, yes."

"Well, I don't think we want to be covering anything up here."

He said quickly, "I'm not covering anything up." The words came out almost before he realized it. He heard his voice, high-pitched, tight.

"No, no," Meredith said soothingly. "I didn't mean to suggest you were. It's just that these technical issues are hard for some of us to grasp. We're looking for a translation into layman's terms of just where we are. If you can do that for us."

"I've been trying to do that," he said. He knew he sounded defensive. But he couldn't help it.

"Yes, Tom, I know you have," Meredith said, her voice still soothing. "But for example: if the laser read-write heads are out of sync with the m-subset instructions off the controller chip, what is that going to mean for us, in terms of down time?"

She was just grandstanding, demonstrating her facility with tech-talk, but her words threw him off balance anyway. Because the laser heads were read-only, not read-write, and they had nothing to do with the m-subset off the controller chip. The position controls all came off the x-subset. And the x-subset was licensed code from Sony, part of the driver code that every company used in their CD drives.

To answer without embarrassing her, he had to move into fantasy, where nothing he could say was true. "Well," he said, "you raise a good point, Meredith. But I think the m-subset should be a relatively simple problem, assuming the laser heads are tracking to tolerance. Perhaps three or four days to fix."

He glanced quickly at Cherry and Lewyn, the only people in the room who would know that Sanders had just spoken gibberish. Both men nodded sagely as they listened. Cherry even rubbed his chin.

Johnson said, "And do you anticipate a problem with the asynchronous tracking signals from the mother board?"

Again, she was mixing everything up. The tracking signals came from the power source, and were regulated by the controller chip. There wasn't a mother board in the drive units. But by now he was in the swing. He answered quickly: "That's certainly a consideration, Meredith, and we should check it thoroughly. I expect we'll find that the asynchronous signals may be phase-shifted, but nothing more than that."

"A phase-shift is easy to repair?"

"Yes, I think so."

Nichols cleared his throat. "I feel this is an in-house technical issue," he said. "Perhaps we should move on to other matters. What's next on the agenda?"

Garvin said, "We've scheduled a demo of the video compression just down the hall."

"Fine. Let's do that."

Chairs scraped back. Everyone stood up, and they filed out of the room. Meredith was slower to close up her files. Sanders stayed behind for a moment, too.

When they were alone he said, "What the hell was all that about?"

"All what?"

"All that gobbledygook about controller chips and read heads. You don't know what you were talking about."

"Oh yes I do," she said angrily. "I was fixing the mess that you made." She leaned over the table and glared at him. "Look, Tom. I decided to take your advice last night, and tell the truth about the drive. This morning I said there were severe problems with it, that you were very knowledgeable, and you would tell them what the problems were. I set it up, for you to say what you told me you wanted to say. But then you came in and announced there were no problems of significance."

"But I thought we agreed last night—"

"These men aren't fools, and we're not going to be able to fool them." She snapped her briefcase shut. "I reported in good faith what you told me. And then you said I didn't know what I was talking about."

He bit his lip, trying to control his anger.

"I don't know what you think is going on

here," she said. "These men don't care about technical details. They wouldn't know a drive head from a dildo. They're just looking to see if anybody's in charge, if anybody has a handle on the problems. They want reassurance. And you didn't reassure them. So I had to jump in and fix it with a lot of techno-bullshit. I had to clean up after you. I did the best I could. But let's face it: you didn't inspire confidence today, Tom. Not at all."

"Goddamn it," he said. "You're just talking about appearances. Corporate appearances in a corporate meeting. But in the end somebody has to actually build the damn drive—"

"I'll say—"

"And I've been running this division for eight years, and running it damn well—"

"Meredith." Garvin stuck his head in the door. They both stopped talking.

"We're waiting, Meredith," he said. He turned and looked coldly at Sanders.

She picked up her briefcase and swept out of the room.

Sanders went immediately downstairs to Blackburn's office. "I need to see Phil."

Sandra, his assistant, sighed. "He's pretty busy today."

"I need to see him now."

"Let me check, Tom." She buzzed the inner office. "Phil? It's Tom Sanders." She listened a moment. "He says go right in."

Sanders went into Blackburn's office and closed the door. Blackburn stood up behind his desk and ran his hands down his chest. "Tom. I'm glad you came down."

They shook hands briefly. "It isn't working out with Meredith," Sanders said at once. He was still angry from his encounter with her.

"Yes, I know."

"I don't think I can work with her."

Blackburn nodded. "I know. She already told me."

"Oh? What'd she tell you?"

"She told me about the meeting last night, Tom."

Sanders frowned. He couldn't imagine that she had discussed that meeting. "Last night?"

"She told me that you sexually harassed her."

"I *what*?"

"Now, Tom, don't get excited. Meredith's assured me she's not going to press charges. We can handle it quietly, in house. That will be best for everyone. In fact, I've just been going over the organization charts, and—"

"Wait a minute," Sanders said. "She's saying *I* harassed *her*?"

Blackburn stared at him. "Tom. We've been friends a long time. I can assure you, this doesn't have to be a problem. It doesn't have to get around the company. Your wife doesn't need to know. As I said, we can handle this quietly. To the satisfaction of everyone involved."

"Wait a minute, it's not true—"

"Tom, just give me a minute here, please. The most important thing now is for us to separate the two of you. So you aren't reporting to her. I think a lateral promotion for you would be ideal."

"Lateral promotion?"

"Yes. There's an opening for technical vice president in the cellular division in Austin. I want to transfer you there. You'll go with the same seniority, salary, and benefit package. Everything the same, except you'll be in Austin and you won't have to have any direct contact with her. How does that sound?"

"Austin."

"Yes."

"Cellular."

"Yes. Beautiful weather, nice working conditions . . . university town . . . chance to get your family out of this rain . . ."

Sanders said, "But Conley's going to sell off Austin."

Blackburn sat down behind his desk. "I can't imagine where you heard that, Tom," he said calmly. "It's completely untrue."

"You sure about that?"

"Absolutely. Believe me, selling Austin is the last thing they'd do. Why, it makes no sense at all."

"Then why are they inventorying the plant?"

"I'm sure they're going over the whole operation with a fine-tooth comb. Look, Tom. Conley's worried about cash flow after the acquisition, and the Austin plant is, as you know, very profitable. We've given them the figures. Now they're verifying them, making sure they're real. But there's no chance they would sell it. Cellular is only going to grow, Tom. You know that. And that's why I think a vice presidency there in Austin is an excellent career opportunity for you to consider."

"But I'd be leaving the Advanced Products Division?"

"Well, yes. The whole point would be to move you out of this division."

"And then I wouldn't be in the new company when it spins off."

"That's true."

Sanders paced back and forth. "That's completely unacceptable."

"Well, let's not be hasty," Blackburn said. "Let's consider all the ramifications."

"Phil," he said. "I don't know what she told you, but—"

"She told me the whole story—"

"But I think you should know—"

"And I want you to know, Tom," Blackburn said, "that I don't have any judgment about what may have happened. That's not my concern or my interest. I'm just trying to solve a difficult problem for the company."

"Phil. Listen. I didn't do it."

"I understand that's probably how you feel, but—"

"I didn't harass her. She harassed me."

"I'm sure," Blackburn said, "it may have *seemed* like that to you at the time, but—"

"Phil, I'm telling you. She did everything but rape me." He paced angrily. "Phil: *she* harassed *me.*"

Blackburn sighed and sat back in his chair. He tapped his pencil on the corner of his desk. "I have to tell you frankly, Tom. I find that difficult to believe."

"It's what happened."

"Meredith's a beautiful woman, Tom. A very vital, sexy woman. I think it's natural for a man to, uh, lose control."

"Phil, you aren't hearing me. She harassed me."

Blackburn gave a helpless shrug. "I hear you, Tom. I just . . . I find that difficult to picture."

"Well, she did. You want to hear what really happened last night?"

"Well." Blackburn shifted in his chair. "Of course I want to hear your version. But the thing is, Tom, Meredith Johnson is very well connected in this company. She has impressed a lot of extremely important people."

"You mean Garvin."

"Not only Garvin. Meredith has built a power base in several areas."

"Conley-White?"

Blackburn nodded. "Yes. There, too."

"You don't want to hear what I say happened?"

"Of course I do," Blackburn said, running his hands through his hair. "Absolutely, I do. And I want to be scrupulously fair. But I'm trying to tell you that no matter what, we're going to have to make some transfers here. And Meredith has important allies."

"So it doesn't matter what I say."

Blackburn frowned, watching him pace. "I understand that you are upset. I can see that. And you're a valued person in this company. But what I'm trying to do here, Tom, is to get you to look at the situation."

"What situation?" Sanders said.

Blackburn sighed. "Were there any witnesses, last night?"

"No."

"So it's your word against hers."

"I guess so."

"In other words, it's a pissing match."

"So? That's no reason to assume I'm wrong, and she's right."

"Of course not," Blackburn said. "But look at the situation. A man claiming sexual harassment against a woman is, well, pretty unlikely. I don't think there's ever been a case in this company. It doesn't mean it couldn't happen. But it does means that it'd be very uphill for you—even if Meredith wasn't so well connected." He paused. "I just don't want to see you get hurt in this."

"I've already been hurt."

"Again, we're talking about feelings here. Conflicting claims. And unfortunately, Tom, no witnesses." He rubbed his nose, tugged at his lapels.

"You move me out of the APD, and I'm hurt. Because I won't get to be part of the new company. The company I worked on for twelve years."

"That's an interesting legal position," Blackburn said.

"I'm not talking about a legal position. I'm talking about—"

"Look. Tom. Let me review this with Garvin.

Meanwhile, why don't you go off and think this Austin offer over. Think about it carefully. Because no one wins in a pissing match. You may hurt Meredith, but you'll hurt yourself much more. That's my concern here, as your friend."

"If you were my friend—" Sanders began.

"I *am* your friend," Blackburn said. "Whether you know it at this moment, or not." He stood up behind his desk. "You don't need this splashed all over the papers. Your wife doesn't need to hear about this, or your kids. You don't need to be the gossip of Bainbridge for the rest of the summer. That isn't going to do you any good at all."

"I understand that, but—"

"But we have to face reality, Tom," Blackburn said. "The company is faced with conflicting claims. What's happened has happened. We have to go on from here. And all I'm saying is, I'd like to resolve this quickly. So think it over. Please. And get back to me."

After Sanders left, Blackburn called Garvin. "I just talked with him," he told Garvin.

"And?"

"He says it was the other way around. That she harassed him."

"Christ," Garvin said. "What a mess."

"Yes. But on the other hand, it's what you'd expect him to say," Blackburn said. "It's the usual response in these cases. The man always denies it."

"Yeah. Well. This is dangerous, Phil."

"I understand."

"I don't want this thing to blow up on us."

"No, no."

"There's nothing more important right now than getting this thing resolved."

"I understand, Bob."

"You made him the Austin offer?"

"Yes. He's thinking it over."

"Will he take it?"

"My guess is no."

"And did you push it?"

"Well, I tried to convey to him that we weren't going to back down on Meredith. That we were going to support her through this."

"Damn right we are," Garvin said.

"I think he was clear about that. So let's see what he says when he comes back to us."

"He wouldn't go off and file, would he?"

"He's too smart for that."

"We hope," Garvin said irritably, and hung up.

*L*ook *at the situation.*

Sanders stood in Pioneer Park and leaned against a pillar, staring at the light drizzle. He was replaying the meeting with Blackburn.

Blackburn hadn't even been willing to listen to Sanders's version. He hadn't let Sanders tell him. Blackburn already knew what had happened.

She's a very sexy woman. It's natural for a man to lose control.

That was what everyone at DigiCom would think. Every single person in the company would have that view of what had happened. Blackburn had said he found it difficult to believe that Sanders had been harassed. Others would find it difficult, too.

Blackburn had told him it didn't matter what happened. Blackburn was telling him that Johnson was well connected, and that nobody would believe a man had been harassed by a woman.

Look at the situation.

They were asking him to leave Seattle, leave the APG. No options, no big payoff. No return for his twelve long years of work. All that was gone.

Austin. Baking hot, dry, brand-new.

Susan would never accept it. Her practice in

Seattle was successful; she had spent many years building it. They had just finished remodeling the house. The kids liked it here. If Sanders even suggested a move, Susan would be suspicious. She'd want to know what was behind it. And sooner or later, she would find out. If he accepted the transfer, he would be confirming his guilt to his wife.

No matter how he thought about it, how he tried to put it together in his mind, Sanders could see no good outcome. He was being screwed.

I'm your friend, Tom. Whether you know it right now or not.

He recalled the moment at his wedding when Blackburn, his best man, said he wanted to dip Susan's ring in olive oil because there was always a problem about getting it on the finger. Blackburn in a panic, in case some little moment in the ceremony went wrong. That was Phil: always worried about appearances.

Your wife doesn't need to hear about this.

But Phil was screwing him. Phil, and Garvin behind him. They were both screwing him. Sanders had worked hard for the company for many years, but now they didn't give a damn about him. They were taking Meredith's side, without any question. They didn't even want to hear his version of what had happened.

As Sanders stood in the rain, his sense of shock slowly faded. And with it, his sense of loyalty. He started to get angry.

He took out his phone and placed a call.

"Mr. Perry's office."

"It's Tom Sanders calling."

"I'm sorry, Mr. Perry is in court. Can I give him a message?"

"Maybe you could help me. The other day he mentioned that you have a woman there who handles sexual harassment cases."

"We have several attorneys who do that, Mr. Sanders."

"He mentioned a Hispanic woman." He was trying to remember what else Perry had said about her. Something about being sweet and demure? He couldn't recall for sure.

"That would be Ms. Fernandez."

"I wonder if you could connect me," Sanders said.

Fernandez's office was small, her desk stacked high with papers and legal briefs in neat piles, a computer terminal in the corner. She stood up as he came in. "You must be Mr. Sanders."

She was a tall woman in her thirties, with straight blond hair and a handsome, aquiline face. She was dressed in a pale, cream-colored suit. She had a direct manner and a firm handshake. "I'm Louise Fernandez. How can I help you?"

She wasn't at all what he had expected. She wasn't sweet and demure at all. And certainly not Hispanic. He was so startled that without thinking he said, "You're not what I—"

"Expected?" She raised an eyebrow. "My father's from Cuba. We left there when I was a child. Please sit down, Mr. Sanders." She turned and walked back around her desk.

He sat down, feeling embarrassed. "Anyway, thank you for seeing me so quickly."

"Not at all. You're John Perry's friend?"

"Yes. He mentioned the other day that you, uh, specialized in these cases."

"I do labor law, primarily constructive termination and Title VII suits."

"I see." He felt foolish that he had come. He was taken aback by her brisk manner and elegant appearance. In fact, she reminded him very much of Meredith. He felt certain that she would not be sympathetic to his case.

She put on horn-rimmed glasses and peered at him across the desk. "Have you eaten? I can get you a sandwich if you like."

"I'm not hungry, thanks."

She pushed a half-eaten sandwich to the side of her desk. "I'm afraid I have a court appearance in an hour. Sometimes things get a bit rushed." She got out a yellow legal pad and set it before her. Her movements were quick, decisive.

Sanders watched her, sure she was the wrong person. He should never have come here. It was all a mistake. He looked around the office. There was a neat stack of bar charts for a courtroom appearance.

Fernandez looked up from the pad, her pen poised. It was one of those expensive fountain pens. "Would you like to tell me the situation?"

"Uh . . . I'm not sure where to begin."

"We could start with your full name and address, and your age."

"Thomas Robert Sanders." He gave his address.

"And your age?"

"Forty-one."

"Occupation?"

"I'm a division manager at Digital Communications. The Advanced Products Division."

"How long have you been at that company?"

"Twelve years."

"Uh-huh. And in your present capacity?"

"Eight years."

"And why are you here today, Mr. Sanders?"

"I've been sexually harassed."

"Uh-huh." She showed no surprise. Her expression was completely neutral. "You want to tell me the circumstances?"

"My boss, ah, came on to me."

"And the name of your boss?"

"Meredith Johnson."

"Is that a man or a woman?"

"A woman."

"Uh-huh." Again, no sign of surprise. She continued making notes steadily, the pen scratching. "When did this happen?"

"Last night."

"What were the exact circumstances?"

He decided not to mention the merger. "She has just been appointed my new boss, and we had several things to go over. She asked if we could meet at the end of the day."

"She requested this meeting?"

"Yes."

"And where did the meeting take place?"

"In her office. At six o'clock."

"Anybody else present?"

"No. Her assistant came in briefly, at the start of the meeting, then left. Before anything happened."

"I see. Go on."

"We talked for a while, about business, and we had some wine. She had gotten some wine. And then she came on to me. I was over by the window and suddenly she started kissing me. Then pretty soon we were sitting on the couch. And then she started, uh . . ." He hesitated. "How much detail do you want?"

"Just the broad strokes for now." She bit her sandwich. "You say you were kissing."

"Yes."

"And she initiated this?"

"Yes."

"What was your reaction when she did that?"

"I was uncomfortable. I'm married."

"Uh-huh. What was the general atmosphere in the meeting, prior to this kiss?"

"It was a regular business meeting. We were talking about business. But all the time, she was making, uh, suggestive remarks."

"Like what."

"Oh, about how good I looked. How I was in shape. How glad she was to see me."

"How glad she was to see you," Fernandez repeated, with a puzzled look.

"Yes. We knew each other before."

"You had a prior relationship?"

"Yes."

"When was that?"

"Ten years ago."

"And were you married then?"

"No."

"Did you both work for the same company at that time?"

"No. I did, but she worked for another company."

"And how long did your relationship last?"

"About six months."

"And have you kept up contact?"

"No. Not really."

"Any contact at all?"

"Once."

"Intimate?"

"No. Just, you know, hello in the hallway. At the office."

"I see. In the last eight years, have you ever been to her house or apartment?"

"No."

"Dinners, drinks after work, anything?"

"No. I really haven't seen her at all. When she joined the company, she was in Cupertino, in Operations. I was in Seattle, in Advanced Products. We didn't have much contact."

"So during this time, she wasn't your superior?"

"No."

"Give me a picture of Ms. Johnson. How old?"

"Thirty-five."

"Would you characterize her as attractive?"

"Yes."

"Very attractive?"

"She was a Miss Teenage something as a kid."

"So you would say she's very attractive." The pen scratched on the legal pad.

"Yes."

"And how about other men—would you say they find her very attractive?"

"Yes."

"What about her manner with regard to sexual matters? Does she make jokes? Sexual jokes, innuendoes, ribald comments?"

"No, never."

"Body language? Flirtatious? Does she touch people?"

"Not really. She certainly knows she's good-looking, and she can play on that. But her manner is . . . kind of cool. She's the Grace Kelly type."

"They say Grace Kelly was very sexually active, that she had affairs with most of her leading men."

"I wouldn't know."

"Uh-huh. What about Ms. Johnson, does she have affairs inside the company?"

"I wouldn't know. I haven't heard anything."

Fernandez flipped to a new page on her pad. "All right. And how long has she been your supervisor? Or is she your supervisor?"

"Yes, she is. One day."

For the first time, Fernandez looked surprised. She glanced at him, and took another bite of her sandwich. "One day?"

"Yes. Yesterday was the first day of a new company organization. She had just been appointed."

"So the day she is appointed, she meets with you, in the evening."

"Yes."

"All right. You were telling me, you were sitting on the couch and she was kissing you. And what happened then?"

"She unzipped—well, first of all, she started rubbing me."

"Your genitals."

"Yes. And kissing me." He found himself sweating. He wiped his forehead with his hand.

"I understand this is difficult. I'll try to make this as brief as possible," Fernandez said. "And then?"

"Then, she unzipped my pants, and started rubbing me with her hand."

"Was your penis exposed?"

"Yes."

"Who exposed it?"

"She took it out."

"So she took your penis out of your pants, and

then rubbed it with her hand, is that right?" She peered at him over her glasses, and for a moment he glanced away in embarrassment. But when he looked back at her, he saw that she was not the least embarrassed, that her manner was more than clinical, more than professional—that she was in some deep way detached, and very cold.

"Yes," he said. "That's what happened."

"And what was your reaction?"

"Well." He gave an embarrassed shrug. "It worked."

"You were sexually aroused."

"Yes."

"Did you say anything to her?"

"Like what?"

"I'm just asking whether you said anything to her."

"Like what? I don't know."

"Did you say anything at all?"

"I said something, I don't know. I was feeling very uncomfortable."

"Do you remember what you said?"

"I think I just kept saying 'Meredith,' trying to get her to stop, you know, but she kept interrupting me, or kissing me."

"Did you say anything else besides 'Meredith'?"

"I don't remember."

"How did you feel about what she was doing?"

"I felt uncomfortable."

"Why?"

"I was afraid of getting involved with her, because she was my boss now, and because I was married now and I didn't want any complications in my life. You know, an office affair."

"Why not?" Fernandez asked.

The question took him aback. "Why *not?*"

"Yes." She looked at him directly, her eyes cool, appraising. "After all, you're alone with a beautiful woman. Why not have an affair?"

"Jesus."

"It's a question most people would ask."

"I'm married."

"So what? Married people have affairs all the time."

"Well," he said. "For one thing, my wife is a lawyer and very suspicious."

"Do I know her?"

"Her name is Susan Handler. She's with Lyman, King."

Fernandez nodded. "I've heard of her. So. You were afraid that she would find out."

"Sure. I mean, you have an affair in the office, and everybody's going to know. There isn't any way to keep it quiet."

"So you were concerned about this becoming known."

"Yes. But that wasn't the main reason."

"What was the main reason?"

"She was my boss. I didn't like the position I

was in. She was, you know . . . well, she had the right to fire me. If she wanted to. So it was like I *had* to do it. I was very uncomfortable."

"Did you tell her that?"

"I tried."

"How did you try?"

"Well, I just tried."

"Would you say that you indicated to her that her advances were not welcome?"

"Eventually, yes."

"How is that?"

"Well, eventually, we continued this . . . whatever you call it, foreplay or whatever, and she had her panties off, and—"

"I'm sorry. How did she come to have her panties off?"

"I took them off."

"Did she ask you to do that?"

"No. But I got pretty worked up at one point, I was going to do it, or at least I was thinking about doing it."

"You were going to have intercourse." Her voice again cool. The pen scratching.

"Yes."

"You were a willing participant."

"For a while there. Yes."

"In what way were you a willing participant?" she asked. "What I mean is, did you initiate touching her body or breast or genitals without her encouragement?"

"I don't know. She was pretty much encouraging everything."

"I am asking, did you volunteer. Did you do it on your own. Or did she, for example, take your hand and place it on her—"

"No. I did it on my own."

"What about your earlier reservations?"

"I was worked up. Excited. I didn't care at that point."

"All right. Go on."

He wiped his forehead. "I'm being very honest with you."

"That's exactly what you should be. It's the best thing all around. Please go on."

"And she was lying on the couch with her skirt pulled up, and she wanted me to enter her, to . . . and she was sort of moaning, you know, saying, 'No, no,' and suddenly I had this feeling again that I didn't want to do this, so I said, 'Okay, let's not,' and I got off the couch and started getting dressed."

"You broke off from the encounter yourself."

"Yes."

"Because she had said, 'no'?"

"No, that was just an excuse. Because I was feeling uneasy at that point."

"Uh-huh. So you got off the couch and started to get dressed . . ."

"Yes."

"And did you say anything at that time? To explain your actions?"

"Yes. I said that I didn't think this was a good idea, and I didn't feel good about it."

"And how did she respond?"

"She got very angry. She started throwing things at me. Then she started hitting me. And scratching me."

"Do you have any marks?"

"Yes."

"Where are they?"

"On my neck and chest."

"Have they been photographed yet?"

"No."

"All right. Now when she scratched you, how did you respond?"

"I just tried to get dressed and get out of there."

"You didn't respond directly to her attack?"

"Well, at one point I pushed her back, to get her away from me, and she tripped on a table and fell on the floor."

"You make it sound like pushing her was self-defense on your part."

"It was. She was ripping the buttons off my shirt. I had to go home, and I didn't want my wife to see my shirt, so I pushed her away."

"Did you ever do anything that was *not* self-defense?"

"No."

"Did you hit her at any time?"

"No."

"You're sure about that?"

"Yes."

"All right. What happened then?"

"She threw a wineglass at me. But by then I was pretty much dressed. I went and got my phone from her windowsill, and then I went—"

"I'm sorry. You got your phone? What phone is that?"

"I had a cellular phone." He took it out of his pocket and showed her. "We all carry them in the company, because we make them. And I had been using the phone to make a call from her office, when she started kissing me."

"Were you in the middle of a call when she started kissing you?"

"Yes."

"Whom were you talking to?"

"An answering machine."

"I see." She was clearly disappointed. "Go on, please."

"So I went and got my phone and got the hell out of there. She was screaming that I couldn't do this to her, that she would kill me."

"And you responded how?"

"Nothing. I just left."

"And this was at what time?"

"About six forty-five."

"Did anybody see you leave?"

"The cleaning lady."

"Do you happen to know her name?"

"No."

"Ever seen her before?"

"No."

"Do you think she worked for your company?"

"She had a company uniform on. You know, for the maintenance firm that cleans up our offices."

"Uh-huh. And then?"

He shrugged. "I went home."

"Did you tell your wife what happened?"

"No."

"Did you tell anybody what happened?"

"No."

"Why not?"

"I guess I was in shock."

She paused and looked back over her notes. "All right. You say you were sexually harassed. And you have described a very direct overture by this woman. Since she was your boss, I would have thought you'd feel yourself at some risk in turning her down."

"Well. I was concerned. Sure. But I mean, don't I have the right to turn her down? Isn't that what this is about?"

"Certainly you have that right. I'm asking about your state of mind."

"I was very upset."

"Yet you did not want to tell anybody what

had happened? You did not want to share this upsetting experience with a colleague? A friend? A family member, perhaps a brother? Anybody at all?"

"No. It didn't even occur to me. I didn't know how to deal with what— I guess I was in shock. I just wanted it to go away. I wanted to think it had never happened."

"Did you make any notes?"

"No."

"All right. Now, you mentioned that you didn't tell your wife. Would you say you concealed it from your wife?"

He hesitated. "Yes."

"Do you often conceal things from her?"

"No. But in this instance, you know, involving an old girlfriend, I didn't think she would be sympathetic. I didn't want to deal with her about this."

"Have you had other affairs?"

"This wasn't an affair."

"I'm asking a general question. In terms of your relationship to your wife."

"No. I haven't had affairs."

"All right. I advise you to tell your wife at once. Make a full and complete disclosure. Because I promise you that she will find out, if she hasn't done so already. However difficult it may be to tell her, your best chance to preserve your relationship is to be completely honest with her."

"Okay."

"Now, going back to last night. What happened next?"

"Meredith Johnson called the house and spoke to my wife."

Fernandez's eyebrows went up. "I see. Did you expect that to happen?"

"God, no. It scared the hell out of me. But apparently she was friendly, and just called to say that the morning meeting was rescheduled for eight-thirty. Today."

"I see."

"But when I got to work today, I found that the meeting had actually been scheduled for eight."

"So you arrived late, and were embarrassed, and so on."

"Yes."

"And you believe that it was a setup."

"Yes."

Fernandez glanced at her watch. "I'm afraid I'm running out of time. Bring me up to date about what happened today quickly, if you can."

Without mentioning Conley-White, he described the morning meeting briefly and his subsequent humiliation. His argument with Meredith. His conversation with Phil Blackburn. The offer of a lateral transfer. The fact that the transfer would deny him the benefits of a possible spin-off. His decision to seek advice.

Fernandez asked few questions and wrote

steadily. Finally, she pushed the yellow pad aside.

"All right. I think I have enough to get the picture. You're feeling slighted and ignored. And your question is, do you have a harassment case?"

"Yes," he said, nodding.

"Well. Arguably you do. It's a jury case, and we don't know what would happen if we went to trial. But based on what you have told me here, I have to advise you that your case is not strong."

Sanders felt stunned. "Jesus."

"I don't make the law. I'm just telling you frankly, so you can arrive at an informed decision. Your situation is not good, Mr. Sanders."

Fernandez pushed back from her desk and began to stuff papers into her briefcase. "I have five minutes, but let me review for you what sexual harassment actually is, under the law, because many clients aren't clear about it. Title VII of the Civil Rights Act of 1964 made sex discrimination in the workplace illegal, but as a practical matter what we call sexual harassment was not defined for many years. Since the middle nineteen-eighties, the Equal Employment Opportunities Commission has, under Title VII, produced guidelines to define sexual harassment. In the last few years, these EEOC guidelines have been further clarified by case law. So the definitions are quite explicit. According to the law, for a complaint to qualify as sexual harassment, the behavior must contain three elements. First, it must be sexual. That means, for example, that making a profane or scatological joke is not sexual harassment, even though a listener may find it offensive. The conduct must be sexual in nature. In your case, there's no doubt about the explicitly sexual element, from what you have told me."

"Okay."

"Second, the behavior must be unwelcome. The courts distinguish between behavior that is voluntary and behavior that is welcome. For example, a person may be having a sexual relationship with a superior and it's obviously voluntary—no one's holding a gun to the person's head. But the courts understand that the employee may feel that they have no choice but to comply, and therefore the sexual relationship was not freely entered into—it's not welcome.

"To determine if behavior is really unwelcome, the courts look at the surrounding behavior in broad terms. Did the employee make sexual jokes in the workplace, and thus indicate that such jokes from others were welcome? Did the employee routinely engage in sexual banter, or sexual teasing with other employees? If the employee engaged in an actual affair, did they allow the supervisor into their apartment, did they visit the supervisor in the hospital, or see them at times when they didn't strictly have to, or engage in other actions that would suggest that they were actively and willingly participating in the relationship. In addition, the courts look to see if the employee ever told the supervisor the behavior was unwelcome, if the employee complained to anyone else about the relationship or tried to take any action to evade the unwelcome situation. That consideration becomes more significant when the employee is highly placed, and presumably more free to act."

"But I didn't tell anybody."

"No. And you didn't tell her, either. At least, not explicitly, so far as I can determine."

"I didn't feel I could."

"I understand you didn't. But it's a problem for your case. Now, the third element in sexual harassment is discrimination on the basis of gender. The most common is quid pro quo—the exchange of sexual favors in return for keeping your job or getting a promotion. The threat of that may be explicit or implied. I believe you said it was your understanding that Ms. Johnson had the ability to fire you?"

"Yes."

"How did you gain that understanding?"

"Phil Blackburn told me."

"Explicitly?"

"Yes."

"And what about Ms. Johnson? Did she make any offer contingent on sex? Did she make any reference to her ability to fire you, in the course of the evening?"

"Not exactly, but it was there. It was always in the air."

"How did you know?"

"She said things like 'As long as we're working together, we might as well have a little fun.' And she talked about wanting to have an affair during company trips we would make together to Malaysia, and so on."

"You interpreted this as an implied threat to your job?"

"I interpreted it to mean that if I wanted to get along with her, I had better go along with her."

"And you didn't want to do that?"

"No."

"Did you say so?"

"I said I was married, and that things had changed between us."

"Well, under most circumstances, that exchange alone would probably serve to establish your case. If there were witnesses."

"But there weren't."

"No. Now, there is a final consideration, which we call hostile working environment. This is ordinarily invoked in situations where an individual is harassed in a pattern of incidents that may not in themselves be sexual but that cumulatively amount to harassment based on gender. I don't believe you can claim hostile work environment on this single incident."

"I see."

"Unfortunately, the incident you describe is simply not as clear-cut as it might be. We would then turn to ancillary evidence of harassment. For example, if you were fired."

"I think in effect I have been fired," Sanders said. "Because I'm being pulled out of the division, and I won't get to participate in the spin-off."

"I understand. But the company's offer to transfer you laterally makes things complicated. Because the company can argue—very successfully, I think—that it does not owe you anything more than a lateral transfer. That it has never promised you the golden egg of a spin-off. That such a spin-off is in any case speculative, intended to occur at some future time, and it might never happen. That the company is not required to compensate you for your hopes—for some vague expectation of a future that might never occur. And therefore the company will claim that a lateral transfer is fully acceptable, and that you are being unreasonable if you turn it down. That you are in effect quitting, not being fired. It will place the burden back on you."

"That's ridiculous."

"Actually, it's not. Suppose, for example, you found out that you had terminal cancer and were going to die in six months. Would the company be required to pay the proceeds of the spin-off to your survivors? Clearly, no. If you're working in the company when it spins off, you participate. If you're not, you don't. The company has no broader obligation."

"You're saying I might as well have cancer."

"No, I'm saying that you're angry and you feel the company owes you something that the court will not agree it does. In my experience, sexual harassment claims often have this quality. People come in feeling angry and wronged, and they think they have rights that they simply don't have."

He sighed. "Would it be different if I were a woman?"

"Basically, no. Even in the most clear-cut situations—the most extreme and outrageous situations—sexual harassment is notoriously difficult to prove. Most cases occur as yours has: behind closed doors, with no witnesses. It's one person's word against another's. In that circumstance, where there is no clear-cut corroborating evidence, there is often a prejudice against the man."

"Uh-huh."

"Even so, one-fourth of all sexual harassment cases are brought by men. Most of those are brought against male bosses, but one-fifth are brought against women. And the number is increasing all the time, as we have more women bosses in the workplace."

"I didn't know that."

"It isn't much discussed," she said, peering over

her glasses. "But it's happening. And from my point of view, it's to be expected."

"Why do you say that?"

"Harassment is about power—the undue exercise of power by a superior over a subordinate. I know there's a fashionable point of view that says women are fundamentally different from men, and that women would never harass an employee. But from where I sit, I've seen it all. I've seen and heard everything that you can imagine—and a lot that you wouldn't believe if I told you. That gives me another perspective. Personally, I don't deal much in theory. I have to deal with the facts. And on the basis of facts, I don't see much difference in the behavior of men and women. At least, nothing that you can rely on."

"Then you believe my story?"

"Whether I believe you is not at issue. What's at issue is whether you realistically have a case, and therefore what you should do in your circumstances. I can tell you that I've heard it all before. You're not the first man I've been asked to represent, you know."

"What do you advise me to do?"

"I can't advise you," Fernandez said briskly. "The decision you face is much too difficult. I can only lay out the situation." She pushed her intercom button. "Bob, tell Richard and Eileen to bring the car around. I'll meet them in front of the building." She turned back to Sanders.

"Let me review your problems," she said. She ticked them off on her fingers. "One: you claim that you got into an intimate situation with a younger, very attractive woman but you turned her down. In the absence of witnesses or corroborating evidence, that isn't going to be an easy story to sell to a jury.

"Two: if you bring a lawsuit, the company will fire you. You're looking at three years before you come to trial. You have to think about how you'll support yourself during that time, about how you'll make your house payments, and your other expenses. I might take you on a contingency basis, but you'll still have to pay all direct costs throughout the trial. That will be a minimum of one hundred thousand dollars. I don't know whether you'll want to mortgage your house to pay for it. But it has to be dealt with.

"Three: a lawsuit will bring all this out into the open. It'll be in the papers and on the evening news for years before the trial begins. I can't adequately describe how destructive an experience that is—for you, and for your wife and family. Many families don't survive the pre-trial period intact. There are divorces, suicides, illnesses. It's *very* difficult.

"Four: because of the offer of lateral transfer, it's not clear what we can claim as damages. The company will claim that you have no case, and we'll have to fight it. But even with a stunning victory, you may end up with only a couple of hundred thousand dollars after expenses and fees and three years of your life. And of course the company can appeal, delaying payment further.

"Five: if you bring a lawsuit, you'll never work in this industry again. I know it's not supposed to work that way, but as a practical matter, you'll never be hired for another job. That's just how it goes. It would be one thing if you were fifty-five. But you're only forty-one. I don't know if you want to make that choice, at this point in your life."

"Jesus." He slumped back in the chair.

"I'm sorry, but these are the facts of litigation."

"But it's so unjust."

She put on her raincoat. "Unfortunately, the law has nothing to do with justice, Mr. Sanders," she said. "It's merely a method for dispute resolution." She snapped her briefcase shut and extended her hand. "I'm sorry, Mr. Sanders. I wish it were different. Please feel free to call me again if you have any further questions."

She hurried out of the office, leaving him sitting there. After a moment the assistant came in. "Can I do anything for you?"

"No," Sanders said, shaking his head slowly. "No, I was just leaving."

In the car, driving to the courthouse, Louise Fernandez recounted Sanders's story to the two junior lawyers traveling with her. One lawyer, a woman, said, "You don't really believe him?"

"Who knows?" Fernandez said. "It was behind closed doors. There's never a way to know."

The young woman shook her head. "I just can't believe a woman would act that way. So aggressively."

"Why not?" Fernandez said. "Suppose this wasn't a case of harassment. Suppose this was a question of implied promise between a man and a woman. The man claims that behind closed doors he was promised a big bonus, but the woman denies it. Would you assume that the man was lying because a woman wouldn't act that way?"

"Not about that, no."

"In that situation, you'd think that anything was possible."

"But this isn't a contract," the woman said. "This is sexual behavior."

"So you think women are unpredictable in their contractual arrangements, but stereotypical in their sexual arrangements?"

The woman said, "I don't know if *stereotypical* is the word I'd use."

"You just said that you can't believe a woman would act aggressively in sex. Isn't that a stereotype?"

"Well, no," the woman said. "It's not a stereotype, because it's true. Women are different from men when it comes to sex."

"And black people have rhythm," Fernandez said. "Asians are workaholics. And Hispanics don't confront . . ."

"But this is different. I mean, there are studies about this. Men and women don't even talk to each other the same way."

"Oh, you mean like the studies that show that women are less good at business and strategic thinking?"

"No. Those studies are wrong."

"I see. Those studies are wrong. But the studies about sexual differences are right?"

"Well, sure. Because sex is fundamental. It's a primal drive."

"I don't see why. It's used for all sorts of purposes. As a way of relating, a way of placating, a way of provoking, as an offer, as a weapon, as a threat. It can be quite complicated, the ways sex is used. Haven't you found that to be true?"

The woman crossed her arms. "I don't think so."

Speaking for the first time, the young man said, "So what'd you tell this guy? Not to litigate?"

"No. But I told him his problems."

"What do you think he should do?"

"I don't know," Fernandez said. "But I know what he should have done."

"What?"

"It's terrible to say it," she said. "But in the real world? With no witnesses? Alone in the office with his boss? He probably should have shut up and fucked her. Because right now, that poor bastard has no options at all. If he's not careful, his life is over."

Sanders walked slowly back down the hill toward Pioneer Square. The rain had stopped, but the afternoon was still damp and gray. The wet pavement beneath his feet sloped steeply downward. Around him the tops of the skyscrapers disappeared into the low-hanging, chilly mist.

He was not sure what he had expected to hear from Louise Fernandez, but it was certainly not a detailed account of the possibility of his being fired, mortgaging his house, and never working again.

Sanders felt overwhelmed by the sudden turn that his life had taken, and by a realization of the precariousness of his existence. Two days ago, he was an established executive with a stable position and a promising future. Now he faced disgrace, humiliation, loss of his job. All sense of security had vanished.

He thought of all the questions Fernandez had asked him—questions that had never occurred to him before. Why hadn't he told anyone. Why hadn't he made notes. Why hadn't he told Meredith explicitly that her advances were unwelcome. Fernandez operated in a world of rules and distinctions that he did not understand, that had never crossed his mind. And now those distinctions turned out to be vitally important.

Your situation is not good, Mr. Sanders.

And yet . . . how could he have prevented this? What should he have done instead? He considered the possibilities.

Suppose he had called Blackburn right after the meeting with Meredith, and had told him in detail that Meredith had harassed him. He could have called from the ferry, lodged his complaint before she lodged hers. Would it have made a difference? What would Blackburn have done?

He shook his head, thinking about it. It seemed unlikely that anything would make a difference. Because in the end, Meredith was tied in to the power structure of the company in a way that Sanders was not. Meredith was a corporate player; she had power, allies. That was the message—the final message—of this situation. Sanders didn't count. He was just a technical guy, a cog in the corporate wheels. His job was to get along with his new boss, and he had failed to do that. Whatever he did now was just whining. Or worse: ratting on the boss. Whistle-blowing. And nobody liked a whistle-blower.

So what could he have done?

As he thought about it, he realized that he couldn't have called Blackburn right after the meeting because his cellular phone had gone dead, its power drained.

He had a sudden image of a car—*a man and a woman in a car, driving to a party.* Somebody had told him something once . . . a story about some people in a car.

It teased him. He couldn't quite get it.

There were plenty of reasons why the phone might be dead. The most likely explanation was nicad memory. The new phones used rechargeable nickel-cadmium batteries, and if they didn't completely discharge between uses, the batteries could reset themselves at a shorter duration. You never knew when it was going to show up. Sanders had had to throw out batteries before because they developed a short memory.

He took out his phone, turned it on. It glowed brightly. The battery was holding up fine today.

But there was something . . .

Driving in a car.

Something he wasn't thinking about.

Going to a party.

He frowned. He couldn't get it. It hung at the back of his memory, too dim to recover.

But it started him thinking: what else wasn't he getting? Because as he considered the whole situation, he began to have the nagging sense that there was something else that he was overlooking. And he had the feeling that Fernandez had overlooked it, too. Something hadn't come up in her questions to him. Something that everybody was taking for granted, even though—

Meredith.

Something about Meredith.

She had accused him of harassment. She had gone to Blackburn and accused him the next morning. Why would she do that? No doubt she felt guilty about what had happened at the meeting. And perhaps she was afraid Sanders would accuse her, so she decided to accuse him first. Her accusation was understandable in that light.

But if Meredith really had power, it didn't make sense to raise the sexual issue at all. She could just as easily have gone to Blackburn and said, Listen, it isn't working out with Tom. I can't deal with him. We have to make a change. And Blackburn would have done it.

Instead, she had accused him of harassment. And that must have been embarrassing to her. Because harassment implied a loss of control. It meant that she had not been able to control her subordinate in a meeting. Even if something unpleasant did happen, a boss would never mention it.

Harassment is about power.

It was one thing if you were a lowly female assistant fondled by a stronger, powerful man. But in this case Meredith was the boss. She had all the power. Why would she claim harassment by Sanders? Because the fact was, subordinates didn't harass their bosses. It just didn't happen. You'd have to be crazy to harass your boss.

Harassment is about power—the undue exercise of power by a superior over a subordinate.

For her to claim sexual harassment was, in an odd way, to admit that she was subordinate to Sanders. And she would never do that. Quite the contrary: Meredith was new to her job, eager to prove that she was in control of the situation. So her accusation made no sense—unless she was using it as a convenient way to destroy him. Sexual harassment had the advantage of being a charge that was difficult to recover from. You were presumed guilty until proven innocent—and it was hard to prove innocence. It tarnished any man, no matter how frivolous the accusation. In that sense, harassment was a very powerful accusation. The most powerful accusation she could make.

But then, she said that she wasn't going to press charges. And the question was—

Why not?

Sanders stopped on the street.

That was it.

She's assured me, she's not going to press charges.

Why wasn't Meredith going to press charges?

At the time that Blackburn said that, Sanders had never questioned it. Louise Fernandez had never questioned it. But the fact was, Meredith's refusal to press charges made no sense at all. She had already accused him. Why not press it? Why not carry it to its conclusion?

Maybe Blackburn had talked her out of it. Blackburn was always so concerned about appearances.

But Sanders didn't think that was what had happened. Because a formal accusation could still be handled quietly. It could be processed inside the company.

And from Meredith's standpoint, there were real advantages to a formal accusation. Sanders was popular at DigiCom. He had been with the company a long time. If her goal was to get rid of him, to banish him to Texas, why not defuse the inevitable corporate grumbling by letting the accusation work its way through the company grapevine? Why not make it official?

The more Sanders thought about it, the more it seemed that there was only one explanation: Meredith wasn't going to press charges because she couldn't.

She couldn't, because she had some other problem.

Some other consideration.

Something else was going on.

We can handle it quietly.

Slowly, Sanders began to see everything differently. In the meeting earlier that day, Blackburn hadn't been ignoring him or slighting him. Not at all: Blackburn was scrambling.

Blackburn was scared.

We can handle it quietly. It's best for everyone.

What did he mean, best for everyone?

What problem did Meredith have?

What problem *could* she have?

The more Sanders thought about it, the more it seemed that there could be only one possible reason why she wasn't pressing charges against him.

He took out his phone, called United Airlines, and booked three round-trip tickets to Phoenix.

And then he called his wife.

Y ou goddamn son of a bitch," Susan said.

They were sitting in a corner table at Il Terrazzo. It was two o'clock; the restaurant was nearly deserted. Susan had listened to him for half an hour, without interruption or comment. He told her everything that had happened in his meeting with Meredith, and everything that had happened that morning. The Conley-White meeting. The conversation with Phil. The conversation with Fernandez. Now he had finished. She stared at him.

"I could really learn to despise you, you know that? You son of a bitch, why didn't you tell me she was your ex-girlfriend?"

"I don't know," he said. "I didn't want to go into it."

"You didn't want to go into it? Adele and Mary Anne are talking to me on the phone all day, and they know, but I don't? It's humiliating, Tom."

"Well," he said, "you know you've been upset a lot lately, and—"

"Cut the crap, Tom," she said. "This has nothing to do with me. You didn't tell me because you didn't want to."

"Susan, that's not—"

"Yes it is, Tom. I was asking you about her, last night. You could have told me if you wanted to. But you didn't." She shook her head. "Son of a bitch. I can't believe what an asshole you are. You've made a real mess of this. Do you realize what a mess this is?"

"Yes," he said, hanging his head.

"Don't act contrite with me, you asshole."

"I'm sorry," he said.

"You're sorry? Fuck you, you're sorry. Jesus Christ. I can't believe you. What an asshole. You spent the night with your goddamned *girlfriend*."

"I didn't spend the night. And she's not my girlfriend."

"What do you mean? She was your big heart-throb."

"She wasn't my 'big heartthrob.' "

"Oh yeah? Then why wouldn't you tell me?" She shook her head. "Just answer one question. Did you fuck her or not?"

"No. I didn't."

She stared at him intently, stirring her coffee. "You're telling me the truth?"

"Yes."

"Nothing left out? No inconvenient parts skipped?"

"No. Nothing."

"Then why would she accuse you?"

"What do you mean?" he said.

"I mean, there must be a reason she accused you. You must have done something."

"Well, I didn't. I turned her down."

"Uh-huh. Sure." She frowned at him. "You know, this is not just about you, Tom. This involves your whole family: me and the kids."

"I understand that."

"Why didn't you tell me? If you told me last night, I could have helped you."

"Then help me now."

"Well, there isn't much we can do now," Susan said, with heavy sarcasm. "Not after she's gone to Blackburn and made an accusation first. Now you're finished."

"I'm not so sure."

"Trust me, you haven't got a move," she said. "If you go to trial, it'll be living hell for at least three years, and I personally don't think you can win. You're a man bringing a charge of harassment against a woman. They'll laugh you out of court."

"Maybe."

"Trust me, they will. So you can't go to trial. What can you do? Move to Austin. Jesus."

"I keep thinking," Sanders said. "She accused me of harassment, but now she isn't pressing charges. And I keep thinking, Why isn't she pressing charges?"

"Who *cares*?" Susan said, with an irritable

wave of the hand. "It could be any of a million reasons. Corporate politics. Or Phil talked her out of it. Or Garvin. It doesn't matter why. Tom, face the facts: *you have no move*. Not now, you stupid son of a bitch."

"Susan, will you settle down?"

"Fuck you, Tom. You're dishonest and irresponsible."

"Susan—"

"We've been married five years. I deserve better than this."

"Will you take it easy? I'm trying to tell you: I think I *do* have a move."

"Tom. You *don't*."

"I think I do. Because this is a very dangerous situation," Sanders said. "It's dangerous for everybody."

"What does that mean?"

"Let's assume that Louise Fernandez told me the truth about my lawsuit."

"She did. She's a good lawyer."

"But she wasn't looking at it from the company's standpoint. She was looking at it from the plaintiff's standpoint."

"Yeah, well, you're a plaintiff."

"No, I'm not," he said. "I'm a *potential* plaintiff."

There was a moment of silence.

Susan stared at him. Her eyes scanned his face.

She frowned. He watched her put it together. "You're kidding."

"No."

"You must be out of your mind."

"No. Look at the situation. DigiCom's in the middle of a merger with a very conservative East Coast company. A company that's already pulled out of one merger because an employee had a little bad publicity. Supposedly this employee used some rough language while firing a temp secretary, and then Conley-White pulled out. They're very skittish about publicity. Which means the last thing anybody at DigiCom wants is a sexual harassment suit against the new female vice president."

"Tom. Do you realize what you're saying?"

"Yes," he said.

"If you do this, they're going to go *crazy.* They're going to try to destroy you."

"I know."

"Have you talked to Max about this? Maybe you should."

"The hell with Max. He's a crazy old man."

"I'd ask him. Because this isn't really your thing, Tom. You were never a corporate infighter. I don't know if you can pull this off."

"I think I can."

"It'll be nasty. In a day or so, you're going to wish you had taken the Austin job."

"Fuck it."

"It'll get really mean, Tom. You'll lose your friends."

"Fuck it."

"Just so you're ready."

"I am." Sanders looked at his watch. "Susan, I want you to take the kids and visit your mother for a few days." Her mother lived in Phoenix. "If you go home now and pack, you can make the eight o'clock flight at Sea-Tac. I've booked three seats for you."

She stared at him, as if she were seeing a stranger. "You're really going to do this . . . ," she said slowly.

"Yes. I am."

"Oh boy." She bent over, picked up her purse from the floor, and pulled out her day organizer.

He said, "I don't want you or the kids to be involved. I don't want anybody pushing a news camera in their faces, Susan."

"Well, just a minute . . ." She ran her finger down her appointments. "I can move that . . . And . . . conference call . . . Yes." She looked up. "Yes. I can leave for a few days." She glanced at her watch. "I guess I better hurry and pack."

He stood up and walked outside the restaurant with her. It was raining; the light on the street was gray and bleak. She looked up at him and kissed him on the cheek. "Good luck, Tom. Be careful."

He could see that she was frightened. It made him frightened, too.

"I'll be okay."

"I love you," she said. And then she walked quickly away in the rain. He waited for a moment to see if she looked back at him, but she never did.

Walking back to his office, he suddenly realized how alone he felt. Susan was leaving with the kids. He was on his own now. He had imagined he would feel relieved, free to act without restraint, but instead he felt abandoned and at risk. Chilled, he thrust his hands into the pockets of his raincoat.

He hadn't handled the lunch with Susan well. And she would be going off, mulling over his answers.

Why didn't you tell me?

He hadn't answered that well. He hadn't been able to express the conflicting feelings he had experienced last night. The unclean feeling, and the guilt, and the sense that he had somehow done something wrong, even though he hadn't done anything wrong.

You could have told me.

He hadn't done anything wrong, he told himself. But then why hadn't he told her? He had no answer to that. He passed a graphics shop, and a plumbing supply store with white porcelain fixtures in a window display.

You didn't tell me because you didn't want to.

But that made no sense. Why wouldn't he want

to tell her? Once again, his thoughts were interrupted by images from the past: the white garter belt . . . a bowl of popcorn. . . . the stained-glass flower on the door to his apartment.

Cut the crap, Tom. This has nothing to do with me.

Blood in the white bathroom sink, and Meredith laughing about it. Why was she laughing? He couldn't remember now; it was just an isolated image. A stewardess putting a tray of airline food in front of him. A suitcase on the bed. The television sound turned off. The stained-glass flower, in gaudy orange and purple.

Have you talked to Max?

She was right about that, he thought. He should talk to Max. And he would, right after he gave Blackburn the bad news.

Sanders was back at his office at two-thirty. He was surprised to find Blackburn there, standing behind Sanders's desk, talking on his phone. Blackburn hung up, looking a little guilty. "Oh, Tom. Good. I'm glad you're back." He walked back around Sanders's desk. "What have you decided?"

"I've thought this over very carefully," Sanders said, closing the door to the hallway.

"And?"

"I've decided to retain Louise Fernandez of Marin, Howard to represent me."

Blackburn looked puzzled. "To represent you?"

"Yes. In the event it becomes necessary to litigate."

"Litigate," Blackburn said. "On what basis would you litigate, Tom?"

"Sexual harassment under Title VII," Sanders said.

"Oh, Tom," Blackburn said, making a mournful face. "That would be unwise. That would be very unwise. I urge you to reconsider."

"I've reconsidered all day," Sanders said. "But the fact is, Meredith Johnson harassed me, she made advances to me and I turned her down. Now she's a woman scorned, and she is being vindictive toward me. I'm prepared to sue if it comes to that."

"Tom . . ."

"That's it, Phil. That's what'll happen if you transfer me out of the division."

Blackburn threw up his hands. "But what do you expect us to do? Transfer Meredith?"

"Yes," Sanders said. "Or fire her. That's the usual thing one does with a harassing supervisor."

"But you forget: she's accused you of harassment, too."

"She's lying," Sanders said.

"But there are no witnesses, Tom. No evidence either way. You and she are both our trusted employees. How do you expect us to decide who to believe?"

"That's your problem, Phil. All I have to say is, I'm innocent. And I'm prepared to sue."

Blackburn stood in the middle of the room, frowning. "Louise Fernandez is a smart attorney. I can't believe she recommended this course of action to you."

"No. This is my decision."

"Then it's very unwise," Blackburn said. "You are putting the company in a very difficult position."

"The company is putting me in a difficult position."

"I don't know what to say," Phil said. "I hope this doesn't force us to terminate you."

Sanders stared at him, meeting his gaze evenly. "I hope not, too," he said. "But I don't have confidence that the company has taken my complaint seriously. I'll fill out a formal charge of sexual harassment with Bill Everts in HR later today. And I'm asking Louise to draw up the necessary papers to file with the state Human Rights Commission."

"Christ."

"She should file first thing tomorrow morning."

"I don't see what the rush is."

"There's no rush. It's just a filing. To get the complaint on record. I'm required to do that."

"But this is very serious, Tom."

"I know it, Phil."

"I'd like to ask you to do me a favor, as your friend."

"What's that?"

"Hold off the formal complaint. At least, with the HRC. Give us a chance to conduct an in-house investigation before you take this outside."

"But you aren't conducting an in-house investigation, Phil."

"Yes, we are."

"You didn't even want to hear my side of the story this morning. You told me it didn't matter."

"That's not true," Blackburn said. "You misunderstood me entirely. Of course it matters. And I assure you, we will hear your story in detail as part of our investigation."

"I don't know, Phil," Sanders said. "I don't see how the company can be neutral on this issue. It seems everything is stacked against me. Everybody believes Meredith and not me."

"I assure you that is not the case."

"It certainly seems like it. You told me this morning how well connected she is. How many allies she has. You mentioned that several times."

"Our investigation will be scrupulous and impartial. But in any case it seems reasonable to ask you to wait for the outcome before filing with a state agency."

"How long do you want me to wait?"

"Thirty days."

Sanders laughed.

"But that's the standard time for a harassment investigation."

"You could do it in a day, if you wanted to."

"But you must agree, Tom, that we're very busy right now, with all the merger meetings."

"That's your problem, Phil. I have a different problem. I've been unjustly treated by my superior, and I feel I have a right, as a long-standing senior employee, to see my complaint resolved promptly."

Blackburn sighed. "All right. Let me get back to you," he said. He hurried out of the room.

Sanders slumped in his chair and stared into space.

It had begun.

Fifteen minutes later, Blackburn met with Garvin in the fifth-floor executive conference room. Also present at the meeting were Stephanie Kaplan and Bill Everts, the head of Human Resources at DigiCom.

Blackburn began the meeting by saying, "Tom Sanders has retained outside counsel and is threatening litigation over Meredith Johnson."

"Oh, Christ," Garvin said.

"He's claiming sexual harassment."

Garvin kicked the leg of the table. "That son of a bitch."

Kaplan said, "What does he say happened?"

"I don't have all the details yet," Blackburn said. "But in essence he claims that Meredith made sexual overtures to him in her office last night, that he turned her down, and that now she is being vindictive."

Garvin gave a long sigh. "Shit," he said. "This is just what I didn't want to happen. This could be a *disaster*."

"I know, Bob."

Stephanie Kaplan said, "Did she do it?"

"Christ," Garvin said. "Who knows in these situations. That's always the question." He turned to Everts. "Has Sanders come to you about this?"

"Not yet, no. I imagine he will."

"We have to keep it in-house," Garvin said. "That's essential."

"Essential," Kaplan said, nodding. "Phil has to make sure it stays in-house."

"I'm trying," Blackburn said. "But Sanders is talking about filing tomorrow with the HRC."

"That's a public filing?"

"Yes."

"How soon is it made public?"

"Probably within forty-eight hours. Depending on how fast HRC does the paperwork."

"Christ," Garvin said. "Forty-eight hours? What's the matter with him? Doesn't he realize what he's doing?"

Blackburn said, "I think he does. I think he knows exactly."

"Blackmail?"

"Well. Pressure."

Garvin said, "Have you talked to Meredith?"

"Not since this morning."

"Somebody's got to talk to her. I'll talk to her. But how are we going to stop Sanders?"

Blackburn said, "I asked him to hold off the HRC filing, pending our investigation, for thirty days. He said no. He said we should be able to conduct our investigation in one day."

"Well, he got that right," Garvin said. "For all

kinds of reasons, we damn well better conduct the investigation in one day."

"Bob, I don't know if that's possible," Blackburn said. "We have significant exposure here. The corporation is required by law to conduct a thorough and impartial investigation. We can't appear to be rushed or—"

"Oh, for Christ's sake," Garvin said. "I don't want to hear this legal pissing and moaning. What are we talking about? Two people, right? And no witnesses, right? So there's just two people. How long does it take to interview two people?"

"Well, it may not be that simple," Blackburn said, with a significant look.

"I'll tell you what's simple," Garvin said. "This is what's simple. Conley-White is a company obsessed with its public image. They sell textbooks to school boards that believe in Noah's ark. They sell magazines for kids. They have a vitamin company. They have a health-food company that markets baby foods. Rainbow Mush or something. Now Conley-White's buying our company, and in the middle of the acquisition a high-profile female executive, the woman in line to become CEO within two years, is accused of seeking sexual favors from a married man. You know what they're going to do if that gets out? They're going to *bail*. You know that Nichols is looking for any excuse to weasel out of this thing. This is perfect for him. Christ."

DISCLOSURE

"But Sanders has already questioned our impartiality," Blackburn said. "And I'm not sure how many people know about the, ah, prior questions that we—"

"Quite a few," Kaplan said. "And didn't it come up at an officers' meeting last year?"

"Check the minutes," Garvin said. "We have no legal problem with current corporate officers, is that right?"

"That's right," Blackburn said. "Current corporate officers cannot be questioned or deposed on these matters."

"And we haven't lost any corporate officers in the last year? Nobody retired or moved?"

"No."

"Okay. So fuck him." Garvin turned to Everts. "Bill, I want you to go back through the HR records, and look carefully at Sanders. See if he's dotted every *i* and crossed every *t*. If he hasn't, I want to know."

"Right," Everts said. "But my guess is he's clean."

"All right," Garvin said, "let's assume that he is. What's it going to take to make Sanders go away? What does he want?"

Blackburn said, "I think he wants his job, Bob."

"He can't have his job."

"Well, that's the problem," Blackburn said.

Garvin snorted. "What's our liability, assuming he ever got to trial?"

"I don't think he has a case, based on what happened in that office. Our biggest liability would come from any perceived failure to respect due process and conduct a thorough investigation. Sanders could win on that alone, if we're not careful. That's my point."

"So we'll be careful. Fine."

"Now, guys," Blackburn said. "I feel strongly obliged to insert a note of caution. The extreme delicacy of this situation means that we have to be mindful of the details. As Pascal once said, 'God is in the details.' And in this case, the competing balance of legitimate legal claims forces me to admit it's unclear precisely what our best—"

"Phil," Garvin said. "Cut the crap."

Kaplan said, "Mies."

Blackburn said, "What?"

"Mies van der Rohe said, 'God is in the details.' "

"Who gives a shit?" Garvin said, pounding the table. "The point is, Sanders has no case—he just has us by the balls. And he knows it."

Blackburn winced. "I wouldn't phrase it exactly that way, but—"

"But that's the fucking situation."

"Yes."

Kaplan said, "Tom's smart, you know. A little naïve, but smart."

"Very smart," Garvin said. "Remember, I trained him. Taught him all he knows. He's going to be a big problem." He turned to Blackburn. "Get to the bottom line. What're we dealing with? Impartiality, right?"

"Yes . . ."

"And we want to move him out."

"Right."

"Okay. Will he accept mediation?"

"I don't know. I doubt it."

"Why not?"

"Ordinarily, we only use mediation to resolve settlement packages for employees who are leaving."

"So?"

"I think that's how he'll view it."

"Let's try, anyway. Tell him it's nonbinding, and see if we can get him to accept it on that basis. Give him three names and let him pick one. Mediate it tomorrow. Do I need to talk to him?"

"Probably. Let me try first, and you back up."

"Okay."

Kaplan said, "Of course, if we go to an outside mediator, we introduce an unpredictable element."

"You mean the mediator could find against us? I'll take the risk," Garvin said. "The important thing is to get the thing resolved. Quietly—and fast. I don't want Ed Nichols backpedaling on me. We have a press conference scheduled for Friday noon. I want this issue dead and buried by then, and I want Meredith Johnson announced as the new head of the division on Friday. Everybody clear on what's going to happen?"

They said they were.

"Then do it," Garvin said, and walked out of the room. Blackburn hurried after him.

In the hallway outside, Garvin said to Blackburn, "Christ, what a mess. Let me tell you. I'm very unhappy."

"I know," Blackburn said mournfully. He was shaking his head sadly.

"You really screwed the pooch on this one, Phil. Christ. You could have handled this one better. A *lot* better."

"How? What could I have done? He says that she hustled him, Bob. It's a serious matter."

"Meredith Johnson is vital to the success of this merger," Garvin said flatly.

"Yes, Bob. Of course."

"We must keep her."

"Yes, Bob. But we both know that in the past she has—"

"She has proven herself an outstanding piece of executive talent," Garvin said, interrupting him. "I won't allow these ridiculous allegations to jeopardize her career."

Blackburn was aware of Garvin's unswerving support of Meredith. For years, Garvin had had a blind spot for Johnson. Whenever criticisms of Johnson arose, Garvin would somehow change the subject, shift to something else. There was no reasoning with him. But now Blackburn felt he had to try. "Bob," he said. "Meredith's only human. We know she has her limitations."

"Yes," Garvin said. "She has youth. Enthusiasm. Honesty. Unwillingness to play corporate games. And of course, she's a woman. That's a real limitation, being a woman."

"But Bob—"

"I tell you, I can't stomach the excuses anymore," Garvin said. "We don't have women in high corporate positions here. Nobody does. Corporate America is rooms full of men. And whenever I talk about putting a woman in, there's always a 'But Bob' that comes up. The hell with it, Phil. We've got to break the glass ceiling sometime."

Blackburn sighed. Garvin was shifting the subject again. He said, "Bob, nobody's disagreeing with—"

"Yes, they are. You're disagreeing, Phil. You're giving me excuses why Meredith isn't suitable. And I'm telling you that if I had named some other woman, there'd be other excuses why that other woman isn't suitable. And I tell you, I'm tired of it."

Blackburn said, "We've got Stephanie. We've got Mary Anne."

"Tokens," Garvin said, with a dismissing wave. "Sure, let the CFO be a woman. Let a couple of the midrange execs be women. Throw the broads a bone. The fact remains. You can't tell me that a bright, able young woman starting out in business isn't held back by a hundred little *reasons*, oh such good *reasons*, why she shouldn't be advanced, why she shouldn't attain a major position of power. But in the end, it's just prejudice. And it has to stop. We have to give these bright young women a decent opportunity."

Blackburn said, "Well, Bob. I just think it would be prudent for you to get Meredith's view of this situation."

"I will. I'll find out what the hell happened. I know she'll tell me. But this thing still has to be resolved."

"Yes, it does, Bob."

"And I want you to be clear. I expect you to do whatever is necessary to get it resolved."

"Okay, Bob."

"*Whatever* is necessary," Garvin said. "Put the pressure on Sanders. Make sure he feels it. Rattle his cage, Phil."

"Okay, Bob."

"I'll deal with Meredith. You just take care of Sanders. I want you to rattle his fucking cage until he's black and blue."

Bob." Meredith Johnson stood at one of the center tables in the Design Group laboratory, going over the torn-apart Twinkle drives with Mark Lewyn. She came over when she saw Garvin standing to one side. "I can't tell you how sorry I am about all this business with Sanders."

"We're having some problems with it," Garvin said.

"I keep going over what happened," she said. "Wondering what I should have done. But he was angry and out of control. He had too much to drink, and he behaved badly. Not that we all haven't done that at some time in our lives, but . . ." She shrugged. "Anyway, I'm sorry."

"Apparently, he's going to file a harassment charge."

"That's unfortunate," she said. "But I suppose it's part of the pattern—trying to humiliate me, to discredit me with the people in the division."

"I won't let that happen," Garvin said.

"He resented my getting the job, and he couldn't deal with having me as his superior. He had to try and put me in my place. Some men are like that." She shook her head sadly. "For all the talk about the new male sensibility, I'm afraid very few men are like you, Bob."

Garvin said, "My concern now, Meredith, is that his filing may interfere with the acquisition."

"I can't see why that would be a problem," she said. "I think we can keep it under control."

"It's a problem, if he files with the state HRC."

"You mean he's going to go *outside?*" she asked.

"Yes. That's exactly what I mean."

Meredith stared off into space. For the first time, she seemed to lose her composure. She bit her lip. "That could be very awkward."

"I'll say. I've sent Phil to see him, to ask if we can mediate. With an experienced outside person. Someone like Judge Murphy. I'm trying to arrange it for tomorrow."

"Fine," Meredith said. "I can clear my schedule for a couple of hours tomorrow. But I don't know what we can expect to come out of it. He won't admit what happened, I'm sure. And there isn't any record, or any witnesses."

"I wanted you to fill me in," Garvin said, "on exactly what did happen, last night."

"Oh, Bob," she sighed. "I blame myself, every time I go over it."

"You shouldn't."

"I know, but I do. If my assistant hadn't gone off to rent her apartment, I could have buzzed her in, and none of this would have happened."

"I think you better tell me, Meredith."

"Of course, Bob." She leaned toward him and spoke quietly, steadily, for the next several minutes. Garvin stood beside her, shaking his head angrily as he listened.

Don Cherry put his Nikes up on Lewyn's desk. "Yeah? So Garvin came in. Then what happened?"

"So Garvin's standing over there in the corner, hopping up and down from one foot to the other, the way he does. Waiting to be noticed. He won't come over, he's waiting to be noticed. And Meredith's talking to me about the Twinkle drive that I have spread all over the table, and I'm showing her what we've found is wrong with the laser heads—"

"She gets all that?"

"Yeah, she seems okay. She's not Sanders, but she's okay. Fast learner."

"And better perfume than Sanders," Cherry said.

"Yeah, I like her perfume," Lewyn said. "Anyway—"

"Sanders's perfume leaves a lot to be desired."

"Yeah. Anyway, pretty soon Garvin gets tired of hopping, and he gives a discreet little cough, and Meredith notices Garvin and she goes 'Oh,' with a little thrill in her voice, you know that little sharp intake of breath?"

"Uh-oh," Cherry said. "Are we talking humparoonie here or what?"

"Well, that's the *thing*," Lewyn said. "She goes running over to him, and he holds out his arms to her, and I tell you it looks like that ad where the two lovers run toward each other in slow motion."

"Uh-oh," Cherry said. "Garvin's wife is going to be pissed."

"But that's the thing," Lewyn said. "When they finally get together, standing there side by side, it isn't that way at all. They're talking, and she's sort of cooing and batting her eyes at him, and he's such a tough guy he doesn't acknowledge it, but it's working on him."

"She's seriously cute, that's why," Cherry said. "I mean face it, she's got an outstanding molded case, with superior fit and finish."

"But the thing is, it's not like lovers at all. I'm staring, trying not to stare, and I tell you, it's not lovers. It's something else. It's almost like father-daughter, Don."

"Hey. You can fuck your daughter. Millions do."

"No, you know what I think? I think Bob sees himself in her. He sees something that reminds him of himself when he was younger. Some kind of energy or something. And I tell you, she plays it, Don. He crosses his arms, she crosses hers. He leans against the wall, she leans against the wall. She matches him exactly. And from a distance, I'm telling you: *she looks like him*, Don."

"No . . ."

"Yes. Think about it."

"It'd have to be from a *very* long distance," Cherry said. He took his feet off the table, and got up to leave. "So what're we saying here? Nepotism in disguise?"

"I don't know. But Meredith's got some kind of rapport with him. It isn't pure business."

"Hey," Cherry said. "Nothing's pure business. I learned that one a long time ago."

Louise Fernandez came into her office, and dropped her briefcase on the floor. She thumbed through a stack of phone messages and turned to Sanders. "What's going on? I have three calls this afternoon from Phil Blackburn."

"That's because I told him I had retained you as my attorney, that I was prepared to litigate my claim. And I, uh, suggested that you were filing with the HRC in the morning."

"I couldn't possibly file tomorrow," she said. "And I wouldn't recommend that we do so now, in any event. Mr. Sanders, I take false statements very seriously. Don't ever characterize my actions again."

"I'm sorry," he said. "But things are happening very fast."

"Just so we are clear. I don't like it, and if it happens again, you'll be looking for new counsel." That coldness again, the sudden coldness. "Now. So you told Blackburn. What was his response?"

"He asked me if I would mediate."

"Absolutely not," Fernandez said.

"Why not?"

"Mediation is invariably to the benefit of the company."

"He said it would be nonbinding."

"Even so. It amounts to free discovery on their part. There's no reason to give it to them."

"And he said you could be present," he said.

"Of course I can be present, Mr. Sanders. That's no concession. You must have an attorney present at all times or the mediation will be invalid."

"Here are the three names he gave me, as possible mediators." Sanders passed her the list.

She glanced at it briefly. "The usual suspects. One of them is better than the other two. But I still don't—"

"He wants to do the mediation tomorrow."

"Tomorrow?" Fernandez stared at him, and sat back in her chair. "Mr. Sanders, I'm all for a timely resolution, but this is ridiculous. We can't be ready by tomorrow. And as I said, I don't recommend that you agree to mediate under any circumstances. Is there something here I don't know?"

"Yes," he said.

"Let's have it."

He hesitated.

She said, "Any communication you make to me is privileged and confidential."

"All right. DigiCom is about to be acquired by a New York company called Conley-White."

"So the rumors are true."

"Yes," he said. "They intend to announce the merger at a press conference on Friday. And they intend to announce Meredith Johnson as the new vice president of the company, on Friday."

"I see," she said. "So that's Phil's urgency."

"Yes."

"And your complaint presents an immediate and serious problem for him."

He nodded. "Let's say it comes at a very sensitive time."

She was silent for a moment, peering at him over her reading glasses. "Mr. Sanders, I misjudged you. I had the impression you were a timid man."

"They're forcing me to do this."

"Are they." She gave him an appraising look. Then she pushed the intercom button. "Bob, let me see my calendar. I have to clear some things. And ask Herb and Alan to come in. Tell them to drop whatever they're doing. This is more important." She pushed the papers aside. "Are all the mediators on this list available?"

"I assume so."

"I'm going to request Barbara Murphy. Judge Murphy. You won't like her, but she'll do a better job than the others. I'll try and set it up for the afternoon if I can. We need the time. Otherwise, late morning. You realize the risk you're taking? I assume you do. This is a very dangerous game you've decided to play." She pushed the intercom. "Bob? Cancel Roger Rosenberg. Cancel Ellen at six. Remind me to call my husband and tell him I won't be home for dinner." She looked at Sanders. "Neither will you. Do you need to call home?"

"My wife and kids are leaving town tonight."

She raised her eyebrows. "You told her everything?"

"Yes."

"You *are* serious."

"Yes," he said. "I'm serious."

"Good," she said. "You're going to need to be. Let's be frank, Mr. Sanders. What you have embarked upon is not strictly a legal procedure. In essence, you're playing the pressure points."

"That's right."

"Between now and Friday, you're in a position to exert considerable pressure on your company."

"That's right."

"And they on you, Mr. Sanders. They on you."

He found himself in a conference room, facing five people, all taking notes. Seated on either side of Fernandez were two young lawyers, a woman named Eileen and a man named Richard. Then there were two investigators, Alan and Herb: one tall and handsome; the other chubby, with a pockmarked face and a camera hanging around his neck.

Fernandez made Sanders go over his story again, in greater detail. She paused frequently to ask questions, noting down times, names, and specific details. The two lawyers never said anything, although Sanders had the strong impression that the young woman was unsympathetic to him. The two investigators were also silent, except at specific points. After Sanders mentioned Meredith's assistant, Alan, the handsome one, said, "Her name again?"

"Betsy Ross. Like in the flag."

"She's on the fifth floor?"

"Yes."

"What time does she go home?"

"Last night, she left at six-fifteen."

"I may want to meet her casually. Can I go up to the fifth floor?"

"No. All visitors are stopped at reception in the downstairs lobby."

"What if I'm delivering a package? Would Betsy take delivery of a package?"

"No. Packages go to central receiving."

"Okay. What about flowers? Would they be delivered directly?"

"Yes, I guess so. You mean, like flowers for Meredith?"

"Yes," Alan said.

"I guess you could deliver those in person."

"Fine," Alan said, and made a note.

They stopped him a second time when he mentioned the cleaning woman he had seen on leaving Meredith's office.

"DigiCom uses a cleaning service?"

"Yes. AMS—American Management Services. They're over on—"

"We know them. On Boyle. What time do the cleaning crews enter the building?"

"Usually around seven."

"And this woman you didn't recognize. Describe her."

"About forty. Black. Very slender, gray hair, sort of curly."

"Tall? Short? What?"

He shrugged. "Medium."

Herb said, "That's not much. Can you give us anything else?"

Sanders hesitated. He thought about it. "No. I didn't really see her."

"Close your eyes," Fernandez said.

He closed them.

"Now take a deep breath, and put yourself back. It's yesterday evening. You have been in Meredith's office, the door has been closed for almost an hour, you have had your experience with her, now you are leaving the room, you are going out . . . How does the door open, in or out?"

"It opens in."

"So you pull the door open . . . you walk out . . . Fast or slow?"

"I'm walking fast."

"And you go into the outer room . . . What do you see?"

Through the door. Into the outer room, elevators directly ahead. Feeling disheveled, off balance, hoping there is no one to see him. Looking to the right at Betsy Ross's desk: clean, bare, chair pulled up to the edge of the desk. Notepad. Plastic cover on the computer. Desk light still burning.

Eyes swinging left, a cleaning woman at the other assistant's desk. Her big gray cleaning cart stands alongside her. The cleaning woman is lifting a trash basket to empty it into the plastic sack that hangs open from one end of the cart. The woman pauses in mid-lift, stares at him curiously. He is wondering how long she has been there, what she has heard from inside the room. A tinny radio on the cart is playing music.

"I'll fucking kill you for this!" Meredith calls after him.

The cleaning woman hears it. He looks away from her, embarrassed, and hurries toward the elevator. Feeling almost panic. He pushes the button.

"Do you see the woman?" Fernandez said.

"Yes. But it was so fast . . . And I didn't want to look at her." Sanders shook his head.

"Where are you now? At the elevator?"

"Yes."

"Can you see the woman?"

"No. I didn't want to look at her again."

"All right. Let's go back. No, no, keep your eyes closed. We'll do it again. Take a deep breath, and let it out slowly . . . Good . . . This time you're going to see everything in slow motion, like a movie. Now . . . come out through the door . . . and tell me when you see her for the first time."

Coming through the door. Everything slow. His head moving gently up and down with each footstep. Into the outer room. The desk to the right, tidy, lamp on. To the left, the other desk, the cleaning woman raising the—

"I see her."

"All right, now freeze what you see. Freeze it like a photograph."

"Okay."

"Now look at her. You can look at her now."

Standing with the trash basket in her hand. Staring at him, a bland expression. She's about forty. Short hair, curls. Blue uniform, like a hotel maid. A silver chain around her neck—no, hanging eyeglasses.

"She wears glasses around her neck, on a metal chain."

"Good. Just take your time. There's no rush. Look her up and down."

"I keep seeing her face . . ." *Staring at him. A bland expression.*

"Look away from her face. Look her up and down."

The uniform. Spray bottle clipped to her waist. Knee-length blue skirt. White shoes. Like a nurse. No. Sneakers. No. Thicker—running shoes. Thick soles. Dark laces. Something about the laces.

"She's got . . . sort of running shoes. Little old lady running shoes."

"Good."

"There's something funny about the laces."

"Can you see what's funny?"

"No. They're dark. Something funny. I . . . can't tell."

"All right. Open your eyes."

He looked at the five of them. He was back in the room. "That was weird," he said.

"If there was time," Fernandez said, "I would have a professional hypnotist take you through the entire evening. I've found it can be very useful. But there's no time. Boys? It's five o'clock. You better get started."

The two investigators collected their notes and left.

"What are they going to do?"

"If we were litigating this," Fernandez said, "we would have the right to depose potential witnesses—to question individuals within the company who might have knowledge bearing on the case. Under the present circumstances, we have no right to interrogate anybody, because you're entering into private mediation. But if one of the DigiCom assistants chooses to have a drink with a handsome delivery man after work, and if the conversation happens to turn to gossip about sex in the office, well, that's the way the cookie crumbles."

"We can use that information?"

Fernandez smiled. "Let's see what we find out first," she said. "Now, I want to go back over several points in your story, particularly starting at the time you decided not to have intercourse with Ms. Johnson."

"Again?"

"Yes. But I have a few things to do first. I need to call Phil Blackburn and arrange tomorrow's sessions. And I have some other things to check on. Let's break now and meet again in two hours. Meanwhile, have you cleaned out your office?"

"No," he said.

"You better clean it out. Anything personal or incriminating, get it out. From now on, expect your desk drawers to be gone through, your files to be searched, your mail to be read, your phone messages checked. Every aspect of your life is now public."

"Okay."

"So, go through your desk and your files. Remove anything of a personal nature."

"Okay."

"On your office computer, if you have any passwords, change them. Anything in electronic data files of a personal nature, get it out."

"Okay."

"Don't just remove it. Make sure you erase it, so it's unrecoverable."

"Okay."

"It's not a bad idea to do the same thing at home. Your drawers and files and computer."

"Okay." He was thinking: at home? Would they really break into his home?

"If you have any sensitive materials that you want to store, bring them to Richard here," she said, pointing to the young lawyer. "He'll have them taken to a safe-deposit box where they'll be kept for you. Don't tell me. I don't want to know anything about it."

"Okay."

"Now. Let's discuss the telephone. From now

on, if you have any sensitive calls to make, don't use your office phone, your cellular phone, or your phone at home. Use a pay phone, and don't put it on a charge card, even your personal charge card. Get a roll of quarters and use them instead."

"You really think this is necessary?"

"I know it is necessary. Now. Is there anything in your past conduct with this company which might be said to be out of order?" She was peering at him over her glasses.

He shrugged. "I don't think so."

"Anything at all? Did you overstate your qualifications on your original job application? Did you abruptly terminate any employee? Have you had any kind of inquiry about your behavior or decisions? Were you ever the subject of an internal company investigation? And even if you weren't, did you ever, to your knowledge, do anything improper, however small or apparently minor?"

"Jesus," he said. "It's been twelve years."

"While you are cleaning out, think about it. I need to know anything that the company might drag up about you. Because if they can, they will."

"Okay."

"And one other point. I gather from what you've told me that nobody at your company is entirely clear why Johnson has enjoyed such a rapid rise among the executives."

"That's right."

"Find out."

"It won't be easy," Sanders said. "Everybody's talking about it, and nobody seems to know."

"But for everybody else," Fernandez said, "it's just gossip. For you, it's vital. We need to know where her connections are and why they exist. If we know that, we have a chance of pulling this thing off. But if we don't, Mr. Sanders, they're probably going to tear us apart."

He was back at DigiCom at six. Cindy was cleaning up her desk and was about to leave.

"Any calls?" he said, as he went into his office.

"Just one," she said. Her voice was tight.

"Who was that?"

"John Levin. He said it was important." Levin was an executive with a hard drive supplier. Whatever Levin wanted, it could wait.

Sanders looked at Cindy. She seemed tense, almost on the verge of tears.

"Something wrong?"

"No. Just a long day." A shrug: elaborate indifference.

"Anything I should know about?"

"No. It's been quiet. You didn't have any other calls." She hesitated. "Tom, I just want you to know, I don't believe what they are saying."

"What are they saying?" he asked.

"About Meredith Johnson."

"What about her?"

"That you sexually harassed her."

She blurted it out, and then waited. Watching him, her eyes moving across his face. He could see her uncertainty. Sanders felt uneasy in turn that this woman he had worked alongside for so many years would now be so openly unsure of him.

He said firmly, "It's not true, Cindy."

"Okay. I didn't think it was. It's just that everybody is—"

"There's no truth to it at all."

"Okay. Good." She nodded, put the call book in the desk drawer. She seemed eager to leave. "Did you need me to stay?"

"No."

"Good night, Tom."

"Good night, Cindy."

He went into his office and closed the door behind him. He sat behind his desk and looked at it a moment. Nothing seemed to have been touched. He flicked on his monitor, and began going through the drawers, rummaging through, trying to decide what to take out. He glanced up at the monitor, and saw that his e-mail icon was blinking. Idly, he clicked it on.

NUMBER OF PERSONAL MESSAGES: 3. DO YOU WANT TO READ THEM NOW?

He pressed the key. A moment later, the first message came up.

SEALED TWINKLE DRIVES ARE ON THEIR WAY TO YOU TODAY DHL. YOU SHOULD HAVE THEM TO-

MORROW. HOPE YOU FIND SOMETHING . . . JAFAR
IS STILL SEVERELY ILL. THEY SAY HE MAY DIE.

ARTHUR KAHN

He pressed the key, and another message came up.

THE WEENIES ARE STILL SWARMING DOWN HERE.
ANY NEWS YET?

EDDIE

Sanders couldn't worry about Eddie now. He pushed the key, and the third message came up.

I GUESS YOU HAVEN'T BEEN READING BACK ISSUES
OF COMLINE. STARTING FOUR YEARS AGO.

AFRIEND

Sanders stared at the screen. ComLine was DigiCom's in-house newsletter—an eight-page monthly, filled with chatty accounts of hirings and promotions and babies born. The summer schedule for the softball team, things like that. Sanders never paid any attention to it and couldn't imagine why he should now.

And who was "Afriend"?

He clicked the REPLY button on the screen.

CAN'T REPLY - SENDER ADDRESS NOT AVAILABLE

He clicked the SENDER INFO button. It should give him the name and address of the person sending the e-mail message. But instead he saw dense rows of type:

FROM UU5.PSI.COM!UWA.PCM.COM.EDU!CHARON
TUE JUN 16 04:43:31 REMOTE FROM DCCSYS
RECEIVED: FROM UUPSI5 BY DCCSYS.DCC.COM ID
AA02599; TUE, 16 JUN 4:42:19 PST
RECEIVED: FROM UWA.PCM.COM.EDU BY UU5.PSI.-
COM (5.65B/4.0.071791-PSI/PSINET)
ID AA28153; TUE, 16 JUN 04:24:58 -0500
RECEIVED: FROM RIVERSTYX.PCM.COM.EDU BY
UWA.PCM.COM.EDU (4.1/SMI-4.1)
ID AA15969; TUE, 16 JUN 04:24:56 PST
RECEIVED: BY   RIVERSTYX.PCM.COM.EDU
(920330.SGI/5.6)
ID AA00448; TUE, 16 JUN 04:24:56 -0500
DATE: TUE, 16 JUN 04:24:56 -0500
FROM: CHARON@UWA.PCM.COM.EDU (AFRIEND)
MESSAGE-ID: < 9212220924.AA90448@RIVER-
STYX.PCM.COM.EDU >
TO: TSANDERS@DCC.COM

Sanders stared. The message hadn't come to him from inside the company at all. He was looking at an Internet routing. Internet was the vast worldwide computer network connecting universities, corporations, government agencies, and private users. Sanders wasn't knowledgeable about the Internet, but it appeared that the message from "Afriend," network name CHARON, had originated from UWA.PCM.COM.EDU, wherever that was. Apparently some kind of educational institution. He pushed the PRINT SCREEN button, and made a mental note to turn this one over to Bosak. He needed to talk to Bosak anyway.

He went down the hall and got the sheet as it came out of the printer. Then he went back to his office and stared at the screen. He decided to try a reply to this person.

FROM: TSANDERS@DCC.COM
TO: CHARON@UWA.PCM.COM.EDU

ANY HELP GREATLY APPRECIATED.

SANDERS

He pushed the SEND button. Then he deleted both the original message and his own reply.

SORRY, YOU CANNOT DELETE THIS MAIL.

Sometimes e-mail was protected with a flag that prevented it from being deleted.
He typed: UNPROTECT MAIL.

THE MAIL IS UNPROTECTED.

He typed: DELETE MAIL.

SORRY, YOU CANNOT DELETE THIS MAIL.

What the hell is this? he thought. The system must be hanging up. Maybe it had been stymied by the Internet address. He decided to delete the message from the system at the control level.

He typed: SYSTEM.

WHAT LEVEL?

He typed: SYSOP.

SORRY, YOUR PRIVILEGES DO NOT INCLUDE SYSOP CONTROL.

"Christ," he said. They'd gone in and taken away his privileges. He couldn't believe it.

He typed: SHOW PRIVILEGES.

SANDERS, THOMAS L.
PRIOR USER LEVEL: 5 (SYSOP)
USER LEVEL CHANGE: TUE JUNE 16 4:50 PM PST
CURRENT USER LEVEL: 0 (ENTRY)
NO FURTHER MODIFICATIONS

There it was: they had locked him out of the system. User level zero was the level that assistants in the company were given.

Sanders slumped back in the chair. He felt as if he had been fired. For the first time, he began to realize what this was going to be like.

Clearly, there was no time to waste. He opened his desk drawer, and saw at once that the pens and pencils were neatly arranged. Someone had already been there. He pulled open the file drawer below. Only a half-dozen files were there; the others were all missing.

They had already gone through his desk.

Quickly, he got up and went out to the big filing cabinets behind Cindy's desk. These cabinets were locked, but he knew Cindy kept the key in her desk. He found the key, and unlocked the current year's files.

The cabinet was empty. There were no files there at all. They had taken everything.

He opened the cabinet for the previous year: empty.

The year before: empty.

All the others: empty.

Jesus, he thought. No wonder Cindy had been so cool. They must have had a gang of workmen up there with trolleys, cleaning everything out during the afternoon.

Sanders locked the cabinets again, replaced the key in Cindy's desk, and headed downstairs.

The press office was on the third floor. It was deserted now except for a single assistant, who was closing up. "Oh. Mr. Sanders. I was just getting ready to leave."

"You don't have to stay. I just wanted to check some things. Where do you keep the back issues of ComLine?"

"They're all on that shelf over there." She pointed to a row of stacked issues. "Was there anything in particular?"

"No. You go ahead home."

The assistant seemed reluctant, but she picked up her purse and headed out the door. Sanders went to the shelf. The issues were arranged in six-month stacks. Just to be safe, he started ten stacks back—five years ago.

He began flipping through the pages, scanning the endless details of game scores and press releases on production figures. After a few minutes, he found it hard to pay attention. And of course he didn't know what he was looking for, although he assumed it was something about Meredith Johnson.

He went through two stacks before he found the first article.

NEW MARKETING ASSISTANT NAMED

Cupertino, May 10: DigiCom President Bob Garvin today announced the appointment of Meredith Johnson as Assistant Director of Marketing and Promotion for Telecommunications. She will report to Howard Gottfried in M and P. Ms. Johnson, 30, came to us from her position as Vice President for Marketing at Conrad Computer Systems of Sunnyvale. Before that, she was a senior administrative assistant at the Novell Network Division in Mountain View.

Ms. Johnson, who has degrees from Vassar College and Stanford Business School, was recently married to Gary Henley, a marketing executive at CoStar. Congratulations! As a new arrival to DigiCom, Ms. Johnson . . .

He skipped the rest of the article; it was all PR fluff. The accompanying photo was standard B-school graduate: against a gray background with light coming from behind one shoulder, it showed a young woman with shoulder-length hair in a pageboy style, a direct businesslike stare just shy of harsh, and a firm mouth. But she looked considerably younger than she did now.

Sanders continued to thumb through the issues. He glanced at his watch. It was almost seven, and he wanted to call Bosak. He came to the end of the year, and the pages were nothing but Christmas stuff. A picture of Garvin and his family ("Merry Christmas from the Boss! Ho Ho Ho!") caught his attention because it showed Bob with his former wife, along with his three college-age kids, standing around a big tree.

Had Garvin been going out with Emily yet? Nobody ever knew. Garvin was cagey. You never knew what he was up to.

Sanders went to the next stack, for the following year. January sales predictions. ("Let's get out and make it happen!") Opening of the Austin plant to manufacture cellular phones; a photo of Garvin in harsh sunlight, cutting the ribbon. A profile of Mary Anne Hunter that began, "Spunky, athletic Mary Anne Hunter knows what she wants out of life . . ." They had called her "Spunky" for weeks afterward, until she begged them to give it up.

Sanders flipped pages. Contract with the Irish government to break ground in Cork. Second-quarter sales figures. Basketball team scores against Aldus. Then a black box:

JENNIFER GARVIN

Jennifer Garvin, a third-year student at Boalt Hall School of Law in Berkeley, died on March 5 in an automobile accident in San Francisco. She was twenty-four years old. Jennifer had been accepted to the firm of Harley, Wayne and Myers following her graduation. A memorial service was held at the Presbyterian Church of Palo Alto for friends of the family and her many classmates. Those wishing to make memorial donations should send contributions to Mothers Against Drunk Drivers. All of us at Digital Communications extend our deepest sympathy to the Garvin family.

Sanders remembered that time as difficult for everyone. Garvin was snappish and withdrawn, drinking too much, and frequently absent from work. Not long afterward, his marital difficulties became public; within two years, he was divorced, and soon after that he married Emily Chen, a young executive in her twenties. But there were other changes, too. Everyone agreed: Garvin was no longer the same boss after the death of his daughter.

Garvin had always been a scrapper, but now he became protective, less ruthless. Some said that Garvin was stopping to smell the roses, but that wasn't it at all. He was newly aware of the arbitrariness of life, and it led him to control things, in a way that hadn't been true before. Garvin had always been Mr. Evolution: put it on the shore and see if it eats or dies. It made him a heartless administrator but a remarkably fair boss. If you did a good job, you were recognized. If you couldn't cut it, you were gone. Everybody understood the rules. But after Jennifer died, all that changed. Now he had overt favorites among staff and programs, and he nurtured those favorites and neglected others, despite the evidence in front of his face. More and more, he made business decisions arbitrarily. Garvin wanted events to turn out the way he intended them to. It gave him a new kind of fervor, a new sense of what the company should be. But it was also a more difficult place to work. A more political place.

It was a trend that Sanders had ignored. He continued to act as if he still worked at the old DigiCom—the company where all that mattered were results. But clearly, that company was gone.

Sanders continued thumbing through the magazines. Articles about early negotiations for a plant in Malaysia. A photo of Phil Blackburn in Ireland, signing an agreement with the city of Cork. New production figures for the Austin plant. Start of production of the A22 cellular model. Births and deaths and promotions. More DigiCom baseball scores.

JOHNSON TO TAKE OPERATIONS POST

Cupertino, October 20: Meredith Johnson has been named new Assistant Manager for Division Operations in Cupertino, replacing the very popular Harry Warner, who retired after fifteen years of service. The shift to Ops Manager takes Johnson out of marketing, where she has been very effective for the last year, since joining the company. In her new position, she will work closely with Bob Garvin on international operations for DigiCom.

But it was the accompanying picture that caught Sanders's attention. Once again, it was a formal head shot, but Johnson now looked completely different. Her hair was light blond. Gone was the neat business-school pageboy. She wore her hair short, in a curly, informal style. She was wearing much less makeup and smiling cheerfully. Overall, the effect was to make her appear much more youthful, open, innocent.

Sanders frowned. Quickly, he flipped back through the issues he had already looked at. Then he went back to the previous stack, with its year-end Christmas pictures: "Merry Christmas from the Boss! Ho Ho Ho!"

He looked at the family portrait. Garvin standing behind his three children, two sons and a daughter. That must be Jennifer. His wife, Harriet, stood to one side. In the picture, Garvin was smiling, his hand resting lightly on his daughter's shoulder, and she was tall and athletic-looking, with short, light blond, curly hair.

"I'll be damned," he said aloud.

He thumbed back quickly to the first article, to look at the original picture of Johnson. He compared it to the later one. There was no doubt about what she had done. He read the rest of the first article:

As a new arrival to DigiCom, Ms. Johnson brings her considerable business acumen, her sparkling humor, and her sizzling softball pitch. She's a major addition to the DigiCom team! Welcome, Meredith!

Her admiring friends are never surprised to learn that Meredith was once a finalist in the Miss Teen Connecticut contest. In her student days at Vassar, Meredith was a valued member of both the tennis team and the debating society. A member of Phi Beta Kappa, she took her major in psychology, with a minor in abnormal psych. Hope you won't be needing that around here, Meredith! At Stanford, she obtained her MBA with honors, graduating near the top of her class. Meredith told us, "I am delighted to join DigiCom and I look forward to an exciting career with this forward-looking company." We couldn't have said it better, Ms. Johnson!

"No shit," Sanders said. He had known almost none of this. From the start, Meredith had been based in Cupertino; Sanders never saw her. The one time he had run into her was soon after her arrival, before she changed her hair. Her hair— and what else?

He looked carefully at the two pictures. Something else was subtly different. Had she had plastic surgery? It was impossible to know. But her appearance was definitely changed between the two portraits.

He moved through the remaining issues of the magazine quickly now, convinced that he had learned what there was to know. Now he skimmed only the headlines:

**GARVIN SENDS JOHNSON TO TEXAS
FOR AUSTIN PLANT OVERSIGHT**

**JOHNSON WILL HEAD NEW
OPERATIONS REVIEW UNIT**

**JOHNSON NAMED OPERATIONS VEEP
TO WORK DIRECTLY UNDER GARVIN**

**JOHNSON: TRIUMPH IN MALAYSIA
LABOR CONFLICT NOW RESOLVED**

**MEREDITH JOHNSON OUR RISING STAR
A SUPERB MANAGER; HER SKILL IN
TECHNICAL AREAS VERY STRONG**

This final headline ran above a lengthy profile of Johnson, well placed on the second page of the magazine. It had appeared in ComLine only two issues ago. Seeing it now, Sanders realized that the article was intended for internal consumption— softening up the beachhead before the June landing. This article was a trial balloon that Cupertino had floated, to see if Meredith would be acceptable to run the technical divisions in Seattle. The only trouble was, Sanders never saw it. And nobody had ever mentioned it to him.

The article stressed the technical savvy that Johnson had acquired during her years with the company. She was quoted as saying, "I began my career working in technical areas, back with Novell. The technical fields have always been my first love; I'd love to go back to it. After all, strong technical innovation lies at the heart of a forward-looking company like DigiCom. Any good manager here must be able to run the technical divisions."

There it was.

He looked at the date: May 2. Published six weeks ago. Which meant that the article had been written at least two weeks before that.

As Mark Lewyn had suspected, Meredith Johnson knew she was going to be the head of the Advanced Products Division at least two months ago. Which meant, in turn, that Sanders had never been under consideration to become division head. He had never had a chance.

It was a done deal.

Months ago.

Sanders swore, took the articles over to the xerox machine and copied them, then put the stacks back on the shelf, and left the press office.

He got on the elevator. Mark Lewyn was there. Sanders said, "Hi, Mark." Lewyn didn't answer. Sanders pushed the button for the ground floor.

The doors closed.

"I just hope you know what the fuck you're doing," Lewyn said angrily.

"I think I do."

"Because you could fuck this thing up for everybody. You know that?"

"Fuck what up?"

"Just because you got your ass in the sling, it's not our problem."

"Nobody said it was."

"I don't know what's the matter with you," Lewyn said. "You're late for work, you don't call me when you say you will . . . What is it, trouble at home? More shit with Susan?"

"This has nothing to do with Susan."

"Yeah? I think it does. You've been late two days running and even when you're here, you walk around like you're dreaming. You're in fucking dreamland, Tom. I mean, what the hell were you doing, going to Meredith's office at night, anyway?"

"She asked me to come to her office. She's the boss. You're saying I shouldn't have gone?"

Lewyn shook his head in disgust. "This innocent act is a lot of crap. Don't you take any responsibility for anything?"

"What—"

"Look, Tom, everybody in the company knows that Meredith is a shark. Meredith Manmuncher, they call her. The Great White. Everybody knows she's protected by Garvin, that she can do what she wants. And what she wants is to play grabass with cute guys who show up in her office at the end of the day. She has a couple of glasses of wine, she gets a little flushed, and she wants service. A delivery boy, a trainee, a young account guy. Whatever. And nobody can say a word because Garvin thinks she walks on water. So, how come everybody else in the company knows it but you?"

Sanders was stunned. He did not know how to answer. He stared at Lewyn, who stood very close to him, his body hunched, hands in his pockets. He could feel Lewyn's breath on his face. But he could hardly hear Lewyn's words. It was as if they came to him from a great distance.

"Hey, Tom. You walk the same halls, you breathe the same air as the rest of us. You know who's doing what. You go marching up there to her office . . . and you know damned well what's coming. Meredith's done everything but announce to the world that she wants to suck your dick. All day long, she's touching your arm, giving you those *meaningful* little looks and squeezes. Oh, *Tom.* So *nice* to see you again. And now you tell me you didn't know what was coming in that office? *Fuck* you, Tom. You're an asshole."

The elevator doors opened. Before them, the ground-floor lobby was deserted, growing dark in the fading light of the June evening. A soft rain fell outside. Lewyn started toward the exit, then turned back. His voice echoed in the lobby.

"You realize," he said, "that you're acting like one of those women in all this. The way they always go, 'Who, me? I never intended that.' The way they go, 'Oh, it's not *my* responsibility. I never thought if I got drunk and kissed him and went to his room and lay down on his bed that he'd fuck me. Oh dear me no.' It's bullshit, Tom. Irresponsible bullshit. And you better think about what I'm saying, because there's a lot of us who have worked every bit as hard as you have in this company, and we don't want to see you screw up this merger and this spin-off for the rest of us. You want to pretend you can't tell when a woman's coming on to you, that's fine. You want to screw up your own life, it's your decision. But you screw up mine, and I'm going to fucking put you away."

Lewyn stalked off. The elevator doors started to close. Sanders stuck his hand out; the doors closed on his fingers. He jerked his hand, and the doors opened again. He hurried out into the lobby after Lewyn.

He grabbed Lewyn on the shoulder. "Mark, wait, listen—"

"I got nothing to say to you. I got kids, I got responsibilities. You're an asshole."

Lewyn shrugged Sanders's arm off, pushed open the door, and walked out. He strode quickly away, down the street.

As the glass doors closed, Sanders saw a flash of blond in the moving reflection. He turned.

"I thought that was a little unfair," Meredith Johnson said. She was standing about twenty feet behind him, near the elevators. She was wearing gym clothes—navy tights, and a sweatshirt—and she carried a gym bag in her hand. She looked beautiful, overtly sexual in a certain way. Sanders felt tense: there was no one else in the lobby. They were alone.

"Yes," Sanders said. "I thought it was unfair."

"I meant, to women," Meredith said. She swung the gym bag over her shoulder, the movement raising her sweatshirt and exposing her bare abdomen above her tights. She shook her head and pushed her hair back from her face. She paused a moment, and then she began to speak. "I want to tell you I'm sorry about all this," she said. She moved toward him in a steady, confident way, almost stalking. Her voice was low. "I never wanted any of this, Tom." She came a little closer, approaching slowly, as if he were an animal that might be frightened away. "I have only the warmest feelings for you." Still closer. "Only the warmest." Closer. "I can't help it, Tom, if I still want you." Closer. "If I did anything to offend you, I apologize." She was very close now, her body almost touching his, her breasts inches from his arm. "I'm truly sorry, Tom," she said softly. She seemed filled with emotion, her breasts rising and falling, her eyes moist and pleading as she looked up at him. "Can you forgive me? Please? You know how I feel about you."

He felt all the old sensations, the old stirrings. He clenched his jaw. "Meredith. The past is past. Cut it out, will you?"

She immediately changed her tone and gestured to the street. "Listen, I have a car here. Can I drop you somewhere?"

"No, thanks."

"It's raining. I thought you might want a lift."

"I don't think it's a good idea."

"Only because it's raining."

"This is Seattle," he said. "It rains all the time here."

She shrugged, walked to the door, and leaned her weight against it, thrusting out her hip. Then she looked back at him and smiled. "Remind me never to wear tights around you. It's embarrassing: you make me wet."

Then she turned away, pushed through the

door, and walked quickly to the waiting car, getting in the back. She closed the door, looked back at him, and waved cheerfully. The car drove off.

Sanders unclenched his hands. He took a deep breath and let it out slowly. His whole body was tense. He waited until the car was gone, then went outside. He felt the rain on his face, the cool evening breeze.

He hailed a taxi. "The Four Seasons Hotel," he said to the driver.

Riding in the taxi, Sanders stared out the window, breathing deeply. He felt as though he couldn't get his breath. He had been badly unnerved by the meeting with Meredith. Especially coming so close after his conversation with Lewyn.

Sanders was distressed by what Lewyn had said, but you could never take Mark too seriously. Lewyn was an artistic hothead who handled his creative tensions by getting angry. He was angry about something most of the time. Lewyn liked being angry. Sanders had known him a long time. Personally, he had never understood how Adele, Mark's wife, put up with it. Adele was one of those wonderfully calm, almost phlegmatic women who could talk on the phone while her two kids crawled all over her, tugging at her, asking her questions. In a similar fashion, Adele just let Lewyn rage while she went on about her business. In fact, everyone just let Lewyn rage, because everyone knew that, in the end, it didn't mean anything.

Yet, it was also true that Lewyn had a kind of instinct for public perceptions and trends. That was the secret of his success as a designer. Lewyn would say, "Pastel colors," and everybody would groan and say that the new design colors looked like hell. But two years later, when the products were coming off the line, pastel colors would be just what everybody wanted. So Sanders was forced to admit that what Lewyn had said about him, others would soon be saying. Lewyn had said the company line: that Sanders was screwing up the chances for everybody else.

Well, screw them, he thought.

As for Meredith—he had had the distinct feeling that she had been toying with him in the lobby. Teasing him, playing with him. He could not understand why she was so confident. Sanders was making a very serious allegation against her. Yet she behaved as if there was no threat at all. She had a kind of imperviousness, an indifference, that made him deeply uneasy. It could only mean she knew that she had Garvin's backing.

The taxi pulled into the turnaround of the hotel. He saw Meredith's car up ahead. She was talking to the driver. She looked back and saw him.

There was nothing to do but get out and walk toward the entrance.

"Are you following me?" she said, smiling.

"No."

"Sure?"

"Yes, Meredith. I'm sure."

They went up the escalator from the street to

the lobby. He stood behind her on the escalator. She looked back at him. "I wish you were."

"Yeah. Well, I'm not."

"It would have been nice," she said. She smiled invitingly.

He didn't know what to say; he just shook his head. They rode the rest of the way in silence until they came to the high ornate lobby. She said, "I'm in room 423. Come and see me anytime." She headed toward the elevators.

He waited until she was gone, then crossed the lobby and turned left to the dining room. Standing at the entrance, he saw Dorfman at a corner table, eating dinner with Garvin and Stephanie Kaplan. Max was holding forth, gesturing sharply as he spoke. Garvin and Kaplan both leaned forward, listening. Sanders was reminded that Dorfman had once been a director of the company—according to the stories, a very powerful director. It was Dorfman who had persuaded Garvin to expand beyond modems into cellular telephony and wireless communications, back in the days when nobody could see any link between computers and telephones. The link was obvious now but obscure in the early 1980s, when Dorfman had said, "Your business is not hardware. Your business is communications. Your business is access to information."

Dorfman had shaped company personnel as well. Supposedly, Kaplan owed her position to his glowing endorsement. Sanders had come to Seattle on Dorfman's recommendation. Mark Lewyn had been hired because of Dorfman. And any number of vice presidents had vanished over the years because Dorfman found them lacking in vision or stamina. He was a powerful ally or a lethal opponent.

And his position at the time of the merger was equally strong. Although Dorfman had resigned as a director years before, he still owned a good deal of DigiCom stock. He still had Garvin's ear. And he still had the contacts and prestige within the business and financial community that made a merger like this much simpler. If Dorfman approved the terms of the merger, his admirers at Goldman, Sachs and at First Boston would raise the money easily. But if Dorfman was dissatisfied, if he hinted that the merger of the two companies did not make sense, then the acquisition might unravel. Everyone knew it. Everyone understood very well the power he wielded—especially Dorfman himself.

Sanders hung back at the entrance to the restaurant, reluctant to come forward. After a while, Max glanced up and saw him. Still talking, he shook his head fractionally: *no*. Then, as he continued to talk, he made a subtle motion with his hand, tapping his watch. Sanders nodded, and went back into the lobby and sat down. He had the stack of ComLine photocopies on his lap. He browsed through them, studying again the way Meredith had changed her appearance.

A few minutes later, Dorfman rolled out in his wheelchair. "So, Thomas. I am glad you are not bored with your life."

"What does that mean?"

Dorfman laughed and gestured to the dining room. "They're talking of nothing else in there. The only topic this evening is you and Meredith. Everyone is so excited. So *worried.*"

"Including Bob?"

"Yes, of course. Including Bob." He wheeled closer to Sanders. "I cannot really speak to you now. Was there something in particular?"

"I think you ought to look at this," Sanders said, handing Dorfman the photocopies. He was thinking that Dorfman could take these pictures to Garvin. Dorfman could make Garvin understand what was really going on.

Dorfman examined them in silence a moment. "Such a lovely woman," he said. "So beautiful . . ."

"Look at the differences, Max. Look at what she did to herself."

Dorfman shrugged. "She changed her hair. Very flattering. So?"

"I think she had plastic surgery as well."

"It wouldn't surprise me," Dorfman said. "So many women do, these days. It is like brushing their teeth, to them."

"It gives me the creeps."

"Why?" Dorfman said.

"Because it's underhanded, that's why."

"What's underhanded?" Dorfman said, shrugging. "She is resourceful. Good for her."

"I'll bet Garvin has no idea what she's doing to him," Sanders said.

Dorfman shook his head. "I'm not concerned about Garvin," he said. "I'm concerned about you, Thomas, and this outrage of yours—hmm?"

"I'll tell you why I'm outraged," Sanders said. "Because this is the kind of sneaky shit that a woman can pull but a man can't. She changes her appearance, she dresses and acts like Garvin's daughter, and that gives her an advantage. Because I sure as hell can't act like his daughter."

Dorfman sighed, shaking his head. "Thomas. Thomas."

"Well, I can't. Can I?"

"Are you enjoying this? You seem to be enjoying this outrage."

"I'm not."

"Then give it up," Dorfman said. He turned his wheelchair to face Sanders. "Stop talking this nonsense, and face what is true. Young people in organizations advance by alliances with powerful, senior people. True?"

"Yes."

"And it is always so. At one time, the alliance was formal—an apprentice and master, or a pupil and tutor. It was arranged, yes? But today, it is not formal. Today, we speak of mentors. Young people in business have mentors. True?"

"Okay . . ."

"So. How do young people attach themselves to a mentor? What is the process? First, by being agreeable, by being helpful to the senior person, doing jobs that need to be done. Second, by being attractive to the older person—imitating their attitudes and tastes. Third, by advocacy—adopting their agenda within the company."

"That's all fine," Sanders said. "What does it have to do with plastic surgery?"

"Do you remember when you joined DigiCom in Cupertino?"

"Yes, I remember."

"You came over from DEC. In 1980?"

"Yes."

"At DEC, you wore a coat and tie every day. But when you joined DigiCom, you saw that Garvin wore jeans. And soon, you wore jeans, too."

"Sure. That was the style of the company."

"Garvin liked the Giants. You began to go to games in Candlestick Park."

"He was the boss, for Christ's sake."

"And Garvin liked golf. So you took up golf, even though you hated it. I remember you complained to me about how much you hated it. Chasing the stupid little white ball."

"Listen. I didn't have plastic surgery to make myself look like his kid."

"*Because you didn't have to*, Thomas," Dorfman said. He threw up his hands in exasperation. "Can you not see this point? Garvin liked brash, aggressive young men who drank beer, who swore, who chased women. And you did all those things in those days."

"I was young. That's what young men do."

"No, Thomas. That's what Garvin liked young men to do." Dorfman shook his head. "So much of this is unconscious. Rapport is unconscious, Thomas. But the task of building rapport is different, depending on whether you are the same sex as that person, or not. If your mentor is a man, you may act like his son, or brother, or father. Or you may act like that man when he was younger—you may remind him of himself. True? Yes, you see that. Good.

"But if you are a woman, everything is different. Now you must be your mentor's daughter, or lover, or wife. Or perhaps sister. In any case, very different."

Sanders frowned.

"I see this often, now that men are starting to work for women. Many times men cannot structure the relationship because they do not know how to act as the subordinate to a woman. Not with comfort. But in other cases, men slip easily into a role with a woman. They are the dutiful son, or the substitute lover or husband. And if they do it well, the women in the organization become angry, because they feel that they cannot compete as son or lover or husband to the boss. So they feel that the man has an advantage."

Sanders was silent.

"Do you understand?" Dorfman said.

"You're saying it happens both ways."

"Yes, Thomas. It is inevitable. It is the process."

"Come on, Max. There's nothing inevitable about it. When Garvin's daughter died, it was a personal tragedy. He was upset, and Meredith took advantage of—"

"*Stop,*" Dorfman said, annoyed. "Now you want to change human nature? There are always tragedies. And people always take advantage. This is nothing new. Meredith is intelligent. It is delightful to see such an intelligent, resourceful woman who is also beautiful. She is a gift from God. She is delightful. This is your trouble, Thomas. And it has been a long time coming."

"What does that—"

"And instead of dealing with your trouble, you waste your time with these . . . *trivialities.*" He handed back the pictures. "These are not important, Thomas."

"Max, will you—"

"You were never a good corporate player, Thomas. It was not your strength. Your strength was that you could take a technical problem and grind it down, push the technicians, encourage them and bully them, and finally get it solved. You could make it work. Is that not so?"

Sanders nodded.

"But now you abandon your strengths for a game that does not suit you."

"Meaning what?"

"You think that by threatening a lawsuit, you put pressure on her and on the company. In fact, you played into her hands. You have let her define the game, Thomas."

"I had to do something. She broke the law."

"She broke the law," Dorfman mimicked him, with a sarcastic whine. "Oh me, oh my. And you are so defenseless. I am filled with sorrow for your plight."

"It's not easy. She's well connected. She has strong supporters."

"Is that so? Every executive with strong supporters has also strong detractors. And Meredith has her share of detractors."

"I tell you, Max," Sanders said, "she's dangerous. She's one of those MBA image people, focused on image, everything image, never substance."

"Yes," Dorfman said, nodding approvingly. "Like so many young executives today. Very skilled with images. Very interested in manipulating that reality. A fascinating trend."

"I don't think she's competent to run this division."

"And what if she is not?" Dorfman snapped. "What difference does it make to you? If she's incompetent, Garvin will eventually acknowledge it and replace her. But by then, you will be long gone. Because you will lose this game with her, Thomas. She is better at politics than you. She always was."

Sanders nodded. "She's ruthless."

"Ruthless, schmoothless. She is *skilled*. She has an instinct. You lack it. You will lose everything if you persist this way. And you will deserve the fate that befalls you because you have behaved like a fool."

Sanders was silent. "What do you recommend I do?"

"Ah. So now you want advice?"

"Yes."

"Really?" He smiled. "I doubt it."

"Yes, Max. I do."

"All right. Here is my advice. Go back, apologize to Meredith, apologize to Garvin, and resume your job."

"I can't."

"Then you don't want advice."

"I can't do that, Max."

"Too much pride?"

"No, but—"

"You are infatuated with the anger. How dare

this woman act this way. She has broken the law, she must be brought to justice. She is dangerous, she must be stopped. You are filled with *delicious*, righteous indignation. True?"

"Oh, hell, Max. I just can't do it, that's all."

"Of course you can do it. You mean you *won't*."

"All right. I won't."

Dorfman shrugged. "Then what do you want from me? You come to ask my advice in order not to take it? This is nothing special." He grinned. "I have a lot of other advice you won't take, either."

"Like what?"

"What do you care, since you won't take it?"

"Come on, Max."

"I'm serious. You won't take it. We are wasting our time here. Go away."

"Just tell me, will you?"

Dorfman sighed. "Only because I remember you from the days when you had sense. First point. Are you listening?"

"Yes, Max. I am."

"First point: you know everything you need to know about Meredith Johnson. So forget her now. She is not your concern."

"What does that mean?"

"Don't interrupt. Second point. Play your own game, not hers."

"Meaning what?"

"Meaning, solve the problem."

"Solve what problem? The lawsuit?"

Dorfman snorted and threw up his hands. "You are impossible. I am wasting my time."

"You mean drop the lawsuit?"

"Can you understand English? *Solve the problem*. Do what you do well. Do your job. Now go away."

"But Max—"

"Oh, I can't do anything for you," Dorfman said. "It's your life. You have your own mistakes to make. And I must return to my guests. But try to pay attention, Thomas. Do not sleep through this. And remember, all human behavior has a reason. All behavior is solving a problem. Even *your* behavior, Thomas."

And he spun in his wheelchair and went back to the dining room.

Fucking Max, he thought, walking down Third Street in the damp evening. It was infuriating, the way Max would never just say what he meant.

This is your trouble, Thomas. And it has been a long time coming.

What the hell was that supposed to mean?

Fucking Max. Infuriating and frustrating and exhausting, too. That was what Sanders remembered most about the sessions he used to have, when Max was on the DigiCom board. Sanders would come away exhausted. In those days, back in Cupertino, the junior execs had called Dorfman "The Riddler."

All human behavior is solving a problem. Even your behavior, Thomas.

Sanders shook his head. It made no sense at all. Meanwhile, he had things to do. At the end of the street, he stepped into a phone booth and dialed Gary Bosak's number. It was eight o'clock. Bosak would be home, just getting out of bed and having coffee, starting his working day. Right now, he would be yawning in front of a half-dozen modems and computer screens as he began to dial into all sorts of databases.

The phone rang, and a machine said, "You have reached NE Professional Services. Leave a message." And a beep.

"Gary, this is Tom Sanders. I know you're there, pick up."

A click, and then Bosak said, "Hey. The last person I thought I'd hear from. Where're you calling from?"

"Pay phone."

"Good. How's it going with you, Tom?"

"Gary, I need some things done. Some data looked up."

"Uh . . . Are we talking things for the company, or private things?"

"Private."

"Uh . . . Tom. I'm pretty busy these days. Can we talk about this next week?"

"That's too late."

"But the thing is, I'm pretty busy now."

"Gary, what is this?"

"Tom, come on. You know what this is."

"I need help, Gary."

"Hey. And I'd love to help you. But I just got a call from Blackburn who told me that if I had anything to do with you, anything at all, I could expect the FBI going through my apartment at six a.m. tomorrow morning."

"Christ. When was this?"

"About two hours ago."

Two hours ago. Blackburn was way ahead of him. "Gary . . ."

"Hey. You know I always liked you, Tom. But not this time. Okay? I got to go."

Click.

F rankly, none of this surprises me," Fernandez said, pushing aside a paper plate. She and Sanders had been eating sandwiches in her office. It was nine p.m., and the offices around them were dark, but her phone was still ringing, interrupting them frequently. Outside, it had begun to rain again. Thunder rumbled, and Sanders saw flashes of summer lightning through the windows.

Sitting in the deserted law offices, Sanders had the feeling that he was all alone in the world, with nobody but Fernandez and the encroaching darkness. Things were happening quickly; this person he had never met before today was fast becoming a kind of lifeline for him. He found himself hanging on every word she said.

"Before we go on, I want to emphasize one thing," Fernandez said. "You were right not to get in the car with Johnson. You are not to be alone with her ever again. Not even for a few moments. Not ever, under any circumstances. Is that clear?"

"Yes."

"If you do, it will destroy your case."

"I won't."

"All right," she said. "Now. I had a long talk

with Blackburn. As you guessed, he's under tremendous pressure to get this matter resolved. I tried to move the mediation session to the afternoon. He implied that the company was ready to deal and wanted to get started right away. He's concerned about how long the negotiations will take. So we'll start at nine tomorrow."

"Okay."

"Herb and Alan have been making progress. I think they'll be able to help us tomorrow. And these articles about Johnson may be useful, too," she said, glancing at the photocopies of the Com-Line pieces.

"Why? Dorfman says they're irrelevant."

"Yes, but they document her history in the company, and that gives us leads. It's something to work on. So is this e-mail from your friend." She frowned at the sheet of printout. "This is an Internet address."

"Yes," he said, surprised that she knew.

"We do a lot of work with high-technology companies. I'll have somebody check it out." She put it aside. "Now let's review where we are. You couldn't clean out your desk because they were already there."

"Right."

"And you would have cleaned out your computer files, but you've been shut out of the system."

"Yes."

"Which means that you can't change any-thing."

"That's right. I can't do anything. It's like I'm an assistant."

She said, "Were you going to change any files?"

He hesitated. "No. But I would have, you know, looked around."

"Nothing in particular you were aware of?"

"No."

"Mr. Sanders," she said, "I want to emphasize that I have no judgment here. I'm simply trying to prepare for what may happen tomorrow. I want to know what surprises they'll have for us."

He shook his head. "There isn't anything in the files that's embarrassing to me."

"You've thought it over carefully?"

"Yes."

"Okay," she said. "Then considering the early start, I think you better get some sleep. I want you sharp tomorrow. Will you be able to sleep?"

"Jeez, I don't know."

"Take a sleeping pill if you need to."

"I'll be okay."

"Then go home and go to bed, Mr. Sanders. I'll see you in the morning. Wear a coat and tie to-morrow. Do you have some kind of a blue coat?"

"A blazer."

"Fine. Wear a conservative tie and a white shirt. No after-shave."

"I never dress like that at the office."

"This is not the office, Mr. Sanders. That's just the point." She stood up and shook his hand. "Get some sleep. And try not to worry. I think everything is going to be fine."

"I bet you say that to all your clients."

"Yes, I do," she said. "But I'm usually right. Get some sleep, Tom. I'll see you tomorrow."

He came home to a dark, empty house. Eliza's Barbie dolls lay in an untidy heap on the kitchen counter. One of his son's bibs, streaked with green baby food, was on the counter beside the sink. He set up the coffeemaker for the morning and went upstairs. He walked past the answering machine but neglected to look at it, and failed to notice the blinking light.

Upstairs, when he undressed in the bathroom, he saw that Susan had taped a note to the mirror. "Sorry about lunch. I believe you. I love you. S."

It was just like Susan to be angry and then to apologize. But he was glad for the note and considered calling her now. But it was nearly midnight in Phoenix, which meant it was too late. She'd be asleep.

Anyway, as he thought about it, he realized that he didn't want to call her. As she had said at the restaurant, this had nothing to do with her. He was alone in this. He'd stay alone.

Wearing just shorts, he padded into his little office. There were no faxes. He switched on his computer and waited while it came up.

The e-mail icon was blinking. He clicked it.

TRUST NOBODY.

AFRIEND

Sanders shut off the computer and went to bed.

WEDNESDAY

In the morning, he took comfort in his routine, dressing quickly while listening to the television news, which he turned up loud, trying to fill the empty house with noise. He drove into town at 6:30, stopping at the Bainbridge Bakery to buy a pull-apart and a cup of cappuccino before going down to the ferry.

As the ferry pulled away from Winslow, he sat toward the stern, so he would not have to look at Seattle as it approached. Lost in his thoughts, he stared out the window at the gray clouds hanging low over the dark water of the bay. It looked like it would rain again today.

"Bad day, huh?" a woman said.

He looked up and saw Mary Anne Hunter, pretty and petite, standing with her hands on her hips, looking at him with concern. Mary Anne lived on Bainbridge, too. Her husband was a marine biologist at the university. She and Susan were good friends, and often jogged together. But he didn't often see Mary Anne on the ferry because she usually went in early.

"Morning, Mary Anne."

"What I can't understand is how they got it," she said.

"Got what?" Sanders said.

"You mean you haven't seen it? Jesus. You're in the papers, Tom." She handed him the newspaper under her arm.

"You're kidding."

"No. Connie Walsh strikes again."

Sanders looked at the front page, but saw nothing. He began flipping through quickly.

"It's in the Metro section," she said. "The first opinion column on the second page. Read it and weep. I'll get more coffee." She walked away.

Sanders opened the paper to the Metro section.

AS I SEE IT
by Constance Walsh

MR. PIGGY AT WORK

The power of the patriarchy has revealed itself again, this time in a local high-tech firm I'll call Company X. This company has appointed a brilliant, highly competent woman to a major executive position. But many men in the company are doing their damnedest to get rid of her.

One man in particular, let's call him Mr. Piggy, has been especially vindictive. Mr. Piggy can't tolerate a woman supervisor, and for weeks he has been running a bitter campaign of innuendo inside the company to keep it from happening. When that failed, Mr. Piggy claimed that his new boss sexually assaulted him, and nearly raped him, in her offices. The blatant hostility of this claim is matched only by its absurdity.

Some of you may wonder how a woman could rape a man. The answer is, of course, she can't. Rape is a crime of violence. It is exclusively a crime of males, who use rape with appalling frequency to keep women in their place. That is the deep truth of our society, and of all other societies before ours.

For their part, women simply do not oppress men. Women are powerless in the hands of men. And to claim that a woman committed rape is absurd. But that didn't stop Mr. Piggy, who is interested only in smearing his new supervisor. He's even bringing a formal charge of sexual harassment against her!

In short, Mr. Piggy has the nasty habits of a typical patriarch. As you might expect, they appear everywhere in his life. Although Mr. Piggy's wife is an outstanding attorney, he pressures her to give up her job and stay home with the kids. After all, Mr. Piggy doesn't want his wife out in the business world, where she might hear about his affairs with young women and his excessive drinking. He probably figures his new female supervisor wouldn't approve of that, either. Maybe she won't allow him to be late to work, as he so often is.

So Mr. Piggy has made his underhanded move, and another talented businesswoman sees her career unfairly jeopardized. Will she be able to keep the pigs in the pen at Company X? Stay tuned for updates.

"Christ," Sanders said. He read it through again.

Hunter came back with two cappuccinos in paper cups. She pushed one toward him. "Here. Looks like you need it."

"How did they get the story?" he said.

Hunter shook her head. "I don't know. It looks to me like there's a leak inside the company."

"But who?" Sanders was thinking that if the story made the paper, it must have been leaked by three or four p.m. the day before. Who in the company even knew that he was considering a harassment charge at that time?

"I can't imagine who it could be," Hunter said. "I'll ask around."

"And who's Constance Walsh?"

"You never read her? She's a regular columnist at the *PostIntelligencer*," Hunter said. "Feminist perspectives, that kind of thing." She shook her head. "How is Susan? I tried to call her this morning, and there's no answer at your house."

"Susan's gone away for a few days. With the kids."

Hunter nodded slowly. "That's probably a good idea."

"We thought so."

"She knows about this?"

"Yes."

"And is it true? Are you charging harassment?"

"Yes."

"Jesus."

"Yes," he said, nodding.

She sat with him for a long time, not speaking. She just sat with him. Finally she said, "I've known you for a long time. I hope this turns out okay."

"Me, too."

There was another long silence. Finally, she pushed away from the table and got up.

"See you later, Tom."

"See you, Mary Anne."

He knew what she was feeling. He had felt it himself, when others in the company had been accused of harassment. There was suddenly a distance. It didn't matter how long you had known the person. It didn't matter if you were friends. Once an accusation was made, everybody pulled away. Because the truth was, you never knew what had happened. You couldn't afford to take sides—even with your friends.

He watched her walk away, a slender, compact

figure in exercise clothes, carrying a leather briefcase. She was barely five feet tall. The men on the
ferry were so much larger. He remembered that
she had once told Susan that she took up running
because of her fear of rape. "I'll just outrun
them," she had said. Men didn't know anything
about that. They didn't understand that fear.

But there was another kind of fear that only
men felt. He looked at the newspaper column with
deep and growing unease. Key words and phrases
jumped out at him:

Vindictive . . . bitter . . . can't tolerate a wo-
man . . . blatant hostility . . . rape . . . crime of
males . . . smearing his supervisor . . . affairs with
young women . . . excessive drinking . . . late
to work . . . unfairly jeopardized . . . pigs in the pen.

These characterizations were more than inaccu-
rate, more than unpleasant. They were dangerous.
And it was exemplified by what happened to John
Masters—a story that had reverberated among
many senior men in Seattle.

Masters was fifty, a marketing manager at MicroSym. A stable guy, solid citizen, married
twenty-five years, two kids—the older girl in college, the younger girl a junior in high school. The
younger girl starts to have trouble with school,
her grades go down, so the parents send her to a
child psychologist. The child psychologist listens

to the daughter and then says, You know, this is the typical story of an abused child. Do you have anything like that in your past?

Gee, the girl says, I don't think so.

Think back, the psychologist says.

At first the girl resists, but the psychologist keeps at her: Think back. Try to remember. And after a while, the girl starts to recall some vague memories. Nothing specific, but now she thinks it's possible. Maybe Daddy did do something wrong, way back when.

The psychologist tells the wife what is suspected. After twenty-five years together, the wife and Masters have some anger between them. The wife goes to Masters and says, Admit what you did.

Masters is thunderstruck. He can't believe it. He denies everything. The wife says, You're lying, I don't want you around here. She makes him move out of the house.

The older daughter flies home from college. She says, What is this madness? You know Daddy didn't do anything. Come to your senses. But the wife is angry. The daughter is angry. And the process, once set in motion, can't be stopped.

The psychologist is required by state law to report any suspected abuse. She reports Masters to the state. The state is required by law to conduct an investigation. Now a social worker is talking to the daughter, the wife, and Masters. Then to the family doctor. The school nurse. Pretty soon, everybody knows.

Word of the accusation gets to MicroSym. The company suspends him from his job, pending the outcome. They say they don't want negative publicity.

Masters is seeing his life dissolve. His younger daughter won't talk to him. His wife won't talk to him. He's living alone in an apartment. He has money problems. Business associates avoid him. Everywhere he turns, he sees accusing faces. He is advised to get a lawyer. And he is so shattered, so uncertain, he starts going to a shrink himself.

His lawyer makes inquiries; disturbing details emerge. It turns out that the particular psychologist who made the accusation uncovers abuse in a high percentage of her cases. She has reported so many cases that the state agency has begun to suspect bias. But the agency can do nothing; the law requires that all cases be investigated. The social worker assigned to the case has been previously disciplined for her excessive zeal in pursuing questionable cases and is widely thought to be incompetent, but the state cannot fire her for the usual reasons.

The specific accusation—never formally presented—turns out to be that Masters molested his daughter in the summer of her third grade. Masters thinks back, has an idea. He gets his old canceled checks out of storage, digs up his old business calendars. It turns out that his daughter was at a camp in Montana that whole summer. When she came home in August, Masters was on a business trip in Germany. He did not return from Germany until after school had started again.

He had never even seen his daughter that summer.

Masters's shrink finds it significant that his daughter would locate the abuse at the one time when abuse was impossible. The shrink concludes that the daughter felt abandoned and has translated that into a memory of abuse. Masters confronts the wife and daughter. They listen to the evidence and admit that they must have the date wrong, but remain adamant that the abuse occurred.

Nevertheless, the facts about the summer schedule lead the state to drop its investigation, and MicroSym reinstates Masters. But Masters has missed a round of promotions, and a vague cloud of prejudice hangs over him. His career has been irrevocably damaged. His wife never reconciles, eventually filing for divorce. He never again sees his younger daughter. His older daughter, caught between warring family factions, sees less of him as time goes on. Masters lives alone, struggles to rebuild his life, and suffers a near-fatal heart attack. After his recovery, he sees a few friends, but now he is morose and drinks too much, a poor companion. Other men avoid him. No one has an answer to his constant question: What did I do wrong? What should I have done instead? How could I have prevented this?

Because, of course, he could not have prevented it. Not in a contemporary climate where men were assumed to be guilty of anything they were accused of.

Among themselves, men sometimes talked of suing women for false accusations. They talked of penalties for damage caused by those accusations. But that was just talk. Meanwhile, they all changed their behavior. There were new rules now, and every man knew them:

Don't smile at a child on the street, unless you're with your wife. Don't ever touch a strange child. Don't ever be alone with someone else's child, even for a moment. If a child invites you into his or her room, don't go unless another adult, preferably a woman, is also present. At a party, don't let a little girl sit on your lap. If she tries, gently push her aside. If you ever have occasion to see a naked boy or girl, look quickly away. Better yet, leave.

And it was prudent to be careful around your own children, too, because if your marriage went sour, your wife might accuse you. And then your past conduct would be reviewed in an unfavorable light: "Well, he was such an affectionate father—

perhaps a little *too* affectionate." Or, "He spent so much time with the kids. He was always hanging around the house . . ."

This was a world of regulations and penalties entirely unknown to women. If Susan saw a child crying on the street, she picked the kid up. She did it automatically, without thinking. Sanders would never dare. Not these days.

And of course there were new rules for business, as well. Sanders knew men who would not take a business trip with a woman, who would not sit next to a female colleague on an airplane, who would not meet a woman for a drink in a bar unless someone else was also present. Sanders had always thought such caution was extreme, even paranoid. But now, he was not so sure.

The sound of the ferry horn roused Sanders from his thoughts. He looked up and saw the black pilings of the Colman Dock. The clouds were still dark, still threatening rain. He stood, belted his raincoat, and headed downstairs to his car.

On his way to the mediation center, he stopped by his office for a few minutes to pick up background documentation on the Twinkle drive. He thought it might be necessary in the morning's work. But he was surprised to see John Conley in his office, talking with Cindy. It was 8:15 in the morning.

"Oh, Tom," Conley said. "I was just trying to arrange an appointment with you. Cindy tells me that you have a very busy schedule and may be out of the office most of the day."

Sanders looked at Cindy. Her face was tight. "Yes," he said, "at least for the morning."

"Well, I only need a few minutes."

Sanders waved him into the office. Conley went in, and Sanders closed the door.

"I'm looking forward to the briefing tomorrow for John Marden, our CEO," Conley said. "I gather you'll be speaking then."

Sanders nodded vaguely. He had heard nothing about a briefing. And tomorrow seemed very far away. He was having trouble concentrating on what Conley was saying.

"But of course we'll all be asked to take a position on some of these agenda items," Conley said.

"And I'm particularly concerned about Austin."

"Austin?"

"I mean, the sale of the Austin facility."

"I see," Sanders said. So it was true.

"As you know, Meredith Johnson has taken an early and strong position in favor of the sale," Conley said. "It was one of the first recommendations she gave us, in the early stages of shaping this deal. Marden's worried about cash flow after the acquisition; the deal's going to add debt, and he's worried about funding high-tech development. Johnson thought we could ease the debt load by selling off Austin. But I don't feel myself competent to judge the pros and cons on this. I was wondering what your view was."

"On a sale of the Austin plant?"

"Yes. Apparently there's tentative interest from both Hitachi and Motorola. So it's quite possible that it could be liquidated quickly. I think that's what Meredith has in mind. Has she discussed it with you?"

"No," Sanders said.

"She probably has a lot of ground to cover, settling in to her new job," Conley said. He was watching Sanders carefully as he spoke. "What do you think about a sale?"

Sanders said, "I don't see a compelling reason for it."

"Apart from cash-flow issues, I think her argument is that manufacturing cellular phones has become a mature business," Conley said. "As a technology, it's gone through its exponential growth phase, and it's now approaching a commodity. The high profits are gone. From now on, there will be only incremental sales increases, against increasing severe foreign competition. So, telephones aren't likely to represent a major income source in the future. And of course there's the question of whether we should be manufacturing in the States at all. A lot of DigiCom's manufacturing is already offshore."

"That's all true," Sanders said. "But it's beside the point. First of all, cellular phones may be reaching market saturation, but the general field of wireless communications is still in its infancy. We're going to see more and more wireless office nets and wireless field links in the future. So the market is still expanding, even if telephony is not. Second, I would argue that wireless is a major part of our company's future interest, and one way to stay competitive is to continue to make products and sell them. That forces you to maintain contact with your customer base, to keep knowledgeable about their future interests. I wouldn't opt out now. If Motorola and Hitachi see a business there, why don't we? Third, I think that we have an obligation—a social obligation, if you will—to keep high-paying skilled jobs in the U.S. Other countries don't export good jobs. Why should we? Each of our offshore manufacturing decisions has been made for a specific reason, and, personally, I hope we start to move them back here. Because there are many hidden costs in off-shore fabrication. But most important of all, even though we are primarily a development unit here—making new products—we need manufacturing. If there's anything that the last twenty years has shown us, it's that design and manufacturing are all one process. You start splitting off the design engineers from the manufacturing guys and you'll end up with bad design. You'll end up with General Motors."

He paused. There was a brief silence. Sanders hadn't intended to speak so strongly; it just came out. But Conley just nodded thoughtfully. "So you believe selling Austin would hurt the development unit."

"No question about it. In the end, manufacturing is a discipline."

Conley shifted in his seat. "How do you think Meredith Johnson feels on these issues?"

"I don't know."

"Because you see, all this raises a related question," Conley said. "Having to do with executive judgment. To be frank, I've heard some rumblings in the division about her appointment. In terms of whether she really has a good enough grasp of the issues to run a technical division."

Sanders spread his hands. "I don't feel I can say anything."

"I'm not asking you to," Conley said. "I gather she has Garvin's support."

"Yes, she does."

"And that's fine with us. But you know what I'm driving at," Conley said. "The classic problem in acquisitions is that the acquiring company doesn't really understand what they are buying, and they kill the goose that lays the golden egg. They don't intend to; but they do. They destroy the very thing they want to acquire. I'm concerned that Conley-White not make a mistake like that."

"Uh-huh."

"Just between us. If this issue comes up in the meeting tomorrow, would you take the position you just took?"

"Against Johnson?" Sanders shrugged. "That could be difficult." He was thinking that he probably wouldn't be at the meeting tomorrow. But he couldn't say that to Conley.

"Well." Conley extended his hand. "Thanks for your candor. I appreciate it." He turned to go. "One last thing. It'd be very helpful if we had a handle on the Twinkle drive problem by tomorrow."

"I know it," Sanders said. "Believe me, we're working on it."

"Good."

Conley turned, and left. Cindy came in. "How are you today?"

"Nervous."

"What do you need me to do?"

"Pull the data on the Twinkle drives. I want copies of everything I took Meredith Monday night."

"It's on your desk."

He scooped up a stack of folders. On top was a small DAT cartridge. "What's this?"

"That's your video link with Arthur from Monday."

He shrugged, and dropped it in his briefcase.

Cindy said, "Anything else?"

"No." He glanced at his watch. "I'm late."

"Good luck, Tom," she said.

He thanked her and left the office.

Driving in morning rush-hour traffic, Sanders realized that the only surprise in his encounter with Conley was how sharp the young lawyer was. As for Meredith, her behavior didn't surprise him at all. For years, Sanders had fought the B-school mentality that she exemplified. After watching these graduates come and go, Sanders had finally concluded that there was a fundamental flaw in their education. They had been trained to believe that they were equipped to manage anything. But there was no such thing as general managerial skills and tools. In the end, there were only specific problems, involving specific industries and specific workers. To apply general tools to specific problems was to fail. You needed to know the market, you needed to know the customers, you needed to know the limits of manufacturing and the limits of your own creative people. None of that was obvious. Meredith couldn't see that Don Cherry and Mark Lewyn needed a link to manufacturing. Yet time and again, Sanders had been shown a prototype and had asked the one significant question: It looks fine, but can you make it on a production line? Can you build it, reliably and quickly, for a price? Sometimes they could, and sometimes they couldn't. If you took away that question, you changed the entire organization. And not for the better.

Conley was smart enough to see that. And smart enough to keep his ear to the ground. Sanders wondered how much Conley knew of what he hadn't said in their meeting. Did he also know about the harassment suit? It was certainly possible.

Christ, Meredith wanted to sell Austin. Eddie had been right all along. He considered telling him, but he really couldn't. And in any case, he had more pressing things to worry about. He saw the sign for the Magnuson Mediation Center and turned right. Sanders tugged at the knot on his tie, and pulled into a space in the parking lot.

The Magnuson Mediation Center was located just outside Seattle, on a hill overlooking the city. It consisted of three low buildings arranged around a central courtyard where water splashed in fountains and pools. The entire atmosphere was designed to be peaceful and relaxing, but Sanders was tense when he walked up from the parking lot and found Fernandez pacing.

"You see the paper today?" she said.

"Yeah, I saw it."

"Don't let it upset you. This is a very bad tactical move on their part," she said. "You know Connie Walsh?"

"No."

"She's a bitch," Fernandez said briskly. "Very unpleasant and very capable. But I expect Judge Murphy to take a strong position on it in the sessions. Now, this is what I worked out with Phil Blackburn. We'll begin with your version of the events of Monday night. Then Johnson will tell hers."

"Wait a minute. Why should I go first?" Sanders said. "If I go first, she'll have the advantage of hearing—"

"You are the one bringing the claim so you are

obligated to present your case first. I think it will be to our advantage," Fernandez said. "This way Johnson will testify last, before lunch." They started toward the center building. "Now, there are just two things you have to remember. First, always tell the truth. No matter what happens, just tell the truth. Exactly as you remember it even if you think it hurts your case. Okay?"

"Okay."

"Second, don't get mad. Her lawyer will try to make you angry and trap you. Don't fall for it. If you feel insulted or start to get mad, request a five-minute break to consult with me. You're entitled to that, whenever you want. We'll go outside and cool off. But whatever you do, keep cool, Mr. Sanders."

"Okay."

"Good." She swung open the door. "Now let's go do it."

The mediation room was wood-paneled and spare. He saw a polished wooden table with a pitcher of water and glasses and some notepads; in the corner, a sideboard with coffee and a plate of pastries. Windows opened out on a small atrium with a fountain. He heard the sound of soft gurgling water.

The DigiCom legal team was already there, ranged along one side of the table. Phil Blackburn, Meredith Johnson, an attorney named Ben Heller, and two other grim-faced female attorneys. Each woman had an imposing stack of xeroxed papers before her on the table.

Fernandez introduced herself to Meredith Johnson, and the two women shook hands. Then Ben Heller shook hands with Sanders. Heller was a florid, beefy man with silver hair, and a deep voice. Well connected in Seattle, he reminded Sanders of a politician. Heller introduced the other women, but Sanders immediately forgot their names.

Meredith said, "Hello, Tom."

"Meredith."

He was struck by how beautiful she looked. She wore a blue suit with a cream-colored blouse.

With her glasses and her blond hair pulled back, she looked like a lovely but studious schoolgirl. Heller patted her hand reassuringly, as if speaking to Sanders had been a terrible ordeal.

Sanders and Fernandez sat down opposite Johnson and Heller. Everybody got out papers and notes. Then there was an awkward silence, until Heller said to Fernandez, "How'd that King Power thing turn out?"

"We were pleased," Fernandez said.

"They fixed an award yet?"

"Next week, Ben."

"What are you asking?"

"Two million."

"Two *million*?"

"Sexual harassment's serious business, Ben. Awards are going up fast. Right now the average verdict is over a million dollars. Especially when the company behaves that badly."

At the far end of the room, a door opened and a woman in her mid-fifties entered. She was brisk and erect, and wore a dark blue suit not very different from Meredith's.

"Good morning," she said. "I'm Barbara Murphy. Please refer to me as Judge Murphy, or Ms. Murphy." She moved around the room, shaking hands with everyone, then took a seat at the head of the table. She opened her briefcase and took out her notes.

"Let me tell you the ground rules for our sessions here," Judge Murphy said. "This is not a court of law, and our proceedings won't be recorded. I encourage everyone to maintain a civil and courteous tone. We're not here to make wild accusations or to fix blame. Our goal is to define the nature of the dispute between the parties, and to determine how best to resolve that dispute.

"I want to remind everyone that the allegations made on both sides are extremely serious and may have legal consequences for all parties. I urge you to treat these sessions confidentially. I particularly caution you against discussing what is said here with any outside person or with the press. I have taken the liberty of speaking privately to Mr. Donadio, the editor of the *Post-Intelligencer,* about the article that appeared today by Ms. Walsh. I reminded Mr. Donadio that all parties in 'Company X' are private individuals and that Ms. Walsh is a paid employee of the paper. The risk of a defamation suit against the *P-I* is very real. Mr. Donadio seemed to take my point."

She leaned forward, resting her elbows on the table. "Now then. The parties have agreed that Mr. Sanders will speak first, and he will then be questioned by Mr. Heller. Ms. Johnson will speak next, and will be questioned by Ms. Fernandez. In the interest of time, I alone will have the right to ask questions during the testimony of the principals, and I will set limits on the questions of opposing attorneys. I'm open to some discussion, but I ask your cooperation in letting me exercise judgment and keep things moving. Before we begin, does anybody have any questions?"

Nobody did.

"All right. Then let's get started. Mr. Sanders, why don't you tell us what happened, from your point of view."

Sanders talked quietly for the next half hour. He began with his meeting with Blackburn, where he learned that Meredith was going to be the new vice president. He reported the conversation with Meredith after her speech, in which she suggested a meeting about the Twinkle drive. He told what happened in the six o'clock meeting in detail.

As he spoke, he realized why Fernandez had insisted he tell this story over and over, the day before. The flow of events came easily to him now; he found that he could talk about penises and vaginas without hesitation. Even so, it was an ordeal. He felt exhausted by the time he described leaving the room and seeing the cleaning woman outside.

He then told about the phone call to his wife, and the early meeting the next morning, his subsequent conversation with Blackburn, and his decision to press charges.

"That's about it," he finished.

Judge Murphy said, "I have some questions before we go on. Mr. Sanders, you mentioned that wine was drunk during the meeting."

"Yes."

"How much wine would you say you had?"

"Less than a glass."

"And Ms. Johnson? How much would you say?"

"At least three glasses."

"All right." She made a note. "Mr. Sanders, do you have an employment contract with the company?"

"Yes."

"What is your understanding of what the contract says about transferring you or firing you?"

"They can't fire me without cause," Sanders said. "I don't know what it says about transfers. But my point is that by transferring me, they might as well be firing me—"

"I understand your point," Murphy said, interrupting him. "I'm asking about your contract. Mr. Blackburn?"

Blackburn said, "The relevant clause refers to 'equivalent transfer.' "

"I see. So it is arguable. Fine. Let's go on. Mr. Heller? Your questions for Mr. Sanders, please."

Ben Heller shuffled his papers and cleared his throat. "Mr. Sanders, would you like a break?"

"No, I'm fine."

"All right. Now, Mr. Sanders. You mentioned that when Mr. Blackburn told you on Monday morning that Ms. Johnson was going to be the new head of the division, you were surprised."

"Yes."

"Who did you think the new head would be?"

"I didn't know. Actually, I thought I might be in line for it."

"Why did you think that?"

"I just assumed it."

"Did anybody in the company, Mr. Blackburn or anybody else, lead you to think you were going to get the job?"

"No."

"Was there anything in writing to suggest you would get the job?"

"No."

"So when you say you assumed it, you were drawing a conclusion based on the general situation at the company, as you saw it."

"Yes."

"But not based on any real evidence?"

"No."

"All right. Now, you've said that when Mr. Blackburn told you that Ms. Johnson was going to get the job, he also told you that she could choose new division heads if she wanted, and you told him you interpreted that to mean Ms. Johnson had the power to fire you?"

"Yes, that's what he said."

"Did he characterize it in any way? For example, did he say it was likely or unlikely?"

"He said it was unlikely."

"And did you believe him?"

"I wasn't sure what to believe, at that point."

"Is Mr. Blackburn's judgment on company matters reliable?"

"Ordinarily, yes."

"But in any case, Mr. Blackburn did say that Ms. Johnson had the right to fire you."

"Yes."

"Did Ms. Johnson ever say anything like that to you?"

"No."

"She never made any statement that could be interpreted as an offer contingent upon your performance, including sexual performance?"

"No."

"So when you say that during your meeting with her you felt that your job was at risk, that was not because of anything Ms. Johnson actually said or did?"

"No," Sanders said. "But it was in the situation."

"You *perceived* it as being in the situation."

"Yes."

"As you had earlier perceived that you were in line for a promotion, when in fact you were not? The very promotion that Ms. Johnson ended up getting?"

"I don't follow you."

"I'm merely observing," Heller said, "that perceptions are subjective, and do not have the weight of fact."

"Objection," Fernandez said. "Employee perceptions have been held valid in contexts where the reasonable expectation—"

"Ms. Fernandez," Murphy said, "Mr. Heller hasn't challenged the validity of your client's perceptions. He has questioned their accuracy."

"But surely they are accurate. Because Ms. Johnson was his superior, and she could fire him if she wanted to."

"That's not in dispute. But Mr. Heller is asking whether Mr. Sanders has a tendency to build up unjustified expectations. And that seems to me entirely relevant."

"But with all due respect, Your Honor—"

"Ms. Fernandez," Murphy said, "we're here to clarify this dispute. I'm going to let Mr. Heller continue. Mr. Heller?"

"Thank you, Your Honor. So to summarize, Mr. Sanders: Although you felt your job was on the line, you never got that sense from Ms. Johnson?"

"No, I didn't."

"Or from Mr. Blackburn?"

"No."

"Or, in fact, from anyone else?"

"No."

"All right. Let's turn to something else. How did it happen that there was wine at the six o'clock meeting?"

"Ms. Johnson said that she would get a bottle of wine."

"You didn't ask her to do that?"

"No. She volunteered to do it."

"And what was your reaction?"

"I don't know." He shrugged. "Nothing in particular."

"Were you pleased?"

"I didn't think about it one way or the other."

"Let me put it a different way, Mr. Sanders. When you heard that an attractive woman like Ms. Johnson was planning to have a drink with you after work, what went through your head?"

"I thought I better do it. She's my boss."

"That's all you thought?"

"Yes."

"Did you mention to anyone that you wanted to be alone with Ms. Johnson in a romantic setting?"

Sanders sat forward, surprised. "No."

"Are you sure about that?"

"Yes." Sanders shook his head. "I don't know what you're driving at."

"Isn't Ms. Johnson your former lover?"

"Yes."

"And didn't you want to resume your intimate relationship?"

"No, I did not. I was just hoping we would be able to find some way to be able to work together."

"Is that difficult? I would have thought it'd be quite easy to work together, since you knew each other so well in the past."

"Well, it's not. It's quite awkward."

"Is it? Why is that?"

"Well. It just is. I had never actually worked with her. I knew her in a totally different context, and I just felt awkward."

"How did your prior relationship with Ms. Johnson end, Mr. Sanders?"

"We just sort of . . . drifted apart."

"You had been living together at the time?"

"Yes. And we had our normal ups and downs. And finally, it just didn't work out. So we split up."

"No hard feelings?"

"No."

"Who left whom?"

"It was sort of mutual, as I recall."

"Whose idea was it to move out?"

"I guess . . . I don't really remember. I guess it was mine."

"So there was no awkwardness or tension about how the affair ended, ten years ago."

"No."

"And yet you felt there was awkwardness now?"

"Sure," Sanders said. "Because we had one kind of relationship in the past, and now we were going to have another kind of relationship."

"You mean, now Ms. Johnson was going to be your superior."

"Yes."

"Weren't you angry about that? About her appointment?"

"A little. I guess."

"Only a little? Or perhaps more than a little?"

Fernandez sat forward and started to protest. Murphy shot her a warning look. Fernandez put her fists under her chin and said nothing.

"I was a lot of things," Sanders said. "I was angry and disappointed and confused and worried."

"So in your mind, although you were feeling many different and confusing feelings, you're certain that you did not, under any circumstances, contemplate having sex with Ms. Johnson that night."

"No."

"It never crossed your mind?"

"No."

There was a pause. Heller shuffled his notes, then looked up. "You're married, are you not, Mr. Sanders?"

"Yes, I am."

"Did you call your wife to tell her you had a late meeting?"

"Yes."

"Did you tell her with whom?"

"No."

"Why not?"

"My wife is sometimes jealous about my past relationships. I didn't see any reason to cause her anxiety or make her upset."

"You mean, if you told her you were having a late meeting with Ms. Johnson, your wife might think that you would renew your sexual acquaintance."

"I don't know what she would think," Sanders said.

"But in any case, you didn't tell her about Ms. Johnson."

"No."

"What did you tell her?"

"I told her I had a meeting and I would be home late."

"How late?"

"I told her it might run to dinner or after."

"I see. Had Ms. Johnson suggested dinner to you?"

"No."

"So you presumed, when you called your wife, that your meeting with Ms. Johnson might be a long one?"

"No," Sanders said. "I didn't. But I didn't know exactly how long it would be. And my wife doesn't like me to call once and say I'll be an hour late, and then call again to say it'll be two hours. That annoys her. So it's easier for her if I just tell her I may be home after dinner. That way, she doesn't expect me and doesn't wait for me; and if I get home early, it's great."

"So this is your usual policy with your wife."

"Yes."

"Nothing unusual."

"No."

"In other words, your usual procedure is to lie to your wife about events at the office because in your view she can't take the truth."

"Objection," Fernandez said. "What's the relevance?"

"That's not it at all," Sanders continued, angrily.

"How is it, Mr. Sanders?"

"Look. Every marriage has its own way to work things out. This is ours. It makes things smoother, that's all. It's about scheduling at home, not about lying."

"But wouldn't you say that you lied when you failed to tell your wife you were seeing Ms. Johnson that night?"

"Objection," Fernandez said.

Murphy said, "I think this is *quite* enough, Mr. Heller."

"Your Honor, I'm trying to show that Mr. Sanders intended to consummate an encounter with Ms. Johnson, and that all his behavior is consistent with that. And in addition, to show that he routinely treats women with contempt."

"You haven't shown that, you haven't even laid

a groundwork for that," Murphy said. "Mr. Sanders has explained his reasons, and in the absence of contrary evidence I accept them. Do you have contrary evidence?"

"No, Your Honor."

"Very well. Bear in mind that inflammatory and unsubstantiated characterizations do not assist our mutual efforts at resolution."

"Yes, Your Honor."

"I want everyone here to be clear: these proceedings are potentially damaging to all parties—not only in their outcome, but in the conduct of the proceedings themselves. Depending on the outcome, Ms. Johnson and Mr. Sanders may find themselves working together in some capacity in the future. I will not permit these proceedings to unnecessarily poison such future relationships. Any further unwarranted accusations will cause me to halt these proceedings. Does anyone have any questions about what I've just said?"

No one did.

"All right. Mr. Heller?"

Heller sat back. "No further questions, Your Honor."

"All right," Judge Murphy said. "We'll break for five minutes, and return to hear Ms. Johnson's version."

Y ou're doing fine," Fernandez said. "You're doing very well. Your voice was strong. You were clear and even. Murphy was impressed. You're doing fine." They were standing outside, by the fountains in the courtyard. Sanders felt like a boxer between rounds, being worked over by his trainer. "How do you feel?" she asked. "Tired?"

"A little. Not too bad."

"You want coffee?"

"No, I'm okay."

"Good. Because the hard part is coming up. You're going to have to be very strong when she gives her version. You won't like what she says. But it's important that you stay calm."

"Okay."

She put her hand on his shoulder. "By the way, just between us: How *did* the relationship end?"

"To tell the truth, I can't remember exactly."

Fernandez looked skeptical. "But this was important, surely . . ."

"It was almost ten years ago," Sanders said. "To me, it feels like another lifetime."

She was still skeptical.

"Look," Sanders said. "This is the third week in June. What was going on in your love life the third week of June, ten years ago? Can you tell me?"

Fernandez was silent, frowning.

"Were you married?" Sanders prompted.

"No."

"Met your husband yet?"

"Uh, let's see . . . no . . . not until . . . I must have met my husband . . . about a year later."

"Okay. Do you remember who you were seeing before him?"

Fernandez was silent. Thinking.

"How about *anything* that happened between you and a lover in June, ten years ago?"

She was still silent.

"See what I mean?" Sanders said. "Ten years is a long time. I remember the affair with Meredith, but I'm not clear about the last few weeks of it. I don't remember the details of how it ended."

"What do you remember?"

He shrugged. "We had more fights, more yelling. We were still living together, but somehow, we began to arrange our schedules so that we never saw each other. You know how that happens. Because when we did run into each other, we fought.

"And finally one night, we had a big argument while we were getting dressed to go to a party. Some formal party for DigiCom. I remember I had to wear a tux. I threw my cuff links at her and then I couldn't find them. I had to get down on the floor and look. But once we were driving to the party, we sort of calmed down, and we started talking about breaking up. In this very ordinary way. Very reasonable way. It just came out. Both of us. Nobody shouted. And in the end, we decided it was best if we broke it off."

Fernandez was looking at him thoughtfully. "That's it?"

"Yeah." He shrugged. "Except we never got to the party."

Something at the back of his mind. *A couple in a car, going to a party. Something about a cellular phone. All dressed up, going to the party and they make a call, and—*

He couldn't get it. It hung in his memory, just beyond recollection.

The woman made a call on the cellular phone, and then . . . Something embarrassing afterward . . .

"Tom?" Fernandez said, shaking his shoulder. "Looks like our time is about up. Ready to go back?"

"I'm ready," he said.

As they were heading back to the mediation room, Heller came over. He gave Sanders an oily smile, then turned to Fernandez. "Counselor," he said. "I wonder if this is the time to talk about settlement."

"Settlement?" Fernandez said, showing elaborate surprise. "Why?"

"Well, things aren't going so well for your client, and—"

"Things are going fine for my client—"

"And this whole inquiry will only get more embarrassing and awkward for him, the longer it continues—"

"My client isn't embarrassed at all—"

"And perhaps it is to everyone's advantage to end it now."

Fernandez smiled. "I don't think that's my client's wish, Ben, but if you have an offer to make, we will of course entertain it."

"Yes. I have an offer."

"All right."

Heller cleared his throat. "Considering Tom's current compensation base and associated benefits package, and taking into consideration his lengthy service with the company, we're prepared to settle for an amount equal to several years of compensation. We'll add an allowance for your fees and other miscellaneous expenses of termination, the cost of a headhunter to relocate to a new position, and all direct costs that may be associated with moving his household, and all together make it four hundred thousand dollars. I think that's very generous."

"I'll see what my client says," Fernandez said. She took Sanders by the arm, and walked a short distance away. "Well?"

"No," Sanders said.

"Not so fast," she said. "That's a pretty reasonable offer. It's as much as you're likely to get in court, without the delay and expenses."

"No."

"Want to counter?"

"No. Fuck him."

"I think we should counter."

"Fuck him."

Fernandez shook her head. "Let's be smart, not angry. What do you hope to gain from all this, Tom? There must be a figure you would accept."

"I want what I'll get when they take the company public," Sanders said. "And that's somewhere between five and twelve million."

"You *think*. It's a speculative estimate for a future event."

"That's what it'll be, believe me."

Fernandez looked at him. "Would you take five million now?"

"Yes."

"Alternatively, would you take the compensation package he outlined, plus the stock options you would get at the time of the offering?"

Sanders considered that. "Yes."

"All right. I'll tell him."

She walked back across the courtyard to Heller. The two spoke briefly. After a moment, Heller turned on his heel and stalked away.

Fernandez came back, grinning. "He didn't go for it." They headed back inside. "But I'll tell you one thing: this is a good sign."

"It is?"

"Yes. If they want to settle before Johnson gives her testimony, it's a very good sign."

In view of the acquisition," Meredith Johnson said, "I felt it was important that I meet with all the division heads on Monday." She spoke calmly and slowly, looking at everyone seated around the table in turn. Sanders had the sense of an executive giving a presentation. "I met with Don Cherry, Mark Lewyn, and Mary Anne Hunter during the afternoon. But Tom Sanders said he had a very busy schedule, and asked if we could meet at the end of the day. At his request, I scheduled the meeting with Tom at six o'clock."

He was amazed at the cool way that she lied. He had expected her to be effective, but he was still astonished to see her in action.

"Tom suggested that we could have a drink as well, and go over old times. That wasn't really my style, but I agreed. I was especially concerned to establish good relations with Tom, because I knew he was disappointed he had not gotten the job, and because we had a past history. I wanted our working relationship to be cordial. For me to refuse a drink with him seemed . . . I don't know—standoffish, or stiff. So I said yes.

"Tom came to the office at six o'clock. We had a glass of wine, and talked about the problems with the Twinkle drive. However, from the outset he kept making comments of a personal nature that I considered inappropriate—for example, comments about my appearance, and about how often he thought about our past relationship. Reference to sexual incidents in the past, and so on."

Son of a bitch. Sanders's whole body was tense. His hands were clenched. His jaw was tight.

Fernandez leaned over and put her hand on his wrist.

Meredith Johnson was saying, ". . . had some calls from Garvin and others. I took them at my desk. Then my assistant came in and asked if she could leave early, to deal with some personal matters. I said she could. She left the room. That was when Tom came over and suddenly started kissing me."

She paused for a moment, looking around the room. She met Sanders's eyes with a steady gaze.

"I was taken aback by his sudden and unexpected overture," she said, staring evenly at him. "At first, I tried to protest, and to defuse the situation. But Tom is much larger than I am. Much stronger. He pulled me over onto the couch and started to disrobe, and to take my clothes off as well. As you can imagine, I was horrified and frightened. The situation was out of control, and the fact that it was happening made our future working relationship very difficult. To say nothing of how I felt personally, as a woman. I mean, to be assaulted in this way."

Sanders stared at her, trying desperately to control his anger. He heard Fernandez, at his ear. *"Breathe."* He took a deep breath and let it out slowly. He had not been aware until then that he was holding his breath.

"I kept trying to make light of it," Meredith continued, "to make jokes, to get free. I was trying to say to him, Oh, come on Tom, let's not do this. But he was determined. And when he tore my underwear off, when I heard the sound of the cloth ripping, I realized that I could not get out of this situation in any diplomatic way. I had to acknowledge that Mr. Sanders was raping me and I became very scared and very angry. When he moved away from me on the couch, to free his penis from his trousers, prior to penetration, I kneed him in the groin. He rolled off the couch, onto the floor. Then he got to his feet, and I got to my feet.

"Mr. Sanders was angry that I had refused his advances. He started shouting at me, and then he hit me, knocking me down onto the floor. But by then I was angry, too. I remember saying, 'You can't do this to me,' and swearing at him. But I can't say I remember everything that he said or that I said. He came back at me one more time, but by then I had my shoes in my hand, and I hit him in the chest with my high heels, trying to drive him away. I think I tore his shirt. I'm not sure. I was so angry by then, I wanted to kill him. I'm sure I scratched him. I remember I said I wanted to kill him. I was so angry. Here it was my first day in this new job, I was under so much pressure, I was trying to do a good job and this . . . this *thing* had happened that ruined our relationship and was going to cause a lot of trouble for everybody in the company. He went off in an angry rage. After he left, the question for me was how to handle it."

She paused, shaking her head, apparently lost in the emotions of that moment.

Heller said gently, "How did you decide to handle it?"

"Well, it's a problem. Tom's an important employee, and he is not an easy person to replace. Furthermore, in my judgment it would not be wise to make a replacement in the middle of the acquisition. My first impulse was to see if we could forget the whole thing. After all, we're both adults. I was personally embarrassed, but I thought that Tom would probably be embarrassed, too, when he sobered up and had a chance to think it over. And I thought that maybe we could just go on from there. After all, awkward things happen sometimes. People can overlook them.

"So when the meeting time changed, I called his

house to tell him. He wasn't there, but I had a very pleasant conversation with his wife. It was clear from our conversation that she did not know that Tom had been meeting me, or that Tom and I knew each other from the past. Anyway, I gave his wife the new meeting time, and asked her to tell Tom.

"The next day, at the meeting, things did not go well. Tom showed up late, and changed his story about the Twinkle drive, minimizing the problems and contradicting me. He was clearly undercutting my authority in a corporate meeting and I could not permit that. I went directly to Phil Blackburn and told him everything that had happened. I said I did not want to press formal charges, but I made it clear that I could not work with Tom and that a change would have to be made. Phil said he would talk to Tom. And eventually it was decided that we would try to mediate a resolution."

She sat back, and placed her hands flat on the table. "That's all, I think. That's everything." She looked around at everyone, meeting their eyes in turn. Very cool, very controlled.

It was a spectacular performance, and in Sanders it produced a quite unexpected effect: he felt guilty. He felt as if he had done the things that she said he had done. He felt sudden shame, and looked down at the table, hanging his head.

Fernandez kicked him in the ankle, hard. He

jerked his head up, wincing. She was frowning at him. He sat up.

Judge Murphy cleared her throat. "Evidently," she said, "we are presented with two entirely incompatible reports. Ms. Johnson, I have only a few questions before we go on."

"Yes, Your Honor?"

"You're an attractive woman. I'm sure you've had to fend off your share of unwanted approaches in the course of your business career."

Meredith smiled. "Yes, Your Honor."

"And I'm sure you have developed some skill at it."

"Yes, Your Honor."

"You've said you were aware of tensions from your past relationship with Mr. Sanders. Considering those tensions, I would have thought that a meeting held in the middle of the day, without wine, would have been more professional—would have set a better tone."

"I'm sure that's correct in hindsight," Meredith said. "But at the time, this was all in the context of the acquisition meetings. Everybody was busy. I was just trying to fit the meeting with Mr. Sanders in before the Conley-White sessions the next day. That's all I was thinking about. Schedules."

"I see. And after Mr. Sanders left your office, why didn't you call Mr. Blackburn, or someone else in the company, to report what had happened?"

"As I said, I was hoping it could all be overlooked."

"Yet the episode you describe," Murphy said, "is a serious breach of normal business behavior. As an experienced manager, you must have known the chance of a good working relationship with Mr. Sanders was nil. I would have thought you'd feel obliged to report what happened to a superior at once. And from a practical standpoint, I would have thought you'd want to go on record as soon as possible."

"As I said, I was still hoping." She frowned, thinking. "You know, I guess . . . I felt responsible for Tom. As an old friend, I didn't want to be the reason why he lost his job."

"On the other hand, you are the reason why he lost his job."

"Yes. Again, in hindsight."

"I see. All right. Ms. Fernandez?"

"Thank you, Your Honor." Fernandez turned in her chair to face Johnson. "Ms. Johnson, in a situation like this, when private behavior occurs behind closed doors, we need to look at surrounding events where we can. So I'll ask you a few questions about surrounding events."

"Fine."

"You've said that when you made the appointment with Mr. Sanders, he requested wine."

"Yes."

"Where did the wine come from, that you drank that night?"

"I asked my assistant to get it."

"This is Ms. Ross?"

"Yes."

"She's been with you a long time?"

"Yes."

"She came up with you from Cupertino?"

"Yes."

"She is a trusted employee?"

"Yes."

"How many bottles did you ask Ms. Ross to buy?"

"I don't remember if I specified a particular number."

"All right. How many bottles did she get?"

"Three, I think."

"Three. And did you ask your assistant to buy anything else?"

"Like what?"

"Did you ask her to buy condoms?"

"No."

"Do you know if she bought condoms?"

"No, I don't."

"In fact, she did. She bought condoms from the Second Avenue Drugstore."

"Well, if she bought condoms," Johnson said, "it must have been for herself."

"Do you know of any reason why your assistant would say she bought the condoms for you?"

"No," Johnson said, speaking slowly. She was thinking it over. "I can't imagine she would do that."

"Just a moment," Murphy said, interrupting. "Ms. Fernandez, are you alleging that the assistant *did* say that she bought the condoms for Ms. Johnson?"

"Yes, Your Honor. We are."

"You have a witness to that effect?"

"Yes, we do."

Sitting beside Johnson, Heller rubbed the bottom of his lip with one finger. Johnson showed no reaction at all. She didn't even blink. She just continued to gaze calmly at Fernandez, waiting for the next question.

"Ms. Johnson, did you instruct your assistant to lock the door to your office when Mr. Sanders was with you?"

"I most certainly did not."

"Do you know if she locked the door?"

"No, I don't."

"Do you know why she would tell someone that you ordered her to lock the door?"

"No."

"Ms. Johnson. Your meeting with Mr. Sanders was at six o'clock. Did you have any appointments later that day?"

"No. His was the last."

"Isn't it true that you had a seven o'clock appointment that you canceled?"

"Oh. Yes, that's true. I had one with Stephanie Kaplan. But I canceled it because I wasn't going to have the figures ready for her to go over. There wasn't time to prepare."

"Are you aware that your assistant told Ms. Kaplan that you were canceling because you had another meeting that was going to run late?"

"I don't know what my assistant said to her," Meredith replied, showing impatience for the first time. "We seem to be talking a great deal about my assistant. Perhaps you should be asking her these questions."

"Perhaps we should. I'm sure it can be arranged. All right. Let's turn to something else. Mr. Sanders said he saw a cleaning woman when he left your office. Did you also see her?"

"No. I stayed in my office after he had gone."

"The cleaning woman, Marian Walden, says she overheard a loud argument prior to Mr. Sanders's departure. She says she heard a man say, 'This isn't a good idea, I don't want to do this,' and she heard a woman say, 'You fucking bastard, you can't leave me like this.' Do you recall saying anything like that?"

"No. I recall saying, 'You can't do this to me.' "

"But you don't recall saying, 'You can't leave me like this.' "

"No, I do not."

"Ms. Walden is quite clear that was what you said."

"I don't know what Ms. Walden thought she heard," Johnson said. "The doors were closed the entire time."

"Weren't you speaking quite loudly?"

"I don't know. Possibly."

"Ms. Walden said you were shouting. And Mr. Sanders has said you were shouting."

"I don't know."

"All right. Now, Ms. Johnson, you said that you informed Mr. Blackburn that you could not work with Mr. Sanders after the unfortunate Tuesday morning meeting, is that right?"

"Yes. That's right."

Sanders sat forward. He suddenly realized that he had overlooked that, while Meredith was making her original statement. He had been so upset, he hadn't realized that she had lied about when she saw Blackburn. Because Sanders had gone to Blackburn's office right after the meeting—and Blackburn already knew.

"Ms. Johnson, what time would you say you went to see Mr. Blackburn?"

"I don't know. After the meeting."

"About what time?"

"Ten o'clock."

"Not earlier?"

"No."

Sanders glanced over at Blackburn, who sat rigidly at the end of the table. He looked tense, and bit his lip.

Fernandez said, "Shall I ask Mr. Blackburn to confirm that? I imagine his assistant has a log, if he has difficulty with exact memory."

There was a short silence. She looked over at Blackburn. "No," Meredith said. "No. I was confused. What I meant to say was I talked to Phil after the initial meeting, and before the second meeting."

"The initial meeting being the one at which Sanders was absent? The eight o'clock meeting."

"Yes."

"So Mr. Sanders's behavior at the second meeting, where he contradicted you, could not have been relevant to your decision to speak to Mr. Blackburn. Because you had already spoken to Mr. Blackburn by the time that meeting took place."

"As I say, I was confused."

"I have no more questions of this witness, Your Honor."

Judge Murphy closed her notepad. Her expression was bland and unreadable. She looked at her watch. "It's now eleven-thirty. We will break for lunch for two hours. I'm allowing extra time so that counsel can meet to review the situation and to decide how the parties wish to proceed." She stood up. "I am also available if counsel wish to meet with me for any reason. Otherwise, I'll see you all back here at one-thirty sharp. Have a pleasant and productive lunch." She turned and walked out of the room.

Blackburn stood and said, "Personally, I'd like to meet with opposing counsel, right now."

Sanders glanced over at Fernandez.

Fernandez gave the faintest of smiles. "I'm amenable to that, Mr. Blackburn," she said.

The three lawyers stood beside the fountain. Fernandez was talking animatedly to Heller, their heads close together. Blackburn was a few paces away, a cellular phone pressed to his ear. Across the courtyard, Meredith Johnson talked on another phone, gesturing angrily as she talked.

Sanders stood off to one side by himself, and watched. There was no question in his mind that Blackburn would seek a settlement. Piece by piece, Fernandez had torn Meredith Johnson's version apart: demonstrating that she had ordered her assistant to buy wine, to buy condoms, to lock the door when Sanders was there, and to cancel later appointments. Clearly, Meredith Johnson was not a supervisor surprised by a sexual overture. She had been planning it all afternoon. Her crucial reaction—her angry statement that "You can't leave me"—had been overheard by the cleaning woman. And she had lied about the timing and motivation of her report to Blackburn.

There could be no doubt in anyone's mind that Meredith was lying. The only question now was what Blackburn and DigiCom would do about it. Sanders had sat through enough management sensitivity seminars on sexual harassment to know what the company's obligation was. They really had no choice.

They would have to fire her.

But what would they do about Sanders? That was another question entirely. He had the strong intuition that by bringing this accusation, he had burned his bridges at the company; he would never be welcomed back. Sanders had shot down Garvin's pet bird, and Garvin would not forgive him for it.

So: they wouldn't let him back. They would have to pay him off.

"They're calling it quits already, huh?"

Sanders turned and saw Alan, one of the investigators, coming up from the parking lot. Alan had glanced over at the lawyers and quickly appraised the situation.

"I think so," Sanders said.

Alan squinted at the lawyers. "They should. Johnson has a problem. And a lot of people in the company know about it. Especially her assistant."

Sanders said, "You talked to her last night?"

"Yeah," he said. "Herb found the cleaning woman and got her taped. And I had a late night with Betsy Ross. She's a lonely lady, here in a new town. She drinks too much, and I taped it all."

"Did she know that?"

"She doesn't have to," Alan said. "It's still admissible." He watched the lawyers for a moment.

"Blackburn must be shitting staples about now."

Louise Fernandez was stalking across the courtyard, grim-faced, hunched over. "God*damn* it," she said, as she came up.

"What happened?" Sanders said.

Fernandez shook her head. "They won't make a deal."

"They won't make a deal?"

"That's right. They just deny every point. Her assistant bought wine? That was for Sanders. Her assistant bought condoms? That was for the assistant. The assistant says she bought them for Johnson? The assistant is an unreliable drunk. The cleaning lady's report? She couldn't know what she heard, she had the radio on. And always the constant refrain, 'You know, Louise, this won't stand up in court.' And Bulletproof Betty is on the phone, running the whole thing. Telling everybody what to do." Fernandez swore. "I have to tell you. This is the kind of shit male executives pull. They look you right in the eye and say, 'It never happened. It just isn't there. You have no case.' It burns my ass. *Damn* it!"

"Better get some lunch, Louise," Alan said. To Sanders he said, "She sometimes forgets to eat."

"Yeah, fine. Sure. Eat." They started toward the parking lot. She was walking fast, shaking her head. "I can't understand how they can take this position," she said. "Because I know—I could see it in Judge Murphy's eyes—that she didn't think there'd be an afternoon session at all. Judge Murphy heard the evidence and concluded it's all over. So did I. But it's not over. Blackburn and Heller aren't moving *one inch*. They're not going to settle. They're basically inviting us to sue."

"So we'll sue," Sanders said, shrugging.

"Not if we're smart," Fernandez said. "Not *now*. This is exactly what I was afraid would happen. They got a lot of free discovery, and we got nothing. We're back to square one. And they have the next three years to work on that assistant, and that cleaning lady, and anything else we come up with. And let me tell you: in three years we won't even be able to *find* that assistant."

"But we have her on tape . . ."

"She still has to appear in court. And believe me, she never will. Look, DigiCom has huge exposure. If we show that DigiCom didn't respond in a timely and adequate fashion to what they knew about Johnson, they could be liable for extremely large damages. There was a case on point last month in California: nineteen point four million dollars, found for the plaintiff. With exposure like that, take my word for it: the assistant will be unavailable. She'll be on vacation in Costa Rica for the rest of her life."

"So what do we do?" Sanders said.

"For better or worse, we're committed now. We've taken this line and we have to continue it. Somehow, we have to force them to come to terms," she said. "But we're going to need something else to do that. You got anything else?"

Sanders shook his head. "No, nothing."

"Hell," Fernandez said. "What's going on? I thought DigiCom was worried about this allegation becoming public before they finished the acquisition. I thought they had a publicity problem."

Sanders nodded. "I thought they did, too."

"Then there's something we don't understand. Because Heller and Blackburn both act like they couldn't care less what we do. Now why is that?"

A heavyset man with a mustache walked past them, carrying a sheaf of papers. He looked like a cop.

"Who's he?" Fernandez said.

"Never seen him before."

"They were calling on the phone for somebody. Trying to locate somebody. That's why I ask."

Sanders shrugged. "What do we do now?"

"We eat," Alan said.

"Right. Let's go eat," Fernandez said, "and forget it for a while."

In the same moment, a thought popped into his mind: *Forget that phone.* It seemed to come from nowhere, like a command:

Forget that phone.

Walking beside him, Fernandez sighed. "We still have things we can develop. It's not over yet. You've still got things, right, Alan?"

"Absolutely," Alan said. "We've hardly begun. We haven't gotten to Johnson's husband yet, or to her previous employer. There's lots of stones left to turn over and see what crawls out."

Forget that phone.

"I better check in with my office," Sanders said, and took out his cellular phone to dial Cindy.

A light rain began to fall. They came to the cars in the parking lot. Fernandez said, "Who's going to drive?"

"I will," Alan said.

They went to his car, a plain Ford sedan. Alan unlocked the doors, and Fernandez started to get in. "And I thought that at lunch today we would be going to have a party," she said.

Going to a party . . .

Sanders looked at Fernandez sitting in the front seat, behind the rain-spattered windshield. He held the phone up to his ear and waited while the call went through to Cindy. He was relieved that his phone was working correctly. Ever since Monday night when it went dead, he hadn't trusted it completely. But it seemed to be fine. Nothing wrong with it at all.

The couple was going to a party and she made a call on a cellular phone. From the car . . .

Forget that phone.

Cindy said, "Mr. Sanders's office."

And when she called, she got an answering ma-

chine. She left a message on the answering machine. And then she hung up.

"Hello? Mr. Sanders's office. Hello?"

"Cindy, it's me."

"Oh, hi, Tom." Still reserved.

"Any messages?" he said.

"Uh, yes, let me look at the book. You had a call from Arthur in KL, he wanted to know if the drives arrived. I checked with Don Cherry's team; they got them. They're working on them now. And you had a call from Eddie in Austin; he sounded worried. And you had another call from John Levin. He called you yesterday, too. And he said it was important."

Levin was the executive with a hard drive supplier. Whatever was on his mind, it could wait.

"Okay. Thanks, Cindy."

"Are you going to be back in the office today? A lot of people are asking."

"I don't know."

"John Conley from Conley-White called. He wanted to meet with you at four."

"I don't know. I'll see. I'll call you later."

"Okay." She hung up.

He heard a dial tone.

And then she had hung up.

The story tugged at the back of his mind. The two people in the car. Going to the party. Who had told him that story? How did it go?

On her way to the party, Adele had made a call from the car and then she had hung up.

Sanders snapped his fingers. Of course! Adele! The couple in the car had been Mark and Adele Lewyn. And they had had an embarrassing incident. It was starting to come back to him now.

Adele had called somebody and gotten the answering machine. She left a message, and hung up the phone. Then she and Mark talked in the car about the person Adele had just called. They made jokes and unflattering comments for about fifteen minutes. And later they were very embarrassed . . .

Fernandez said, "Are you just going to stand there in the rain?"

Sanders didn't answer. He took the cellular phone down from his ear. The keypad and screen glowed bright green. Plenty of power. He looked at the phone and waited. After five seconds, it clicked itself off; the screen went blank. That was because the new generation of phones had an auto-shutdown feature to conserve battery power. If you didn't use the phone or press the keypad for fifteen seconds, the phone shut itself off. So it wouldn't go dead.

But his phone had gone dead in Meredith's office.

Why?

Forget that phone.

Why had his cellular phone failed to shut itself off? What possible explanation could there be? Mechanical problems: one of the keys stuck, keeping the phone on. It had been damaged when he dropped it, when Meredith first kissed him. The battery was low because he forgot to charge it the night before.

No, he thought. The phone was reliable. There was no mechanical fault. And it was fully charged.

No.

The phone had worked correctly.

They made jokes and unflattering comments for about fifteen minutes.

His mind began to race, with scattered fragments of conversation coming back to him.

"Listen, why didn't you call me last night?"

"I did, Mark."

Sanders was certain that he had called Mark Lewyn from Meredith's office. Standing in the parking lot in the rain, he again pressed L-E-W on his keypad. The phone turned itself back on, the little screen flashing LEWYN and Mark's home number.

"There wasn't any message when I got home."

"I talked to your answering machine, about six-fifteen."

"I never got a message."

Sanders was sure that he had called Lewyn and

had talked to his answering machine. He remembered a man's voice saying the standard message, "Leave a message when you hear the tone."

Standing there with the phone in his hand, staring at Lewyn's phone number, he pressed the SEND button. A moment later, the answering machine picked up. A woman's voice said, "Hi, you've reached Mark and Adele at home. We're not able to come to the phone right now, but if you leave a message, we'll call you back." *Beep.*

That was a different message.

He *hadn't* called Mark Lewyn that night.

Which could only mean he hadn't pressed L-E-W that night. Nervous in Meredith's office, he must have pressed something else. He had gotten somebody else's answering machine.

And his phone had gone dead.

Because . . .

Forget that phone.

"Jesus Christ," he said. He suddenly put it together. He knew exactly what had happened. And it meant that there was the chance that—

"Tom, are you all right?" Fernandez said.

"I'm fine," he said. "Just give me a minute. I think I've got something important."

He hadn't pressed L-E-W.

He had pressed something else. Something very close, probably one letter off. With fumbling fingers, Sanders pushed L-E-L. The screen stayed blank: he had no number stored for that combination. L-E-M. No number stored. L-E-S. No number stored. L-E-V.

Bingo.

Printed across the little screen was:

LEVIN

And a phone number for John Levin.

Sanders had called John Levin's answering machine that night.

John Levin called. He said it was important.

I'll bet he did, Sanders thought.

He remembered now, with sudden clarity, the exact sequence of events in Meredith's office. He had been talking on the phone and she said, "Forget that phone," and pushed his hand down as she started kissing him. He had dropped the phone on the windowsill as they kissed, and left it there.

Later on, when he left Meredith's office, buttoning his shirt, he had picked up the cellular phone from the sill, but by then it was dead. Which could only mean that it had remained constantly on for almost an hour. It had remained on during the entire incident with Meredith.

In the car, when Adele finished the call, she hung the phone back in the cradle, She didn't press the END *button, so the phone line stayed open, and their entire conversation was recorded on the person's answering machine. Fifteen minutes of jokes and personal commentary, all recorded on his answering machine.*

And Sanders's phone had been dead because the line stayed open. The whole conversation had been recorded.

Standing in the parking lot, he quickly dialed John Levin's number. Fernandez got out of the car and came over to him. "What's going on?" Fernandez said. "Are we going to lunch, or what?"

"Just a minute."

The call went through. A click of the pickup, then a man's voice: "John Levin."

"John, it's Tom Sanders."

"Well, hey there, Tom boy!" Levin burst out laughing. "My *man*! Are you having a red-hot sex life these days, or what? I tell you, Tom, my ears were burning."

Sanders said, "Was it recorded?"

"Jesus Christ, Tom, you better believe it. I came in Tuesday morning to check my messages, and I tell you, it went on for half an hour, I mean—"

"John—"

"Whoever said married life was dull—"

"John. Listen. *Did you keep it?*"

There was a pause. Levin stopped laughing. "Tom, what do you think I am, a pervert? Of *course* I kept it. I played it for the whole office. They loved it!"

"John. Seriously."

Levin sighed. "Yeah. I kept it. It sounded like you might be having a little trouble, and . . . I don't know. Anyway, I kept it."

"Good. Where is it?"

"Right here on my desk," Levin said.

"John, I want that tape. Now listen to me: this is what I want you to do."

Driving in the car, Fernandez said, "I'm waiting."

Sanders said, "There's a tape of the whole meeting with Meredith. It was all recorded."

"How?"

"It was an accident. I was talking to an answering machine," he said, "and when Meredith started kissing me, I put the phone down but didn't end the call. So the phone stayed connected to the answering machine. And everything we said went right onto the answering machine."

"Hot damn," Alan said, slapping the steering wheel as he drove.

"This is an audio tape?" Fernandez said.

"Yes."

"Good quality?"

"I don't know. We'll see. John's bringing it to lunch."

Fernandez rubbed her hands together. "I feel better already."

"Yes?"

"Yes," she said. "Because if it's any good at all, we can really draw blood."

John Levin, florid and jovial, pushed away his plate and drained the last of his beer. "Now that's what I call a meal. *Excellent* halibut." Levin weighed nearly three hundred pounds, and his belly pressed up against the edge of the table.

They were sitting in a booth in the back room of McCormick and Schmick's on First Avenue. The restaurant was noisy, filled with the lunch-time business crowd. Fernandez pressed the headphones to her ears as she listened to the tape on a Walkman. She had been listening intently for more than half an hour, making notes on a yellow legal pad, her food still uneaten. Finally she got up. "I have to make a call."

Levin glanced at Fernandez's plate. "Uh . . . do you want that?"

Fernandez shook her head, and walked away.

Levin grinned. "Waste not, want not," he said, and pulled the plate in front of him. He began to eat. "So Tom, are you in shit or what?"

"Deep shit," Sanders said. He stirred a cappuccino. He hadn't been able to eat lunch. He watched Levin wolf down great bites of mashed potatoes.

"I figured that," Levin said. "Jack Kerry over

at Aldus called me this morning and said you were suing the company because you refused to jump some woman."

"Kerry is an asshole."

"The worst," Levin nodded. "The absolute worst. But what can you do? After Connie Walsh's column this morning, everybody's been trying to figure out who Mr. Piggy is." Levin took another huge bite of food. "But how'd she get the story in the first place? I mean, she's the one who broke it."

Sanders said, "Maybe you told her, John."

"Are you kidding?" Levin said.

"You had the tape."

Levin frowned. "You keep this up, Tom, you're going to piss me off." He shook his head. "No, you ask me, it was a woman who told her."

"What woman knew? Only Meredith, and she wouldn't tell."

"I'll bet you anything it'll turn out to be a woman," Levin said. "If you ever find out— which I doubt." He chewed thoughtfully. "Swordfish is a little rubbery. I think we should tell the waiter." He looked around the room. "Uh, Tom."

"Yes?"

"There's a guy standing over there, hopping from one foot to the other. I think maybe you know him."

Sanders looked over his shoulder. Bob Garvin

was standing by the bar, looking at him expectantly. Phil Blackburn stood a few paces behind.

"Excuse me," Sanders said, and he got up from the table.

Garvin shook hands with Sanders. "Tom. Good to see you. How are you holding up with all this?"

"I'm okay," Sanders said.

"Good, good." Garvin placed his hand in a fatherly way on Sanders's shoulder. "It's nice to see you again."

"Nice to see you too, Bob."

Garvin said, "There's a quiet place in the corner over there. I asked them for a couple of cappuccinos. We can talk for a minute. Is that okay?"

"That's fine," Sanders said. He was well acquainted with the profane, angry Garvin. This cautious, polite Garvin made him uneasy.

They sat in the corner of the bar. Garvin settled into his chair and faced him.

"Well, Tom. We go way back, you and I."

"Yes, we do."

"Those damn trips to Seoul, eating that crappy food, and your ass hurting like hell. You remember all that."

"Yes, I do."

"Yeah, those were the days," Garvin said. He was watching Sanders carefully. "Anyway, Tom, we know each other, so I'm not going to bullshit

you. Let me just put all the cards on the table,"
Garvin said. "We've got a problem here, and it's
got to be solved before it turns into a real mess for
everybody. I want to appeal to your better judgment about how we proceed from here."

"My better judgment?" Sanders said.

"Yes," Garvin said. "I'd like to look at this
thing from all sides."

"How many sides are there?"

"There are at least two," Garvin said, with a
smile. "Look, Tom. I'm sure it's no secret that
I've supported Meredith inside our company. I've
always believed that she's got talent and the kind
of executive vision that we want for the future.
I've never seen her do anything before that would
suggest otherwise. I know she's only human, but
she's very talented and I support her."

"Uh-huh . . ."

"Now perhaps in this case . . . perhaps it is true
that she's made a mistake. I don't know."

Sanders said nothing. He just waited, staring at
Garvin's face. Garvin was doing a convincing impression of an open-minded man. Sanders didn't
buy it.

"In fact, let's say she has," Garvin said. "Let's
say she did make a mistake."

"She did, Bob," Sanders said, firmly.

"All right. Let's say she did. An error of judgment, let's call it. An oversteppping of bounds. The

point is, Tom, faced with a situation like this, I still strongly support her."

"Why?"

"Because she's a woman."

"What does that have to do with it?"

"Well, women in business have traditionally been excluded from executive positions, Tom."

"Meredith hasn't been excluded," Sanders said.

"And after all," Garvin said, "she's young."

"She's not that young," Sanders said.

"Sure she is. She's practically a college kid. She just got her MBA a couple of years ago."

"Bob," Sanders said. "Meredith Johnson's thirty-five. She's not a kid at all."

Garvin did not seem to hear that. He looked at Sanders sympathetically. "Tom, I can understand that you were disappointed about the job," he said. "And I can understand that in your eyes, Meredith made a mistake in the way she approached you."

"She didn't approach me, Bob. She jumped me."

Garvin showed a flash of irritation. "You're no kid either, you know."

"That's right, I'm not," Sanders said. "But I *am* her employee."

"And I know she holds you in the highest regard," Garvin said, settling back in his chair. "As does everybody in the company, Tom. You're vital to our future. You know it, I know it. I want to keep our team together. And I keep coming back to the idea that we have to make allowances for women. We have to cut them a little slack."

"But we're not talking about women," Sanders said. "We're talking about one particular woman."

"Tom—"

"And if a man had done what she did, you wouldn't be talking about cutting him slack. You'd fire him, and throw him out on his ass."

"Possibly so."

"Well, that's the problem," Sanders said.

Garvin said, "I'm not sure I follow you there, Tom." His tone carried a warning: Garvin didn't like being disagreed with. Over the years, as his company grew in wealth and success, Garvin had grown accustomed to deference. Now, approaching retirement, he expected obedience and agreement. "We have an obligation to attain equality," Garvin said.

"Fine. But equality *means* no special breaks," Sanders said. "Equality means treating people the same. You're asking for *in*equality toward Meredith, because you won't do what you would do to a man—fire him."

Garvin sighed. "If it was a clear case, Tom, I would. But I understand this particular situation isn't so clear."

Sanders considered telling him about the tape.

Something made him hold back. He said, "I think it is."

"But there are always differences of opinion on these matters," Garvin said, leaning across the bar. "That's a fact, isn't it? Always a difference of opinion. Tom. Look: what did she do that was so bad? I mean, really. She made a pass? Fine. You could have decided it was flattering. She's a beautiful woman, after all. There are worse things that could happen. A beautiful woman puts her hand on your knee. Or you could have just said, no thank you. You could have handled it any number of ways. You're a grown-up. But this . . . *vindictiveness*. Tom. I have to tell you. I'm surprised at you."

Sanders said, "Bob, she broke the law."

"That really remains to be seen, doesn't it?" Garvin said. "You can throw open your personal life for a jury to inspect, if that's what you want to do. I wouldn't want to do it, myself. And I don't see that it helps anybody to take this into court. It's a no-win situation, all around."

"What're you saying?"

"You don't want to go to court, Tom." Garvin's eyes were narrow, dangerous.

"Why not?"

"You just don't." Garvin took a deep breath. "Look. Let's stay on track here. I've talked to Meredith. She feels as I do, that this thing has gotten out of hand."

"Uh-huh . . ."

"And I'm talking to you now, too. Because my hope, Tom, is that we can put this to rest, and go back to the way things were—now hear me out, please—go back to the way things were, before this unfortunate misunderstanding happened. You stay at your job, Meredith stays at hers. You two continue to work together like civilized adults. You move forward and build the company, take it public, and everybody makes a pile of money a year down the line. What's wrong with that?"

Sanders felt something like relief, and a sense of normalcy returning. He longed to escape from the lawyers and from the tension of the last three days. To sink back into the way things were seemed as appealing as a warm bath.

"I mean, look at it this way, Tom. Right after this thing happened on Monday night, nobody blew the whistle. You didn't call anybody. Meredith didn't call anybody. I think you both wanted this thing to go away. Then there was an unfortunate mix-up the next day, and an argument that needn't have happened. If you'd been on time for the meeting, if you and Meredith had been in sync on the story, none of this would have happened. You two would still be working together, and whatever happened between you would remain your private business. Instead, we have this. It's all a big mistake, really. So why not just forget it and go forward? And get rich. Tom? What's wrong with that?"

"Nothing," Sanders said, finally.

"Good."

"Except it won't work," Sanders said.

"Why not?"

A dozen answers flashed through his mind: Because she's not competent. Because she's a snake. Because she's a corporate player, all image, and this is a technical division that has to get out the product. Because she's a liar. Because I have no respect for her. Because she'll do it again. Because she has no respect for me. Because you're not treating me fairly. Because she's your pet. Because you chose her over me. Because . . .

"Things have gone too far," he said.

Garvin stared at him. "Things can go back."

"No, Bob. They can't."

Garvin leaned forward. His voice dropped. "Listen you little *feringi* pissant. I know exactly what's going on here. I took you in when you didn't know *bulkogi* from bullshit. I gave you your start, I gave you help, I gave you opportunities, all along the line. Now you want to play rough? Fine. You want to see the shit come down? Just fucking wait, Tom." He stood up.

Sanders said, "Bob, you've never been willing to listen to reason on the subject of Meredith Johnson."

"Oh, you think *I* have a problem with Mere-

dith?" Garvin laughed harshly. "Listen, Tom: she
was your girlfriend, but she was smart and independent, and you couldn't handle her. You were
pissed when she dropped you. And now, all these
years later, you're going to pay her back. That's
what this is about. It has nothing to do with business ethics or breaking the law or sexual harassment or any other damned thing. It's personal,
and it's petty. And you're so full of shit your eyes
are brown."

And he stalked out of the restaurant, pushing
angrily past Blackburn. Blackburn remained behind for a moment, staring at Sanders, and then
hurried after his boss.

As Sanders walked back to his table, he passed a booth with several guys from Microsoft, including two major assholes from systems programming. Someone made a snorting pig sound.

"Hey Mr. Piggy," said a low voice.

"Suwee! Suwee!"

"Couldn't get it up, huh?"

Sanders walked on a few paces, then turned back. "Hey, guys," he said. "At least I'm not bending over and grabbing my ankles in late-night meetings with—" and he named a Programming head at Microsoft.

They all roared with laughter.

"Whoa ho!"

"Mr. Piggy speaks!"

"Oink oink."

Sanders said, "What're you guys doing in town, anyway? They run short on K-Y jelly in Redmond?"

"Whoa!"

"The Piggy is pissed!"

They were doubled over, laughing like college kids. They had a big pitcher of beer on the table. One of them said, "If Meredith Johnson pulled off her pants for me, I sure wouldn't call the police about it."

"No way, Jose!"

"Service with a smile!"

"Hard charger!"

"Ladies *first!*"

"Ka-jung! Ka-jung!"

They pounded the table, laughing.

Sanders walked away.

O utside the restaurant, Garvin paced back and forth angrily on the pavement. Blackburn stood with the phone at his ear.

"Where is that fucking car?" Garvin said.

"I don't know, Bob."

"I told him to *wait.*"

"I know, Bob. I'm trying to get him."

"Christ Almighty, the simplest things. Can't even get the fucking cars to work right."

"Maybe he had to go to the bathroom."

"So? How long does that take? Goddamn Sanders. Could you believe him?"

"No, I couldn't, Bob."

"I just don't understand. He won't deal with me on this. And I'm bending over backward here. I offer him his job back, I offer him his stock back, I offer him everything. And what does he do? Jesus."

"He's not a team player, Bob."

"You got that right. And he's not willing to meet us. We've got to get him to come to the table."

"Yes we do, Bob."

"He's not feeling it," Garvin said. "That's the problem."

"The story ran this morning. It can't have made him happy."

"Well, he's not feeling it."

Garvin paced again.

"There's the car," Blackburn said, pointing down the street. The Lincoln sedan was driving toward them.

"Finally," Garvin said. "Now look, Phil. I'm tired of wasting time on Sanders. We tried being nice, and it didn't work. That's the long and the short of it. So what are we going to do, to make him feel it?"

"I've been thinking about that," Phil said. "What's Sanders doing? I mean really doing? He's smearing Meredith, right?"

"Goddamn right."

"He didn't hesitate to smear her."

"He sure as hell didn't."

"And it's not true, what he's saying about her. But the thing about a smear is that it doesn't have to be true. It just has to be something people are willing to believe is true."

"So?"

"So maybe Sanders needs to see what that feels like."

"Like what feels like? What're you talking about?"

Blackburn stared thoughtfully at the approaching car. "I think that Tom's a violent man."

"Oh hell," Garvin said, "he's not. I've known him for years. He's a pussycat."

"No," Blackburn said, rubbing his nose. "I disagree. I think he's violent. He was a football player in college, he's a rough-and-tumble sort of guy. Plays football on the company team, knocks people around. He has a violent streak. Most men do, after all. Men are violent."

"What kind of shit is this?"

"And you have to admit, he was violent to Meredith," Blackburn continued. "Shouting. Yelling. Pushing her. Knocking her over. Sex and violence. A man out of control. He's much bigger than she is. Just stand them side by side, anybody can see the difference. He's much bigger. Much stronger. All you have to do is look, and you see he is a violent abusive man. That nice exterior is just a cover. Sanders is one of those men who take out their hostility by beating up defenseless women."

Garvin was silent. He squinted at Blackburn. "You'll never make this fly."

"I think I can."

"Nobody in their right mind'll buy it."

Blackburn said, "I think somebody will."

"Yeah? Who?"

"Somebody," Blackburn said.

The car pulled up to the curb. Garvin opened the door. "Well, all I know," he said, "is that we need to get him to negotiate. We need to apply pressure to bring him to the table."

Blackburn said, "I think that can be arranged."

Garvin nodded. "It's in your hands, Phil. Just make sure it happens." He got in the car. Blackburn got in the car after Garvin. Garvin said to the driver, "Where the fuck have you been?"

The door slammed shut. The car drove off.

Sanders drove with Fernandez in Alan's car back to the mediation center. Fernandez listened to Sanders's report of the conversation with Garvin, shaking her head. "You never should have seen him alone. He couldn't have behaved that way if I was there. Did he really say you have to make allowances for women?"

"Yes."

"That's noble of him. He's found a virtuous reason why we should protect a harasser. It's a nice touch. Everyone should sit back and allow her to break the law because she's a woman. Very nice."

Sanders felt stronger hearing her words. The conversation with Garvin had rattled him. He knew that Fernandez was working on him, building him back up, but it worked anyway.

"The whole conversation is ridiculous," Fernandez said. "And then he threatened you?"

Sanders nodded.

"Forget it. It's just bluster."

"You're sure?"

"Absolutely," she said. "Just talk. But at least now you know why they say men just don't get it. Garvin gave you the same lines that every corporate guy has been giving for years: Look at it from the harasser's point of view. What did they do that was so wrong. Let bygones be bygones. Everybody just go back to work. We'll be one big happy family again."

"Incredible," Alan said, driving the car.

"It is, in this day and age," Fernandez said. "You can't pull that stuff anymore. How old is Garvin, anyway?"

"Almost sixty."

"That helps explain it. But Blackburn should have told him it's completely unacceptable. According to the law, Garvin really doesn't have any choice. At a minimum, he has to transfer Johnson, not you. And almost certainly, he should fire her."

"I don't think he will," Sanders said.

"No, of course he won't."

"She's his favorite," Sanders said.

"More to the point, she's his vice president," Fernandez said. She stared out the window as they went up the hill toward the mediation center. "You have to realize, all these decisions are about power. Sexual harassment is about power, and so is the company's resistance to dealing with it. Power protects power. And once a woman gets up in the power structure, she'll be protected by the structure, the same as a man. It's like the way doctors won't testify against other doctors. It doesn't matter if the doctor is a man or a woman.

Doctors just don't want to testify against other doctors. Period. And corporate executives don't want to investigate claims against other executives, male or female."

"So it's just that women haven't had these jobs?"

"Yes. But they're starting to get them now. And now they can be as unfair as any man ever was."

"Female chauvinist sows," Alan said.

"Don't you start," Fernandez said.

"Tell him the figures," Alan said.

"What figures?" Sanders said.

"About five percent of sexual harassment claims are brought by men against women. It's a relatively small figure. But then, only five percent of corporate supervisors are women. So the figures suggest that women executives harass men in the same proportion as men harass women. And as more women get corporate jobs, the percentage of claims by men is going up. Because the fact is, harassment is a power issue. And power is neither male nor female. Whoever is behind the desk has the opportunity to abuse power. And women will take advantage as often as men. A case in point being the delightful Ms. Johnson. And her boss isn't firing her."

"Garvin says it's because the situation isn't clear."

"I'd say that tape is pretty damn clear," Fernandez said. She frowned. "Did you tell him about the tape?"

"No."

"Good. Then I think we can wrap this case up in the next two hours."

Alan pulled into the parking lot and parked the car. They all got out.

"All right," Fernandez said. "Let's see where we are with her significant others. Alan. We've still got her previous employer—"

"Conrad Computer. Right. We're on it.

"And also the one before that."

"Symantec."

"Yes. And we have her husband—"

"I've got a call into CoStar for him."

"And the Internet business? 'Afriend'?"

"Working on it."

"And we have her B-school, and Vassar."

"Right."

"Recent history is the most important. Focus on Conrad and the husband."

"Okay," Alan said. "Conrad's a problem, because they supply systems to the government and the CIA. They gave me some song and dance about neutral reference policy and nondisclosure of prior employees."

"Then get Harry to call them. He's good on negligent referral. He can shake them up if they continue to stonewall."

"Okay. He may have to."

Alan got back in the car. Fernandez and Sanders started walking up to the mediation center. Sanders said, "You're checking her past companies?"

"Yes. Other companies don't like to give damaging information on prior employees. For years, they would never give anything at all except the dates of employment. But now there's something called compelled self-publication, and something called negligent referral. A company can be liable now for failing to reveal a problem with a past employee. So we can try to scare them. But in the end, they may not give us the damaging information we want."

"How do you know they have damaging information to give?"

Fernandez smiled. "Because Johnson is a harasser. And with harassers, there's always a pattern. It's never the first time."

"You think she's done this before?"

"Don't sound so disappointed," Fernandez said. "What did you think? That she did all this because she thought you were so cute? I guarantee you she has done it before." They walked past the fountains in the courtyard toward the door to the center building. "And now," Fernandez said, "let's go cut Ms. Johnson to shreds."

Precisely at one-thirty, Judge Murphy entered the mediation room. She looked at the seven silent people sitting around the table and frowned. "Has opposing counsel met?"

"We have," Heller said.

"With what result?" Murphy said.

"We have failed to reach a settlement," Heller said.

"Very well. Let's resume." She sat down and opened her notepad. "Is there further discussion relating to the morning session?"

"Yes, Your Honor," Fernandez said. "I have some additional questions for Ms. Johnson."

"Very well. Ms. Johnson?"

Meredith Johnson put on her glasses. "Actually, Your Honor, I would like to make a statement first."

"All right."

"I've been thinking about the morning session," Johnson said, speaking slowly and deliberately, "and Mr. Sanders's account of the events of Monday night. And I've begun to feel that there may be a genuine misunderstanding here."

"I see." Judge Murphy spoke absolutely without inflection. She stared at Meredith. "All right."

"When Tom first suggested a meeting at the end of the day, and when he suggested that we have some wine, and talk over old times, I'm afraid I may have unconsciously responded to him in a way that he might not have intended."

Judge Murphy didn't move. Nobody was moving. The room was completely still.

"I believe it is correct to say that I took him at his word, and began to imagine a, uh, romantic interlude. And to be frank, I was not opposed to that possibility. Mr. Sanders and I had a very special relationship some years ago, and I remembered it as a very exciting relationship. So I believe it is fair to say that I was looking forward to our meeting, and that perhaps I presumed that it would lead to an encounter. Which I was, unconsciously, quite willing to have occur."

Alongside Meredith, Heller and Blackburn sat completely stone-faced, showing no reaction at all. The two female attorneys showed no reaction. This had all been worked out in advance, Sanders realized. What was going on? Why was she changing her story?

Johnson cleared her throat, then continued in the same deliberate way. "I believe it is correct to say that I was a willing participant in all the events of the evening. And it may be that I was too forward, at one point, for Mr. Sanders's taste. In the heat of the moment, I may have overstepped the bounds of propriety and my position in the

company. I think that's possible. After serious
reflection, I find myself concluding that my own
recollection of events and Mr. Sanders's recollection of events are in much closer agreement than
I had earlier recognized."

There was a long silence. Judge Murphy said
nothing. Meredith Johnson shifted in her chair,
took her glasses off, then put them back on again.

"Ms. Johnson," Murphy said finally, "do I understand you to say that you are now agreeing to
Mr. Sanders's version of the events on Monday
night?"

"In many respects, yes. Perhaps in most
respects."

Sanders suddenly realized what had happened:
they knew about the tape.

But how could they know? Sanders himself had
learned of it only two hours ago. And Levin had
been out of his office, having lunch with them. So
Levin couldn't have told them. How could they
know?

"And, Ms. Johnson," Murphy said, "are you
also agreeing to the charge of harassment by Mr.
Sanders?"

"Not at all, Your Honor. No."

"Then I'm not sure I understand. You've
changed your story. You say you now agree that
Mr. Sanders's version of the events is correct in
most respects. But you do not agree that he has a
claim against you?"

"No, Your Honor. As I said, I think it was all a misunderstanding."

"A *misunderstanding*," Murphy repeated, with an incredulous look on her face.

"Yes, Your Honor. And one in which Mr. Sanders played a very active role."

"Ms. Johnson. According to Mr. Sanders, you initiated kissing over his protests; you pushed him down on the couch over his protests; you unzipped his trousers and removed his penis over his protests; and you removed your own clothing over his protests. Since Mr. Sanders is your employee, and dependent on you for employment, it is difficult for me to comprehend why this is not a clear-cut and indisputable case of sexual harassment on your part."

"I understand, Your Honor," Meredith Johnson said calmly. "And I realize I have changed my story. But the reason I say it is a misunderstanding is that from the beginning, I genuinely believed that Mr. Sanders was seeking a sexual encounter with me, and that belief guided my actions."

"You do not agree that you harassed him."

"No, Your Honor. Because I thought I had clear *physical* indications that Mr. Sanders was a willing participant. At times he certainly took the lead. So now, I have to ask myself why he would take the lead—and then so suddenly withdraw. I don't know why he did that. But I believe he

shares responsibility for what happened. That is
why I feel that, at the very least, we had a genuine
misunderstanding. And I want to say that I am
sorry—truly, deeply sorry—for my part in this
misunderstanding."

"You're sorry." Murphy looked around the
room in exasperation. "Can anyone explain to me
what is going on? Mr. Heller?"

Heller spread his hands. "Your Honor, my client told me what she intended to do here. I consider it a very brave act. She is a true seeker after
truth."

"Oh, spare me," Fernandez said.

Judge Murphy said, "Ms. Fernandez, considering this radically different statement from Ms.
Johnson, would you like a recess before you proceed with your questions?"

"No, Your Honor. I am prepared to go forward now," Fernandez said.

"I see," Murphy said, puzzled. "All right.
Fine." Judge Murphy clearly felt that there was
something everyone else in the room knew that
she didn't.

Sanders was still wondering how Meredith
knew about the tape. He looked over at Phil
Blackburn, who sat at one end of the table, his
cellular phone before him. He was rubbing the
phone nervously.

Phone records, Sanders thought. That must be
it.

DigiCom would have had somebody—most probably Gary Bosak—going through all of Sanders's records, looking for things to use against him. Bosak would have checked all the calls made on Sanders's cellular phone. When he did that, he would have discovered a call that lasted forty-five minutes on Monday night. It would stand out: a whopping big duration and charge. And Bosak must have looked at the time of the call and figured out what had happened. He'd realize that Sanders hadn't been talking on the phone during that particular forty-five minutes on Monday night. Therefore, there could only be one explanation. The call was running to an answering machine, which meant there was a tape. And Johnson knew it, and had adjusted her story accordingly. That was what had made her change.

"Ms. Johnson," Fernandez said. "Let's clear up a few factual points first. Are you now saying that you *did* send your assistant to buy wine and condoms, that you *did* tell her to lock the door, and that you *did* cancel your seven o'clock appointment in anticipation of a sexual encounter with Mr. Sanders?"

"Yes, I did."

"In other words, you lied earlier."

"I presented my point of view."

"But we are not talking about a point of view. We are talking about facts. And given this set of facts, I'm curious to know why you feel that Mr. Sanders shares responsibility for what happened in that room Monday night."

"Because I felt . . . I felt that Mr. Sanders had come to my office with the clear intention of having sex with me, and he later denied any such intention. I felt he had set me up. He led me on, and then accused me, when I had done nothing more than simply respond to him."

"You feel he set you up?"

"Yes."

"And that's why you feel he shares responsibility?"

"Yes."

"In what way did he set you up?"

"Well, I think it's obvious. Things had gone very far along, when he suddenly got off the couch and said he was not going to proceed. I'd say that was a setup."

"Why?"

"Because you can't go so far and then just stop. That's obviously a hostile act, intended to embarrass and humiliate me. I mean . . . anyone can see that."

"All right. Let's review that particular moment in detail," Fernandez said. "As I understand it, we're talking about the time when you were on the couch with Mr. Sanders, with both of you in a state of partial undress. Mr. Sanders was crouched on his knees on the couch, his penis was exposed, and you were lying on your back with your panties removed and your legs spread, is that correct?"

"Basically. Yes." She shook her head. "You make it sound so . . . crude."

"But that was the situation at that moment, was it not?"

"Yes. It was."

"Now, at that moment, did you say, 'No, no, please,' and did Mr. Sanders reply, 'You're right, we shouldn't be doing this,' and then get off the couch?"

"Yes," she said. "That's what he said."

"Then what was the misunderstanding?"

"When I said, 'No, no,' I meant, 'No, don't wait.' Because he was waiting, sort of teasing me, and I wanted him to go ahead. Instead, he got off the couch, which made me very angry."

"Why?"

"Because I wanted him to do it."

"But Ms. Johnson, you said, 'No, no.' "

"I know what I said," she replied irritably, "but in that situation, it's perfectly clear what I was really saying to him."

"Is it?"

"Of course. He knew exactly what I was saying to him, but he chose to ignore it."

"Ms. Johnson, have you ever heard the phrase, 'No means no'?"

"Of course, but in this situation—"

"I'm sorry, Ms. Johnson. Does no mean no, or not?"

"Not in this case. Because at that time, lying on that couch, it was absolutely clear what I was really saying to him."

"You mean it was clear to you."

Johnson became openly angry. "It was clear to him, too," she snapped.

"Ms. Johnson. When men are told that 'no means no,' what does that mean?"

"I don't know." She threw up her hands in irritation. "I don't know what you're trying to say."

"I'm trying to say that men are being told that they must take women at their literal word. That no means no. That men cannot assume that no means maybe or yes."

"But in this particular situation, with all our clothes off, when things had gone so far—"

"What does that have to do with it?" Fernandez said.

"Oh, come off it," Johnson said. "When people are getting together, they begin with little touches, then little kisses, then a little petting, then some more petting. Then the clothes come off, and you're touching various private parts, and so on. And pretty soon you have an expectation about what's going to happen. And you don't turn back. To turn back is a hostile act. That's what he did. He set me up."

"Ms. Johnson. Isn't it true that women claim the right to turn back at any point, up to the moment of actual penetration? Don't women claim the unequivocal right to change their minds?"

"Yes, but in this instance—"

"Ms. Johnson. If women have the right to change their minds, don't men as well? Can't Mr. Sanders change his mind?"

"It was a hostile act." Her face had a fixed, stubborn look. "He set me up."

"I'm asking whether Mr. Sanders has the same rights as a woman in this situation. Whether he has the right to withdraw, even at the last moment."

"No."

"Why?"

"Because men are different."

"How are they different?"

"Oh, for Christ's sake," Johnson said angrily. "What are we talking about here? This is Alice in Wonderland. Men and women are *different*. Everybody knows that. Men can't control their impulses."

"Apparently Mr. Sanders could."

"Yes. As a hostile act. Out of his desire to humiliate me."

"But what Mr. Sanders actually said at the time was, 'I don't feel good about this.' Isn't that true?"

"I don't remember his exact words. But his behavior was very hostile and degrading toward me as a woman."

"Let's consider," Fernandez said, "who was hostile and degrading toward whom. Didn't Mr. Sanders protest the way things were going earlier in the evening?"

"Not really. No."

"I thought he had." Fernandez looked at her notes. "Early on, did you say to Mr. Sanders, 'You look good' and 'You always had a nice hard tush'?"

"I don't know. I might have. I don't remember."

"And what did he reply?"

"I don't remember."

Fernandez said, "Now, when Mr. Sanders was talking on the phone, did you come up, push it out of his hand, and say, 'Forget that phone'?"

"I might have. I don't really remember."

"And did you initiate kissing at that point?"

"I'm not really sure. I don't think so."

"Well, let's see. How else could it have occurred? Mr. Sanders was talking on his cellular phone, over by the window. You were on another phone at your desk. Did he interrupt his call, set down his phone, come over, and start kissing you?"

She paused for a moment. "No."

"Then who initiated the kissing?"

"I guess I did."

"And when he protested and said, 'Meredith,' did you ignore him, press on, and say, 'God, I've wanted you all day. I'm so hot, I haven't had a decent fuck'?" Fernandez repeated these statements in a flat uninflected monotone, as if reading from a transcript.

"I may have . . . I think that might be accurate. Yes."

Fernandez looked again at her notes. "And then, when he said, 'Meredith, wait,' again clearly speaking in a tone of protest, did you say, 'Oh, don't talk, no, no, oh Jesus'?"

"I think . . . possibly I did."

"On reflection, would you say these comments by Mr. Sanders were protests that you ignored?"

"If they were, they were not very clear protests. No."

"Ms. Johnson. Would you characterize Mr. Sanders as fully enthusiastic throughout the encounter?"

Johnson hesitated a moment. Sanders could almost see her thinking, trying to decide how much the tape would reveal. Finally she said, "He was enthusiastic sometimes, not so much at other times. That's my point."

"Would you say he was ambivalent?"

"Possibly. Somewhat."

"Is that a yes or a no, Ms. Johnson?"

"Yes."

"All right. So Mr. Sanders was ambivalent throughout the session. He's told us why: because he was being asked to embark on an office affair with an old girlfriend who was now his boss. And because he was now married. Would you consider those valid reasons for ambivalence?"

"I suppose so."

"And in this state of ambivalence, Mr. Sanders was overwhelmed at the last moment with the feeling that he didn't want to go forward. And he told you how he felt, simply and directly. So, why would you characterize that as a 'setup'? I think we have ample evidence that it is just the opposite—an uncalculated, rather desperate human response to a situation which you entirely controlled. This was not a reunion of old lovers, Ms. Johnson, though you prefer to think it was. This was not a meeting of equals at all. The fact is, you are his superior and you controlled every aspect of the meeting. You arranged the time, bought the wine, bought the condoms, locked the door—and then you blamed your employee when he failed to please you. That is how you continue to behave now."

"And you're trying to put his behavior in a good light," Johnson said. "But what I'm saying is that as a practical matter, waiting to the last minute to stop makes people very angry."

"Yes," Fernandez said. "That's how many men feel, when women withdraw at the last minute.

But women say a man has no right to be angry, because a woman can withdraw at any time. Isn't that true?"

Johnson rapped her fingers on the table irritably. "Look," she said. "You're trying to make some kind of federal case here, by trying to obscure basic facts. What did I do that was so wrong? I made him an offer, that's all. If Mr. Sanders wasn't interested, all he had to do was say, 'No.' But he never said that. Not once. Because he intended to *set me up*. He's angry he didn't get the job and he's retaliating the only way he can—by smearing me. This is nothing but guerrilla warfare and character assassination. I'm a successful woman in business, and he resents my success and he's out to get me. You're saying all kinds of things to avoid that central and unavoidable fact."

"Ms. Johnson. The central and unavoidable fact is that you're Mr. Sanders's superior. And your behavior toward him was illegal. And it *is* in fact a federal case."

There was a short silence.

Blackburn's assistant came into the room and handed him a note. Blackburn read the note and passed it to Heller.

Murphy said, "Ms. Fernandez? Are you ready to explain what's going on to me now?"

"Yes, Your Honor. It turns out there is an audio tape of the meeting."

"Really? Have you heard it?"

"I have, Your Honor. It confirms Mr. Sanders's story."

"Are you aware of this tape, Ms. Johnson?"

"No, I am not."

"Perhaps Ms. Johnson and her attorney would like to hear it, too. Perhaps we should all hear it," Murphy said, looking directly at Blackburn.

Heller put the note in his pocket and said, "Your Honor, I'd like to request a ten-minute recess."

"Very well, Mr. Heller. I'd say this development warrants it."

Outside in the courtyard, black clouds hung low. It was threatening to rain again. Over by the fountains, Johnson huddled with Heller and Blackburn. Fernandez watched them. "I just don't understand this," she said. "There they all are, talking again. What is there to talk about? Their client lied, and then changed her story. There's no question that Johnson's guilty of sexual harassment. We have it recorded on tape. So what are they talking about?"

Fernandez stared for a moment, frowning. "You know, I have to admit it. Johnson's a hell of a smart woman," she said.

"Yes," Sanders said.

"She's quick and she's cool."

"Uh-huh."

"Moved up the corporate ladder fast."

"Yes."

"So . . . how'd she let herself get into this situation?"

"What do you mean?" Sanders said.

"I mean, what's she doing coming on to you the very first day at work? And coming on so strongly? Leaving herself open to all these problems? She's too smart for that."

Sanders shrugged.

"You think it's just because you're irresistible?" Fernandez said. "With all due respect, I doubt it."

He found himself thinking of the time he first knew Meredith, when she was doing demos, and the way she used to cross her legs whenever she was asked a question she couldn't answer. "She could always use sex to distract people. She's good at that."

"I believe it," Fernandez said. "So what is she distracting us from now?"

Sanders had no answer. But his instinct was that something else was going on. "Who knows how people really are in private?" he said. "I once knew this woman, she looked like an angel, but she liked bikers to beat her up."

"Uh-huh," Fernandez said. "That's fine. I'm not buying it for Johnson. Because Johnson strikes me as very controlled, and her behavior with you was not controlled."

"You said it yourself, there's a pattern."

"Yeah. Maybe. But why the first day? Why right away? I think she had another reason."

Sanders said, "And what about me? Do you think I had another reason?"

"I assume you did," she said, looking at him seriously. "But we'll talk about that later."

Alan came up from the parking lot, shaking his head.

"What've you got?" Fernandez said.

"Nothing good. We're striking out every-where," he said. He flipped open his notepad. "Okay. Now, we've checked out that Internet address. The message originated in the 'U District.' And 'Afriend' turns out to be Dr. Arthur A. Friend. He's a professor of inorganic chemistry at the University of Washington. That name mean anything to you?"

"No," Sanders said.

"I'm not surprised. At the moment, Professor Friend is in northern Nepal on a consulting job for the Nepalese government. He's been there for three weeks. He's not expected back until late July. So it probably isn't him sending the messages anyway."

"Somebody's using his Internet address?"

"His assistant says that's impossible. His office is locked while he's away, and nobody goes in there except her. So nobody has access to his computer terminal. The assistant says she goes in once a day and answers Dr. Friend's e-mail, but otherwise the computer is off. And nobody knows the password but her. So I don't know."

"It's a message coming out of a locked office?" Sanders said, frowning.

"I don't know. We're still working on it. But for the moment, it's a mystery."

"All right, fine," Fernandez said. "What about Conrad Computer?"

"Conrad has taken a very hard position. They

will only release information to the hiring company, meaning DigiCom. Nothing to us. And they say that the hiring company has not requested it. When we pushed, Conrad called DigiCom themselves, and DigiCom told them they weren't interested in any information Conrad might have."

"Hmmm."

"Next, the husband," Alan said. "I talked to someone who worked in his company, CoStar. Says the husband hates her, has lots of bad things to say about her. But he's in Mexico on vacation with his new girlfriend until next week."

"Too bad."

"Novell," Alan said. "They keep only the last five years current. Prior to that, records are in cold storage at headquarters in Utah. They have no idea what they'll show, but they're willing to get them out if we'll pay for it. It'll take two weeks."

Fernandez shook her head. "Not good."

"No."

"I have a strong feeling that Conrad Computer is sitting on something," Fernandez said.

"Maybe, but we'll have to sue to get it. And there's no time." Alan looked across the courtyard at the others. "What's happening now?"

"Nothing. They're hanging tough."

"Still?"

"Yeah."

"Jesus," Alan said. "Who's she got behind her?"

"I'd love to know," Fernandez said.

Sanders flipped open his cellular phone and checked in with his office. "Cindy, any messages?"

"Just two, Tom. Stephanie Kaplan asked if she could meet with you today."

"She say why?"

"No. But she said it wasn't important. And Mary Anne has come by twice, looking for you."

"Probably wants to skin me," Sanders said.

"I don't think so, Tom. She's about the only one who—she's very concerned about you, I think."

"Okay. I'll call her."

He started to dial Mary Anne's number when Fernandez nudged him in the ribs. He looked over and saw a slender, middle-aged woman walking up from the parking lot toward them.

"Buckle up," Fernandez said.

"Why? Who's that?"

"That," Fernandez said, "is Connie Walsh."

Connie Walsh was about forty-five years old, with gray hair and a sour expression. "Are you Tom Sanders?"

"That's right."

She pulled out a tape recorder. "Connie Walsh, from the *Post-Intelligencer*. Can we talk for a moment?"

"Absolutely not," Fernandez said.

Walsh looked over at her.

"I'm Mr. Sanders's attorney."

"I know who you are," Walsh said, and turned back to Sanders. "Mr. Sanders, our paper's going with a story on this discrimination suit at Digi-Com. My sources tell me that you are accusing Meredith Johnson of sex discrimination, is that correct?"

"He has no comment," Fernandez said, stepping between Walsh and Sanders.

Walsh looked past her shoulder and said, "Mr. Sanders, is it also true that you and she are old lovers, and that your accusation is a way to even the score?"

"He has no comment," Fernandez said.

"It looks to me like he does," Walsh said. "Mr. Sanders, you don't have to listen to her. You can say something if you want to. And I really think you should take this opportunity to defend yourself. Because my sources are also saying that you physically abused Ms. Johnson in the course of your meeting. These are very serious charges people are making against you, and I imagine you'll want to respond. What do you have to say to her allegations? Did you physically abuse her?"

Sanders started to speak, but Fernandez shot him a warning glance, and put her hand on his chest. She said to Walsh, "Has Ms. Johnson made these allegations to you? Because she was the only other one besides Mr. Sanders who was there."

"I'm not free to say. I have the story from very well-informed sources."

"Inside or outside the company?"

"I really can't say."

"Ms. Walsh," Fernandez said, "I am going to forbid Mr. Sanders to talk to you. And you better check with the *P-I* counsel before you run any of these unsubstantiated allegations."

"They're not unsubstantiated, I have very reliable—"

"If there is any question in your counsel's mind, you might have her call Mr. Blackburn and he will explain what your legal position is in this matter."

Walsh smiled bleakly. "Mr. Sanders, do you want to make a comment?"

Fernandez said, "Just check with your counsel, Ms. Walsh."

"I will, but it won't matter. You can't squash this. Mr. Blackburn can't squash this. And speaking personally, I have to say I don't know how you can defend a case like this."

Fernandez leaned close to her, smiled, and said, "Why don't you step over here with me, and I'll explain something to you."

She walked with Walsh a few yards away, across the courtyard.

Alan and Sanders remained where they were. Alan sighed. He said, "Wouldn't you give anything to know what they were saying right now?"

Connie Walsh said, "It doesn't matter what you say. I won't give you my source."

"I'm not asking for your source. I'm simply informing you that your story is wrong—"

"Of course you'd say that—"

"And that there's documentary evidence that it's wrong."

Connie Walsh paused. She frowned. "Documentary evidence?"

Fernandez nodded slowly. "That's right."

Walsh thought it over. "But there can't be," she said. "You said it yourself. They were alone in the room. It's his word against hers. There's no documentary evidence."

Fernandez shook her head, and said nothing.

"What is it? A tape?"

Fernandez smiled thinly. "I really can't say."

"Even if there is, what can it show? That she pinched his butt a little? She made a couple of jokes? What's the big deal? Men have been doing that for hundreds of years."

"That's not the issue in this—"

"Give me a break. So this guy gets a little pinch, and he starts screaming bloody murder. That's not normal behavior in a man. This guy obviously hates and demeans women. That's clear, just to look at him. And there's no question: he hit her, in that meeting. The company had to call a doctor to examine her for a concussion. And I have several reliable sources that tell me he's known to be physically abusive. He and his wife have had trouble for years. In fact, she's left town with the kids and is going to file for divorce." Walsh was watching Fernandez carefully as she said it.

Fernandez just shrugged.

"It's a fact. The wife has left town," Walsh said flatly. "Unexpectedly. She took the kids. And nobody knows where she went. Now, you tell me what that means."

Fernandez said, "Connie, all I can do is advise you in my capacity as Mr. Sanders's attorney that documentary evidence contradicts your sources about this harassment charge."

"Are you going to show me this evidence?"

"Absolutely not."

"Then how do I know it exists?"

"You don't. You only know I have informed you of its existence."

"And what if I don't believe you?"

Fernandez smiled. "These are the decisions a journalist must make."

"You're saying it'd be reckless disregard."

"If you go with your story, yes."

Walsh stepped back. "Look. Maybe you've got some kind of a technical legal case here, and maybe you don't. But as far as I'm concerned, you're just another minority woman trying to get ahead with the patriarchy by getting down on her knees. If you had any self-respect you wouldn't be doing their dirty work for them."

"Actually, Connie, the person who seems to be caught in the grip of the patriarchy is you."

"That's a lot of crap," Walsh said. "And let me tell you, you're not going to evade the facts here. He led her on, and then he beat her up. He's an ex-lover, he's resentful, and he's violent. He's a typical man. And let me tell you, before I'm through, he'll wish he had never been born."

Sanders said, "Is she going to run the story?"

"No," Fernandez said. She stared across the courtyard at Johnson, Heller, and Blackburn. Connie Walsh had gone over to Blackburn and was talking to him. "Don't get distracted by this," Fernandez said. "It's not important. The main issue is: what're they going to do about Johnson."

A moment later, Heller came toward them. He said, "We've been going over things on our side, Louise."

"And?"

"We've concluded that we see no purpose to further mediation and are withdrawing, as of now. I've informed Judge Murphy that we will not continue."

"Really. And what about the tape?"

"Neither Ms. Johnson nor Mr. Sanders knew they were being taped. Under law, one party must know the interaction is being recorded. Therefore the tape is inadmissible."

"But Ben—"

"We argue that the tape should be disallowed, both from this mediation and from any subsequent legal proceeding. We argue that Ms. Johnson's characterization of the meeting as a misunderstanding between consenting adults is the correct one, and that Mr. Sanders bears a responsibility for that misunderstanding. He was an active participant, Louise, no way around it. He took her panties off. Nobody held a gun to his head. But since there was fault on both sides, the proper thing is for the two parties to shake hands, let go of all animosity, and return to work. Apparently Mr. Garvin has already proposed this to Mr. Sanders, and Mr. Sanders has refused. We believe that under the circumstances Mr. Sanders is acting unreasonably and that if he does not reconsider in a timely manner, he should be fired for his refusal to show up for work."

"Son of a bitch," Sanders said.

Fernandez laid a restraining hand on his arm. "Ben," she said calmly. "Is this a formal offer of reconciliation and return to the company?"

"Yes, Louise."

"And what are the sweeteners?"

"No sweeteners. Everybody just goes back to work."

"The reason I ask," Fernandez said, "is that I believe I can successfully argue that Mr. Sanders was aware the tape was being made, and thus it is indeed admissible. I will argue further that it is admissible under discovery of public records over common carriers as defined in *Waller* v. *Herbst*. I will argue further that the company knew of Ms. Johnson's long history of harassment, and has

failed to take proper steps to investigate her behavior, either prior to this incident, or now. And
I will argue that the company was derelict in protecting Mr. Sanders's reputation when it leaked
the story to Connie Walsh."

"Wait a minute here—"

"I will argue that the company had a clear reason for leaking it: they desired to cheat Mr. Sanders out of his well-deserved reward for more than
a decade of service to the company. And you've
got an employee in Ms. Johnson who has had
some trouble before. I will claim defamation and
ask for punitive damages of sufficient magnitude
to send a message to corporate America. I'll ask
for sixty million dollars, Ben. And you'll settle for
forty million—the minute I get the judge to allow
the jury to hear this tape. Because we both know
that when the jury hears that tape, they will take
about five seconds to find against Ms. Johnson
and the company."

Heller shook his head. "You've got a lot of long
shots there, Louise. I don't think they'll ever let
that tape be played in court. And you're talking
about three years from now."

Fernandez nodded slowly. "Yes," she said.
"Three years is a long time."

"You're telling me, Louise. Anything can
happen."

"Yes, and frankly, I'm worried about that tape.

So many untoward things can happen with evidence that is so scandalous. I can't guarantee somebody hasn't made a copy already. It'd be terrible if one fell into the hands of KQEM, and they started playing it over the radio."

"Christ," Heller said. "Louise, I can't believe you said that."

"Said what? I'm merely expressing my legitimate fears," Fernandez said. "I'd be derelict if I did not let you know my concerns. Let's face facts here, Ben. The cat's out of the bag. The press already has this story. Somebody leaked it to Connie Walsh. And she printed a story that's very damaging to Mr. Sanders's reputation. And it seems that somebody is still leaking, because now Connie is planning to write some unfounded speculation about physical violence by my client. It's unfortunate that someone on your side should have chosen to talk about this case. But we both know how it is with a hot story in the press—you never know where the next leak will come from."

Heller was uneasy. He glanced back at the others by the fountain. "Louise, I don't think there's any movement over there."

"Well, just talk to them."

Heller shrugged, and walked back.

"What do we do now?" Sanders said.

"We go back to your office."

"We?"

"Yes," Fernandez said. "This isn't the end. More is going to happen today, and I want to be there when it does."

Driving back, Blackburn talked on the car phone with Garvin. "The mediation's over. We called it off."

"And?"

"We're pushing Sanders hard to go back to work. But he's not responding so far. He's hanging tough. Now he's threatening punitive damages of sixty million dollars."

"Christ," Garvin said. "Punitive damages on what basis?"

"Defamation from corporate negligence dealing with the fact that we supposedly knew that Johnson had a history of harassment."

"I never knew of any history," Garvin said. "Did you know of any history, Phil?"

"No," Blackburn said.

"Is there any documentary evidence of such a history?"

"No," Blackburn said. "I'm sure there isn't."

"Good. Then let him threaten. Where did you leave it with Sanders?"

"We gave him until tomorrow morning to rejoin the company at his old job or get out."

"All right," Garvin said. "Now let's get serious. What have we got on him?"

"We're working on that felony charge," Blackburn said. "It's early, but I think it's promising."

"What about women?"

"There isn't any record on women. I know Sanders was screwing one of his assistants a couple of years back. But we can't find the records in the computer. I think he went in and erased them."

"How could he? We blocked his access."

"He must have done it some time ago. He's a cagey guy."

"Why the hell would he do it some time ago, Phil? He had no reason to expect any of this."

"I know, but we can't find the records now." Blackburn paused. "Bob, I think we should move up the press conference."

"To when?"

"Late tomorrow."

"Good idea," Garvin said. "I'll arrange it. We could even do it noon tomorrow. John Marden is flying in in the morning," he said, referring to Conley-White's CEO. "That'll work out fine."

"Sanders is planning to string this out until Friday," Blackburn said. "Let's just beat him to the punch. We've got him blocked as it is. He can't get into the company files. He can't get access to Conrad or anything else. He's isolated. He can't possibly come up with anything damaging between now and tomorrow."

"Fine," Garvin said. "What about the reporter?"

"I think she'll break the story on Friday," Blackburn said. "She already has it, I don't know where from. But she won't be able to resist trashing Sanders. It's too good a story; she'll go with it. And he'll be dead meat when she does."

"That's fine," Garvin said.

Meredith Johnson came off the fifth-floor elevator at DigiCom and ran into Ed Nichols. "We missed you at the morning meetings," Nichols said.

"Yeah, I had some things to take care of," she said.

"Anything I should know?"

"No," she said. "It's boring. Just some technical matters about tax exemptions in Ireland. The Irish government wants to expand local content at the Cork plant and we're not sure we can. This has been going on for more than a year."

"You look a little tired," Nichols said, with concern. "A little pale."

"I'm okay. I'll be happy when this is all over."

"We all will," Nichols said. "You have time for dinner?"

"Maybe Friday night, if you're still in town," she said. She smiled. "But really, Ed. It's just tax stuff."

"Okay, I believe you."

He waved and went down the hallway. Johnson went into her office.

She found Stephanie Kaplan there, working at the computer terminal on Johnson's desk. Kaplan looked embarrassed. "Sorry to use your computer. I was just running over some accounts while I waited for you."

Johnson threw her purse on the couch. "Listen, Stephanie," she said. "Let's get something straight right now. I'm running this division, and nobody's going to change that. And as far as I'm concerned, this is the time when a new vice president decides who's on their side, and who isn't. Somebody supports me, I'll remember. Somebody doesn't, I'll deal with that, too. Do we understand each other?"

Kaplan came around the desk. "Yes, sure, Meredith."

"Don't fuck with me."

"Never entered my mind, Meredith."

"Good. Thank you, Stephanie."

"No problem, Meredith."

Kaplan left the office. Johnson closed the door behind her and went directly to her computer terminal and stared intently at the screen.

Sanders walked through the corridors of DigiCom with a sense of unreality. He felt like a stranger. The people who passed him in the halls looked away and brushed past him, saying nothing.

"I don't exist," he said to Fernandez.

"Never mind," she said.

They passed the main part of the floor, where people worked in chest-high cubicles. Several pig grunts were heard. One person sang softly, "Because I used to fuck her, but it's all over now . . ."

Sanders stopped and turned toward the singing. Fernandez grabbed his arm.

"Never mind," she said.

"But Christ . . ."

"Don't make it worse than it is."

They passed the coffee machine. Beside it, someone had taped up a picture of Sanders. They had used it for a dartboard.

"Jesus."

"Keep going."

As he came to the corridor leading to his office, he saw Don Cherry coming the other way.

"Hi, Don."

"You screwed up bad on this one, Tom." He shook his head and walked on.

Even Don Cherry.

Sanders sighed.

"You knew this was going to happen," Fernandez said.

"Maybe."

"You did. This is the way it works."

Outside his office, Cindy stood up when she saw him. She said, "Tom, Mary Anne asked you to call her as soon as you got in."

"Okay."

"And Stephanie said to say never mind, she found out whatever she needed to know. She said, uh, not to call her."

"Okay."

He went in the office and closed the door. He sat down behind his desk and Fernandez sat opposite him. She took her cellular phone out of her briefcase, and dialed. "Let's get one thing squared away—Ms. Vries's office please . . . Louise Fernandez calling."

She cupped her hand over the phone. "This shouldn't take— Oh, Eleanor? Hi, Louise Fernandez. I'm calling you about Connie Walsh. Uh-huh . . . I'm sure you've been going over it with her. Yes, I know she feels strongly. Eleanor, I just wanted to confirm to you that there is a tape of the event, and it substantiates Mr. Sanders's version rather than Ms. Johnson's. Actually, yes, I could do that. Entirely off the record? Yes, I could. Well, the problem with Walsh's source is that the company now has huge liability and if you print a story that's wrong—even if you got it from a source—I think they have an action against you. Oh yes, I think absolutely Mr. Blackburn would sue. He wouldn't have any choice. Why don't you—I see. Uh-huh. Well, that could change, Eleanor. Uh-huh. And don't forget that Mr. Sanders is considering defamation right now, based on the Mr. Piggy piece. Yes, why don't you do that. Thank you."

She hung up and turned to Sanders. "We went to law school together. Eleanor is very competent and very conservative. She'd never have allowed the story in the first place, and would never have considered it now, if she didn't place a lot of reliance on Connie's source."

"Meaning?"

"I'm pretty sure I know who gave her the story," Fernandez said. She was dialing again.

"Who?" Sanders said.

"Right now, the important thing is Meredith Johnson. We've got to document the pattern, to demonstrate that she has harassed employees before. Somehow we've got to break this deadlock with Conrad Computer." She turned away. "Harry? Louise. Did you talk to Conrad? Uh-huh. And?" A pause. She shook her head irritably. "Did you explain to them about their liabilities? Uh-huh. Hell. So what's our next move? Because we've got a time problem here, Harry, that's what I'm concerned about."

While she was talking, Sanders turned to his monitor. The e-mail light was flashing. He clicked it.

YOU HAVE 17 MESSAGES WAITING.

Christ. He could only imagine. He clicked the READ button. They flashed up in order.

FROM: DON CHERRY, CORRIDOR PROGRAMMING TEAM

TO: ALL SUBJECTS

WE HAVE DELIVERED THE VIE UNIT TO CONLEY-WHITE'S PEOPLE. THE UNIT IS NOW ACTIVE INTO THEIR COMPANY DB SINCE THEY GAVE US THE HOOKS TODAY. JOHN CONLEY ASKED THAT IT BE DELIVERED TO A SUITE AT THE FOUR SEASONS HOTEL BECAUSE THEIR CEO IS ARRIVING THURSDAY MORNING AND WILL SEE IT THEN. ANOTHER PROGRAMMING TRIUMPH BROUGHT TO YOU BY THE SWELL FOLKS AT VIE.

DON THE MAGNIFICENT

Sanders flipped to the next one.

FROM: DIAGNOSTICS GROUP
TO: APG TEAM

ANALYSIS OF TWINKLE DRIVES. THE PROBLEM
WITH THE CONTROLLER TIMING LOOP DOES NOT
SEEM TO COME FROM THE CHIP ITSELF. WE VERI-
FIED MICRO-FLUCTUATIONS IN CURRENT FROM
THE POWER UNIT WHICH WAS APPARENTLY
ETCHED WITH SUBSTANDARD OR INADEQUATE RE-
SISTANCES ON THE BOARD BUT THIS IS MINOR AND
DOES NOT EXPLAIN OUR FAILURE TO MEET SPECS.
ANALYSIS IS CONTINUING.

Sanders viewed the message with a sense of
detachment. It didn't really tell him anything. Just
words that concealed the underlying truth: they
still didn't know what the problem was. At another time, he'd be on his way down to the Diagnostics team, to ride them hard to get to the
bottom of it. But now . . . He shrugged and went
to the next message.

FROM: BASEBALL CENTRAL
TO: ALL PLAYERS
RE: NEW SUMMER SOFTBALL SCHEDULE

DOWNLOAD FILE BB.72 TO GET THE NEW REVISED
SUMMER SCHEDULE. SEE YOU ON THE FIELD!

He heard Fernandez say on the phone, "Harry,
we've got to crack this one somehow. What time

do they close their offices in Sunnyvale?" Sanders
went to the next message.

> NO MORE GROUP MESSAGES. DO YOU WANT TO
> READ PERSONAL MESSAGES?

He clicked the icon.

> WHY DON'T YOU JUST ADMIT YOU ARE GAY?
>
> (UNSIGNED)

He didn't bother to see where it had come from.
They would probably have manually entered it as
coming from Garvin's address, or something like
that. He could check the real address inside the
system, but not without the access privileges they
had taken away. He went to the next message.

> SHE'S BETTER LOOKING THAN YOUR ASSISTANT,
> AND YOU DIDN'T SEEM TO MIND SCREWING HER.
>
> (UNSIGNED)

Sanders clicked to the next one.

> YOU SLIMY WEASEL - GET OUT OF THIS COMPANY.
>
> YOUR BEST ADVICE

Christ, he thought. The next one:

LITTLE TOMMY HAD A PECKER
HE PLAYED WITH EVERY DAY
BUT WHEN A LADY TRIED TO TOUCH IT
LITTLE TOMMY SAID GO AWAY.

The verses ran on, down to the bottom of the screen, but Sanders didn't read the rest. He clicked and went on.

IF YOU WEREN'T FUCKING YOUR DAUGHTER SO MUCH YOU MIGHT BE ABLE TO

He clicked again. He was clicking faster and faster, going through the messages.

GUYS LIKE YOU GIVE MEN A BAD NAME YOU ASS-HOLE.

BORIS

Click.

YOU FILTHY LYING MALE PIG

Click.

HIGH TIME SOMEBODY STUCK IT TO THE WHINING BITCHES. I'M TIRED OF THE WAY THEY BLAME EV-ERYBODY BUT THEIRSELVES. TITS AND BLAME ARE SEX-LINKED TRAITS. THEY'RE BOTH ON THE X-CHROMOSOME.

KEEP ON TRUCKIN'

He went through them, no longer reading. Eventually he was going so fast he almost missed one of the later ones:

JUST RECEIVED WORD THAT MOHAMMED JAFAR IS DYING. HE'S STILL IN THE HOSPITAL, AND NOT EXPECTED TO SURVIVE UNTIL MORNING. I GUESS MAYBE THERE'S SOMETHING TO THIS SORCERY BUSINESS, AFTER ALL.

ARTHUR KAHN

Sanders stared at the screen. A man dying of sorcery? He couldn't begin to imagine what had really happened. The very idea seemed to belong to another world, not his. He heard Fernandez say, "I don't care, Harry, but Conrad has information relevant to the pattern, and somehow we have to get it out of them."

Sanders clicked to the final message.

YOU'RE CHECKING THE WRONG COMPANY.

AFRIEND

Sanders twisted the monitor around so Fernandez could see it. She frowned as she talked on the phone. "Harry, I got to go. Do what you can." She hung up. "What does it mean, we're checking the wrong company? How does this friend even know what we're doing? When did this come in?"

Sanders looked at the message headers. "One-twenty this afternoon."

Fernandez made a note on her legal pad. "That was about the time Alan was talking to Conrad. And Conrad called DigiCom, remember? So this message has to be coming from inside DigiCom."

"But it's on the Internet."

"Wherever it appears to be coming from, it's actually from somebody inside the company trying to help you."

His immediate thought, out of nowhere, was *Max*. But that didn't make any sense. Dorfman was tricky, but not in this way. Besides, Max wasn't knowledgeable about the minute-to-minute workings of the company.

No, this was somebody who wanted to help Sanders but who didn't want the help to be traced back.

"You're checking the wrong company . . ." he repeated aloud.

Could it be someone at Conley-White? Hell, he thought, it could be anybody.

"What does it mean, we're checking the wrong company?" he said. "We're checking all her past employers, and we're having a very difficult—"

He stopped.

You're checking the wrong company.

"I must be an idiot," he said. He started typing at his computer.

"What is it?" Fernandez said.

"They've restricted my access, but I still should be able to get this," he said, typing quickly.

"Get what?" she said, puzzled.

"You say harassers have a pattern, right?"

"Right."

"It shows up again and again, right?"

"Right."

"And we're checking her past employers, to get information about past episodes of harassment."

"Right. And failing."

"Yes. But the thing is," Sanders said, "she's worked here for the last four years, Louise. We're checking the wrong company."

He watched as the computer terminal flashed:

SEARCHING DATABASE

And then, after a moment, he turned the screen so Fernandez could see:

Digital Communications Data Reference Search Report

DB 4: Human Resources (Sub 5/Employee Records)
Search Criteria:
1. Disposition: Terminated a/o Transferred a/o Resigned
2. Supervisor: Johnson, Meredith
3. Other Criteria: males only

Summary Search Results:

Michael Tate: 5/9/89

       Terminate   Drug Use   HR RefMed

Edwin Sheen: 7/5/89
       Resign   Alt Employment   D-Silicon
William Rogin: 11/9/89
       Transfer   Own Request   Austin
Frederic Cohen: 4/2/90
       Resign   Alt Employment   Squire Sx
Robert Ely: 6/1/90
       Transfer   Own Request   Seattle
Michael Backes: 8/11/90
       Transfer   Own Request   Malaysia
Peter Saltz: 1/4/91
       Resign   Alt Employment   Novell
Ross Wald: 8/5/91
       Transfer   Own Request   Cork
Richard Jackson: 11/14/91
       Resign   Alt Employment   Aldus
James French: 2/2/92
       Transfer   Own Request   Austin

Fernandez scanned the list. "Looks like working for Meredith Johnson can be hazardous to your job. You're looking at the classic pattern: people last only a few months, and then resign or ask to be transferred elsewhere. Everything voluntary. Nobody ever fired, because that might trigger a wrongful termination suit. Classic. You know any of these people?"

"No," Sanders said, shaking his head. "But three of them are in Seattle," he said.

"I only see one."

"No, Aldus is here. And Squire Systems is out

in Bellevue. So Richard Jackson and Frederic Cohen are up here, too."

"You have any way to get details of termination packages on these people?" she said. "That would be helpful. Because if the company paid anybody off, then we have a de facto case."

"No." Sanders shook his head. "Financial data is beyond minimal access."

"Try anyway."

"But what's the point? The system won't let me."

"Do it," Fernandez said.

He frowned. "You think they're monitoring me?"

"I guarantee it."

"Okay." He typed in the parameters and pressed the search key. The answer came back:

FINANCIAL DATABASE SEARCH IS BEYOND LEVEL (0) ACCESS

He shrugged. "Just as I thought. No cigar."

"But the point is, we asked the question," Fernandez said. "It'll wake them right up."

Sanders was heading toward the bank of elevators when he saw Meredith coming toward him with three Conley-White executives. He turned quickly, then went to the stairwell and started walking down the four flights to the street level. The stairwell was deserted.

One flight below, the door opened and Stephanie Kaplan appeared and started coming up the stairs. Sanders was reluctant to speak to her; Kaplan was, after all, the chief financial officer and close to both Garvin and Blackburn. In the end, he said casually, "How's it going, Stephanie."

"Hello, Tom." Her nod to him was cool, reserved.

Sanders continued past her, going down a few more steps, when he heard her say, "I'm sorry this is so difficult for you."

He paused. Kaplan was one flight above him, looking down. There was no one else in the stairwell.

He said, "I'm managing."

"I know you are. But still, it must be hard. So much going on at once, and nobody giving you information. It must be confusing to try to figure everything out."

Nobody giving you information?

"Well, yes," he said, speaking slowly. "It is hard to figure things out, Stephanie."

She nodded. "I remember when I first started out in business," she said. "I had a woman friend who got a very good job in a company that didn't usually hire women executives. In her new position, she had a lot of stress and crises. She was proud of the way she was dealing with the problems. But it turned out she'd only been hired because there was a financial scandal in her division, and from the beginning they were setting her up to take the fall. Her job was never about any of the things she thought it was. She was a patsy. And she was looking the wrong way when they fired her."

Sanders stared at her. Why was she telling him this? He said, "That's an interesting story."

Kaplan nodded. "I've never forgotten it," she said.

On the stairs above, a door clanged open, and they heard footsteps descending. Without another word, Kaplan turned and continued up.

Shaking his head, Sanders continued down.

In the newsroom of the Seattle *Post-Intelligencer*, Connie Walsh looked up from her computer terminal and said, "You've got to be kidding."

"No, I'm not," Eleanor Vries said, standing over her. "I'm killing this story." She dropped the printout back on Walsh's desk.

"But you know who my source is," Walsh said. "And you know Jake was listening in to the entire conversation. We have very good notes, Eleanor. Very complete notes."

"I know."

"So, given the source, how can the company possibly sue?" Walsh said. "Eleanor: *I have the fucking story.*"

"You have *a* story. And the paper faces a substantial exposure already."

"Already? From what?"

"The Mr. Piggy column."

"Oh, for Christ's sake. There's no way to claim identification from that column."

Vries pulled out a xerox of the column. She had marked several passages in yellow highlighter. "Company X is said to be a high-tech company in Seattle that just named a woman to a high position. Mr. Piggy is said to be her subordinate. He is said to have brought a sexual harassment action. Mr. Piggy's wife is an attorney with young children. You say Mr. Piggy's charge is without merit, that he is a drunk and a womanizer. I think Sanders can absolutely claim identification and sue for defamation."

"But this is a column. An opinion piece."

"This column alleges facts. And it alleges them in a sarcastic and wildly overstated manner."

"It's an opinion piece. Opinion is protected."

"I don't think that's certain in this case at all. I'm disturbed that I allowed this column to run in the first place. But the point is, we cannot claim to be absent malice if we allow further articles to go out."

Walsh said, "You have no guts."

"And you're very free with other people's guts," Vries said. "The story's killed and that's final. I'm putting it in writing, with copies to you, Marge, and Tom Donadio."

"Fucking lawyers. What a world we live in. This story needs to be told."

"Don't screw around with this, Connie. I'm telling you. Don't."

And she walked away.

Walsh thumbed through the pages of the story. She had been working on it all afternoon, polishing it, refining it. Getting it exactly right. And now she wanted the story to run. She had no patience with legal thinking. This whole idea of protecting rights was just a convenient fiction. Because when you got right down to it, legal thinking was just narrow-minded, petty, self-protective—the kind of thinking that kept the power structure firmly in place. And in the end, fear served the power structure. Fear served men in power. And if there was anything that Connie Walsh believed to be true of herself, it was that she was not afraid.

After a long time, she picked up the phone and dialed a number. "KSEA-TV, good afternoon."

"Ms. Henley, please."

Jean Henley was a bright young reporter at Seattle's newest independent TV station. Walsh had spent many evenings with Henley, discussing the problems of working in the male-dominated mass media. Henley knew the value of a hot story in building a reporter's career.

This story, Walsh told herself, would be told. One way or another, it would be told.

Robert Ely looked up at Sanders nervously. "What do you want?" he asked. Ely was young, not more than twenty-six, a tense man with a blond mustache. He was wearing a tie and was in his shirtsleeves. He worked in one of the partitioned cubicles at the back of DigiCom's Accounting Department in the Gower Building.

"I want to talk about Meredith," Sanders said. Ely was one of the three Seattle residents on his list.

"Oh God," Ely said. He glanced around nervously. His Adam's apple bobbed. "I don't—I don't have anything to say."

"I just want to talk," Sanders said.

"Not *here*," Ely said.

"Then let's go to the conference room," Sanders said. They walked down the hall to a small conference room, but a meeting was being held there. Sanders suggested they go to the little cafeteria in the corner of Accounting, but Ely told him that wouldn't be private. He was growing more nervous by the minute.

"Really, I have nothing to tell you," he kept saying. "There's nothing, really nothing."

Sanders knew he had better find a quiet place at

once, before Ely bolted and ran. They ended up in the men's room—white tile, spotlessly clean. Ely leaned against a sink. "I don't know why you are talking to me. I don't have anything I can tell you."

"You worked for Meredith, in Cupertino."

"Yes."

"And you left there two years ago?"

"Yes."

"Why did you leave?"

"Why do you think?" Ely said, in a burst of anger. His voice echoed off the tiles. "You know why, for Christ's sake. Everybody knows why. She made my life hell."

"What happened?" Sanders asked.

"What happened." Ely shook his head, remembering. "Every day, every day. 'Robert, would you stay late, we have some things to go over.' After a while, I tried to make excuses. Then she would say, 'Robert, I'm not sure you're showing the proper dedication to this company.' And she would put little comments in my performance review. Subtle little negative things. Nothing that I could complain about. But they were there. Piling up. 'Robert, I think you need my help here. Why don't you see me after work.' 'Robert, why don't you drop by my apartment and we'll discuss it. I really think you should.' I was—it was terrible. The, uh, person I was living with did not, uh . . . I was in a real bind."

"Did you report her?"

Ely laughed harshly. "Are you kidding? She's practically a member of Garvin's *family*."

"So you just put up with it . . ."

Ely shrugged. "Finally, the person I was living with got another job. When he came up here, I transferred, too. I mean, of course I wanted to go. It just worked out all around."

"Would you make a statement about Meredith now?"

"Not a chance."

"You realize," Sanders said, "that the reason she gets away with it is that nobody reports her."

Ely pushed away from the sink. "I have enough problems in my life without going public on this." He went to the door, paused, and turned back. "Just so you're clear: I've got nothing to say on the subject of Meredith Johnson. If anybody asks, I'll say our working relationship was correct at all times. And I'll also say that I never met you."

Meredith Johnson? Of course I remember her," Richard Jackson said. "I worked for her for more than a year." Sanders was in Jackson's office on the second floor of the Aldus Building, on the south side of Pioneer Square. Jackson was a good-looking man of thirty, with the hearty manner of an ex-athlete. He was a marketing manager at Aldus; his office was friendly, cluttered with product boxes for graphics programs: Intellidraw, Freehand, SuperPaint, and Pagemaker.

"Beautiful and charming woman," Jackson said. "Very intelligent. Always a pleasure."

Sanders said, "I was wondering why you left."

"I was offered this job, that's why. And I've never regretted it. Wonderful job. Wonderful company. I've had a great experience here."

"Is that the only reason you left?"

Jackson laughed. "You mean, did Meredith Manmuncher come on to me?" he said. "Hey, is the Pope Catholic? Is Bill Gates rich? Of *course* she came on to me."

"Did that have anything to do with your leaving?"

"No, no," Jackson said. "Meredith came on to

everybody. She's sort of an equal opportunity employer, in that respect. She chased *everybody*. When I first started in Cupertino, she had this little gay guy she used to chase around the table. Terrorized the poor bastard. Little skinny nervous guy. Christ, she used to make him tremble."

"And you?"

Jackson shrugged. "I was a single guy, just starting out. She was beautiful. It was okay with me."

"You never had any difficulties?"

"Never. Meredith was fabulous. Shitty lay, of course. But you can't have everything. She's a very intelligent, very beautiful woman. Always dressed great. And she liked me, so she took me to all these functions. I met people, made contacts. It was great."

"So you saw nothing wrong?"

"Not a damn thing," Jackson said. "She could get a little bossy. That got old. There were a couple of other women I was seeing, but I always had to be on call for her. Even at the last minute. That could be irritating sometimes. You begin to think your life is not your own. And she's got a mean temper sometimes. But what the hell. You do what you have to do. Now I'm assistant manager here at thirty. I'm doing great. Great company. Great town. Great future. And I owe it to her. She's great."

Sanders said, "You were an employee of the company at the time that you were having your relationship, isn't that right?"

"Yeah, sure."

"Isn't she required by company policy to report any relationship with an employee? Did she report her relationship with you?"

"Christ, no," Jackson said. He leaned across his desk. "Let's get one thing straight, just between you and me. I think Meredith is great. If you have a problem with her, it's your problem. I don't know what it could be. You used to live with her, for Christ's sake. So there can't be any surprises. Meredith likes to fuck guys. She likes to tell them to do this, do that. She likes to order them around. That's who she is. And I don't see anything wrong with it."

Sanders said, "I don't suppose you'd—"

"Make a statement?" Jackson said. "Get serious. Listen, there's a lot of bullshit around now. I hear things like, 'You can't go out with the people you work with.' Christ, if I couldn't go out with the people I worked with, I'd still be a virgin. That's all anybody can go out with—the people you work with. That's the only people you get to know. And sometimes those people are your superiors. Big deal. Women screw men and get ahead. Men screw women and get ahead. Everybody's going to screw everybody else anyway, if they can. Because they want to. I mean, women are just as hot as men. They want it just like we do. That's real life. But you get some people who are pissed off, so they file a complaint, and say, 'Oh no, you can't do that to me.' I'm telling you, it's all bullshit. Like these sensitivity training seminars we all have to go to. Everybody sits there with their hands in their laps like a fucking Red Guard meeting, learning the correct way to address your fellow workers. But afterward everybody goes out and fucks around, the same as they always did. The assistants go, 'Oh, Mr. Jackson, have *you* been to the *gym*? You look so *strong*.' Batting their eyelashes. So what am I supposed to do? You can't make rules about this. People get hungry, they eat. Doesn't matter how many meetings they attend. This is all a gigantic jerk off. And anybody who buys into it is an asshole."

"I guess you answered my question," Sanders said. He got up to leave. Obviously, Jackson wasn't going to help him.

"Look," Jackson said. "I'm sorry you've got a problem here. But everyone's too damned sensitive these days. I see people now, kids right out of college, and they really think they should never experience an unpleasant moment. Nobody should ever say anything they don't like, or tell a joke they don't like. But the thing is, nobody can make the world be the way they want it to be all the time. Things always happen that embarrass you or piss you off. That's life. I hear women telling jokes about men every day. Offensive jokes. Dirty jokes. I don't get bent out of shape. Life is great. Who has time for this crap? Not me."

Sanders came out of the Aldus Building at five o'clock. Tired and discouraged, he trudged back toward the Hazzard Building. The streets were wet, but the rain had stopped, and the afternoon sunlight was trying to break through the clouds.

He was back in his office ten minutes later. Cindy was not at her desk, and Fernandez was gone. He felt deserted and alone and hopeless. He sat down and dialed the final number on his list.

"Squire Electronic Data Systems, good evening."

Sanders said, "Frederic Cohen's office, please."

"I'm sorry, Mr. Cohen has gone for the day."

"Do you know how I could reach him?"

"I'm afraid I don't. Do you want to leave voice mail?"

Damn, he thought. What was the point? But he said, "Yes, please."

There was a click. Then, "Hi, this is Fred Cohen. Leave a message at the tone. If it's after hours, you can try me on my car phone at 502-8804 or my home at 505-9943."

Sanders jotted the numbers down. He dialed the car phone first. He heard a crackle of static, then:

"I know, honey, I'm sorry I'm late, but I'm on my way. I just got tied up."

"Mr. Cohen?"

"Oh." A pause. "Yes. This is Fred Cohen."

"My name is Tom Sanders. I work over at Digi-Com, and—"

"I know who you are." The voice sounded tense.

"I understand you used to work for Meredith Johnson."

"Yes. I did."

"I wonder if I could talk to you."

"What about?"

"About your experiences. Working for her."

There was a long pause. Finally, Cohen said, "What would be the point of that?"

"Well, I'm in a sort of a dispute with Meredith now, and—"

"I know you are."

"Yes, and you see, I would like to—"

"Look. Tom. I left DigiCom two years ago. Whatever happened is ancient history now."

"Well, actually," Sanders said, "it's not, because I'm trying to establish a pattern of behavior and—"

"I know what you're trying to do. But this is very touchy stuff, Tom. I don't want to get into it."

"If we could just talk," Sanders said. "Just for a few minutes."

"Tom." Cohen's voice was flat. "Tom, I'm married now. I have a wife. She's pregnant. I don't have anything to say about Meredith Johnson. Nothing at all."

"But—"

"I'm sorry. I've got to go."

Click.

Cindy came back in as he was hanging up the phone. She pushed a cup of coffee in front of him. "Everything okay?"

"No," he said. "Everything is terrible." He was reluctant to admit, even to himself, that he had no more moves left. He had approached three men, and they had each refused to establish a pattern of behavior for him. He doubted that the other men on the list would behave differently. He found himself thinking of what his wife, Susan, had said two days before. *You have no moves.* Now, after all this effort, it turned out to be true. He was finished. "Where's Fernandez?"

"She's meeting with Blackburn."

"What?"

Cindy nodded. "In the small conference room. They've been there about fifteen minutes now."

"Oh, Christ."

He got up from his desk and went down the hall. He saw Fernandez sitting with Blackburn in the conference room. Fernandez was making notes on her legal pad, head bent deferentially. Blackburn was running his hands down his lapels and looking upward as he spoke. He seemed to be dictating to her.

Then Blackburn saw him, and waved him over. Sanders went into the conference room. "Tom," Blackburn said, with a smile. "I was just coming to see you. Good news: I think we've been able to resolve this situation. I mean, really resolve it. Once and for all."

"Uh-huh," Sanders said. He didn't believe a word of it. He turned to Fernandez.

Fernandez looked up from her legal pad slowly. She appeared dazed. "That's the way it looks."

Blackburn stood and faced Sanders. "I can't tell you how pleased I am, Tom. I've been working on Bob all afternoon. And he's finally come to face reality. The plain fact is, the company has a problem, Tom. And we owe you a debt of gratitude for bringing it so clearly to our attention. This can't go on. Bob knows he has to deal with it. And he will."

Sanders just stared. He couldn't believe what he was hearing. But there was Fernandez, nodding and smiling.

Blackburn smoothed his tie. "But as Frank Lloyd Wright once said, 'God is in the details.' You know, Tom, we have one small immediate problem, a political problem, having to do with the merger. We're asking your help with the briefing tomorrow for Marden, Conley's CEO. But after that . . . well, you've been badly wronged,

Tom. This company has wronged you. And we recognize that we have an obligation to make it up to you, whatever way we can."

Still disbelieving it, Sanders said harshly, "What exactly are we talking about?"

Blackburn's voice was soothing. "Well, Tom, at this point, that's really up to you," he said. "I've given Louise the parameters of a potential deal, and all the options that we would agree to. You can discuss it with her and get back to us. We'll sign any interim papers you require, of course. All that we ask in return is that you attend the meeting tomorrow and help us to get through the merger. Fair enough?"

Blackburn extended his hand and held it there.

Sanders stared.

"From the bottom of my heart, Tom, I'm sorry for all that has happened."

Sanders shook his hand.

"Thank you, Tom," Blackburn said. "Thank you for your patience, and thank you on behalf of this company. Now, sit down and talk with Louise, and let us know what you decide."

And Blackburn left the room, closing the door softly behind him.

He turned to Fernandez. "What the hell is this all about?"

Fernandez gave a long sigh. "It's called capitulation," she said. "Total and complete capitulation. DigiCom just folded."

Sanders watched Blackburn walk down the hallway away from the conference room. He was filled with confused feelings. Suddenly, he was being told it was all over, and over without a fight. Without blood being spilled.

Watching Blackburn, he had a sudden image of blood in the bathroom sink of his old apartment. And this time, he remembered where it came from. A part of the chronology fell into place.

Blackburn was staying at his apartment during his divorce. He was on edge, and drinking too much. One day he cut himself so badly while shaving that the sink was spattered with blood. Later on, Meredith saw the blood in the sink and on the towels, and she said, "Did one of you guys fuck her while she was having her period?" Meredith was always blunt that way. She liked to startle people, to shock them.

And then, one Saturday afternoon, she walked around the apartment in white stockings and a garter belt and a bra while Phil was watching television. Sanders said to her, "What are you doing that for?"

"Just cheering him up," Meredith replied. She threw herself back on the bed. "Now why don't you cheer me up?" she said. And she pulled her legs back, opening—

"Tom? Are you listening to me?" Fernandez was saying. "Hello? Tom? Are you there?"

"I'm here," Sanders said.

But he was still watching Blackburn, thinking about Blackburn. Now he remembered another time, a few years later. Sanders had started dating Susan, and Phil had dinner with the two of them one night. Susan went to the bathroom. "She's great," Blackburn said. "She's terrific. She's beautiful and she's great."

"But?"

"But . . ." Blackburn had shrugged. "She's a lawyer."

"So?"

"You can never trust a lawyer," Blackburn had said, and laughed. One of his rueful, wise laughs.

You can never trust a lawyer.

Now, standing in the DigiCom conference room, Sanders watched as Blackburn disappeared around a corner. He turned back to Fernandez.

". . . really had no choice," Fernandez was saying. "The whole situation finally became untenable. The fact situation with Johnson is bad. And the tape is dangerous—they don't want it played, and they're afraid it will get out. They have a problem about prior sexual harassment by Johnson; she's done it before, and they know it. Even though none of the men you talked to has agreed to talk, one of them might in the future, and they know it. And of course they've got their chief counsel revealing company information to a reporter."

Sanders said, "What?"

She nodded. "Blackburn was the one who gave the story to Connie Walsh. He acted in flagrant violation of all rules of conduct for an employee of the company. He's a major problem for them. And it all just became too much. These things could bring down the entire company. Looking at it rationally, they had to make a deal with you."

"Yeah," Sanders said. "But none of this is rational, you know?"

"You're acting like you don't believe it," Fernandez said. "Believe it. It just got too big. They couldn't sit on it anymore."

"So what's the deal?"

Fernandez looked at her notes. "You got your whole shopping list. They'll fire Johnson. They'll give you her job, if you want that. Or they'll reinstate you at your present position. Or they'll give you another position in the company. They'll pay you a hundred thousand in pain and suffering and they'll pay my fees. Or they'll negotiate a termination agreement, if you want that. In any case, they'll give you full stock options if and when the division goes public. Whether you choose to remain with the company or not."

"Jesus Christ."

She nodded. "Total capitulation."

"You really believe Blackburn means it?"

You can never trust a lawyer.

"Yes," she said. "Frankly, it's the first thing that has made any sense to me all day. They had to do this, Tom. Their exposure is too great, and the stakes are too high."

"And what about this briefing?"

"They're worried about the merger—as you suspected when all this began. They don't want to blow it with any sudden changes now. So they want you to participate in the briefing tomorrow with Johnson, as if everything was normal. Then early next week, Johnson will have a physical exam as part of her insurance for the new job. The exam will uncover serious health problems, maybe even cancer, which will force a regrettable change in management."

"I see."

He went to the window and looked out at the city. The clouds were higher, and the evening sun was breaking through. He took a deep breath.

"And if I don't participate in the briefing?"

"It's up to you, but I would, if I were you," Fernandez said. "At this point, you really are in a position to bring down the company. And what good is that?"

He took another deep breath. He was feeling better all the time.

"You're saying this is over," he said, finally.

"Yes. It's over, and you've won. You pulled it off. Congratulations, Tom."

She shook his hand.

"Jesus Christ," he said.

She stood up. "I'm going to draw up an instrument outlining my conversation with Blackburn, specifying these options, and send it to him for his signature in an hour. I'll call you when I have it signed. Meanwhile, I recommend you do whatever preparation you need for this meeting tomorrow, and get some much deserved rest. I'll see you tomorrow."

"Okay."

It was slowly seeping into him, the realization that it was over. Really over. It had happened so suddenly and so completely, he was a little dazed.

"Congratulations again," Fernandez said. She folded her briefcase and left.

He was back in his office at about six. Cindy was leaving; she asked if he needed her, and he said he didn't. Sanders sat at his desk and stared out the window for a while, savoring the conclusion of the day. Through his open door, he watched as people left for the night, heading down the hall. Finally he called his wife in Phoenix to tell her the news, but her line was busy.

There was a knock at his door. He looked up and saw Blackburn standing there, looking apologetic. "Got a minute?"

"Sure."

"I just wanted to repeat to you, on a personal level, how sorry I am about all this. In the press of complex corporate problems like this, human values may get lost, despite the best of intentions. While we intend to be fair to everyone, sometimes we fail. And what is a corporation if not a human group, a group of human beings? We're all people, underneath it all. As Alexander Pope once said, 'We're all just human.' So recognizing your own graciousness through all this, I want to say to you . . ."

Sanders wasn't listening. He was tired; all he really heard was that Phil realized he had screwed up, and now was trying to repair things in his usual manner, by sucking up to someone he had earlier bullied.

Sanders interrupted, saying, "What about Bob?" Now that it was over, Sanders was having a lot of feelings about Garvin. Memories going back to his earliest days with the company. Garvin had been a kind of father to Sanders, and he wanted to hear from Garvin now. He wanted an apology. Or something.

"I imagine Bob's going to take a couple of days to come around," Blackburn said. "This was a very difficult decision for him to arrive at. I had to work very hard on him, on your behalf. And now he's got to figure out how to break it to Meredith. All that."

"Uh-huh."

"But he'll eventually talk to you. I know he will. Meanwhile, I wanted to go over a few things about the meeting tomorrow," Blackburn said. "It's for Marden, their CEO, and it's going to be a bit more formal than the way we usually do things. We'll be in the big conference room on the ground floor. It'll start at nine, and go to ten. Meredith will chair the meeting, and she'll call on all the division heads to give a summary of progress and problems in their divisions. Mary Anne first, then Don, then Mark, then you. Everyone will talk three to four minutes. Do it standing. Wear a jacket and tie. Use visuals if you have them, but stay away from technical details. Keep it an overview. In your case, they'll expect to hear mostly about Twinkle."

Sanders nodded. "All right. But there isn't really much new to report. We still haven't figured out what's wrong with the drives."

"That's fine. I don't think anybody expects a solution yet. Just emphasize the success of the prototypes, and the fact that we've overcome production problems before. Keep it upbeat, and keep it moving. If you have a prototype or a mock-up, you might want to bring it along."

"Okay."

"You know the stuff—bright rosy digital future, minor technical glitches won't stand in the way of progress."

"Meredith's okay with that?" he said. He was slightly disturbed to hear that she was chairing the meeting.

"Meredith is expecting all the heads to be upbeat and nontechnical. There won't be a problem."

"Okay," Sanders said.

"Call me tonight if you want to go over your presentation," Blackburn said. "Or in the morning, early. Let's just finesse this session, and then we can move on. Start making changes next week."

Sanders nodded.

"You're the kind of man this company needs,"

Blackburn said. "I appreciate your understanding. And again, Tom, I'm sorry."

He left.

Sanders called down to the Diagnostics Group, to see if they had any further word. But there was no answer. He went out to the closet behind Cindy's desk and took out the AV materials: the big schematic drawing of the Twinkle drive, and the schematic of the production line in Malaysia. He could prop these on easels while he talked.

But as he thought about it, it occurred to him that Blackburn was right. A mock-up or a prototype would be good to have. In fact, he should probably bring one of the drives that Arthur had sent from KL.

It reminded him that he should call Arthur in Malaysia. He dialed the number.

"Mr. Kahn's office."

"It's Tom Sanders calling."

The assistant sounded surprised. "Mr. Kahn is not here, Mr. Sanders."

"When is he expected back?"

"He's out of the office, Mr. Sanders. I don't know when he'll be back."

"I see." Sanders frowned. That was odd. With Mohammed Jafar missing, it was unlike Arthur to leave the plant without supervision.

The assistant said, "Can I give him a message?"

"No message, thanks."

He hung up, went down to the third floor to

Cherry's programming group, and put his card in the slot to let himself in. The card popped back out, and the LED blinked 0000. It took him a moment to realize that they had cut off his access. Then he remembered the other card he had picked up earlier. He pushed it in the slot, and the door opened. Sanders went inside.

He was surprised to find the unit deserted. The programmers all kept strange hours; there was almost always somebody there, even at midnight.

He went to the Diagnostics room, where the drives were being studied. There were a series of benches, surrounded by electronic equipment and blackboards. The drives were set out on the benches, all covered in white cloth. The bright overhead quartz lights were off.

He heard rock-and-roll music from an adjacent room, and went there. A lone programmer in his early twenties was sitting at a console typing. Beside him, a portable radio blared.

Sanders said, "Where is everybody?"

The programmer looked up. "Third Wednesday of the month."

"So?"

"OOPS meets on the third Wednesday."

"Oh." The Object Oriented Programmer Support association, or OOPS, was an association of programmers in the Seattle area. It was started by Microsoft some years earlier, and was partly social and partly trade talk.

Sanders said, "You know anything about what the Diagnostics team found?"

"Sorry." The programmer shook his head. "I just came in."

Sanders went back to the Diagnostics room. He flicked on the lights and gently removed the white cloth that covered the drives. He saw that only three of the CD-ROM drives had been opened, their innards exposed to powerful magnifying glasses and electronic probes on the tables. The remaining seven drives were stacked to one side, still in plastic.

He looked up at the blackboards. One had a series of equations and hastily scribbled data points. The other had a flowchart list that read:

A. Contr. Incompat.
   VLSI?
   pwr?
B. Optic Dysfunct-? voltage reg?/arm?/servo?
C. Laser R/O (a,b,c)
D. Σ Mechanical $\sqrt{}$ $\sqrt{}$
E. Gremlins

It didn't mean much to Sanders. He turned his attention back to the tables, and peered at the test equipment. It looked fairly standard, except that there were a series of large-bore needles lying on the table, and several white circular wafers encased in plastic that looked like camera filters.

There were also Polaroid pictures of the drives in various stages of disassembly; the team had documented their work. Three of the Polaroids were placed in a neat row, as if they might be significant, but Sanders couldn't see why. They just showed chips on a green circuit board.

He looked at the drives themselves, being careful not to disturb anything. Then he turned to the stack of drives that were still wrapped in plastic. But looking closely, he noticed fine, needle-point punctures in the plastic covering four of the drives.

Nearby was a medical syringe and an open notebook. The notebook showed a column of figures:

PPU
7
11 (repeat 11)
5
2

And at the bottom someone had scrawled, "Fucking Obvious!" But it wasn't obvious to Sanders. He decided that he'd better call Don Cherry later tonight, to have him explain it. In the meantime, he took one of the extra drives from the stack to use in the presentation the following morning.

He left the Diagnostics room carrying all his

presentation materials, the easel boards flapping against his legs. He headed downstairs to the ground floor conference room, which had an AV closet where speakers stored visual material before a presentation. He could lock his material away there.

In the lobby, he passed the receptionist's desk, now manned by a black security guard, who watched a baseball game and nodded to Sanders. Sanders went back toward the rear of the floor, moving quietly on the plush carpeting. The hallway was dark, but the lights were on in the conference room; he could see them shining from around the corner.

As he came closer, he heard Meredith Johnson say, "And then what?" And a man's voice answered something indistinct.

Sanders paused.

He stood in the dark corridor and listened. From where he stood, he could see nothing of the room.

There was a moment of silence, and then Johnson said, "Okay, so will Mark talk about design?"

The man said, "Yes, he'll cover that."

"Okay," Johnson said. "Then what about the . . ."

Sanders couldn't hear the rest. He crept forward, moving silently on the carpet, and cautiously peered around the corner. He still could not see into the conference room itself, but there

was a large chrome sculpture in the hallway outside the room, a sort of propeller shape, and in
the reflection of its polished surface he saw Meredith moving in the room. The man with her was
Blackburn.

Johnson said, "So what if Sanders doesn't
bring it up?"

"He will," Blackburn said.

"You're sure he doesn't—that the—" Again,
the rest was lost.

"No, he—no idea."

Sanders held his breath. Meredith was pacing,
her image in the reflection, twisting and distorted.
"So when he does—I will say that this is a—is
that—you mean?"

"Exactly," Blackburn said.

"And if he—"

Blackburn put his hand on her shoulder. "Yes,
you have to—"

"—So—want me to—"

Blackburn said something quiet in reply, and
Sanders heard none of it, except the phrase
"—must demolish him."

"—Can do that—"

"—Make sure—counting on you—"

There was the shrill sound of a telephone. Both
Meredith and Blackburn reached for their pockets. Meredith answered the call, and the two
began to move toward the exit. They were heading toward Sanders.

Panicked, Sanders looked around, and saw a men's room to his right. He slipped inside the door as they came out of the conference room and started down the hallway.

"Don't worry about this, Meredith," Blackburn said. "It'll go fine."

"I'm not worried," she said.

"It should be quite smooth and impersonal," Blackburn said. "There's no reason for rancor. After all, you have the facts on your side. He's clearly incompetent."

"He still can't get into the database?" she said.

"No. He's locked out of the system."

"And there's no way he can get into Conley-White's system?"

Blackburn laughed. "No way in hell, Meredith."

The voices faded, moving down the hallway. Sanders strained to listen, finally heard the click of a door closing. He stepped out of the bathroom into the hallway.

The hallway was deserted. He stared toward the far door.

His own telephone rang in his pocket, the sound so loud it made him jump. He answered it. "Sanders."

"Listen," Fernandez said. "I sent the draft of your contract to Blackburn's office, but it came back with a couple of added statements that I'm not sure about. I think we better meet to discuss them."

"In an hour," Sanders said.

"Why not now?"

"I have something to do first," he said.

Ah, Thomas." Max Dorfman opened the door to his hotel room and immediately wheeled away, back toward the television set. "You have finally decided to come."

"You've heard?"

"Heard what?" Dorfman said. "I am an old man. No one bothers with me anymore. I'm cast by the wayside. By everyone—including you." He clicked off the television set and grinned.

Sanders said, "What have you heard?"

"Oh, just a few things. Rumors, idle talk. Why don't you tell me yourself?"

"I'm in trouble, Max."

"Of course you are in trouble," Dorfman snorted. "You have been in trouble all week. You only noticed now?"

"They're setting me up."

"They?"

"Blackburn and Meredith."

"Nonsense."

"It's true."

"You believe Blackburn can set you up? Philip Blackburn is a spineless fool. He has no principles and almost no brains. I told Garvin to fire him years ago. Blackburn is incapable of original thought."

"Then Meredith."

"Ah. Meredith. Yes. So beautiful. Such lovely breasts."

"Max, please."

"You thought so too, once."

"That was a long time ago," Sanders said.

Dorfman smiled. "Times have changed?" he said, with heavy irony.

"What does that mean?"

"You are looking pale, Thomas."

"I can't figure anything out. I'm scared."

"Oh, you're scared. A big man like you is scared of this beautiful woman with beautiful breasts."

"Max—"

"Of course, you are right to be scared. She has done all these many terrible things to you. She has tricked you and manipulated you and abused you, yes?"

"Yes," Sanders said.

"You have been victimized by her and Garvin."

"Yes."

"Then why were you mentioning to me the flower, hmm?"

He frowned. For a moment he didn't know what Dorfman was talking about. The old man was always so confusing and he liked to be—

"The *flower*," Dorfman said irritably, rapping his knuckles on the wheelchair arm. "The stained-glass flower in your apartment. We were speaking of it the other day. Don't tell me you have forgotten it?"

The truth was that he had, until that moment. Then he remembered the image of the stained-glass flower, the image that had come unbidden to his mind a few days earlier. "You're right. I forgot."

"You *forgot*." Dorfman's voice was heavy with sarcasm. "You expect me to believe that?"

"Max, I did, I—"

He snorted. "You are impossible. I cannot believe you will behave so transparently. You didn't forget, Thomas. You merely chose not to confront it."

"Confront what?"

In his mind, Sanders saw the stained-glass flower, in bright orange and purple and yellow. The flower mounted in the door of his apartment. Earlier in the week, he had been thinking about it constantly, almost obsessing about it, and yet today—

"I cannot bear this charade," Dorfman said. "Of course you remember it all. But you are *determined* not to think of it."

Sanders shook his head, confused.

"Thomas. You told it all to me, ten years ago," Dorfman said, waving his hand. "You *confided* in me. Blubbering. You were very upset at the time. It was the most important thing in your life, at the time. Now you say it is all forgotten?" He shook his head. "You told me that you would take trips with Garvin to Japan and Korea. And when you returned, she would be waiting for you in the apartment. In some erotic costume, or whatever. Some erotic pose. And you told me that sometimes, when you got home, you would see her first through the stained glass. Isn't that what you told me, Thomas? Or do I have it wrong?"

He had it wrong.

It came back to Sanders in a rush then, like a picture zooming large and bright before his eyes. He saw everything, almost as if he was there once again: the steps leading up to his apartment on the second floor, and the sounds he heard as he went up the steps in the middle of the afternoon, sounds he could not identify at first, but then he realized what he was hearing as he came to the landing and looked in through the stained glass and he saw—

"I came back a day early," Sanders said.

"Yes, that's right. You came back *unexpectedly.*"

The glass in patterns of yellow and orange and purple. And through it, her naked back, moving up and down. She was in the living room, on the couch, moving up and down.

"And what did you do?" Dorfman said. "When you saw her?"

"I rang the bell."

"That's right. Very civilized of you. Very non-confrontational and polite. You rang the bell."

In his mind he saw Meredith turning, looking toward the door. Her tangled hair falling across her face. She brushed the hair away from her eyes. Her expression changed as she saw him. Her eyes widened.

Dorfman prodded: "And then what? What did you do?"

"I left," Sanders said. "I went back to the ... I went to the garage and got in my car. I drove for a while. A couple of hours. Maybe more. It was dark when I got back."

"You were upset, naturally."

He came back up the stairs, and again looked in through the stained glass. The living room was empty. He unlocked the door and entered the living room. There was a bowl of popcorn on the couch. The couch was creased. The television was on, soundless. He looked away from the couch and went into the bedroom, calling her name. He found her packing, her open suitcase on the bed. He said, "What are you doing?"

"Leaving," she said. She turned to face him. Her body was rigid, tense. "Isn't that what you want me to do?"

"I don't know," he said.

And then she burst into tears. Sobbing, reaching for a kleenex, blowing her nose loudly, awkwardly, like a child. And somehow in her distress he held his arms out, and she hugged him and said she was sorry, repeating the words, again and again, through her tears. Looking up at him. Touching his face.

And then somehow . . .

Dorfman cackled. "Right on the suitcase, yes? Right there on the suitcase, on her clothes that were being packed, you made your reconciliation."

"Yes," Sanders said, remembering.

"She aroused you. You wanted her back. She excited you. She challenged you. You wanted to possess her."

"Yes . . ."

"Love is wonderful," Dorfman sighed, sarcastic again. "So pure, so innocent. And then you were together again, is that right?"

"Yes. For a while. But it didn't work out."

It was odd, how it had finally ended. He had been so angry with her at first, but he had forgiven her, and he thought that they could go on. They had talked about their feelings, they had expressed their love, and he had tried to go on with the best will in the world. But in the end, neither of them could; the incident had fatally ruptured the relationship, and something vital had been torn from it. It didn't matter how often they told themselves that they could go on. Something else now ruled. The core was dead. They fought more often, managing in this way to sustain the old energy for a while. But finally, it just ended.

"And when it was over," Dorfman said, "that was when you came and talked to me."

"Yes," Sanders said.

"And what did you come to talk to me about?" Dorfman asked. "Or have you 'forgotten' that, too?"

"No. I remember. I wanted your advice."

He had gone to Dorfman because he was considering leaving Cupertino. He was breaking up with Meredith, his life was confused, everything was in disarray, and he wanted to make a fresh start, to go somewhere else. So he was considering moving to Seattle to head the Advanced Projects Division. Garvin had offered him the job in passing one day, and Sanders was thinking about taking it. He had asked Dorfman's advice.

"You were quite upset," Dorfman said. "It was an unhappy ending to a love affair."

"Yes."

"So you might say that Meredith Johnson is the reason you are here in Seattle," Dorfman said. "Because of her, you changed your career, your life. You made a new life here. And many people knew this fact of your past. Garvin knew. And Blackburn knew. That is why he was so careful to ask you if you could work with her. Everyone was so worried about how it would be. But you reassured them, Thomas, didn't you?"

MICHAEL CRICHTON 511

"Yes."

"And your reassurances were false."

Sanders hesitated. "I don't know, Max."

"Come, now. You know *exactly*. It must have been like a bad dream, a nightmare from your past, to hear that this person you had run away from was now coming to Seattle, pursuing you up here, and that she would be your superior in the company. Taking the job that you wanted. That you thought you deserved."

"I don't know . . ."

"Don't you? In your place, I would be angry. I would want to be rid of her, yes? She hurt you once very badly, and you would not want to be hurt again. But what choice did you have? She had the job, and she was Garvin's protégé. She was protected by Garvin's power, and he would not hear a word against her. True?"

"True."

"And for many years you had not been close to Garvin, because Garvin didn't really want you to take the Seattle job in the first place. He had offered it to you, expecting you to turn it down. Garvin likes protégés. He likes admirers at his feet. He does not like his admirers to pack up and leave for another city. So Garvin was disappointed with you. Things were never the same. And now suddenly here was this woman out of your past, a woman with Garvin's backing. So, what choice did you have? What could you do with your anger?"

His mind was spinning, confused. When he thought back to the events of that first day—the rumors, the announcement by Blackburn, the first meeting with her—he did not remember feeling anger. His feelings had been so complicated on that day, but he had not felt anger, he was sure of it . . .

"Thomas, Thomas. Stop dreaming. There is no time for it."

Sanders was shaking his head. He couldn't think clearly.

"Thomas, *you arranged all this*. Whether you admit it or not, whether you are aware of it or not. On some level, what has happened is exactly what you intended. And you made sure it would happen."

He found himself remembering Susan. What had she said at the restaurant?

Why didn't you tell me? I could have helped you.

And she was right, of course. She was an attorney; she could have advised him if he had told her what happened the first night. She would have told him what to do. She could have gotten him out of it. But he hadn't told her.

There's not much we can do now.

"You wanted this confrontation, Thomas."

And then Garvin: *She was your girlfriend, and you didn't like it when she dropped you. So now you want to pay her back.*

"You worked all week to ensure this confrontation."

"Max—"

"So don't tell me you are a victim here. You're not a victim. You call yourself a victim because you don't want to take responsibility for your life. Because you are sentimental and lazy and naïve. You think other people should take care of you."

"Jesus, Max," Sanders said.

"You deny your part in this. You pretend to forget. You pretend to be unaware. And now you pretend to be confused."

"Max—"

"Oh! I don't know why I bother with you. How many hours do you have until this meeting? Twelve hours? Ten? Yet you waste your time talking to a crazy old man." He spun in his wheelchair. "If I were you, I would get to work."

"Meaning what?"

"Well, we know what your intentions are, Thomas. But what are *her* intentions, hmmm? She is solving a problem, too. She has a purpose here. So: what is the problem she is solving?"

"I don't know," Sanders said.

"Clearly. But how will you find out?"

Lost in thought, he walked the five blocks to Il Terrazzo. Fernandez was waiting for him outside. They went in together.

"Oh Christ," Sanders said, as he looked around.

"All the usual suspects," Fernandez said.

In the far section straight ahead, Meredith Johnson was having dinner with Bob Garvin. Two tables away, Phil Blackburn was eating with his wife, Doris, a thin bespectacled woman who looked like an accountant. Near them, Stephanie Kaplan was having dinner with a young man in his twenties—probably her son at the university, Sanders thought. And over to the right, by the window, the Conley-White people were in the midst of a working dinner, their briefcases open at their feet, papers scattered all over the table. Ed Nichols sat with John Conley to his right, and Jim Daly to his left. Daly was speaking into a tiny dictating machine.

"Maybe we should go somewhere else," Sanders said.

"No," Fernandez said. "They've already seen us. We can sit in the corner over there."

Carmine came over. "Mr. Sanders," he said with a formal nod.

"We'd like a table in the corner, Carmine."

"Yes of course, Mr. Sanders."

They sat to one side. Fernandez was staring at Meredith and Garvin. "She could be his daughter," she said.

"Everybody says so."

"It's quite striking."

The waiter brought menus. Nothing on it appealed to Sanders, but they ordered anyway. Fernandez was looking steadily at Garvin. "He's a fighter, isn't he."

"Bob? Famous fighter. Famous tough guy."

"She knows how to play him." Fernandez turned away and pulled papers out of her briefcase. "This is the contract that Blackburn sent back. It is all in order, except for two clauses. First, they claim the right to terminate you if you are shown to have committed a felony on the job."

"Uh-huh." He wondered what they might mean.

"And this second clause claims the right to terminate you if you have 'failed to demonstrate satisfactory performance in the job as measured by industry standards.' What does that mean?"

He shook his head. "They must have something in mind." He told her about the conversation he had overheard in the conference room.

As usual, Fernandez showed no reaction. "Possible," she said.

"Possible? They're going to do it."

"I meant legally. It's possible that they intend something of this sort. And it would work."

"Why?"

"A harassment claim brings up the entire performance of an employee. If there is dereliction, even a very old or minor dereliction, it may be used to dismiss the claim. I had one client who worked for a company for ten years. But the company was able to demonstrate that the employee had lied on the original application form, and the case was dismissed. The employee was fired."

"So this comes down to my performance."

"It may. Yes."

He frowned. What did they have on him?

She is solving a problem, too. So: what is the problem she is solving?

Beside him, Fernandez pulled the tape recorder out of her pocket. "There's a couple of other things I want to go over," she said. "There's something that happens early on in the tape."

"Okay."

"I want you to listen."

She gave the player to him. He held it close to his ear.

He heard his own voice saying clearly, ". . . we'll face that later. I've given her your thoughts, and she's talking to Bob now, so presumably we'll go into the meeting tomorrow taking that position. Well, anyway, Mark, if there is a significant change in all this, I'll contact you before the meeting tomorrow, and—"

"Forget that phone," Meredith's voice said loudly, and then there was the sound of rustling, like fabric, and a sort of hissing sound, and a dull *thunk* as the phone was dropped. The momentary sharp crackle of static.

More rustling. Then silence.

A grunt. Rustling.

As he listened, he tried to imagine the action in the room. They must have moved over to the couch, because now the voices were lower, less distinct. He heard himself say, "Meredith, wait—"

"Oh God," she said, "I've wanted you all day."

More rustling. Heavy breathing. It was hard to be certain what was happening. A little moan from her. More rustling.

She said, "Oh God, you feel so *good*, I can't stand the bastard touching me. Those stupid glasses. Oh! I'm so *hot*, I haven't had a decent fuck—"

More rustling. Static crackle. Rustling. More rustling. Sanders listened with a sense of disappointment. He could not really create images for what was going on—and he had been there. This tape would not be persuasive to someone else. Most of it sounded like obscure noise. With long periods of silence.

"Meredith—"

"*Oooh.* Don't talk. No! No . . ." He heard her gasping, in little breaths.

Then more silence.

Fernandez said, "That's enough."

Sanders put the player down and shut it off. He shook his head.

"You can't tell anything from this. About what was really going on."

"You can tell enough," Fernandez said. "And don't you start worrying about the evidence. That's my job. But you heard her first statements?" She consulted her notepad. "Where she says, 'I've wanted you all day'? And then she says, 'Oh God you feel so good, I can't stand the bastard touching me. Those stupid glasses, oh I'm so hot, I haven't had a decent fuck.' You heard that part?"

"Yes. I heard it."

"Okay. Who is she talking about?"

"Talking about?"

"Yes. Who is the bastard she can't stand touching her?"

"I assume her husband," Sanders said. "We were talking about him earlier. Before the tape."

"Tell me what was said earlier."

"Well, Meredith was complaining about having

to pay alimony to her husband, and then she said her husband was terrible in bed. She said, 'I hate a man who doesn't know what he's doing.' "

"So you think 'I can't stand the bastard touching me' refers to her husband?"

"Yes."

"I don't," Fernandez said. "They were divorced months ago. The divorce was bitter. The husband hates her. He has a girlfriend now; he's taken her to Mexico. I don't think she means the husband."

"Then who?"

"I don't know."

Sanders said, "I suppose it could be anybody."

"I don't think it's just anybody. Listen again. Listen to how she sounds."

He rewound the tape, held the player to his ear. After a moment, he put the player down. "She sounds almost angry."

Fernandez nodded. "Resentful is the term I'd use. She's in the midst of this episode with you, and she's talking about someone else. 'The bastard.' It's as if she wants to pay somebody back. Right at that moment, she's getting even."

Sanders said, "I don't know. Meredith's a talker. She always talked about other people. Old boyfriends, that stuff. She's not what you'd call a romantic."

He remembered one time when they were lying on the bed in the apartment in Sunnyvale, feeling a sort of relaxed glow. A Sunday afternoon. Listening to kids laughing in the street outside. His hand resting on her thigh, feeling the sweat. And in this thoughtful way she said, "You know, I once went out with this Norwegian guy, and he had a curved dick. Curved like a sword, sort of bent over to the side, and he—"

"Jesus, Meredith."

"What's the matter? It's true. He really did."

"Not now."

Whenever this sort of thing happened, she'd sigh, as if she was obliged to put up with his excessive sensitivity. "Why is it that guys always want to think they're the only ones?"

"We don't. We know we're not. Just not now, okay?"

And she'd sigh again . . .

Sitting in the restaurant, Fernandez said, "Even if it's not unusual for her to talk during sex—even if she is indiscreet or distancing—who is she talking about here?"

Sanders shook his head. "I don't know, Louise."

"And she says she can't stand him touching her . . . as if she has no choice. And she mentions his silly glasses." She looked over at Meredith, who was eating quietly with Garvin. "Him?"

"I don't think so."

"Why not?"

"Everybody says no. Everybody says Bob isn't screwing her."

"Everybody could be wrong."

Sanders shook his head. "It'd be incest."

"You're probably right."

The food came. Sanders poked at his pasta *puttanesca*, picking out the olives. He wasn't feeling hungry. Beside him, Fernandez ate heartily. They had ordered the same thing.

Sanders looked over at the Conley-White people. Nichols was holding up a clear plastic sheet of 35-millimeter transparencies. Slides. Of what? he wondered. His half-frame glasses were perched on his nose. He seemed to be taking a long time. Beside him, Conley glanced at his watch and said something about the time. The others nodded. Conley glanced over at Johnson, then turned back to his papers.

Daly said something. ". . . have that figure?"

"It's here," Conley said, pointing to the sheet.

"This is really very good," Fernandez said. "You shouldn't let it get cold."

"Okay." He took a bite. It had no taste. He put the fork down.

She wiped her chin with her napkin. "You know, you never really told me why you stopped. At the end."

"My friend Max Dorfman says I set it all up."

"Uh-huh," Fernandez said.

"Do you think that, too?"

"I don't know. I was just asking what you were feeling, at the time. At the time you pulled away."

He shrugged. "I just didn't want to."

"Uh-huh. Didn't feel like it when you got there, huh?"

"No, I didn't." Then he said, "You really want to know what it was? She coughed."

"She coughed?" Fernandez said.

Sanders saw himself again in the room, his trousers down around his knees, bent over Meredith on the office couch. He remembered thinking, What the hell am I doing? And she had her hands on his shoulders, tugging him toward her. "Oh please . . . No . . . No . . ."

And then she turned her head aside and coughed.

That cough was what did it. That was when he sat back, and said, "You're right," and got off the couch.

Fernandez frowned. "I have to say," Fernandez said. "A cough doesn't seem like a big deal."

"It was." He pushed his plate away. "I mean, you can't cough at a time like that."

"Why? Is this some etiquette I don't know about?" Fernandez said. "No coughing in the clinch?"

"It's not that at all," Sanders said. "It's just what it means."

"I'm sorry, you've lost me. What does a cough mean?"

He hesitated. "You know, women always think that men don't know what's going on. There's this whole idea that men can't find the place, they don't know what to do, all that stuff. How men are stupid about sex."

"I don't think you're stupid. What does a cough mean?"

"A cough means you're not involved."

She raised her eyebrows. "That seems a little extreme."

"It's just a fact."

"I don't know. My husband has bronchitis. He coughs all the time."

"Not at the last moment, he doesn't."

She paused, thinking about it. "Well, he certainly does right afterward. He breaks out in a fit of coughing. We always laugh about how he does that."

"Right after is different. But at the moment, right in the intense moment, I'm telling you— nobody coughs."

More images flashed through his mind. Her cheeks turn red. Her neck is blotchy, or her upper chest. Nipples no longer hard. They were hard at first, but not now. The eyes get dark, sometimes purple below. Lips swollen. Breathing changes. Sudden surging heat. Shift in the hips, shifting rhythm, tension but something else, something liquid. Forehead frowning. Wincing. Biting. So many different ways, but—

"Nobody coughs," he said again.

And then he felt a kind of sudden embarrassment, and pulled his plate back, and took a bite of pasta. He wanted a reason not to say more, because he had the feeling that he had overstepped the rules, that there was still this area, this kind of knowledge, this awareness that everyone pretended didn't exist . . .

Fernandez was staring at him curiously. "Did you read about this somewhere?"

He shook his head, chewing.

"Do men discuss it? Things like this?"

He shook his head, no.

"Women do."

"I know." He swallowed. "But anyway, she coughed, and that was why I stopped. She wasn't involved, and I was very—angry about it, I guess. I mean she was lying there panting and moaning, but she was really uninvolved. And I felt . . ."

"Exploited?"

"Something like that. Manipulated. Sometimes I think maybe if she hadn't coughed right then . . ." Sanders shrugged.

"Maybe I should ask her," Fernandez said, nodding her head in Meredith's direction.

Sanders looked up and saw that she was coming over to their table. "Oh, hell."

"Calmly, calmly. Everything's fine."

Meredith came over, a big smile on her face. "Hello, Louise. Hello, Tom." Sanders started to get up. "Don't get up, Tom, please." She rested her hand on his shoulder, gave it a little squeeze. "I just came by for a moment." She was smiling radiantly. She looked exactly like the confident boss, stopping to say hello to a couple of colleagues. Back at her table, Sanders saw Garvin paying the bill. He wondered if he would come over, too.

"Louise, I just wanted to say no hard feelings," Meredith said. "Everybody had a job to do. I understand that. And I think it served a purpose, clearing the air. I just hope we can go on productively from here."

Meredith was standing behind Sanders's chair as she talked. He had to twist his head and crane his neck to look at her.

Fernandez said, "Don't you want to sit down?"

"Well, maybe for a minute."

Sanders stood to get her a chair. He was thinking that to the Conley people, all this would look exactly right. The boss not wanting to intrude, waiting to be pressed by her co-workers to join them. As he brought the chair, he glanced over and saw that Nichols was looking at them, peering over his glasses. So was young Conley.

Meredith sat down. Sanders pushed the chair in for her. "You want anything?" Fernandez said solicitously.

"I just finished, thanks."

"Coffee? Anything?"

"I'm fine, thanks."

Sanders sat down. Meredith leaned forward. "Bob's been telling me about his plans to take this division public. It's very exciting. It looks like full speed ahead."

Sanders watched her with astonishment.

"Now, Bob has a list of names for the new company. When we spin it off next year. See how these sound to you: SpeedCore, SpeedStar, PrimeCore, Talisan, and Tensor. I think Speed-Core makes racing parts for stock cars. SpeedStar is right on the money—but maybe too right on. PrimeCore sounds like a mutual fund. How about Talisan or Tensor?"

"Tensor is a lamp," Fernandez said.

"Okay. But Talisan is pretty good, I think."

"The Apple-IBM joint venture is called Taligent," Sanders said.

"Oh. You're right. Too close. How about Mi-croDyne? That's not bad. Or ADG, for Advanced Data Graphics? Do either of those work, do you think?"

"MicroDyne is okay."

"I thought so, too. And there was one more . . . AnoDyne."

"That's a painkiller," Fernandez said.

"What is?"

"An anodyne is a painkiller. A narcotic."

"Oh. Forget that. Last one, SynStar."

"Sounds like a drug company."

"Yeah, it does. But we've got a year to come up with a better one. And MicroDyne isn't bad, to start. Sort of combining micro with dynamo. Good images, don't you think?"

Before they could answer, she pushed her chair back. "I've got to go. But I thought you'd like to hear the thinking. Thanks for your input. Good night, Louise. And Tom, I'll see you tomorrow." She shook hands with them both and crossed the room to Garvin. Together she and Garvin went over to the Conley table to say hello.

Sanders stared at her. " 'Good images,' " he repeated. "Christ. She's talking about names for a company, but she doesn't even know what the company is."

"It was quite a show."

"Sure," Sanders said. "She's all show. But it had nothing to do with us. It's for them." He nodded toward the Conley-White people, sitting across the restaurant. Garvin was shaking hands all around, and Meredith was talking to Jim Daly. Daly made a joke and she laughed, throwing her head back, showing her long neck.

"The only reason she talked to us was so that when I get fired tomorrow, she won't be seen as having planned it."

Fernandez was paying the bill. "You want to go?" she said. "I still have some things to check."

"Really? What do you have to check?"

"Alan may have gotten something more for us. There's a possibility."

At the Conley table, Garvin was saying goodbye. He gave a final wave, then crossed the room to talk to Carmine.

Meredith remained at the Conley-White table. She was standing behind John Conley, with her hands resting on his shoulders while she talked to Daly and Ed Nichols. Ed Nichols said something, peering over his glasses, and Meredith laughed, and came around to look over his shoulder at a sheet of figures he was holding. Her head was very close to Nichols. She nodded, talked, pointed to the sheet.

You're checking the wrong company.

Sanders stared at Meredith, smiling and joking with the three men from Conley-White. What had Phil Blackburn said to him yesterday?

The thing is, Tom, Meredith Johnson is very well connected in this company. She has impressed a lot of important people.

Like Garvin.

Not only Garvin. Meredith has built a power base in several areas.

Conley-White?

Yes. There, too.

Alongside him, Fernandez stood up. Sanders stood and said, "You know what, Louise?"

"What?"

"We've been checking the wrong company."

Fernandez frowned, then looked over at the Conley-White table. Meredith was nodding with Ed Nichols and pointing with one hand, her other hand flat on the table for balance. Her fingers were touching Ed Nichols. He was peering at the sheets of data over his glasses.

"Stupid glasses . . ." Sanders said.

No wonder Meredith wouldn't press harassment charges against him. It would have been too embarrassing for her relationship with Ed Nichols. And no wonder Garvin wouldn't fire her. It made perfect sense. Nichols was already uneasy about the merger—his affair with Meredith might be all that was holding it in place.

Fernandez sighed. "You think so? Nichols?"

"Yeah. Why not?"

Fernandez shook her head. "Even if it's true, it doesn't help us. They can argue paramour preference, they can argue lots of things—if there's even an argument that needs to be made. This isn't the first merger made in the sack, you know. I say, forget it."

"You mean to tell me," he said, "that there's nothing improper with her having an affair with someone at Conley-White and being promoted as a result?"

"Nothing at all. At least, not in the strict legal sense. So forget it."

Suddenly he remembered what Kaplan had

said. *She was looking in the wrong direction when they fired her.*

"I'm tired," he said.

"We all are. They look tired, too."

Across the room, the meeting was breaking up. Papers were being put back into briefcases. Meredith and Garvin were chatting with them. They all started leaving. Garvin shook hands with Carmine, who opened the front door for his departing guests.

And then it happened.

There was the sudden harsh glare of quartz lights, shining in from the street outside. The group huddled together, trapped in the light. They cast long shadows back into the restaurant.

"What's going on?" Fernandez said.

Sanders turned to look, but already the group was ducking back inside, closing the door. There was a moment of sudden chaos. They heard Garvin say, "God*damn* it," and spin to Blackburn.

Blackburn stood, a stricken look on his face, and rushed over to Garvin. Garvin was shifting from foot to foot. He was simultaneously trying to reassure the Conley-White people and chew out Blackburn.

Sanders went over. "Everything okay?"

"It's the goddamned press," Garvin said. "KSEA-TV is out there."

"This is an outrage," Meredith said.

"They're asking about some harassment suit," Garvin said, looking darkly at Sanders.

Sanders shrugged.

"I'll speak to them," Blackburn said. "This is just ridiculous."

"I'll say it's ridiculous," Garvin said. "It's an outrage, is what it is."

Everyone seemed to be talking at once, agreeing that it was an outrage. But Sanders saw that Nichols looked shaken. Now Meredith was leading them out of the restaurant the back way, onto the terrace. Blackburn went out the front, into the harsh lights. He held up his hands, like a man being arrested. Then the door closed.

Nichols was saying, "Not good, not good."

"Don't worry, I know the news director over there," Garvin was saying. "I'll put this one away."

Jim Daly said something about how the merger ought to be confidential.

"Don't worry," Garvin said grimly. "It's going to be confidential as hell by the time I get through."

Then they were gone, out the back door, into the night. Sanders went back to the table, where Fernandez was waiting.

"A little excitement," Fernandez said calmly.

"More than a little," Sanders said. He glanced across the room at Stephanie Kaplan, still having dinner with her son. The young man was talking, gesturing with his hands, but Kaplan was staring fixedly at the back door, where the Conley-White people had departed. She had a curious expression on her face. Then, after a moment, she turned back and resumed her conversation with her son.

The evening was black, damp, and unpleasant. He shivered as he walked back to his office with Fernandez.

"How did a television crew get the story?"

"Probably from Walsh," Fernandez said. "But maybe another way. It's really a small town. Anyway, never mind that. You've got to prepare for the meeting tomorrow."

"I've been trying to forget that."

"Yeah. Well, don't."

Ahead they saw Pioneer Square, with windows in the buildings still brightly lit. Many of the companies here had business with Japan, and stayed open to overlap with the first hours of the day in Tokyo.

"You know," Fernandez said, "watching her with those men, I noticed how cool she was."

"Yes. Meredith is cool."

"Very controlled."

"Yes. She is."

"So why did she approach you so overtly—and on her first day? What was the rush?"

What is the problem she is trying to solve? Max had said. Now Fernandez was asking the same thing. Everyone seemed to understand except Sanders.

You're not a victim.

So, solve it, he thought.

Get to work.

He remembered the conversation when Meredith and Blackburn were leaving the conference room.

It should be quite smooth and impersonal. After all, you have the facts on your side. He's clearly incompetent.

He still can't get into the database?

No. He's locked out of the system.

And there's no way he can get into Conley-White's system?

No way in hell, Meredith.

They were right, of course. He couldn't get into the system. But what difference would it make if he could?

Solve the problem, Max had said. *Do what you do best.*

Solve the problem.

"Hell," Sanders said.

"It'll come," Fernandez said.

It was nine-thirty. On the fourth floor, cleaning crews worked in the central partition area. Sanders went into his office with Fernandez. He didn't really know why they were going there. There wasn't anything he could think to do, now.

Fernandez said, "Let me talk to Alan. He might have something." She sat down and began to dial.

Sanders sat behind his desk, and stared at the monitor. On the screen, his e-mail message read:

YOU'RE STILL CHECKING THE WRONG COMPANY.

AFRIEND

"I don't see how," he said, looking at the screen. He felt irritable, playing with a puzzle that everyone could solve except him.

Fernandez said, "Alan? Louise. What have you got? Uh-huh. Uh-huh. Is that . . . Well, that's very disappointing, Alan. No, I don't know, now. If you can, yes. When would you be seeing her? All right. Whatever you can." She hung up. "No luck tonight."

"But we've only got tonight."

"Yes."

Sanders stared at the message on the computer screen. Somebody inside the company was trying to help him. Telling him he was checking the wrong company. The message seemed to imply that there was a way for him to check the other company. And presumably, whoever knew enough to send this message also knew that Sanders had been cut out of the DigiCom system, his privileges revoked.

What could he do?

Nothing.

Fernandez said, "Who do you think this 'Afriend' is?"

"I don't know."

"Suppose you had to guess."

"I don't know."

"What comes into your mind?" she said.

He considered the possibility that 'Afriend' was Mary Anne Hunter. But Mary Anne wasn't really a technical person; her strength was marketing. She wasn't likely to be sending routed messages over the Internet. She probably didn't know what the Internet was. So: not Mary Anne.

And not Mark Lewyn. Lewyn was furious at him.

Don Cherry? Sanders paused, considering that. In a way, this was just like Cherry. But the only time that Sanders had seen him since this began, Cherry had been distinctly unfriendly.

Not Cherry.

Then who else could it be? Those were the only people with executive sysop access in Seattle. Hunter, Lewyn, Cherry. A short list.

Stephanie Kaplan? Unlikely. At heart, Kaplan was plodding and unimaginative. And she didn't know enough about computers to do this.

Was it somebody outside the company? It could be Gary Bosak, he thought. Gary probably felt guilty about having turned his back on Sanders. And Gary had a hacker's devious instincts— and a hacker's sense of humor.

It might very well be Gary.

But it still didn't do Sanders any good.

You were always good at technical problems. That was always your strength.

He pulled out the Twinkle CD-ROM drive, still in plastic. Why would they want it wrapped that way?

Never mind, he thought. Stay focused.

There was something wrong with the drive. If he knew what, he would have the answer. Who would know?

Wrapped in plastic.

It was something to do with the production line. It must be. He fumbled with the material on his desk and found the DAT cartridge. He inserted it into the machine.

It came up, showing his conversation with Arthur Kahn. Kahn was on one side of the screen, Sanders on the other.

Behind Arthur, the brightly lit assembly line beneath banks of fluorescent lights. Kahn coughed, and rubbed his chin. "Hello, Tom. How are you?"

"I'm fine, Arthur," he said.

"Well, good. I'm sorry about the new organization."

But Sanders wasn't listening to the conversation. He was looking at Kahn. He noticed now that Kahn was standing very close to the camera, so close that his features were slightly blurred, out of focus. His face was large, and blocked any clear view of the production line behind him. "You know how I feel personally," Kahn was saying, on the screen.

His face was blocking the line.

Sanders watched a moment more, and then switched the tape off.

"Let's go downstairs," he said.

"You have an idea?"

"Call it a last-ditch hope," he said.

T he lights clicked on, harsh lights shining on the tables of the Diagnostic team. Fernandez said, "What is this place?"

"This is where they check the drives."

"The drives that don't work?"

"Right."

Fernandez gave a little shrug. "I'm afraid I'm not—"

"Me neither," Sanders said. "I'm not a technical person. I can just read people."

She looked around the room. "Can you read this?"

He sighed. "No."

Fernandez said, "Are they finished?"

"I don't know," he said.

And then he saw it. They *were* finished. They had to be. Because otherwise the Diagnostics team would be working all night, trying to get ready for the meeting tomorrow. But they had covered the tables up and gone to their professional association meeting because they were finished.

The problem was solved.

Everybody knew it but him.

That was why they had only opened three

drives. They didn't need to open the others. And they had asked for them to be sealed in plastic . . .

Because . . .

The punctures . . .

"Air," he said.

"Air?"

"They think it's the air."

"What air?" she said.

"The air in the plant."

"The plant in Malaysia?"

"Right."

"This is about air in Malaysia?"

"No. Air in the *plant*."

He looked again at the notebook on the table. "PPU" followed by a row of figures. PPU stood for "particulates per unit." It was the standard measure of air cleanliness in a plant. And these figures, ranging from two to eleven—they were way off. They should be running zero particulates . . . one, at most. These figures were unacceptable.

The air in the plant was bad.

That meant that they would be getting dirt in the split optics, dirt in the drive arms, dirt in the chip joins . . .

He looked at the chips attached to the board.

"Christ," he said.

"What is it?"

"Look."

"I don't see anything."

"There's a space between the chips and the boards. The chips aren't seated."

"It looks okay to me."

"It's not."

He turned to the stacked drives. He could see at a glance that all the chips were seated differently. Some were tight, some had a gap of a few millimeters, so you could see the metal contacts.

"This isn't right," Sanders said. "This should never happen." The fact was that the chips were inserted on the line by automated chip pressers. Every board, every chip should look exactly the same coming off the line. But they didn't. They were all different. Because of that, you could get voltage irregularities, memory allocation problems—all kinds of random stuff. Which was exactly what they were getting.

He looked at the blackboard, the list of the flowchart. One item caught his eye.

D. Σ Mechanical √ √

The Diagnostics team had put two checks beside "Mechanical." The problem with the CD-ROM drives was a mechanical problem. Which meant it was a problem in the production line.

And the production line was his responsibility. He'd designed it, he'd set it up. He'd checked all the specs on that line, from beginning to end.

And now it wasn't working right.

He was sure that it wasn't his fault. Something must have happened after he had set up the line. Somehow it had been changed around, and it didn't work anymore. But what had happened?

To find out, he needed to get onto the databases.

But he was locked out.

There wasn't any way to get online.

Immediately, he thought of Bosak. Bosak could get him on. So, for that matter, could one of the programmers on Cherry's teams. These kids were hackers: they would break into a system for a moment of minor amusement the way ordinary people went out for coffee. But there weren't any programmers in the building now. And he didn't know when they would be back from their meeting. Those kids were so unreliable. Like the kid that had thrown up all over the walker pad. That was the problem. They were just kids, playing with toys like the walker pad. Bright creative kids, fooling around, no cares at all, and—

"Oh, Jesus." He sat forward. "Louise."

"Yes?"

"There's a way to do this."

"Do what?"

"Get into the database." He turned and hurried out of the room. He was rummaging through his pockets, looking for the second electronic passcard.

Fernandez said, "Are we going somewhere?"

"Yes, we are."

"Do you mind telling me where?"

"New York," Sanders said.

The lights flicked on one after another, in long banks. Fernandez stared at the room. "What is this? The exercise room from hell?"

"It's a virtual reality simulator," Sanders said.

She looked at the round walker pads, and all the wires, the cables hanging from the ceiling. "This is how you're going to get to New York?"

"That's right."

Sanders went over to the hardware cabinets. There were large hand-painted signs reading, "Do Not Touch" and "Hands Off, You Little Wonk." He hesitated, looking for the control console.

"I hope you know what you're doing," Fernandez said. She stood by one of the walker pads, looking at the silver headset. "Because I think somebody could get electrocuted with this."

"Yeah, I know." Sanders lifted covers off monitors and put them back on again, moving quickly. He found the master switch. A moment later, the equipment hummed. One after another, the monitors began to glow. Sanders said, "Get up on the pad."

He came over and helped her stand on the walker pad. Fernandez moved her feet experimentally, feeling the balls roll. Immediately, there was a green flash from the lasers. "What was that?"

"The scanner. Mapping you. Don't worry about it. Here's the headset." He brought the headset down from the ceiling and started to place it over her eyes.

"Just a minute." She pulled away. "What is this?"

"The headset has two small display screens. They project images right in front of your eyes. Put it on. And be careful. These things are expensive."

"How expensive?"

"A quarter of a million dollars apiece." He fitted the headset over her eyes and put the headphones over her ears.

"I don't see any images. It's dark in here."

"That's because you're not plugged in, Louise." He plugged in her cables.

"Oh," she said, in a surprised voice. "What do you know . . . I can see a big blue screen, like a movie screen. Right in front of me. At the bottom of the screen there are two boxes. One says 'ON' and one says 'OFF.' "

"Just don't touch anything. Keep your hands on this bar," he said, putting her fingers on the walker handhold. "I'm going to mount up."

"This thing on my head feels funny."

Sanders stepped up onto the second walker pad

and brought the headset down from the ceiling. He plugged in the cable. "I'll be right with you," he said.

He put on the headset.

Sanders saw the blue screen, surrounded by blackness. He looked to his left and saw Fernandez standing beside him. She looked entirely normal, dressed in her street clothes. The video was recording her appearance, and the computer eliminated the walker pad and the headset.

"I can see you," she said, in a surprised voice. She smiled. The part of her face covered by the headset was computer animated, giving her a slightly unreal, cartoonlike quality.

"Walk up to the screen."

"How?"

"Just walk, Louise." Sanders started forward on the walker pad. The blue screen became larger and larger, until it filled his field of vision. He went over to the ON button, and pushed it with his finger.

The blue screen flashed. In huge lettering, stretching wide in front of them, it said:

DIGITAL COMMUNICATIONS DATA SYSTEMS

Beneath that was listed a column of oversize menu items. The screen looked exactly like an ordinary DigiCom monitor screen, the kind on everybody's office desk, now blown up to enormous size.

"A gigantic computer terminal," Fernandez said. "Wonderful. Just what everybody has been hoping for."

"Just wait." Sanders poked at the screen, selecting menu items. There was a kind of *whoosh* and the lettering on the screen curved inward, pulling back and deepening until it formed a sort of funnel that stretched away from them into the distance. Fernandez was silent.

That shut her up, he thought.

Now, as they watched, the blue funnel began to distort. It widened, became rectangular. The lettering and the blue color faded. Beneath his feet, a floor emerged. It looked like veined marble. The walls on both sides became wood paneling. The ceiling was white.

"It's a corridor," she said, in a soft voice.

The Corridor continued to build itself, progressively adding more detail. Drawers and cabinets appeared in the walls. Pillars formed along its length. Other hallways opened up, leading down to other corridors. Large light fixtures emerged from the walls and turned themselves on. Now the pillars cast shadows on the marble floors.

"It's like a library," she said. "An old-fashioned library."

"This part is, yes."

"How many parts are there?"

"I'm not sure." He started walking forward.

She hurried to catch up to him. Through his earphones, he heard the sound of their feet clicking on the marble floor. Cherry had added that—a nice touch.

Fernandez asked, "Have you been here before?"

"Not for several weeks. Not since it was finished."

"Where are we going?"

"I'm not exactly sure. But somewhere in here there's a way to get into the Conley-White database."

She said, "Where are we now?"

"We're in data, Louise. This is all just data."

"This corridor is data?"

"There is no corridor. Everything you see is just a bunch of numbers. It's the DigiCom company database, exactly the same database that people access every day through their computer terminals. Except it's being represented for us as a place."

She walked alongside him. "I wonder who did the decorating."

"It's modeled on a real library. In Oxford, I think."

They came to the junction, with other corridors stretching away. Big signs hung overhead. One said "Accounting." Another said "Human Resources." A third said "Marketing."

"I see," Fernandez said. "We're inside your company database."

"That's right."

"This is amazing."

"Yeah. Except we don't want to be here. Somehow, we have to get into Conley-White."

"How do we do that?"

"I don't know," Sanders said. "I need help."

"Help is here," said a soft voice nearby. Sanders looked over and saw an angel, about a foot high. It was white, and hovered in the air near his head. It held a flickering candle in its hands.

"Goddamn," Louise said.

"I am sorry," the angel said. "Is that a command? I do not recognize 'Goddamn.' "

"No," Sanders said quickly. "It's not a command." He was thinking that he would have to be careful or they would crash the system.

"Very well. I await your command."

"Angel: I need help."

"Help is here."

"How do I enter the Conley-White database?"

"I do not recognize 'the Conley-White database.' "

That made sense, Sanders thought. Cherry's team wouldn't have programmed anything about Conley-White into the Help system. He would have to phrase the question more generally. Sanders said, "Angel: I am looking for a database."

"Very well. Database gateways are accessed with the keypad."

"Where is the keypad?" Sanders said.

"Make a fist with your hand."

Sanders made a fist and a gray pad formed in the air so that he appeared to be holding it. He pulled it toward him and looked at it.

"Pretty neat," Fernandez said.

"I also know jokes," the angel said. "Would you like to hear one?"

"No," Sanders said.

"Very well. I await your command."

Sanders stared at the pad. It had a long list of operator commands, with arrows and push buttons. Fernandez said, "What is that, the world's most complicated TV remote?"

"Just about."

He found a push button marked OTHER DB. That seemed likely. He pressed it.

Nothing happened.

He pressed it again.

"The gateway is opening," the angel announced.

"Where? I don't see anything."

"The gateway is opening."

Sanders waited. Then he realized that the Digi-Com system would have to connect to any remote database. The connection was going through; that was causing a delay.

"Connecting . . . now," the angel said.

The wall of the Corridor began to dissolve. They saw a large gaping black hole, and nothing beyond it.

"That's creepy," Fernandez said.

White wire-frame lines began to appear, outlining a new corridor. The spaces filled, one by one, creating the appearance of solid shapes.

"This one looks different," Fernandez said.

"We're connecting over a T-1 high-speed data line," Sanders said. "But even so, it's much slower."

The Corridor rebuilt itself as they watched. This time the walls were gray. They faced a black-and-white world.

"No color?"

"The system's trying to generate a simpler environment. Color means more data to push around. So this is black and white."

The new corridor added lights, a ceiling, a floor. After a moment, Sanders said, "Shall we go in?"

"You mean, the Conley-White database is in there?"

"That's right," Sanders said.

"I don't know," she said. She pointed: "What about this?"

Directly in front of them was a kind of flowing river of black-and-white static. It ran along the floor, and also along the walls. It made a loud hissing sound.

"I think that's just static off the phone lines."

"You think it's okay to cross?"

"We have to."

He started forward. Immediately, there was a growl. A large dog blocked their path. It had three heads that floated above its body, looking in all directions.

"What's that?"

"Probably a representation of their system security." Cherry and his sense of humor, he thought.

"Can it hurt us?"

"For God's sake, Louise. It's just a cartoon." Somewhere, of course, there was an actual monitoring system running on the Conley-White database. Perhaps it was automatic, or perhaps there was a real person who actually watched users come and go on the system. But now it was nearly one o'clock in the morning in New York. The dog was most likely just an automatic device of some kind.

Sanders walked forward, stepping through the flowing river of static. The dog growled as he approached. The three heads swiveled, watching him as he passed with cartoon eyes. It was a strange sensation. But nothing happened.

He looked back at Fernandez. "Coming?"

She moved forward tentatively. The angel remained behind, hovering in the air.

"Angel, are you coming?"

It didn't answer.

"Probably can't cross a gateway," Sanders said. "Not programmed."

They walked down the gray corridor. It was lined with unmarked drawers on all sides.

"It looks like a morgue," Fernandez said.

"Well, at least we're here."

"This is their company database in New York?"

"Yes. I just hope we can find it."

"Find what?"

He didn't answer her. He walked over to one file cabinet at random and pulled it open. He scanned the folders.

"Building permits," he said. "For some warehouse in Maryland, looks like."

"Why aren't there labels?"

Even as she said it, Sanders saw that labels were slowly emerging out of the gray surfaces. "I guess it just takes time." Sanders turned and looked in all directions, scanning the other labels. "Okay. That's better. HR records are on this wall, over here."

He walked along the wall. He pulled open a drawer.

"Uh-oh," Fernandez said.

"What?"

"Somebody's coming," she said, in an odd voice.

At the far end of the corridor, a gray figure was approaching. It was still too distant to make out details. But it was striding directly toward them.

"What do we do?"

"I don't know," Sanders said.

"Can he see us?"

"I don't know. I don't think so."

"We can see him, but he can't see us?"

"I don't know." Sanders was trying to figure it out. Cherry had installed another virtual system in the hotel. If someone was on that system, then he or she could probably see them. But Cherry had said that his system represented other users as well, such as somebody accessing the database from a computer. And somebody using a computer wouldn't be able to see them. A computer user wouldn't know who else was in the system.

The figure continued to advance. It seemed to come forward in jerks, not smoothly. They saw more detail; they could start to see eyes, a nose, a mouth.

"This is really creepy," Fernandez said.

The figure was still closer. The details were filling in.

"No kidding," Sanders said.

It was Ed Nichols.

Up close, they saw that Nichols's face was represented by a black-and-white photograph wrapped crudely around an egg-shaped head, atop a gray moving body that had the appearance of a mannequin or a puppet. It was a computer-generated figure. Which meant that Nichols wasn't on the virtual system. He was probably using his notebook computer in his hotel room. Nichols walked up to them and continued steadily past them.

"He can't see us."

Fernandez said, "Why does his face look that way?"

"Cherry said that the system pulls a photo from the file and pastes it on users."

The Nichols-figure continued on walking down the corridor, away from them.

"What's he doing here?"

"Let's find out."

They followed him back down the corridor until Nichols stopped at one file cabinet. He pulled it open and began to go through the records. Sanders and Fernandez came up and stood by his shoulder, and watched what he was doing.

The computer-generated figure of Ed Nichols was thumbing through his notes and e-mail. He went back two months, then three months, then six months. Now he began to pull out sheets of paper, which seemed to hang in the air as he read them. Memos. Notations. Personal and Confidential. Copies to File.

Sanders said, "These are all about the acquisition."

More notes came out. Nichols was pulling them quickly, one after another.

"He's looking for something specific."

Nichols stopped. He had found what he was looking for. His gray computer image held it in his hand and looked at it. Sanders read it over his shoulder, and said certain phrases aloud to Fernandez: "Memo dated December 4, last year. 'Met yesterday and today with Garvin and Johnson in Cupertino re possible acquisition of Digi-Com . . .' bla bla . . . 'Very favorable first impression . . . Excellent grounding in critical areas we seek to acquire . . .' bla bla . . . 'Highly capable and aggressive executive staff at all levels. Particularly impressed with competence of Ms. Johnson despite youth.' I'll bet you were impressed, Ed."

The computer-generated Nichols moved down the hall to another drawer and opened it. He didn't find what he wanted and closed it. He went on to another drawer.

Then he began reading again, and Sanders read this one, too: " 'Memo to John Marden. Cost issues re DigiCom acquisition' . . . bla bla . . . 'Concern for high-technology development costs in new company' . . . bla bla . . . Here we are. 'Ms. Johnson has undertaken to demonstrate her fiscal responsibility in new Malaysia operation . . . Suggests savings can be made . . . Expected cost savings . . .' How the hell could she do that?"

"Do what?" Fernandez said.

"Demonstrate fiscal responsibility in the

Malaysia operation? That was my operation."

"Uh-oh," Fernandez said. "You're not going to believe this."

Sanders glanced over at her. Fernandez was staring down the corridor. He turned to look.

Someone else was coming toward them.

"Busy night," he said.

But even from a distance, he could see that this figure was different. The head was more lifelike, and the body was fully detailed. The figure walked smoothly, naturally. "This could be trouble," he said. Sanders recognized him, even from a distance.

"It's John Conley," Fernandez said.

"Right. And he's on the walker pad."

"Which means?"

Conley abruptly stopped in the middle of the corridor, and stared.

"He can see us," Sanders said.

"He can? How?"

"He's on the system we installed in the hotel. That's why he's so detailed. He's on the other virtual system, so he can see us, and we can see him."

"Uh-oh."

"You said it."

Conley moved forward, slowly. He was frowning. He looked from Sanders to Fernandez to Nichols and back to Sanders. He seemed uncertain what to do.

Then he held his finger to his lips, a gesture for silence.

"Can he hear us?" Fernandez whispered.

"No," Sanders said, in a normal voice.

"Can we talk to him?"

"No."

Conley seemed to make a decision. He walked over to Sanders and Fernandez, until he was standing very close. He looked from one to the other. They could see his expression perfectly.

Then he smiled. He extended his hand.

Sanders reached out, and shook it. He didn't feel anything, but through the headset he saw what looked like his hand gripping Conley's.

Then Conley shook Fernandez's hand.

"This is extremely weird," Fernandez said.

Conley pointed toward Nichols. Then he pointed to his own eyes. Then to Nichols again.

Sanders nodded. They all went over to stand beside Nichols as he went through records.

"You mean Conley's watching him, too?"

"Yes."

"So we can all see Nichols . . ."

"Yes."

"But Nichols can't see any of us."

"Right."

The gray computer figure of Ed Nichols was pulling files hastily out of a drawer.

"What's he up to now?" Sanders said. "Ah. Going through expense records. Now he's found one: 'Sunset Shores Lodge, Carmel. December 5 and 6.' Two days after his memo. And look at these expenses. A hundred and ten dollars for breakfast? Somehow I don't think our Ed was alone there."

He looked over at Conley.

Conley shook his head, frowning.

Suddenly, the record Nichols was holding vanished.

"What happened?"

"I think he just deleted it."

Nichols thumbed through other records. He found four more for the Sunset Shores, and deleted them all. They vanished in midair. Then he closed the drawer, turned, and walked away.

Conley remained behind. He looked at Sanders and drew a finger quickly under his throat.

Sanders nodded.

Conley again put his finger to his lips.

Sanders nodded. He would keep quiet. "Come on," Sanders said to Fernandez. "We're done in here." He started back toward the DigiCom Corridor.

She walked alongside him, then said, "I think we have company."

Sanders looked back: Conley was following them.

"It's okay," he said. "Let him come."

They crossed the gateway, past the barking dog, and came back into the Victorian library. Fernandez sighed. "It feels good to be home again, doesn't it?"

Conley was walking along, showing no surprise. But then, he had seen the Corridor before. Sanders walked quickly. The angel floated alongside them.

"But you realize," Fernandez said, "that none of this makes any sense. Because Nichols is the one who's been opposed to the acquisition, and Conley is the one pushing for it."

"That's right," Sanders said. "It's perfect. Nichols is having it off with Meredith. He promotes her behind the scenes as the new head of the division. And how does he hide that fact? By continuously bitching and moaning to anybody who will listen."

"You mean, it's a cover."

"Sure. That's why Meredith never answered his complaints in any of the meetings. She knew he wasn't a real threat."

"And Conley?" she said.

Conley was still walking alongside them.

"Conley genuinely wants the acquisition. And

he wants it to work well. Conley's smart, and I think he realizes that Meredith isn't competent for the job. But Conley sees Meredith as the price of Nichols's support. So Conley has gone along with the choice of Meredith—at least for the time being."

"And what are we doing now?"

"Finding out about the last missing piece."

"Which is?"

Sanders was looking down the hallway marked OPERATIONS. This wasn't really his area of the database, except in specific places of overlap. The files were marked alphabetically. He went down the row until he found DIGICOM/MALAYSIA SA.

He opened it up and searched the file section marked STARTUP. He found his own memos, feasibility studies, site reports, government negotiations, first set specifications, memos from their Singapore suppliers, more government negotiations, all stretching back two years.

"What are you looking for?"

"Building plans."

He expected to see the thick sheets of blueprints and inspection summaries, but instead there was just a thin file. He opened the first sheet, and a three-dimensional image of the factory floated in the air in front of him. It was just an outline at first, but it rapidly filled in and became solid-looking. Sanders, Fernandez, and Conley stood on three sides of it, looking at it. It was like a very large, detailed doll's house. They peered in through the windows.

Sanders pushed a button. The model became transparent, then turned into a cutaway; now they could see the assembly line, the physical plant. A green line—the conveyor belt—started moving, and the machines and workers assembled the CD-ROM drives as the parts came down the line.

"What are you looking for?"

"Revisions." He shook his head. "This is the first set of plans."

The second sheet was marked "Revisions 1/First Set" with the date. He opened it up. The model of the plant seemed to shimmer for a moment, but it remained the same.

"Nothing happened."

The next sheet was marked "Revisions 2/Detail Only." Again, when he opened it, the plant shimmered briefly but was unchanged.

"According to these records, the plant was never revised," Sanders said. "But we know it was."

"What's he doing?" Fernandez said. She was looking at Conley.

Sanders saw that Conley was slowly mouthing words, his facial movements exaggerated.

"He's trying to tell us something," she said to Sanders. "Can you see what it is?"

"No." Sanders watched a moment, but the cartoonlike quality of Conley's face made it impossible to read his lips. Finally Sanders shook his head.

Conley nodded, and took the keypad out of Sanders's hand. He pushed a button marked RE-LATED and Sanders saw a list of related databases flash up in the air. It was an extensive list, including the permits from the Malay government, the architect's notes, the contractor agreements, health and medical inspections, and more. All together, there were about eighty items on the list. Sanders felt sure he would have overlooked the one in the middle of the list that Conley was now pointing to:

OPERATIONS REVIEW UNIT

"What's that?" Fernandez said.

Sanders pressed the name and a new sheet fluttered up. He pushed a button marked SUMMARY and read the sheet aloud: " 'The Operations Review Unit was formed four years ago in Cupertino by Philip Blackburn to address problems not normally within Operations Management purview. The mission of the Review Unit was to improve management efficiency within DigiCom. Over the years, the Operations Review Unit has successfully resolved a number of management problems at DigiCom.' "

"Uh-huh," Fernandez said.

" 'Nine months ago, the Operations Review

Unit, then headed by Meredith Johnson of Cupertino Operations, undertook a review of the proposed manufacturing facility in Kuala Lumpur, Malaysia. The immediate stimulus for the review was a conflict with the Malay government over the number and ethnic composition of workers employed at the proposed facility.' "

"Uh-oh," Fernandez said.

" 'Led by Ms. Johnson, with legal assistance from Mr. Blackburn, the Operations Review Unit had outstanding success in resolving the many problems facing DigiCom's Malaysian operation.' "

"What is this, a press release?" Fernandez said.

"Looks like it," Sanders said. He read on: " 'Specific issues concerned the number and ethnic composition of workers employed at the facility. The original plans called for seventy workers to be employed. Responding to the requests of the Malay government, Operations Review was able to increase the number of workers to eighty-five by reducing the amount of automation at the plant, thus making the facility more suitable to the economy of a developing country.' " Sanders looked over at Fernandez. "And screwing us completely," he said.

"Why?"

He continued: " 'In addition, a cost-savings review generated important fiscal benefits in a number of areas. Costs were reduced with no detriment to product quality at the plant. Air-handling capacity was revised to more appropriate levels, and outsourcing supplier contracts were reallocated, with substantial savings benefit to the company.' " Sanders shook his head. "That's it," he said. "That's the whole ball game."

"I don't understand," Fernandez said. "This makes sense to you?"

"You're damned right it does."

He pushed the DETAIL button for more pages.

"I am sorry," the angel said, "there is no more detail."

"Angel, where are the supporting memos and files?" Sanders knew that there had to be massive paperwork behind these summary changes. The renegotiations with the Malay government alone would fill drawers of files.

The angel said, "I am sorry. There is no more detail available."

"Angel, show me the files."

"Very well."

After a moment, a sheet of pink paper flashed up:

THE DETAIL FILES ON
OPERATIONS REVIEW UNIT/MALAYSIA
HAVE BEEN DELETED
SUNDAY 6/14 AUTHORIZATION DC/C/5905

"Hell," Sanders said.

"What does that mean?"

"Somebody cleaned up," Sanders said. "Just a few days ago. Who knew all this was going to happen? Angel, show me all communications between Malaysia and DC for the past two weeks."

"Do you wish telephone or video links?"

"Video."

"Press V."

He pushed a button, and a sheet uncurled in the air:

Date	Linking	To	Duration	Auth
6/1	A. Kahn > M. Johnson	0812–0814	ACSS
6/1	A. Kahn > M. Johnson	1343–1346	ADSS
6/2	A. Kahn > M. Johnson	1801–1804	DCSC
6/2	A. Kahn > T. Sanders	1822–1826	DCSE
6/3	A. Kahn > M. Johnson	0922–0924	ADSC
6/4	A. Kahn > M. Johnson	0902–0912	ADSC
6/5	A. Kahn > M. Johnson	0832–0832	ADSC
6/7	A. Kahn > M. Johnson	0904–0905	ACSS
6/11	A. Kahn > M. Johnson	2002–2004	ADSC
6/13	A. Kahn > M. Johnson	0902–0932	ADSC
6/14	A. Kahn > M. Johnson	1124–1125	ACSS
6/15	A. Kahn > T. Sanders	1132–1134	DCSE

"Burning up the satellite links," Sanders said, staring at the list. "Arthur Kahn and Meredith Johnson talked almost every day until June fourteenth. Angel, show me these video links."

"The links are not available for viewing except for 6/15."

That had been his own transmission to Kahn, two days earlier. "Where are the others?" A message flashed up:

THE VIDEO FILES ON
OPERATIONS REVIEW UNIT/MALAYSIA
HAVE BEEN DELETED
SUNDAY 6/14 AUTHORIZATION DC/C/5905

Scrubbed again. He was pretty sure who had done it, but he had to be sure. "Angel, how do I check deletion authorization?"

"Press the data you desire," the Angel said.

Sanders pressed the authorization number. A small sheet of paper came upward out of the top sheet and hung in the air:

AUTHORIZATION DC/C/5905 IS
DIGITAL COMMUNICATIONS
CUPERTINO/OPERATIONS EXECUTIVE
SPECIAL PRIVILEGES NOTED
(NO OPERATOR ID NECESSARY)

"It was done by somebody very high up in Operations in Cupertino, a few days ago."

"Meredith?"

"Probably. And it means I'm screwed."

"Why?"

"Because now I know what was done at the Malaysia plant. I know exactly what happened:

Meredith went in and changed the specs. But she's erased the data, right down to her voice transmissions to Kahn. Which means I can't prove any of it."

Standing in the corridor, Sanders poked the sheet, and it fluttered back down, dissolving into the top sheet. He closed his file, put it back in the drawer, and watched the model dissolve and disappear.

He looked over at Conley. Conley gave a little resigned shrug. He seemed to understand the situation. Sanders shook his hand, gripping air, and waved good-bye. Conley nodded and turned to leave.

"Now what?" Fernandez said.

"It's time to go," Sanders said.

The angel began to sing: "It's time to go, so long again till next week's show—"

"Angel, be quiet." The angel stopped singing. He shook his head. "Just like Don Cherry."

"Who's Don Cherry?" Fernandez asked.

"Don Cherry is a living god," the angel said.

They walked back to the entrance to the Corridor and then climbed out of the blue screen.

Back in Cherry's lab, Sanders took off the headset and, after a moment of disorientation, stepped off the walker pad. He helped Fernandez remove her equipment. "Oh," she said, looking around. "We're back in the real world."

"If that's what you call it," he said. "I'm not sure it's that much more real." He hung up her headset and helped her down from the walker pad. Then he turned off the power switches around the room.

Fernandez yawned and looked at her watch. "It's eleven o'clock. What are you going to do now?"

There was only one thing he could think of. He picked up the receiver on one of Cherry's data modem lines and dialed Gary Bosak's number. Sanders couldn't retrieve any data, but perhaps Bosak could—if he could talk him into it. It wasn't much of a hope. But it was all he could think to do.

An answering machine said, "Hi, this is NE Professional Services. I'm out of town for a few days, but leave a message." And then a beep.

Sanders sighed. "Gary, it's eleven o'clock on

Wednesday. I'm sorry I missed you. I'm going home." He hung up.

His last hope.

Gone.

Out of town for a few days.

"Shit," he said.

"Now what?" Fernandez said, yawning.

"I don't know," he said. "I've got half an hour to make the last ferry. I guess I'll go home and try to get some sleep."

"And the meeting tomorrow?" she asked. "You said you need documentation."

Sanders shrugged. "Louise, I've done all that I can do. I know what I'm up against. I'll manage somehow."

"Then I'll see you tomorrow?"

"Yeah," he said. "See you tomorrow."

He felt less sanguine on the ferry going home, looking back at the lights of the city in the rippling black water. Fernandez was right; he ought to be getting the documentation he needed. Max would criticize him, if he knew. He could almost hear the old man's voice: "Oh, so you're *tired?* That's a good reason, Thomas."

He wondered if Max would be at the meeting tomorrow. But he found he couldn't really think about it. He couldn't imagine the meeting. He was too tired to concentrate. The loudspeaker announced that they were five minutes from Winslow, and he went belowdecks to get into his car.

He unlocked the door and slipped behind the wheel. He looked in the rearview mirror and saw a dark silhouette in the backseat.

"Hey," Gary Bosak said.

Sanders started to turn.

"Just keep looking forward," Bosak said. "I'll get out in a minute. Now listen carefully. They're going to screw you tomorrow. They're going to pin the Malaysia fiasco on you."

"I know."

"And if that doesn't work, they're going to hit you with employing me. Invasion of privacy. Felonious activity. All that crap. They've talked to my parole officer. Maybe you've seen him—a fat guy with a mustache?"

Sanders vaguely remembered the man walking up to the mediation center the day before. "I think so, yes. Gary, listen, I need some documents—"

"Don't talk. There's no time. They pulled all the documents relating to the plant off the system. Nothing's there anymore. It's gone. I can't help you." They heard the sound of the ferry horn. All around them, drivers were starting their engines. "But I'm not going down for this felony crap. And you're not, either. Take this." He reached forward, and handed Sanders an envelope.

"What's this?"

"Summary of some work I did for another officer of your company. Garvin. You might want to fax it to him in the morning."

"Why don't you?"

"I'm crossing the border tonight. I have a cousin in BC, I'll stay there for a while. You can leave a message on my machine if it turns out okay."

"All right."

"Stay cool, guy. The shit's really going to hit the fan tomorrow. Lots of changes coming."

Up ahead, the ramp went down with a metallic clang. The traffic officers were directing cars off the ferry.

"Gary. You've been monitoring me?"

"Yeah. Sorry about that. They told me I had to."

"Then who's 'Afriend'?"

Bosak laughed. He opened the door and got out. "I'm surprised at you, Tom. Don't you know who your friends are?"

The cars were beginning to pull out. Sanders saw brake lights on the car ahead of him flash red, and the car began to move.

"Gary—" he said, turning. But Bosak was gone.

He put the car in gear and drove off the ferry.

At the top of the driveway, he stopped to pick up his mail. There was a lot of it; he hadn't checked the mailbox for two days. He drove down to the house and left the car outside the garage. He unlocked the front door and went in. The house seemed empty and cold. It had a lemony odor. Then he remembered that Consuela had probably cleaned up.

He went into the kitchen and set up the coffeemaker for the morning. The kitchen was clean and the children's toys had been picked up; Consuela had definitely been there. He looked at the answering machine.

A red numeral was blinking: 14.

Sanders replayed the calls. The first was from John Levin, asking him to call, saying it was urgent. Then Sally, asking if the kids could arrange a play date. But then the rest were all hang-ups. And as he listened, they all seemed to sound exactly the same—the thin hissing background static of an overseas call and then the abrupt click of disconnection. Again and again.

Someone was trying to call him.

One of the later calls was apparently placed by an operator, because a woman's lilting voice said,

"I'm sorry, there is no answer. Do you wish to leave a message?" And then a man's voice replied, "No." And then disconnection.

Sanders played it back, listening to that "No."

He thought it sounded familiar. Foreign, but still familiar.

"No."

He listened several times but could not identify the speaker.

"No."

One time, he thought the man sounded hesitant. Or was it hurried? He couldn't tell.

"Do you wish to leave a message?"

"No."

Finally he gave up, rewound the machine, and went upstairs to his office. He'd had no faxes. His computer screen was blank. No further help from "Afriend" tonight.

He read through the paper that Bosak had given him in the car. It was a single sheet, a memo addressed to Garvin, containing a report summary on a Cupertino employee whose name was blanked out. There was also a xerox of a check made out to NE Professional Services signed by Garvin.

It was after one when Sanders went into the bathroom and took a shower. He turned the water up hot, held his face close to the nozzle, and felt the stinging spray on his skin. With the sound of the shower roaring in his ears, he almost missed hearing the telephone ringing. He grabbed a towel and ran into the bedroom.

"Hello?"

He heard the static hiss of an overseas connection. A man's voice said, "Mr. Sanders, please."

"This is Mr. Sanders speaking."

"Mr. Sanders, sir," the voice said, "I do not know if you will remember me. This is Mohammed Jafar."

THURSDAY

The morning was clear. Sanders took an early ferry to work and got to his office at eight. He passed the downstairs receptionist and saw a sign that said "Main Conference Room in Use." For a horrified moment he thought that he had again mistaken the time for his meeting, and hurried to look in. But it was Garvin, addressing the Conley-White executives. Garvin was speaking calmly, and the executives were nodding as they listened. Then as he watched, Garvin finished and introduced Stephanie Kaplan, who immediately launched into a financial review with slides. Garvin left the conference room, and immediately his expression turned grim as he walked down the hallway toward the espresso bar at the end of the corridor, ignoring Sanders.

Sanders was about to head upstairs when he heard Phil Blackburn say, "I really feel I have a right to protest the way this matter has been handled."

"Well, you don't," Garvin said angrily. "You don't have any rights at all."

Sanders moved forward, toward the espresso bar. From his position across the hallway, he was able to see into the bar. Blackburn and Garvin were talking by the coffee machines.

"But this is extremely unfair," Blackburn said.

"Fuck unfair," Garvin said. "She named you as the source, you stupid asshole."

"But Bob, you told me—"

"I told you what?" Garvin said, eyes narrowing.

"You told me to handle it. To put pressure on Sanders."

"That's right, Phil. And you told *me* that you were going to take care of it."

"But you knew I talked to—"

"I knew you had done something," Garvin said. "But I didn't know what. Now she's named you as a source."

Blackburn hung his head. "I just think it's extremely unfair."

"Really? But what do you expect me to do? You're the fucking lawyer, Phil. You're the one always sweating about how things look. You tell me. What do I do?"

Blackburn was silent for a moment. Finally he said, "I'll get John Robinson to represent me. He can work out the settlement agreement."

"Okay, fine." Garvin nodded. "That's fine."

"But I just want to say to you, on a personal level, Bob, that I feel my treatment in this matter has been very unfair."

"Goddamn it, Phil, don't talk to me about your

feelings. Your feelings are for sale. Now listen with both ears: Don't go upstairs. Don't clean out your desk. Go right to the airport. I want you on a plane in the next half hour. I want you fucking out of here, right now. Is that clear?"

"I just think you should acknowledge my contribution to the company."

"I am, you asshole," Garvin said. "Now get the fuck out of here, before I lose my temper."

Sanders turned and hurried upstairs. It was hard for him to keep from cheering. Blackburn was fired! He wondered if he should tell anybody; perhaps Cindy, he thought.

But when he got to the fourth floor, the hallways were buzzing; everyone was out of their offices, talking in the corridors. Obviously, rumors of the firing had already leaked. Sanders was not surprised that staffers were in hallways. Even though Blackburn was disliked, his firing would cause widespread uneasiness. Such a sudden change, involving a person so close to Garvin, conveyed to everyone a sense of peril. Everything was at risk.

Outside his office, Cindy said, "Tom, can you believe it? They say Garvin is going to fire Phil."

"You're kidding," Sanders said.

Cindy nodded. "Nobody knows why, but apparently it had something to do with a news crew last night. Garvin's been downstairs explaining it to the Conley-White people."

Behind him, somebody shouted, "It's on the e-mail!" The hallway was instantly deserted; everyone vanished into their offices. Sanders stepped behind his desk and clicked the e-mail icon. But it was slow coming up, probably because every employee in the building was clicking at exactly the same time.

Fernandez came in and said, "Is it true about Blackburn?"

"I guess so," Sanders said. "It's just coming over the e-mail now."

FROM: ROBERT GARVIN, PRESIDENT AND CEO
TO: ALL THE DIGICOM FAMILY

IT IS WITH GREAT SADNESS AND A DEEP SENSE OF PERSONAL LOSS THAT I TODAY ANNOUNCE THE RESIGNATION OF OUR VALUED AND TRUSTED CHIEF CORPORATE COUNSEL, PHILIP A. BLACKBURN. PHIL HAS BEEN AN OUTSTANDING OFFICER OF THIS COMPANY FOR NEARLY FIFTEEN YEARS, A WONDERFUL HUMAN BEING, AND A CLOSE PERSONAL FRIEND AND ADVISOR AS WELL. I KNOW THAT LIKE ME, MANY OF YOU WILL MISS HIS WISE COUNSEL AND GOOD HUMOR PROFOUNDLY IN THE DAYS AND WEEKS TO COME. AND I AM SURE THAT YOU WILL ALL JOIN ME IN WISHING HIM THE BEST OF GOOD FORTUNE IN HIS NEW ENDEAVORS. A HEARTY THANK YOU, PHIL. AND GOOD LUCK.

THIS RESIGNATION IS EFFECTIVE IMMEDIATELY.
HOWARD EBERHARDT WILL SERVE AS ACTING
COUNSEL UNTIL SUCH TIME AS A NEW PERMANENT
APPOINTMENT IS MADE.

ROBERT GARVIN

Fernandez said, "What does it say?"

"It says, 'I fired his sanctimonious ass.' "

"It had to happen," Fernandez said. "Especially since he was the source on the Connie Walsh story."

Sanders said, "How did you know that?"

"Eleanor Vries."

"She told you?"

"No. But Eleanor Vries is a very cautious attorney. All those media attorneys are. The safest way to keep your job is to refuse to let things run. When in doubt, throw it out. So I had to ask myself, why did she let the Mr. Piggy story run, when it's clearly defamatory. The only possible reason is that she felt Walsh had an unusually strong source inside the company—a source that understood the legal implications. A source that, in giving the story, was in essence also saying, we won't sue if you print it. Since high-ranking corporate officers never know anything about law, it means the source could only be a high-ranking lawyer."

"Phil."

"Yes."

"Jesus."

"Does this change your plans?" Fernandez said.

Sanders had been considering that. "I don't think so," he said. "I think Garvin would have fired him later in the day, anyway."

"You sound confident."

"Yeah. I got some ammunition last night. And I hope more today."

Cindy came in and said, "Are you expecting something from KL? A big file?"

"Yes."

"This one's been coming in since 7 a.m. It must be a monster." She put a DAT cartridge on his desk. It was exactly like the DAT cartridge that had recorded his video link with Arthur Kahn.

Fernandez looked at him. He shrugged.

At eight-thirty, he transmitted Bosak's memo to Garvin's private fax machine. Then he asked Cindy to make copies of all the faxes that Mohammed Jafar had sent him the previous night. Sanders had been up most of the night, reading the material that Jafar had sent him. And it made interesting reading.

Jafar of course was not ill; he had never been ill. That had been a little story that Kahn had contrived with Meredith.

He pushed the DAT videocassette into the machine, and turned to Fernandez.

"You going to explain?" she said.

"I hope it'll be self-explanatory," Sanders said. On the monitor, the following appeared:

5 SECONDS TO DIRECT VIDEO LINKUP: DC / M-DC / C

SEN: A. KAHN

REC: M. JOHNSON

On the screen, he saw Kahn at the factory, and then a moment later the screen split and he saw Meredith at her office in Cupertino.

"What is this?" Fernandez said.

"A recorded video communication. From last Sunday."

"I thought the communications were all erased."

"They were, here. But there was still a record in KL. A friend of mine sent it to me."

On the screen, Arthur Kahn coughed. "Uh, Meredith. I'm a little concerned."

"Don't be," Meredith said.

"But we still aren't able to manufacture to specs. We have to replace the air handlers, at the very least. Put in better ones."

"Not now."

"But we have to, Meredith."

"Not yet."

"But those handlers are inadequate, Meredith. We both thought they'd be okay, but they aren't."

"Never mind."

Kahn was sweating. He rubbed his chin nervously. "It's only a matter of time before Tom figures it out, Meredith. He's not stupid, you know."

"He'll be distracted."

"So you say."

"And besides, he's going to quit."

Kahn looked startled. "He is? I don't think he—"

"Trust me. He'll quit. He's going to hate working for me."

Sitting in Sanders's office, Fernandez leaned forward, staring at the screen. She said, "No shit."

Kahn said, "Why will he hate it?"

Meredith said, "Believe me. He will. Tom Sanders will be out in my first forty-eight hours."

"But how can you be sure—"

"What choice does he have? Tom and I have a history. Everybody in the company knows that. If any problem comes up, nobody will believe him. He's smart enough to understand that. If he ever wants to work again, he'll have no choice but to take whatever settlement he's offered and leave."

Kahn nodded, wiping the sweat from his cheek. "And then we say Sanders made the changes at the plant? He'll deny that he did."

"He won't even know. Remember. He'll be gone by then, Arthur."

"And if he isn't?"

"Trust me. He'll be gone. He's married, has a family. He'll go."

"But if he calls me about the production line—"

"Just evade it, Arthur. Be mystified. You can do that, I'm sure. Now, who else does Sanders talk to there?"

"The foreman, sometimes. Jafar. Jafar knows everything, of course. And he's one of those honest sorts. I'm afraid if—"

"Make him take a vacation."

"He just took one."

"Make him take another one, Arthur. I only need a week here."

"Jesus," Kahn said. "I'm not sure—"

She cut in: "Arthur."

"Yes, Meredith."

"This is the time when a new vice president counts favors that will be repaid in the future."

"Yes, Meredith."

"That's all."

The screen went blank. There were white streaking video lines, and then the screen was dark.

"Pretty cut and dried," Fernandez said.

Sanders nodded. "Meredith didn't think the changes would matter, because she didn't know anything about production. She was just cutting costs. But she knew that the changes at the plant would eventually be traced back to her, so she thought she had a way to get rid of me, to make me quit the company. And then she would be able to blame me for the problems at the plant."

"And Kahn went along with it."

Sanders nodded.

"And they got rid of Jafar."

Sanders nodded. "Kahn told Jafar to go visit his cousin in Johore for a week—to get out of town. To make it impossible for me to reach Jafar. But he never thought that Jafar would call me." He glanced at his watch. "Now, where is it?"

"What?"

On the screen, there was a series of tones, and they saw a handsome, dark-skinned newscaster at a desk, facing a camera and speaking rapidly in a foreign language.

"What's this?" Fernandez said.

"The Channel Three evening news, from last December." Sanders got up and pushed a button on the tape machine. The cassette popped out.

"What does it show?"

Cindy came back from the copying machine with wide eyes. She carried a dozen stacks of paper, each neatly clipped. "What're you going to do with this?"

"Don't worry about it," he said.

"But this is outrageous, Tom. What she's done."

"I know," he said.

"Everybody is talking," she said. "The word is that the merger is off."

"We'll see," Sanders said.

With Cindy's help, he began arranging the piles of paper in identical manila folders.

Fernandez said, "What exactly are you going to do?"

"Meredith's problem is that she lies," Sanders said. "She's smooth, and she gets away with it. She's gotten away with it her whole life. I'm going to see if I can get her to make a single, very big lie."

He looked at his watch. It was eight forty-five. The meeting would start in fifteen minutes.

The conference room was packed. There were fifteen Conley-White executives down one side of the table, with John Marden in the middle, and fifteen DigiCom executives down the other side, with Garvin in the middle.

Meredith Johnson stood at the head of the table and said, "Next, we'll hear from Tom Sanders. Tom, I wonder if you could review for us where we stand with the Twinkle drive. What is the status of our production there."

"Of course, Meredith." Sanders stood, his heart pounding. He walked to the front of the room. "By way of background, Twinkle is our code name for a stand-alone CD-ROM drive player which we expect to be revolutionary." He turned to the first of his charts. "CD-ROM is a small laser disk used to store data. It is cheap to manufacture, and can hold an enormous amount of information in any form—words, images, sound, video, and so on. You can put the equivalent of six hundred books on a single small disk, or, thanks to our research here, an hour and a half of video. And any combination. For example, you could make a textbook that combines text, pictures, short movie sequences, animated cartoons, and so on. Production costs will soon be at ten cents a unit."

He looked down the table. The Conley-White people were interested. Garvin was frowning. Meredith looked tense.

"But for CD-ROM to be effective, two things need to happen. First, we need a portable player. Like this." He held up the player, and then passed it down the Conley-White side.

"A five-hour battery, and an excellent screen. You can use it on a train, a bus, or in a class-room—anywhere you can use a book."

The executives looked at it, turned it over in their hands. Then they looked back at Sanders.

"The other problem with CD-ROM technol-ogy," Sanders said, "is that it's slow. It's sluggish getting to all that wonderful data. But the Twin-kle drives that we have successfully made in pro-totype are twice as fast as any other drive in the world. And with added memory for our packing and unpacking images, it is as quick as a small computer. We expect to get the unit cost for these drives down to the price of a video-game unit within a year. And we are manufacturing the drives now. We have had some early problems, but we are solving them."

Meredith said, "Can you tell us more about that? I gather from talking to Arthur Kahn that we're still not clear on why the drives have problems."

"Actually, we are," Sanders said. "It turns out that the problems aren't serious at all. I expect them to be entirely resolved in a matter of days."

"Really." She raised her eyebrows. "Then we've found what the trouble is?"

"Yes, we have."

"That's wonderful news."

"Yes, it is."

"Very good news indeed," Ed Nichols said. "Was it a design problem?"

"No," Sanders said. "There's nothing wrong with the design we made here, just as there was nothing wrong with the prototypes. What we have is a fabrication problem involving the production line in Malaysia."

"What sort of problems?"

"It turns out," Sanders said, "that we don't have the proper equipment on the line. We should be using automatic chip installers to lock the controller chips and the RAM cache on the board, but the Malays on the line have been installing chips by hand. Literally pushing them in with their thumbs. And it turns out that the assembly line is dirty, so we're getting particulate matter in the split optics. We should have level-seven air handlers, but we only have level-five handlers installed. And it turns out that we should be ordering components like hinge rods and clips from one very reliable Singapore supplier, but the components are actually coming from another supplier. Less expensive, less reliable."

Meredith looked uneasy, but only for a moment. "Improper equipment, improper conditions, improper components . . ." She shook her head. "I'm sorry. Correct me if I'm wrong, but didn't you set up that line, Tom?"

"Yes, I did," Sanders said. "I went out to Kuala Lumpur last fall and set it up with Arthur Kahn and the local foreman, Mohammed Jafar."

"Then how is it that we have so many problems?"

"Unfortunately, there was a series of bad judgment calls in setting up the line."

Meredith looked concerned. "Tom, we all know that you're extremely competent. How could this have happened?"

Sanders hesitated.

This was the moment.

"It happened because the line was changed," he said. "The specifications were altered."

"Altered? How?"

"I think that's something for you to explain to this group, Meredith," he said. "Since you ordered the changes."

"I ordered them?"

"That's right, Meredith."

"Tom, you must be mistaken," she said coolly.

"I haven't had anything to do with that Malaysia line."

"Actually, you have," Sanders said. "You made two trips there, in November and December of last year."

"Two trips to Kuala Lumpur, yes. Because you mishandled a labor dispute with the Malaysian government. I went there and resolved the dispute. But I had nothing to do with the actual production line."

"I'd say you're mistaken, Meredith."

"I assure you," she said coldly. "I am not. I had nothing to do with the line, and any so-called changes."

"Actually, you went there and inspected the changes you ordered."

"I'm sorry, Tom. I didn't. I've never even seen the actual line."

On the screen behind her, the videotape of the newscast began to play silently with the sound off. The newscaster in coat and tie speaking to the camera.

Sanders said, "You never went to the plant itself?"

"Absolutely not, Tom. I don't know who could have told you such a thing—or why you would say it now."

The screen behind the newscaster showed the DigiCom building in Malaysia, then the interior of the plant. The camera showed the production lines and an official inspection tour taking place. They saw Phil Blackburn, and alongside him, Meredith Johnson. The camera moved in on her as she chatted with one of the workers.

There was a murmur in the room.

Meredith spun around and looked. "This is outrageous. This is out of context. I don't know where this could have come from—"

"Malaysia Channel Three. Their version of the BBC. I'm sorry, Meredith." The newscast segment finished and the screen went blank. Sanders made a gesture, and Cindy began moving around the table, handing a manila folder to each person.

Meredith said, "Wherever this so-called tape came from—"

Sanders said, "Ladies and gentlemen, if you will open your packets, you will find the first of a series of memos from the Operations Review Unit, which was under the direction of Ms. Johnson in the period in question. I direct your attention to the first memo, dated November eighteenth of last year. You will notice that it has been signed by Meredith Johnson, and it stipulates that the line will be changed to accommodate the labor demands of the Malay government. In particular, this first memo states that automated chip installers will not be included, but that this work will be done by hand. That made the Malay government happy, but it meant we couldn't manufacture the drives."

Johnson said, "But you see, what you are over-looking is that the Malays gave us no choice—"

"In that case, we should never have built the plant there," Sanders said, cutting her off. "Because we can't manufacture the intended product at those revised specifications. The tolerances are inadequate."

Johnson said, "Well, that may be your own opinion—"

"The second memo, dated December third, indicates that a cost-savings review diminished air-handling capacities on the line. Again, this is a variance in the specifications that I established. Again, it is critical—we can't manufacture high-performance drives under these conditions. The long and the short of it is that these decisions doomed the drives to failure."

"Now look," Johnson said. "If anybody believes that the failure of these drives is anything but your—"

"The third memo," Sanders said, "summarizes cost savings from the Operations Review Unit. You'll see that it claims an eleven percent reduction in operating costs. That savings has already been wiped out by fabrication delays, not counting our time-to-market delay costs. Even if we immediately restore the line, this eleven percent savings translates into a production cost increase, over the run, of nearly seventy percent. First year, it's a hundred and ninety percent increase.

"Now the next memo," Sanders said, "explains why this cost-cutting was adopted in the first place. During acquisition talks between Mr. Nichols and Ms. Johnson in the fall of last year, Ms. Johnson indicated she would demonstrate that it was possible to reduce high-technology development costs, which were a source of concern to Mr. Nichols when they were meeting at—"

"Oh *Christ*," Ed Nichols said, staring at the paper.

Meredith pushed forward, stepping in front of Sanders. "Excuse me, Tom," she said, speaking firmly, "but I really must interrupt you. I'm sorry to have to say this, but no one here is fooled by this little charade." She swept her arm wide, encompassing the room. "Or by your so-called evidence." She spoke more loudly. "You weren't present when these management decisions were carefully taken by the best minds in this company. You don't understand the thinking that lies behind them. And the false postures you are striking now, the so-called memos that you are holding up to convince us . . . No one here is persuaded." She gave him a pitying look. "It's all empty, Tom. Empty words, empty phrases. When it comes right down to it, you're all show and no substance. You think you can come in here and second-guess the management team? I'm here to tell you that you can't."

Garvin stood abruptly, and said, "Meredith—"

"Let me finish," Meredith said. She was flushed, angry. "Because this is important, Bob. This is the heart of what is wrong with this division. Yes, there were some decisions taken that may be questionable in retrospect. Yes, we tried innovative procedures which perhaps went too far. But that hardly excuses the behavior we see today. This calculated, manipulative attitude by an individual who will do anything—anything at all—to get ahead, to make a name for herself at the expense of others, who will savage the reputation of anyone who stands in her path—I mean, that stands in *his* path—this ruthless demeanor that we are seeing . . . No one is fooled by this, Tom. Not for a minute. We're being asked to accept the worst kind of fraudulence. And we simply won't do it. It's wrong. This is all wrong. And it is bound to catch up with you. I'm sorry. You can't come here and do this. It simply won't work—it hasn't worked. That's all."

She stopped to catch her breath and looked around the table. Everyone was silent, motionless. Garvin was still standing; he appeared to be in shock. Slowly, Meredith seemed to realize that something was wrong. When she spoke again, her voice was quieter.

"I hope that I have . . . that I have accurately expressed the sentiments of everyone here. That's all I intended to do."

There was another silence. Then Garvin said,

"Meredith, I wonder if you would leave the room for a few minutes."

Stunned, she stared at Garvin for a long moment. Then she said, "Of course, Bob."

"Thank you, Meredith."

Walking very erect, she left the room. The door clicked shut behind her.

John Marden sat forward and said, "Mr. Sanders, please continue with your presentation. In your view, how long will it be until the line is repaired and fully functioning?"

It was noon. Sanders sat in his office with his feet on his desk and stared out the window. The sun was shining brightly on the buildings around Pioneer Square. The sky was clear and cloudless. Mary Anne Hunter, wearing a business suit, came in and said, "I don't get it."

"Get what?"

"That news tape. Meredith must have known about it. Because she was there when they were shooting it."

"Oh, she knew about it, all right. But she never thought I'd get it. And she never thought she'd appear in it. She thought they'd only show Phil. You know—a Muslim country. In a story about executives, they usually just show the men."

"Uh-huh. So?"

"But Channel Three is the government station," Sanders said. "And the story that night was that the government had been only partially successful in negotiating changes in the DigiCom plant—that the foreign executives had been intransigent and uncooperative. It was a story intended to protect the reputation of Mr. Sayad, the finance minister. So the cameras focused on her."

"Because . . ."

"Because she was a woman."

"Foreign she-devil in a business suit? Can't make a deal with a *feringi* woman?"

"Something like that. Anyway, the story focused on her."

"And you got the tape."

"Yeah."

Hunter nodded. "Well," she said, "it's fine with me." She left the room, and Sanders was alone again, staring out the window.

After a while, Cindy came in and said, "The latest word is the acquisition is off."

Sanders shrugged. He was flat, drained. He didn't care.

Cindy said, "Are you hungry? I can get you some lunch."

"I'm not hungry. What are they doing now?"

"Garvin and Marden are talking."

"Still? It's been more than an hour."

"They just brought in Conley."

"Only Conley? Nobody else?"

"No. And Nichols has left the building."

"What about Meredith?"

"Nobody's seen her."

He leaned back in his chair. He stared out the window. His computer gave three beeps.

30 SECONDS TO DIRECT VIDEO LINKUP: DC/M-DC/S
SEN: A. KAHN
REC: T. SANDERS

Kahn was calling. Sanders smiled grimly. Cindy came in and said, "Arthur's going to call."

"I see that."

15 SECONDS TO DIRECT VIDEO LINKUP: DC/M-DC/S

Sanders adjusted his desk lamp and sat back. The screen blossomed, and he saw the shimmering image resolve. It was Arthur, in the plant.

"Oh, Tom. Good. I hope it's not too late," Arthur said.

"Too late for what?" Sanders said.

"I know there's a meeting today. There's something I have to tell you."

"What's that, Arthur?"

"Well, I'm afraid I haven't been entirely straightforward with you, Tom. It's about Meredith. She made changes in the line six or seven months ago, and I'm afraid she intends to blame that on you. Probably in the meeting today."

"I see."

"I feel terrible about this, Tom," Arthur said, hanging his head. "I don't know what to say."

"Don't say anything, Arthur," Sanders said.

Kahn smiled apologetically. "I wanted to tell you earlier. I really did. But Meredith kept saying that you would be out. I didn't know what to do. She said there was a battle coming, and I had better pick the winner."

"You picked wrong, Arthur," Sanders said. "You're fired." He reached up and snapped off the television camera in front of him.

"What're you talking about?"

"You're fired, Arthur."

"But you can't do this to me . . . ," Kahn said. His image faded, began to shrink. "You can't—"

The screen was blank.

Fifteen minutes later, Mark Lewyn came by the office. He tugged at the neck of his black Armani T-shirt. "I think I'm an asshole," he said.

"Yeah. You are."

"It's just . . . I didn't understand the situation," he said.

"That's right, you didn't."

"What're you going to do now?"

"I just fired Arthur."

"Jesus. And what else?"

"I don't know. We'll see how it shakes out."

Lewyn nodded and went away nervously. Sanders decided to let him be nervous for a while. In the end, their friendship would be repaired. Adele and Susan were good friends. And Mark was too talented to replace in the company. But Lewyn could sweat for a while; it'd do him good.

At one o'clock, Cindy came in and said, "The word is Max Dorfman just went into the conference with Garvin and Marden."

"What about John Conley?"

"He's gone. He's with the accountants now."

"Then that's a good sign."

"And the word is Nichols was fired."

"Why do they think that?"

"He flew home an hour ago."

Fifteen minutes later, Sanders saw Ed Nichols walking down the hallway. Sanders got up and went out to Cindy's desk. "I thought you said Nichols went home."

"Well, that's what I heard," she said. "It's crazy. You know what they're saying about Meredith now?"

"What?"

"They say she's staying on."

"I don't believe it," Sanders said.

"Bill Everts told Stephanie Kaplan's assistant that Meredith Johnson is not going to be fired, that Garvin is backing her one hundred percent. Phil is going to take the rap for what happened in Malaysia but Garvin still believes Meredith is young and this shouldn't be held against her. So she's staying in her job."

"I don't believe it."

Cindy shrugged. "That's what they say," she said.

He went back to his office and stared out the window. He told himself it was just a rumor. After a while, the intercom buzzed. "Tom? Meredith Johnson just called. She wants to see you in her office right away."

Bright sunlight streamed in through the big windows on the fifth floor. The assistant outside Meredith's office was away from her desk. The door was ajar. He knocked.

"Come in," Meredith Johnson said.

She was standing, leaning back against the edge of her desk, her arms folded across her chest. Waiting.

"Hello, Tom," she said.

"Meredith."

"Come in. I won't bite."

He came in, leaving the door open.

"I must say that you outdid yourself this morning, Tom. I was surprised at how much you were able to learn in a short time. And it was really quite resourceful, the approach you took in the meeting."

He said nothing.

"Yes, it was a really excellent effort. You feeling proud of yourself?" she said, staring hard at him.

"Meredith . . ."

"You think you've finally paid me back? Well, I have news for you, Tom. You don't know *anything* about what's really going on."

She pushed away from the desk, and as she moved away, he saw a cardboard packing box on the desktop beside the telephone. She walked around behind the desk, and began putting pictures and papers and a pen set into the box.

"This whole thing was Garvin's idea. For three years, Garvin's been looking for a buyer. He couldn't find one. Finally he sent me out, and I found him one. I went through twenty-seven different companies until I got to Conley-White. They were interested, and I sold them hard. I put in the hours. I did whatever I had to do to keep the deal moving forward. *Whatever* I had to do." She pushed more papers into the box angrily.

Sanders watched her.

"Garvin was happy as long as I was delivering Nichols to him on a platter," Johnson said. "He wasn't fussy about how I was doing it. He wasn't even interested. He just wanted it done. I busted my ass for him. Because the chance to get this job was a big break for me, a real career opportunity. Why shouldn't I have it? I did the work. I put the deal together. I *earned* this job. I beat you fairly."

Sanders said nothing.

"But that's not how it turns out, is it. Garvin won't support me when the going gets tough. Everybody said he was like a father to me. But he was just using me. He was just making a deal, any way he could. And that's all he's doing now. Just another fucking deal, and who cares who gets hurt. Everybody moves on. Now I've got to find an attorney to negotiate my severance package. Nobody gives a damn."

She closed the box and leaned on it. "But I beat you, fair and square, Tom. I don't deserve this. I've been screwed by the damned system."

"No you haven't," Sanders said, staring her straight in the eye. "You've been fucking your assistants for years. You've been taking every advantage of your position that you could. You've been cutting corners. You've been lazy. You've been living on image and every third word out of your mouth is a lie. Now you're feeling sorry for yourself. You think the system is what's wrong. But you know what, Meredith? The system didn't screw you. The system *revealed* you, and dumped you out. Because when you get right down to it, you're completely full of shit." He turned on his heel. "Have a nice trip. Wherever you're going."

He left the room, and slammed the door behind him.

He was back in his office five minutes later, still angry, pacing back and forth behind his desk.

Mary Anne Hunter came in, wearing a sweatshirt and exercise tights. She sat down, and put her running shoes up on Sanders's desk. "What're you all worked up about? The press conference?"

"What press conference?"

"They've scheduled a press conference for four o'clock."

"Who says?"

"Marian in PR. Swears it came from Garvin himself. And Marian's assistant has been calling the press and the stations."

Sanders shook his head. "It's too soon." Considering all that had happened, the press conference should not be held until the following day.

"I think so," Hunter said, nodding. "They must be going to announce that the merger has fallen through. You heard what they're saying about Blackburn?"

"No, what?"

"That Garvin made him a million-dollar settlement."

"I don't believe it."

"That's what they say."

"Ask Stephanie."

"Nobody's seen her. Supposedly she went back to Cupertino, to deal with finances now that the merger is off." Hunter got up and walked to the window. "At least it's a nice day."

"Yeah. Finally."

"I think I'll go for a run. I can't stand this waiting."

"I wouldn't leave the building."

She smiled. "Yeah, I guess not." She stood at the window for a while. Finally she said, "Well, what do you know . . ."

Sanders looked up. "What?"

Hunter pointed down toward the street. "Minivans. With antennas on the top. I guess there is going to be a press conference, after all."

They held the press conference at four, in the main downstairs conference room. Strobes flashed as Garvin stood before the microphone, at the end of the table.

"I have always believed," he said, "that women must be better represented in high corporate office. The women of America represent our nation's most important underutilized resource as we go into the twenty-first century. And this is true in high technology no less than in other industries. It is therefore with great pleasure that I announce, as part of our merger with Conley-White Communications, that the new Vice President at Digital Communications Seattle is a woman of great talent, drawn from within the ranks in our Cupertino headquarters. She has been a resourceful and dedicated member of the DigiCom team for many years, and I am sure she will be even more resourceful in the future. I am pleased to introduce now the new Vice President for Advanced Planning, Ms. Stephanie Kaplan."

There was applause, and Kaplan stepped to the microphone and brushed back her shock of gray hair. She wore a dark maroon suit and smiled quietly. "Thank you, Bob. And thanks to everyone who has worked so hard to make this division so great. I want to say particularly that I look forward to working with the outstanding division heads we have here, Mary Anne Hunter, Mark Lewyn, Don Cherry, and, of course, Tom Sanders. These talented people stand at the center of our company, and I intend to work hand in hand with them as we move into the future. As for myself, I have personal as well as professional ties here in Seattle, and I can say no more than that I am delighted, just delighted, to be here. And I look forward to a long and happy time in this wonderful city."

Back in his office, Sanders got a call from Fernandez. "I finally heard from Alan. Are you ready for this? Arthur A. Friend is on sabbatical in Nepal. Nobody goes into his office except his assistant and a couple of his most trusted students. In fact, there's only one student who has been there during the time he is away. A freshman in the chemistry department named Jonathan—"

"Kaplan," Sanders said.

"That's right. You know who he is?" Fernandez said.

"He's the boss's son. Stephanie Kaplan's just been named the new head of the division."

Fernandez was silent for a moment. "She must be a very remarkable woman," she said.

Garvin arranged a meeting with Fernandez at the Four Seasons Hotel. They sat in the small, dark bar off Fourth Avenue in the late afternoon.

"You did a hell of a job, Louise," he said. "But justice was not served, I can tell you that. An innocent woman took the fall for a clever, scheming man."

"Come on, Bob," she said. "Is that why you called me over here? To complain?"

"Honest to God, Louise, this harassment thing has gotten out of hand. Every company I know has at least a dozen of these cases now. Where will it end?"

"I'm not worried," she said. "It'll shake out."

"Eventually, maybe. But meanwhile innocent people—"

"I don't see many innocent people in my line of work," she said. "For example, it's come to my attention that DigiCom's board members were aware of Johnson's problem a year ago and did nothing to address it."

Garvin blinked. "Who told you that? It's completely untrue."

She said nothing.

"And you could never have proved it."

Fernandez raised her eyebrows and said nothing.

"Who said that?" Garvin said. "I want to know."

"Look, Bob," she said. "The fact is, there's a category of behavior that no one condones anymore. The supervisor who grabs genitals, who squeezes breasts in the elevator, who invites an assistant on a business trip but books only one hotel room. All that is ancient history. If you have an employee behaving like that, whether that employee is male or female, gay or straight, you are obliged to stop it."

"Okay, fine, but sometimes it's hard to know—"

"Yes," Fernandez said. "And there's the opposite extreme. An employee doesn't like a tasteless remark and files a complaint. Somebody has to tell her it's not harassment. By then, her boss has been accused, and everybody in the company knows. He won't work with her anymore; there's suspicion, and bad feelings, and it's all a big mess at the company. I see that a lot. That's unfortunate, too. You know, my husband works in the same firm I do."

"Uh-huh."

"After we first met, he asked me out five times. At first I said no, but finally I said yes. We're happily married now. And the other day he said to me that, given the climate now, if we met today, he probably wouldn't ask me out five times. He'd just drop it."

"See? That's what I'm talking about."

"I know. But those situations will settle out eventually. In a year or two, everybody will know what the new rules are."

"Yes, but—"

"But the problem is that there's that third category, somewhere in the middle, between the two extremes," Fernandez said. "Where the behavior is gray. It's not clear what happened. It's not clear who did what to whom. That's the largest category of complaints we see. So far, society's tended to focus on the problems of the victim, not the problems of the accused. But the accused has problems, too. A harassment claim is a weapon, Bob, and there are no good defenses against it. Anybody can use the weapon—and lots of people have. It's going to continue for a while, I think."

Garvin sighed.

"It's like that virtual reality thing you have," Fernandez said. "Those environments that seem real but aren't really there. We all live every day in virtual environments, defined by our ideas. Those environments are changing. It's changed with regard to women, and it's going to start changing with regard to men. The men didn't like it when it changed before, and the women aren't going to like it changing now. And some people will take advantage. But in the final analysis, it'll all work out."

"When? When will it all end?" Garvin said, shaking his head.

"When women have fifty percent of the executive positions," she said. "That's when it will end."

"You know I favor that."

"Yes," Fernandez said, "and I gather you have just appointed an outstanding woman. Congratulations, Bob."

Mary Anne Hunter was assigned to drive Meredith Johnson to the airport, to take a plane back to Cupertino. The two women sat in silence for fifteen minutes, Meredith Johnson hunched down in her trench coat, staring out the window.

Finally, when they were driving past the Boeing plant, Johnson said, "I didn't like it here, anyway."

Choosing her words carefully, Hunter said, "It has its good and bad points."

There was another silence. Then Johnson asked, "Are you a friend of Sanders?"

"Yes."

"He's a nice guy," Johnson said. "Always was. You know, we used to have a relationship."

"I heard that," Hunter said.

"Tom didn't do anything wrong, really," Johnson said. "He just didn't know how to handle a passing remark."

"Uh-huh," Hunter said.

"Women in business have to be perfect all the time, or they just get murdered. One little slip and they're dead."

"Uh-huh."

"You know what I'm talking about."

"Yes," Hunter said. "I know."

There was another long silence. Johnson shifted in her seat.

She stared out the window.

"The system," Johnson said. "That's the problem. I was raped by the fucking system."

S anders was leaving the building, on his way to the airport to pick up Susan and the kids, when he ran into Stephanie Kaplan. He congratulated her on the appointment. She shook his hand and said without smiling, "Thank you for your support."

He said, "Thank you for yours. It's nice to have a friend."

"Yes," she said. "Friendships are nice. So is competence. I'm not going to keep this job very long, Tom. Nichols is out as CFO of Conley, and their number-two man is a modest talent at best. They'll be looking for someone in a year or so. And when I go over there, someone will have to take over the new company here. I imagine it should be you."

Sanders bowed slightly.

"But that's in the future," Kaplan said crisply. "In the meantime, we have to get the work here back on track. This division is a mess. Everyone's been distracted by this merger, and the product lines have been compromised by Cupertino's ineptitude. We've got a lot to do to turn this around. I've set the first production meeting with all the division heads for seven a.m. tomorrow morning. I'll see you then, Tom."

And she turned away.

Sanders stood at the arrivals gate at Sea-Tac and watched the passengers come off the Phoenix plane. Eliza came running up to him, shouting "Daddy!" as she leapt into his arms. She had a suntan.

"Did you have a nice time in Phoenix?"

"It was great, Dad! We rode horses and ate tacos, and guess what?"

"What?"

"I saw a snake."

"A real snake?"

"Uh-huh. A green one. It was *this* big," she said, stretching her hands.

"That's pretty big, Eliza."

"But you know what? Green snakes don't hurt you."

Susan came up, carrying Matthew. She had a suntan, too. He kissed her, and Eliza said, "I told Daddy about the snake."

"How are you?" Susan said, looking at his face.

"I'm fine. Tired."

"Is it finished?"

"Yes. It's finished."

They walked on. Susan slipped her arm around his waist. "I've been thinking. Maybe I'm travel-

ing too much. We ought to spend more time together."

"That'd be nice," he said.

They walked toward the baggage claim. Carrying his daughter, feeling her small hands on his
shoulder, he glanced over and saw Meredith
Johnson standing at the check-in counter of one
of the departure gates. She was wearing a trench
coat. Her hair was pulled back. She didn't turn
and see him.

Susan said, "Somebody you know?"

"No," he said. "It's nobody."

POSTSCRIPT

Constance Walsh was fired by the Seattle *Post-Intelligencer* and sued the paper for wrongful termination and sexual discrimination under Title VII of the Civil Rights Act of 1964. The paper settled out of court.

Philip Blackburn was named chief counsel at Silicon Holographics of Mountain View, California, a company twice as large as DigiCom. He was later elected Chairman of the Ethics Panel of the San Francisco Bar Association.

Edward Nichols took early retirement from Conley-White Communications and moved with his wife to Nassau, Bahamas, where he worked part-time as a consultant to offshore firms.

Elizabeth "Betsy" Ross was hired by Conrad Computers in Sunnyvale, California, and soon after joined Alcoholics Anonymous.

John Conley was named Vice President for Planning at Conley-White Communications. He died in an automobile accident in Patchogue, New York, six months later.

Mark Lewyn was charged with sexual harassment under Title VII by an employee of the Design Group. Although Lewyn was cleared of the charge, his wife filed for divorce not long after the investigation was concluded.

Arthur Kahn joined Bull Data Systems in Kuala Lumpur, Malaysia.

Richard Jackson of Aldus was charged with sexual harassment under Title VII by an employee of American DataHouse, a wholesale distributor for Aldus. After an investigation, Aldus fired Jackson.

Gary Bosak developed a data encryption algorithm, which he licensed to IBM, Microsoft, and Hitachi. He became a multi-millionaire.

Louise Fernandez was appointed to the federal bench. She delivered a lecture to the Seattle Bar Association in which she argued that sexual harassment suits had become increasingly used as a weapon to resolve corporate disputes. She suggested that in the future there might be a need to revise laws or to limit the involvement of attorneys in such matters. Her speech was received coolly.

Meredith Johnson was named Vice President for Operations and Planning at IBM's Paris office. She subsequently married the United States Ambassador to France, Edward Harmon, following his divorce. She has since retired from business.

AFTERWORD

The episode related here is based on a true story. Its appearance in a novel is not intended to deny the fact that the great majority of harassment claims are brought by women against men. On the contrary: the advantage of a role-reversal story is that it may enable us to examine aspects concealed by traditional responses and conventional rhetoric. However readers respond to this story, it is important to recognize that the behavior of the two antagonists mirrors each other, like a Rorschach inkblot. The value of a Rorschach test lies in what it tells us about ourselves.

It is also important to emphasize that the story in its present form is fiction. Because allegations of sexual harassment in the workplace involve multiple, conflicting legal rights, and because such claims now create substantial risk not only for the individuals but for corporations, it has been necessary to disguise the real event with care. All the principals in this case agreed to be interviewed with the understanding that their identities would be concealed. I am grateful to them for their willingness to help clarify the difficult issues inherent in investigations of sexual harassment.

In addition, I am indebted to a number of attorneys, human relations officers, individual employees, and corporate officials who provided valuable perspectives on this evolving issue. It is characteristic of the extreme sensitivity surrounding any discussion of sexual harassment that everyone I talked to asked to remain anonymous.

American Heart Association, *American Heart Association
Cookbook, 5th Edition (Abridged)*
Barbara Taylor Bradford, *Angel* (paper)
Barbara Taylor Bradford, *Remember*
William F. Buckley, Jr., *Tucker's Last Stand*
Leo Buscaglia, Ph.D., *Born for Love*
Michael Crichton, *Disclosure* (paper)
Michael Crichton, *Rising Sun*
Dominick Dunne, *A Season in Purgatory*
Fannie Flagg, *Daisy Fay and the Miracle Man* (paper)
Fannie Flagg, *Fried Green Tomatoes at the
Whistle Stop Cafe* (paper)
Robert Fulghum, *It Was on Fire When I Lay Down
on It* (hardcover and paper)
Robert Fulghum, *Maybe (Maybe Not): Second Thoughts
from a Secret Life*
Robert Fulghum, *Uh-Oh*
Peter Gethers, *The Cat Who Went to Paris*
Martha Grimes, *The End of the Pier*
Martha Grimes, *The Horse You Came In On* (paper)
Lewis Grizzard, *If I Ever Get Back to Georgia, I'm
Gonna Nail My Feet to the Ground*
David Halberstam, *The Fifties* (2 volumes, paper)
Kathryn Harvey, *Stars*
Katharine Hepburn, *Me* (hardcover and paper)
P.D. James, *The Children of Men*
Naomi Judd, *Love Can Build a Bridge* (paper)
Judith Krantz, *Dazzle*
Judith Krantz, *Scruples Two*
John le Carré, *The Night Manager* (paper)

(continued)

John le Carré, *The Secret Pilgrim*
Robert Ludlum, *The Bourne Ultimatum*
Robert Ludlum, *The Road to Omaha*
James A. Michener, *Mexico* (paper)
James A. Michener, *The Novel*
James A. Michener, *The World is My Home* (paper)
Richard North Patterson, *Degree of Guilt*
Louis Phillips, editor, *The Random House Large Print
    Treasury of Best-Loved Poems*
Maria Riva, *Marlene Dietrich* (2 volumes, paper)
Mickey Rooney, *Life Is Too Short*
William Styron, *Darkness Visible*
Margaret Truman, *Murder at the National Cathedral*
Margaret Truman, *Murder at the Pentagon*
Donald Trump with Charles Leerhsen, *Trump: Surviving
    at the Top*
Anne Tyler, *Saint Maybe*
John Updike, *Rabbit at Rest*
Phyllis A. Whitney, *Star Flight* (paper)
Lois Wyse, *Grandchildren Are So Much Fun
    I Should Have Had Them First*

The New York Times Large Print Crossword Puzzles (paper)

Will Weng, editor, Volume 1
Will Weng, editor, Volume 2
Will Weng, editor, Volume 3
Eugene T. Maleska, editor, Volume 4
Eugene T. Maleska, editor, Volume 5
Eugene T. Maleska, editor, Volume 6
Eugene T. Maleska, editor, Volume 7

Eugene T. Maleska, editor, Omnibus Volume 1